the MAKING of
ERIN
BETTENCOURT

a novel

SANDRA CUNHA

To my three favourite ladies:

My sister, Elizabeth (a.k.a. Lizzie Lizard), for being my first best friend.

My niece, Sophia Rose (a.k.a. Soapie Soaps), for coming along when needed the most.

And, especially, Maria Gorete (a.k.a. my mommy), for loving me unconditionally. I miss you and think about you every single day.

PART I
ERIN, GIRL

"My life didn't please me,
so I created my life."
Coco Chanel

ONE

September 2013

I LIKE TO PLAY THIS GAME. I made it up myself, but I play it only once a year.

There are specific instructions to my game. First, I get dressed in jeans and a T-shirt. Then, I pull my hair back into a low ponytail. And finally—this is the crucial element—I put on a pair of dark sunglasses. (Wearing a hat is optional, depending on my mood and level of play.)

My playground is Yorkville: Toronto's hamlet of luxury and splendor. It's where the rich come to show-off that they are indeed rich and where those of lesser financial means come to gawk. This population of gawkers increases a thousandfold in September during the Toronto International Film Festival as Hollywood movie stars descend upon the city and get added to the mix.

And I'm one of them: a gawker, not a movie star. But I *pretend* I'm famous.

Or hope to get mistaken for someone famous. I would even settle for up-and-comer, on the verge of major stardom, currently featuring in independent films.

That is the game.

Once I'm in character, the key is to never make lasting eye contact with anyone. If someone catches my eye, I have to look away quickly—as if I have just been spotted. It's also important to have a coffee cup in my hand at all times. Caffeine is the only reason a celebrity would brave the possible onslaught of crazed fans. I tried having my sister act as my fake publicist one year. She wasn't good at following the rules or staying in character. It's better to play alone.

And so, here I am on this beautiful Saturday afternoon, but I have been walking around for hours, and no one seems to recognize who I am. I mean, who my celebrity lookalike is. My coffee is long gone, and

I'm feeling slightly foolish drinking from an empty cup. I'm questioning whether to invest another five bucks in my game and get a fresh one, but I have completed so many laps around the main loop, most of the gawkers must be on to me.

I'm about to call it quits when I hear, "Anne! Anne! Ms. Hathaway!" I glance over and see a crowd forming...and it's making its way towards me.

Oh, my god. They think I'm Anne Hathaway.

I can't believe this is happening. After years of playing my game, people think I'm somebody famous! Although, I never thought that somebody would be Anne Hathaway. I guess I kind of look like her. My hair is lighter, and my eyes aren't as big, but, maybe, from a distance...

As I'm psyching myself up to play the role of Anne Hathaway, the crowd has found the "real" Anne, standing a few feet away from me.

Of course.

I contemplate joining them, but if I do, I will return to gawker status. Instead, I sneak a candid photo of Anne with my phone and leave her to her fans.

Sigh. There is always next year.

My self-consoling is interrupted by a sudden flash in the distance. I can't make out what it was because the afternoon sun is too strong. But I'm curious now and want to find out, so I head in the flash's direction.

It's only when I'm standing directly in front of it that I see what drew me forward: the glint of a gold lock.

There before me in a store window display is what I have been searching for without realizing it until this very moment: a vintage Chanel 2.55 bag, medium, navy.

I'm not into designer labels. (That could be because I never owned a designer label.) But this bag is different. This bag belonged to my mom.

Okay, not *this* specific bag. My mom had one exactly like it. I remember her wearing it when I was a kid. The ladies would paw at it, asking if it was real.

It was real.

My grandmother passed the bag down to my mom when she got her first job, and it would have been mine, except my mom had to sell it. I was probably thirteen years old at the time, but I can still see her expression as she handed it over to the hairy, gold-chained man who responded to her newspaper ad. She had such a hard time letting it go.

I had forgotten about the bag until today. Now that I have seen it again, I want it back. I *need* it back.

The odd thing is, I never noticed this store before—not that I shop in this area. It's somewhat (totally) out of my budget. Normally, I stay on the street. I'm intimidated even stepping foot into expensive stores, but it looks as though it's a vintage shop, so it can't be that bad.

Mustering up some courage, I go inside, where I find a sales assistant wearing an excessive amount of hot-pink lipstick for daytime hours.

"Excuse me," I say to her. "How much for the Chanel bag in the window? The navy one?"

"You mean, the vintage Chanel 2.55, it's..." She looks me up and down, then says with a smirk, "Two."

"Two hundred?" That is more than I have ever paid for a bag, but with a little cutting back I could—

"No, two *thousand*."

"But—but it's used!"

"It's a classic. It's Chanel."

"Right. Okay, um, thank you," I say, walking away deflated.

So I'm back where I started, standing outside the vintage shop, gazing through the window at my mom's bag. It's gorgeous. It should already be mine. But two grand for a purse? That is insane.

Or is it?

I could charge it to my credit card and promise myself I will pay it off as quickly as possible. It isn't a frivolous purchase. It's an heirloom.

My missing family heirloom.

With hope restored, I turn to reenter the shop.

But then, I remember something. Something very, *very* bad: I had a "plasectomy" last month. That is when you cut up your credit cards into tiny bits. And to top it off, I cancelled them to avoid the temptation of calling the credit card companies to get them back. Now, thanks to debt guru Dave Ramsey, I'm on a cash-only system. (I'm not a big fan of Mr. Ramsey at the moment.) Why couldn't I have waited one more month to find divine financial intervention?

The image of the bag refuses to leave my mind.

Somehow, I find myself back inside the shop, where I tap the same salesgirl on the shoulder. "Um, excuse me?"

She turns and frowns when she realizes it's me.

"Hi, again," I say. "I was wondering...do you have a layaway plan?"

"We don't do lay-a-way," she says, then walks off.

Rude!

Whatever. They can keep their overpriced bag. I turn and leave the shop, managing not to look back.

More than once.

I return to my apartment with zero purchases, one (real) celebrity sighting, and two blisters on my feet. I linger in the hallway before entering. Someone on this floor is having something delicious for dinner tonight. It smells so good.

I drop my crummy old purse in the one luxury of my studio apartment: a walk-in closet. Sometimes I lie down in there and daydream. It's my form of meditation.

If only I could call my sister, Betty, and tell her about the bag. But she is in Boston with her boyfriend, Matt, and I have strict instructions to limit calls to emergency situations. This seems urgent to me, although Betty may not agree with that.

She has been travelling back-and-forth to Boston every weekend for the last few months as Matt is on a consulting project there. They have been dating since high school and are a bit codependent. As for Betty, she is an accountant at one of the Big Four firms. I can never remember which one; probably because I zone out at the very mention of the word accounting. But she likes it. Her actual name is Beatrice, which she doesn't like, so she goes by Betty, and as our last name is Bettencourt, this makes her Betty Bettencourt. It's a crowd-pleaser.

We are twins. Well, what is known as "Irish twins," as we were born within twelve months of each other. (I don't think being Irish is a necessary requirement anymore.) I was born in February, and she came along later that same year in December. Although we couldn't be more different, we are really close. We have been through a lot together. She is my best friend.

And I can't even call to tell her my news.

So I settle for the next best thing: a frozen dinner and a night with my other friends—the ones who live inside the television.

I dozed off sometime between the opening monologue of a *Saturday Night Live* rerun and an infomercial for a gadget that can chop an onion a hundred-and-one different ways. Before I'm tempted to buy this spellbinding gadget, I turn off the television.

Lacking the energy to convert my futon sofa once again into a bed, I leave it as is and vow to keep it permanently in the bed position come the morning. It isn't as if I get many visitors, anyway. I'm also too lazy to get up to wash the makeup off my face and to brush my teeth.

I accept the future consequences and go back to sleep.

Betty's flight comes in at seven. I debated surprising her at the airport, but that would mean giving up one of my precious Sunday evenings. Instead, I catch up on some reading.

I subscribe to a few fashion and gossip magazines. I'm still on the summer issues, and it's practically fall. I'm so deeply immersed in a "How to Get Bikini Ready in Six Weeks" article that I almost don't hear my phone ringing.

It's Betty!

"Hey, Betty Boop," I say when I answer.

"Stop calling me that already."

"You love it."

"No, no, I don't. How was film fest?"

"Good, I saw Anne Hathaway."

"Cool. Did you watch any films this time?"

"Um, no. But you won't believe it, I saw—"

"Hugh Jackman? Was he with Anne? Is he cuter in real life? Was he taller or shorter than you expected?"

"I didn't see Hugh. I saw—"

"Did you finally see Ryan Gosling? Can you stop stalking movie stars now?"

"What? I don't stalk movie stars. *Just listen!* This is important." I take a deep breath and continue, "While I was in Yorkville yesterday, I saw the most beautiful bag. Not any old bag, *the bag*: a vintage Chanel 2.55. And...it was navy!"

"Chanel? Why do you need a Chanel bag? You already have a bunch of purses."

"I don't think you heard me properly. It isn't *any* Chanel bag; it's the 2.55. As in, mom's bag."

"I didn't realize it had a name. How much was it?"

I tell her.

"*Two thousand?* Are you kidding me?" she says, laughing.

"It's our birthright! You can't put a price on a birthright!"

"Are you nuts? You don't have twenty bucks, much less two grand. Forget about it. Go to H&M and buy a purse there. No one will know the difference."

I should have known she wouldn't get it. Betty is pretty frugal. She is the one who told me about this Dave Ramsey guy and his cash-only system that inspired my credit card cutting last month. Ever since she bought a one-bedroom-plus-den condo last year, she has been on a mission to get me on the property ladder. But I don't want a stupid condo, I want the Chanel bag.

"Betty, *please*! I *need* it! It's mom's bag!"

"All right, all right. Relax. It isn't actually mom's bag. I hope you know that. How much do you *really* want it?"

Without a moment's hesitation, I say, "Enough to bring my lunch to work every single day for a year to get it."

"Wow. Okay, let me think of a way for you to buy the bag without wrecking the progress you have made. Give me a couple of days to come up with a plan, but I'm going now because I'm starving." Betty is always hungry.

As soon as I'm off the phone, I feel better. My sister is a financial wizard; she will think of something for sure. She has to. This is meant to be. What are the chances of my finding the bag after all these years?

It's a sign from my mom. She wants me to have it, too. I know it.

TWO

I HATE MONDAYS. I have hated Mondays ever since I began working full time. Not those first couple of weeks when the prospect of getting paid was still exciting, but every Monday after that. I'm not too fond of Tuesdays, Wednesdays, or Thursdays, either. Fridays, I can handle, but only because we are allowed to wear jeans.

Usually, I'm at least fifteen minutes late for work, but on Mondays, it's closer to twenty. It takes me five extra minutes to realize it isn't the weekend anymore. So on this particular Monday, I'm taking my leisurely time getting to the subway station, trying to find a reason I don't need to go to work that I have somehow forgotten. Like it's a statutory holiday. Or my actual purpose in life is to join whatever the Canadian-version of the Peace Corps is, and I should go sign up right now. Random stuff like that.

I also hate the subway. When did I become such a hater? I used to be a happy-go-lucky sort of person before I started working. At least, I think I was. It's hard to remember.

But who could enjoy the subway during rush hour? I become a different person as soon as I pass through the turnstile. My blood pressure immediately goes up—almost as though I'm ready to do battle. And I am. I'm willing to push and shove with the rest of them if it means I can get on the train and not wait for the next one. The next one may never come.

Monday morning rush hour is especially busy, so I stake my ground behind the yellow line, holding out my arms slightly to the side, just slightly, so it isn't obvious. I also act indifferent about getting on the train. That fools them every time. And I always say, "Oops, sorry!" as I'm pushing and shoving people. It makes it easier to get away with.

This is what the subway has turned me into.

And as morbid as it might sound, sometimes as I'm standing behind that yellow line with the crowds pressing against me, I think it wouldn't be so terrible if I fell onto the tracks...or if I jumped. Then, I wouldn't need to worry about going to a job I hate. I wouldn't need to worry about anything at all. But that is a decision you can't come back from, so I wait behind the yellow line.

There is only one good thing when it comes to taking the subway: Suit Guy.

I first met him three years ago. Well, we haven't met in the conventional sense, although we seem to end up in the same subway car, a lot. To increase the chances of serendipitously running into him, I wait farther down the platform than necessary and try to get on the train at a certain time. I almost never see him on Mondays, as I'm extra late, but today is my lucky day because there he is.

He is wearing his navy suit (my favourite), along with monogrammed cufflinks attached to what must be a custom-made shirt. I have figured out one of his initials: "S." I imagine it stands for something that equals his level of refinement. Until I know what that is, he is Suit Guy.

I spoke with him once. There was a seat available, and he asked me if I wanted it. I stuttered that he could have it, as I preferred to stand. He said he preferred to stand, too, and then...he smiled at me. I haven't sat down during morning rush hour since.

That is the closest I have ever been to him. He smelled so good: a concoction of soap and sandalwood. Bliss. But I'm too far away to inhale his intoxicating scent this morning. I can only sneak peeks at him in the train windows whenever we go into a dark tunnel.

Have there ever been eyes more blue?

I sigh loudly, causing some passengers to glance my way. They are probably wondering if I'm going to be "a problem" on their morning commute.

Suit Guy gets off at King station. I got off once and followed him. (Maybe it was more than once.) I'm convinced he is a high-ranking executive or something equally impressive sounding. One of these days, I'm bound to find out.

When I'm not in stalker-girl mode, I get off two stops later at St. Andrew station, which is what I do today.

And so, the race begins to my box in the sky.

On this morning, like every weekday morning before, I walk down the same gloomy, grey corridor.

Carol, our team's administrative assistant, greets me with raised eyebrows. She never says anything, but I know she is keeping track of my lateness.

I enter my cubicle, which is also grey. Why are cubicles almost always grey? It's like walking into bad weather. No one likes bad weather. Imagine how much happier everyone would be to enter a striped or paisley cubicle. (Note to self: invent cubicle wallpaper.)

It usually takes me a good half-hour to settle in properly. First, I turn on my computer. While waiting for it to start up, I check my voicemail. (None.) Once the computer is ready to go, I read my emails: personal, then work-related. Finally, I go online to see what is happening in the world. As in, the latest celebrity gossip.

But this morning, my routine gets interrupted by Carol, who is peering over the wall of my cubicle. (I can't stand when she does that.) I instinctively minimize my computer screen. It's become an ingrained reflex.

"Erin, will you be joining us for the monthly team meeting?"

What she is implying with her pseudo-question is that I couldn't possibly have remembered there is a team meeting this morning. Sure, I had forgotten, but still.

"Of course," I say, giving her a fake smile. "I wouldn't miss it for anything."

She fake-smiles back at me and returns to her desk.

Carol and I have a hate-hate relationship, although we pretend to like each other. It's a half-hearted attempt on both our parts. She has been gunning for my job as sales and marketing coordinator ever since

I started working here, nearly five years ago. *Coordinator*, not manager. Why she would want my job is anyone's guess.

I grab my notebook and head to the office kitchen for some disgusting coffee. My Monday morning extra-tardiness means there wasn't enough time to buy a latte on my way into work. But I need coffee, no matter how bad, to get me through the meeting without falling asleep—which only happened once, but I live in fear of it ever happening again.

The meeting is beginning as I sneak into the boardroom. I quickly take a seat.

"Morning, everyone. I trust you all had a pleasant weekend. Let's keep this brief. I have another meeting in an hour," Bradford, director of sales and marketing—and my boss—says as he commands his troops.

Ah, Bradford. He means well, but he isn't totally with it. He is constantly coming up with "make-do" projects he believes are the most important tasks in the world when they are just "make-do" projects. I think he secretly lives in fear of losing his job, so he has to keep proving his worth. That is my diagnosis, anyway.

These monthly team meetings are the definition of boring. We each have to give an update on what we are working on, and for me that usually isn't much. Carol always goes first. She spends ten minutes going over the office supplies budget, lecturing the team to print double-sided to cut down on paper costs.

"Excellent work, Carol. Way to stay on top of things," Bradford says when she finishes.

Carol beams. (Kiss ass.) She is also the one who decided it was no longer in the budget for us to have donuts at these meetings. (Heartless.) It was the one thing I looked forward to.

"Erin, how is everything coming along with you?"

"Huh? Um, great," I say once I realize Bradford is talking to me. "I'm almost done with that, uh, project you gave me."

Bradford and I have an unspoken agreement. He is frequently in meetings or off on business trips to our U.S. counterpart. I'm sure he knows I spend the majority of my time surfing the web, particularly when he is out of town. But he appears to live by the army mantra of "Don't ask, don't tell." He enjoys the status of having extra soldiers; active service is optional.

"Yes, great." He nods as he looks away uncomfortably. (See? He knows.)

While he questions his next soldier, I daydream about winning the lottery. Wouldn't it be wonderful? I wouldn't need to work anymore. I could buy whatever I wanted, including my mom's Chanel bag.

I let out a loud sigh, and everyone turns towards me.

"Sorry," I mouth, feeling my cheeks burning. At least, I didn't hum the jingle from the lottery commercials like last time.

The meeting ends a gruelling hour later. I contemplate returning to my desk, but go downstairs to grab a latte, instead. It isn't as if I have anything pressing to do. I know I should save that money for my mom's bag, but I feel caffeine falls under the list of necessary expenditures.

When I get back to my desk, there is a stack of documents with a yellow sticky note on top. The note reads: "3x copies by noon. DOUBLE-SIDED! Carol."

God, I can't stand her.

I want to take the stack over to her desk and throw it in her face. She is the administrative assistant. Why do I have to do her crappy work?

Fighting my animalistic urges, I take the stack to the copy room. I have to wait several minutes while Shirley from accounts payable copies some invoices. She tries making small talk, but I'm in no mood for chit-chat after seeing Carol's note.

As my luck would have it, the machine jams with my first copy. I kick it in frustration. Normally, I would try to fix it, but I can't be bothered.

Making sure no one is watching, I leave the copy room and head to the one on the opposite side of the floor. This gives me a weird sense of pleasure in what is turning into yet another depressing day in my world of work.

That can't be right. I could have sworn it was Thursday. But my online calendar confirms it's, unfortunately, only Wednesday.

This week is especially light. I have a minor sales report to complete and a few calls to make. I wonder if anyone would notice if I took a short nap under my desk; doing nothing is tiring. I take a peek underneath, but it's way too dusty—I would be covered in evidence. Someone should clean under there; I could be making good use of that space. Maybe there is a sick room somewhere in the building. I could say I'm feeling lightheaded and need to lie down for a bit. Why haven't I thought of this before?

As I'm searching our company's web portal, my work phone rings.

"Erin Bettencourt," I say, answering in my best phone voice. It's throatier and deeper than my normal voice.

"Hey, it's Betty. Are you sick or something?"

"No, I was just—"

"Using your fake phone voice?" she laughs.

"Yeah." She knows me too well. "What's up?"

"I have a way for you to earn extra money—"

"*Really?* Phew! I've been going by the vintage shop after work every night to make sure mom's bag is still there, but I'm freaking out that someone will buy it. What's your idea? I can't wait to hear it!"

"Then stop talking. *Sheesh.* Remember how you used to babysit in high school? I checked around and found something similar for you."

"Great! When do they need me?" I knew Betty would come through. Did I mention she skipped a grade? She is practically a genius. Sometimes it feels as though she is the older sister.

"Saturday, but there's something you should know."

"What?"

"They aren't kids, and you won't exactly be babysitting."

"What are they, then? And what will I be doing?"

"Three dogs, and you would be walking them. What do you think?"

"What kind of dogs?"

"I thought you were over that."

"What *kind* of dogs?"

"Small dogs. I have seen photos on my coworker's desk. But one of them is a...chihuahua. Don't freak out. You're not a kid anymore."

When I was four, a chihuahua bit me. It was more of a scratch— but equally traumatizing. Ever since then, I try to avoid them.

"Think about it, Erin. It's good money. You should do it."

I mull it over in my mind. I am older (and taller) now. I could probably outrun a chihuahua if the situation called for it. And it is important to face your fears.

"I'll do it!" I say. "What time do I need to get there?"

Betty gives me the time and says she will call me on Saturday morning with the address.

Who knew dog walkers make twenty bucks an hour *per* dog? This could be my new money-making gig for Project Coco. (That is what we have codenamed it.)

How hard can it possibly be?

THREE

Project Coco Fund = $0.00

EVERYTHING IS FUZZY. I'm in a state of total confusion. Moments earlier, I was running down the cobblestone streets of Moscow while being chased by two secret agents. To avoid capture, I had to jump from one building rooftop to another, even performing a forward flip at one point, which both surprised and delighted me I could do. Was it only a dream? It felt so real. Alas, back to my less exciting waking world.

I pick up my phone, trying to make out the time through squinting eyes.

SHIT!

It's 9:32 a.m. I should be at my desk, not in my bed.

Why didn't my alarm go off?

Frantically, I deliberate which parts of my morning routine can be safely skipped. I smell my armpits. No shower. I'm hungry, but there is no time. Hair and makeup? Definitely required.

Stupid! Stupid! How could I have slept in so late?

I run into my walk-in closet and put on a black top and black skirt. (I can't colour-coordinate in this condition.) My teeth get a two-second brushing while I pull my hair back into a low ponytail. I apply some makeup. *Too much blush!* Now I'm sweating, so I swipe on several flicks of deodorant and douse myself in perfume.

Eight minutes later, I'm ready to go. That has to be a personal record. Grabbing my jacket and purse, I head for the door.

Where are my keys?

I swear I put them in my purse last night. Wasting another five minutes, I search for the missing keys. But I can't find them anywhere, so I risk it and leave the door unlocked.

The elevator takes forever to arrive. When it does, Larry, the superintendent, is in there. He is so gross. He is always giving the women in the building "the eye."

"Don't you look flustered—in a bit of a rush?" he asks my breasts.

"A bit, yeah," I say through clenched teeth.

The elevator doors open at what seems like every floor; more and more people keep cramming in. I'm being pressed up against Larry, whose hot breath I can feel on the back of my neck. I'm going to puke or kill them all; it could go either way.

We finally reach ground level. I make it out without puking up my non-existent breakfast or getting a criminal record, then sprint for the front doors.

As I approach the corner of my street, my phone rings.

Crap! It's probably Bradford—or worse, Carol—asking where I am. I check the display. It's just Betty.

"Hey, I can't talk. I'm so late!" I say out of breath as I run across the street, narrowly avoiding getting hit by a car.

"Late? But you don't need to get there until two. How do you know where you're going? I never gave you the address."

"*Address?* What address?" I slow down my pace. Something is beginning to click in my mind.

"For Greta's place, remember? You're walking her dogs this afternoon. Erin, are you okay?"

And then, it hits me. Today is Saturday.

With time once again on my side, I return to my unlocked apartment and take a long, hot bubble bath. I have earned it after this morning's events.

Afterwards, I change into something more dog-friendly. No need to impress the little felines. Wait, felines are cats. I mean, pooches.

Putting on yoga pants and running shoes, I decide this will be my weekly workout. I have been meaning to take-up running, and this is the perfect opportunity to start. I see people running with their dogs all the time...although they rarely have three dogs. And I guess I'm supposed to be dog walking, not dog running. Imagine if one of them has an undiagnosed heart condition that gets triggered by our run. That would be horrible. (And I probably wouldn't get paid.)

I'm not a dog lover—admitting that is sacrilege these days. But I never understood the whole dog infatuation thing. You won't catch me stopping to pet one while *oohing* and *aahing*.

Hold on a second.

Dog lovers will be stopping me to pet the pooches, and some of those lovers will be men, potentially attractive men. I can't wear my sweats!

Rummaging through my closet, I search for something more appropriate, but even with a closet full of clothes, I can't find anything to wear. I settle on a flowy, black tank top with my favourite jeans, casual yet stylish. And, to add a little *je ne sais quoi*, a pair of three-inch, red, fake-suede ankle booties purchased at a half-off sale before the Great Plasectomy. It's somewhat warm for ankle booties, but they make my outfit.

So what if this isn't the standard uniform of those in command of the leash? I seek to defy convention; shake up things in the dog-walking world. Plus, they are small dogs with short legs. How fast can they go?

I get off the subway at Rosedale station. No one ever gets off at Rosedale station. I wonder why this station exists. Maybe it's for "the staff" who take care of the upper class and their offspring (including the four-legged variety).

I approach the house. No, not house, mansion. It's huge. I'm not sure how to get in. There is a gate with a keypad. Betty never said anything about a keypad. Although Greta probably wouldn't give me the code right away, as she hasn't met me, yet. But in a few weeks, when I have bonded with her pups, she will want me to move in and become her official dog nanny. I will live in the guesthouse and have gourmet meals with the family. And I won't need to worry about work or money. I will get to be outside during the day and—

"Hola? Hola?"

A woman's voice coming from the keypad transports me back to reality.

"Um, *hola.* I'm Erin Bettencourt. I'm here to walk the dogs."

"They are expecting you. Please come in."

They are? Wow, smart dogs.

Making my way through the gate, I wobble to the front door. My heels weren't designed for the rough terrain of this interlocking-stone driveway. As I'm searching for the doorbell, the tallest door I have ever seen opens.

A uniformed maid—uh, domestic helper—appears behind the door. Another woman soon appears with perfectly styled white-blonde hair, pulled back into a tight bun. She is wearing a simple yet exquisite ivory pantsuit. She looks great for someone who has to be like fifty.

"Thank you, Maria," she says to the domestic helper.

Maria nods and goes back to her duties.

"You must be Erin. I am Greta," she says with an accent. (Betty mentioned her coworker was Swedish.) "Your sister recommends you highly. I trust you will take great care with my babies. They mean the world to me."

"Yes, of course. I *love* dogs. All dogs. Even the ugly ones, I mean, the less fortunate looking ones."

Stop talking, Erin.

"That is kind. It is my pleasure to introduce you to my babies. This is Huey, over there is Dewey, and...where has Louie gone to? Please give me a moment. My apologies."

She leaves me standing at the massive door. I guess *DuckTales* was popular in Sweden, too. I glance down at the ugliest pug on Earth, slobbering away. Next to him, appearing ready to pounce, is Dewey, the chihuahua. My heart races.

Be cool. He can't jump higher than your thigh from his position.

Greta returns with a terrier in her arms. He is licking her face, and I swear they are French kissing. There is no other way to describe what I'm seeing.

"And this is Louie, my favourite," she whispers this to me because dogs can understand humans. "My babies enjoy taking a special route on their Saturday walk. I asked Maria to print out a map for you. Please do follow the map, or they get quite anxious. And here are the baggies." Greta hands me the map and the baggies.

What do I need baggies for? *Ah, crap.* I forgot that part.

"Don't worry, I will follow your map to the letter, um, latitude," I say. "I'm fully trained in these matters."

"Well, you must be a professional to walk three rambunctious dogs in *those* heels. I expect them back by four for their afternoon nap. Adjö!" She hands me their *DuckTales* colour-coded leashes and closes the enormous door.

I'm now on my own with the chihuahua and his thugs.

Examining the map Greta gave me, I see she wants me to take the dogs to a park that is at least a thirty-minute walk away. And there are instructions about a dog wading pool. I did not wake up this morning to smell of wet dog. Besides, the dogs should be around people who will appreciate their clothes, I mean, their beautiful shiny fur.

Where are their fancy dog clothes? These are rich dogs, and they are running around naked. I wonder if they are embarrassed. The chihuahua might be: She seems to drop her head in shame as we pass a poodle wearing a pink tweed coat-thingy. Wait, the chihuahua is probably a boy given the name Huey—or is he Dewey? Maybe he is gay. He is definitely fashion conscious. I can tell. We may get on better than expected.

As I exit McMansionville, I end up on Yonge Street. There is no way we are going to the dog park. It would be a waste of a gorgeous Saturday afternoon. But where should we go, instead?

I know! We will go to Yorkville and check up on my mom's bag. It's been nearly twenty-four hours since I last laid eyes on it. The vintage shop is practically around the corner from here. Having the dogs with me will make it seem like I live in the neighbourhood. It isn't as if someone would purposefully bring their dogs to Yorkville to show them off. (Or would they?) It's a pity the dogs aren't wearing any clothes. That will affect my credibility a bit. I'm glad I wore my red heels; I wouldn't want people thinking I was hired to walk these dogs.

We pass a small park as we walk south on Yonge Street. So, technically, I took them to the park.

As we approach Yorkville, I decide we will do my usual loop to show-off my new friends before dropping by the vintage shop. That should be enough exercise for these small guys.

A couple stops me as I walk by a café. They are not your typical Yorkville couple—they are wearing Crocs—so I'm hesitant to stop. They ask a bunch of questions about the pug. I make up some stuff, but how am I supposed to know who the breeder was or what diet he is on?

I manage to get away, then take the dogs by Sassafraz, where the elite go to eat. A woman dining at the outdoor patio literally gasps when she sees my brood. She gets up from her chair, dropping the white cloth napkin from her lap, and rushes towards us.

"Oh, my—aren't they darling! Look at that pug! Honey, do you see this cute, little pug?" she asks her husband, who is digging into a piece of steak and oblivious to the fact his wife has left the table.

She returns her attention to me. "We had a pug." Her eyes tear up. "He passed last year."

After I give her my sympathies, I tell her about my goldfish that died when I was eight, and how my sister and I debated for days whether to have a proper burial or to flush it down the toilet. We took so long to decide our mom threw it in the garbage.

She makes a horrified face as I tell her this and backs away, saying something about her food getting cold.

I walk on. I have bigger fish to fry.

And a big fish does appear: a tall, dark, and handsome one. He gives me a sly glance, then bends down to pet, of course, the pug. He is about to make contact when the pug squats and takes a dump. On my shoe.

The guy laughs and walks off. (Jerk.)

This is beyond embarrassing.

I'm in Yorkville with poo on my shoe.

Mortifying...and gross.

I immediately go into emergency response mode. I grab one of the dog baggies and try to get as much of the crap off my shoe as possible. I don't have any water on me, but I doubt the fake-suede could handle it. So I search my purse, finding a random wet wipe. I use it to remove any remaining traces. My new ankle bootie may never be the same, but at least it doesn't look as though there is poo on my shoe anymore.

Having put everything in the nearest garbage bin, I apply a couple of generous rounds of hand sanitizer. I can't help hearing snickers from passersby who witnessed the event. But my new motto is: If I don't look at them, they don't exist.

I'm just about done with this dog-walking business when I remember my original purpose. I cut the walk short and head straight for the vintage shop; practically dragging the mutts behind me.

Trying to think positive thoughts, I visualize myself months from now, wearing my Chanel bag on this same street. Everyone will gaze upon me with admiration and stop to ask about my bag; not some pug that can't control his bowels. This is merely a necessary step to get me to that place. I need to remember that.

As the vintage shop comes into view, I gaze in the direction of the window display to draw strength from my lovely bag, except...it isn't there.

My mom's bag is missing!

Don't panic, Erin! Don't panic!

They may have moved the bag inside the shop. Yes, that is the most likely scenario. I tie the dogs' leashes to the nearest bike post and sprint towards the shop door. Once inside, I glance around frantically.

I can't see it! I can't see it!

"Is there something I can help you with?" (I recognize that voice.) "Oh, it's you." Apparently, the mean salesgirl recognizes me, too.

"There was a vintage Chanel 2.55 bag in your window display yesterday. I was, um, wondering where it is?" I ask, trying to play it cool, but I'm totally hyperventilating at this point.

"Hmm, we sold it."

"You. Sold. My. Chanel. Bag?"

"Yes, an hour ago," she says, beaming.

Evil, stuck-up bitch. I want to punch her in her hot-pink lipstick mouth. But I'm too angry, and I don't know if I would be able to stop if I did. I actually want to cry...because of a purse.

As I go to leave the shop, with my head hanging low, a voice coming from behind me asks, "Excuse me, miss? Did you say you were looking for the Chanel 2.55 bag?"

I give a slight nod without turning around.

"We sent it out for repairs. Nothing major, the clasp needed tweaking. We should have it back in a few weeks."

I quickly turn around. Standing there is an angel, a Betty-White-lookalike angel. Before I can help myself, I give her a hug.

"Thank you," I whisper in her ear.

When I release her, she winks at me.

The mean salesgirl scowls and says, "I thought she said the vintage Chloé." (Yeah, right.)

With disaster averted, I can safely leave the shop. Everything is right in my world again.

The dogs seem anxious as I untie them. They probably thought they had been abandoned. I should be nicer to them; it isn't their fault they got stuck with the one person who doesn't love dogs.

"C'mon, Huey, Dewey, and Louie—let's get you a treat!" I say to win them over.

The chihuahua and pug look up at me nervously. Where is the terrier, um, Louie? I double-check the bike post, but he isn't there.

Oh, my god. I lost her favourite.

FOUR

Project Coco Fund = $0.00

THINK, ERIN, THINK!

If you were a dog, without a dime on you, where would you go? *Where would you go?*

I run around Yorkville, asking people if they have seen a terrier. Most show concern and offer to help, but a few look at me as if I'm an unfit mother. I am an unfit mother. I can't even take care of three little dogs. Louie must be so scared, wandering around lost in this big, busy city. What if he gets attacked by another dog or dog-napped? Without the fancy dog clothes, the dog-nappers might not think he is worth much, but what if they figure out he is rich and lives in McMansionville?

Checking the time, I see it's almost three. I have an hour to find Louie and get the dogs back before my cover is blown.

Why did I ever agree to do this? There has to be an easier way to make money.

Oh, no—Betty!

She is going to hate me! But she should have known this was a bad idea. I hope she doesn't get fired because of this. Greta is fairly high-up at the accounting firm from what Betty has told me.

I sit down on a bench and try to think logically.

What are the facts? One hyperactive dog went missing at approximately 14:45 hours. He has short legs, so he couldn't have gotten outside the city limits in less than a fifteen-minute period. Search area can be confined to the City of Toronto—unless dog-napped, then he could be anywhere.

Other known facts: enjoys chasing tail and wading in doggie pools.

Enjoys wading in doggie pools...maybe he went to the dog park? Is that possible? Could he know how to get there on his own? There is still time to make it to the dog park and back before I have to face the music. It's worth a shot. I will do it for Betty, and for Louie, and for all dogs everywhere! As if on cue, Huey and Dewey both bark at that exact moment.

I get up from the bench and decide we will have to take the subway to save time. I have seen dogs on the subway, so I know they are allowed. They don't even need a token.

As the train pulls into the station, the chihuahua's legs shake. Poor thing, I bet he has never ridden the subway before. He is totally slumming it today. Feeling a new sense of motherly love, I pick up the two dogs and cradle them in my arms.

While on the train, the pug gets all the attention again. I feel bad for the chihuahua now that he is the only one being ignored. I gently pat his head and tell him he is a good boy.

When the train arrives at our stop, I get up and make my way towards the subway doors, still holding onto both dogs. As I do, I hear muffled chuckles.

What is so funny? Why is everyone looking at me?

I glance down and see what they are laughing at. The chihuahua is peeing on my favourite jeans. Not only am I being peed on, but it looks as though *I* peed my pants. These dogs need some serious potty-training. But I don't have time to worry about that now. I will deal with this one day in therapy. I need to find Louie!

I make my way to the park, following the map Greta gave me. My feet are killing me. Why did I wear three-inch heels? Heels that haven't been broken-in properly. Cheap heels that defy the laws of physics. I hobble the remaining way to the park.

The park is huge, and, of course, the wading pool is on the opposite end. I take off my heels and start running. I have to. I'm losing precious time. Whatever infectious disease I get will be treated later. It's the price paid for vanity.

As I get closer to the wading pool, I see dogs everywhere: big dogs, little dogs, skinny dogs, fat dogs. And I can't help thinking how much dogs are like people.

I spot a terrier, but he is wearing a plaid kerchief around his neck, so unless Louie went shopping, that is not him. Maybe Greta wouldn't notice. Or I could get her a new dog. But where would I buy one?

I'm about to ask someone when I see another terrier, splashing in the wading pool, with a green-coloured leash trailing behind him.

LOUIE!

Dropping my ankle booties, I run towards the wading pool while holding on tightly to the other two dogs. I don't want to lose one of them now that I have found Louie.

"Louie! LOUIE! *Get over here!*"

Louie looks over at me, and I swear he gives me a mischievous grin as he paddles to the centre of the pool.

Damn dog. He isn't going to make this easy. But I'm calling his bluff, I have suffered enough for one day.

As I make my way into the pool, I hear a man shout, "Hey, lady! Dogs only! No humans allowed!"

I ignore him.

When I get to Louie, I try to grab his leash while still holding onto the other two dogs. But they are excited and think we are playing a game. I lose hold of Dewey, who paddles over to Louie. It's as if they haven't seen each other in years the way they are carrying on. Huey is wiggling in my arms like crazy, so I let him go.

I give up!

Walking out of the wading pool, I head to a grassy area. On a positive note, it no longer looks as though I peed my pants because they are now completely soaked. I lie on the grass to enjoy the warm afternoon sun and to dry out my jeans.

Just as I'm nodding off, I'm awoken by Louie licking my hand. Soon, Huey and Dewey join him. (They must have mixed up the names in the Swedish version of *DuckTales;* Louie should have been named Huey.)

"You little rascals!" I say, tickling their bellies. "Let's go home!"

I quickly grab their leashes before they take this as a command and dash off again.

We make it back to Greta's castle with a minute to spare.

"My babies! My babies!" she says as they jump all over her. "Thank you for bringing them back in one piece. I hope they were not too much trouble."

"No trouble at all." Luckily, dogs can't talk.

"Well, then, if you are not busy two weeks from today, our regular dog walker is out of—"

"Sorry, I can't. I have plans." (I don't have plans.)

Greta hands me an envelope with my earnings, and I wave goodbye to the little guys as she closes the gigantic door.

Those were the two longest hours of my life. I open the envelope and count six twenty-dollar bills.

But was it worth it?

I got pooped *and* peed on; my new ankle booties are wrecked; I have a potential infectious disease from running barefoot in the park; I almost lost Betty her job (which she won't ever find out about); and I'm convinced I suffered a minor heart attack from the day's events.

So no. Although, conquering my fear of chihuahuas was a nice bonus. At least, it's over, and I made some money to put towards Project Coco.

As I'm walking back across the impossible terrain of the driveway, I smell something bad. It's me. I smell like wet dog.

Yeah, definitely not worth it.

FIVE
Project Coco Fund = $120.00

THIS TIME, I knew I was dreaming. Well, not at first.

I was sitting at my cubicle—work dreams are usually the worst—reading one of my favourite blogs, when I felt a drop of water on my cheek. Except, it wasn't water. It was a cold, silver dime. I thought Carol had lost it and was throwing her loose change at me. When another dime hit my hand, I stood up and looked over my cubicle wall towards her desk, but she was nowhere in sight.

The dimes soon turned into paper bills: five-dollar bills, then tens, twenties, fifties...until a small hill of hundreds was forming.

It was raining money!

Money was coming out of the filing cabinets, the phone, the computer, even the garbage can.

It was everywhere!

I started laughing and dancing around because that is when I realized I was dreaming, and I knew it was a sign: a sign from above. So I began stuffing as much of the money as possible into my shirt and pants.

The best thing about the dream was the overwhelming feeling I had that everything would work out. I would be okay.

But suddenly, instead of raining money, it was raining for real.

That was when I saw her.

Carol was standing in the entryway of my cubicle with a look of pure contempt on her face. She said something, but I couldn't understand what she was saying because everything had gone mute. I could see only her lips moving. I glanced down, and the money had vanished. And then, I could hear again.

What I heard was Carol laughing: a twisted, evil laugh.

—

I know what I need to do now. What I'm meant to do. I have to start a business...from my cubicle.

It makes perfect sense. There is no way I can earn money fast enough to buy my mom's bag in my spare time. I need to make money during working hours, too.

And why shouldn't I start a business from my current job? It isn't as if they appreciate me or pay me that much. I have worked there for almost five years, and I have never been promoted. Sure, I haven't done anything to deserve a promotion, but I haven't been given the chance to, either.

So there is a slight ethical issue. But aren't these the same people, the same company that has squandered my innermost potential by giving me menial, mind-numbing tasks, day-after-day, for years? Exactly. I'm finally taking initiative. Misdirected, perhaps, but initiative nonetheless.

Ethics aside, there is just one small, teeny-tiny problem: I have no idea what sort of business to start.

Think, Erin, think! What are you good at? What are your skills? Strengths?

Clearly, I love brainstorming in the third person. (I can't help it. It makes me feel as though I'm not doing it on my own.)

Hmm...people are always telling me I have nice handwriting. I could do calligraphy and create fancy invitations and certificates, or whatever people need calligraphy for these days.

I Google it.

Dammit. Apparently, it takes years to become an expert. I don't have years.

What else? I like to doodle during meetings. I could start a greeting card business—but that seems as if it would take a long time to get up and running, too. I need something that is low cost with immediate cash flow.

I conduct another Google search, clicking on a link to a site with a list of small business ideas. I scan the page. *Freelance Writer*. If only I could write. *Gift Basket Assembly*. Too suspicious to do at work. *Wedding Photographer*. All my photos are blurry. *Dog Walker*. Yeah, right, maybe if people needed walking.

Wait a minute. People may not need walking, but they need help with other things.

Glancing further down the page, I see it: *Personal Errand Service*.

An errand service sounds perfect for me. It will get me away from my desk every now and again. I have already mastered the art of the extra-long lunch break, and I'm a pro at setting up fake meetings. I can run errands during those times, instead. And it's practically no cost. I can post ads on Craigslist and Kijiji and print some business cards.

All I need is a catchy business name. *Erin Bettencourt Personal Errand Services*. Yawn, boring. *Erin Bettencourt for Hire*. Sounds illegal. *Girl Friday*. Very cool, so it's probably already taken. *Errands by Erin*. Getting there. *Errand Girl*. Errand sounds a lot like Erin.

Erin Girl.

That is it! But I need a tagline so people know what the business is about.

For all your errand needs, call Erin Girl!

It makes me sound like a superhero.

Erin Girl: Saving the day, one errand at a time!

Oh, I like that better.

Making myself a coffee, I settle in for the rest of Sunday afternoon. I spend hours perfecting my ads for Craigslist and Kijiji—being sure to leave dog walking off my list of service offerings. I scratch the idea of business cards because that would involve spending money. I have to keep this operation cheap. As in, no cost.

Later that night, I call Betty to let her know I'm becoming an entrepreneur. She thinks it's a great idea, too. I omit the part about completing errands during working hours. Betty is fairly by the book, so it's for her own benefit.

It will be hard sleeping tonight because tomorrow Erin Girl launches!

The next morning, I get into work bright and early. Okay, on time, which is early for me.

Carol greets me with a raised eyebrow and a barely noticeable half-smile.

I'm shocked.

Maybe getting in on time is what I needed to do to win her favour. However, I'm not so easily fooled. Carol is my biggest obstacle in running my new venture. I will have to cover my tracks, and then add an extra layer of protection. I keep remembering that horrific laugh of hers in my dream. I'm getting shivers just thinking about it.

But there is no way I'm backing down now. I'm too excited. I have to do this. I'm meant to do this.

So I log in to my computer to post my ads only to be informed it needs fifteen minutes to perform a software update that I should have completed ages ago, but as I haven't, it has chosen this moment in time to do the update for me.

This is my reward for coming in early.

I take this as a sign—they are everywhere these days—that I should go downstairs and grab a pre-celebratory latte.

As I walk past Carol, I get a frown. Any favour gained has been lost.

It's taking forever to get my latte as everyone working downtown, with the exclusion of the Carols of the world, seems to be avoiding work by grabbing a hot beverage.

Normally, I enjoy waiting in long lines: I get to listen-in on other people's conversations, check out their outfits, and make general personal judgments. But today, I have a business to launch.

When it's finally my turn, I'm told they are out of lactose-free milk. It isn't even half-past nine! Has everyone become lactose-intolerant overnight? I order a green tea, instead. I will celebrate with a proper drink once the money flows in.

As I'm walking back to my office building, second thoughts creep into my mind. Am I really going to do this? Do I even want to run errands for other people? What if nobody calls? What if they do call, but they turn out to be crazy people who want me to do crazy things for them? What if they yell at me? Or worse. And, although I don't want to think about it, it's possible I could get caught.

But I'm too invested. *I need the bag.* I already feel as if I own it. Even the universe wants me to have it. How likely is it that the bag would be sent off for repairs, allowing me the time to come up with the funds to buy it? The bag needs me, too.

I pick up the pace and get back to my desk at record-speed, where I find my computer ready-and-waiting for me. Before I can change my mind, I post my ads on Craigslist and Kijiji.

Erin Girl has launched.

SIX

Project Coco Fund = $120.00

TWENTY-FOUR HOURS LATER, no one has responded to my ads. What if this doesn't work?

I'm about to consult Google for backup ideas when I'm hit with a sudden craving for a martini—shaken, not stirred—which can mean only one thing: My phone is ringing. (I switched my ringtone to the *James Bond* theme song in light of my new, covert business operation. But the ringtone isn't so covert sounding as it plays loudly across the office floor.)

I quickly answer the call, noticing it's from a blocked number.

"Hi, this is Erin—" I'm about to add "Girl" in case it's a client, but I can't because this is a covert operation.

There is a pause on the other end, then a crackly woman's voice asks, "Is this Erin Girl? The errand service?"

"Yes, yes, it is!" I say excitedly. "How can I help you today?"

"I most certainly hope you can help. My name is Margaret, Mrs. Margaret O'Connor. I need someone to run an errand for me. My son says he is too busy, but he saw your ad on that Gregslist, or whatever it's called. It isn't a big errand, but it's very important."

"No problem, Mrs. O'Connor. Big or small, I can handle it all," I say, then cringe at how cheesy that sounded.

"Oh, goody!" (She bought it.) "I need Fuji apples picked up for me at the store. I forgot to get them when I was out yesterday. Now my knee is acting up, and I can't leave the house. I need exactly seven apples—no more, no less. And they *must* be medium in size with no bruises; that is with *no bruises*."

"Okay, seven, medium, Fuji apples with no bruises." I try to suppress a giggle. Are these the types of errands I will be getting?

33

"They also have to be organic. I eat *only* organic apples. I read an article about pesticides. You know, when I was a child, we didn't have to worry about that sort of thing. We could pick an apple off the tree and eat it right there. But these days, I have to pay extra for the organic kind."

"Uh-huh," I say, jotting down notes. "I will need your address and when you would like the apples delivered by."

She tells me where she lives: Rosedale. *Quelle surprise.* She also tells me the apples have to come from Whole Foods. She only trusts Whole Foods with her pesticide-free, organic apples.

"I will need the apples no later than two this afternoon. I'm hosting my bridge club this evening. Everyone expects me to bake my famous apple pie, and there I go forgetting the most important ingredient. Goodness! I almost forgot something else: How much is this going to cost me?" she asks, her voice taking on a serious tone.

Crap. I'm not sure what to say. I had an approximate rate in mind for my services, but it's different now that I'm on the spot. I mean, she just wants some apples.

"It shouldn't take me more than an hour to complete the errand with delivery, so...ten dollars, plus the cost of the apples?"

Silence. Minutes seem to pass before she says, "All right, then. I suppose that is the price you pay for forgetfulness. I will need to see the receipt, though."

I let out my breath. "Of course! I look forward to meeting you."

Erin Girl has its first client!

This is a great way to kick off things. The timing is perfect. I can go out on my lunch and be back to work without raising any suspicions. Maybe every errand will be this easy.

I start humming to myself.

"Someone is in a good mood," Bradford says, peering over my cubicle wall.

Why do they always do that? I have a door—sort of.

"I am. It's...I'm...loving this weather we are having," I say, trying to come up with something. The weather seems like a safe bet.

"Indeed, indeed. Was that the travel agency on the phone?"

"Um, no—but I confirmed your flight details; everything is in order. I got the flight you requested and printed your itinerary for you. It's right here..."

As I'm rummaging through the papers on my desk, I notice my notes from the call with Mrs. O'Connor in plain view. In my haste to hide them, I knock over my coffee cup, spilling the half-drunk latte contents across my desk.

"Well, that is unfortunate. Looks like your humming is done for the day. Print it again and drop it off on my desk once you have cleaned that up," he says, walking away without offering any help. (Chivalry is dead.)

I grab and try to salvage my notes from the call. I can make out some of what I wrote. Mrs. O'Connor's address is visible, but the type and quantity of apples she requested are completely smudged. I'm almost certain she wanted eight apples...or was it seven? I know they have to be organic and purchased at Whole Foods. But what kind did she want? It wasn't a common apple, definitely not Granny Smith or McIntosh. I would remember if it was one of those.

C'mon, Erin! You just talked to her. What kind of apple did she want?

I go through the letters of the alphabet, hoping that will jog my memory. It's a trick I use that normally works. I go through it again and again. But I can't remember.

I get off the subway at Museum station and walk up Avenue Road until I hit Whole Foods. I shopped here once before. I bought six things, and my bill came to almost seventy dollars. I haven't been back since. I have yet to embrace the organics movement—I still eat hot dogs.

Making my way down the escalator, I take in the store as it appears below. There is something cool about an underground grocery store. It seems illicit somehow. I bet there is a secret code to get black-market stuff at the meat counter.

The produce section has a plethora of apples. I look at the names to see if any spark my memory. I have safely crossed Granny Smith and McIntosh off the list, and anything that isn't organic, but several options remain.

I see a produce guy. Perhaps he will know.

"Excuse me, sir?" (Politeness gets you everywhere.)

"Something I can help you with?"

"I hope so. I have to buy apples for...my grandma. She is baking an apple pie, but I can't seem to remember what kind she needs."

"Why don't you give her a call?"

"Thank you, Sherlock. But if I had 'grandma's' number, I would have already done that. Sadly, I'm new to the business world and forgot that tiny detail."

That is what I want to say. What I actually say is, "She is hard of hearing and doesn't pick up her phone. What type of apple do people buy to make a pie?"

"Granny Smith is a popular—"

"I'm looking for something more exotic."

"How about Pink Lady?"

"That sounds pretty, but I don't think that is what my grandma wanted."

"A delivery of Rome apples just came in. I could go to the back and grab you some."

Maybe that was it? I think the apple had the name of a city or something like that.

"Are they organic?" I ask.

"They are!" he says with pride.

"All right, I will take some of those."

He goes into a backroom while I wander around examining the other apples. There are some named Red Prince, Lady Alice, Royal Gala. They sound so regal. Then, I see Fuji apples, which rings a bell.

But what about the Rome apples? Honestly, I can't be sure if it's either one.

"Here are the Rome apples. How many would you like?" the produce guy asks me as he wheels over a cart with a box of apples on top of it.

"Um, seven. No—make it eight. And only medium-sized ones with no bruises; that is with *no bruises*."

He gives me a funny expression, then picks through them.

As he does, I pick out eight of the Fuji apples. I will have to buy both.

It's past one by the time I get to Mrs. O'Connor's place. Who knew that picking up apples would take so long or that organic apples cost so much? More than a buck a pop!

I ring the doorbell of her quaint townhouse. I was expecting another McMansion, so this puts me somewhat at ease, although I'm worried about the apple situation. I have worked out a complicated scheme to determine what kind of apple she wants without her knowing I have both types hiding behind me.

The door opens. I have to look down to see the sweetest, little, old lady smiling up at me.

"Hello, dear. You must be Erin." She reaches out her hand and pats my arm. (I love her.) "Let me go fetch my purse. They had the Fujis, did they?" she calls from the hallway.

So much for my elaborate plan. "They did. All organic," I say, breathing a sigh of relief. I grab the paper bag behind me with the Fuji apples. I guess I will be eating overpriced Rome apples for the rest of the week.

"Oh, goody!" she says, returning with her purse. "I will need to check the apples and see the receipt."

I hand her the bag, along with the separate receipt I got for the Fuji apples.

She appraises the apples, then says, "Oh, dear," in a tone that implies the worst thing in the world has happened. "There are eight apples in here, not seven. And one of them...one of them has a bruise." She looks at me, horrified. "I won't pay for a bruised apple."

The apples are for a *pie*. I'm not a baker, but I'm guessing a couple of bruises wouldn't be a big deal. Alas, the customer is always right.

"No worries, Mrs. O'Connor. I threw that one in as a bonus in case they got banged up. I will deduct it from your total."

"Let me get my calculator and specs, then," she says, heading back into the townhouse.

I nervously check the time. This is taking longer than I expected.

When she returns, Mrs. O'Connor works out the total and hands me eighteen dollars and forty cents—exactly.

I thank her, then make my way towards the subway station.

Once on the subway, I do some mental calculations and realize I lost money on my first errand run. Not a promising start.

It's almost two o'clock when I get back to the office. I half-walk, half-run to my desk, taking off my jacket as I do. I can't be late for my status meeting with Bradford before he leaves on his business trip. Hopefully, no one noticed I was gone this entire time.

As I approach my cubicle, I see a shadow inside of it. Please don't let it be...

"Carol? What are you doing in here?" I ask, out of breath.

She puts her index finger up to her mouth, then points to my work phone at her ear. I pause in the entryway of my cubicle, not knowing what I should do.

"I'm sorry, sir. You have the wrong number. We are a multinational corporation, not an errand service," she says, rolling her eyes at me. "There is no errand girl here...I'm certain...That is quite all right. Okay, goodbye now." Carol puts the phone back on the receiver and turns to face me from my office chair.

"How strange, that man was looking for an errand service," she says, appraising me through her thick, black-rimmed glasses.

"That is strange," I say innocently. "I had a few calls this week asking for the same thing. My number must be similar to that errand business. Anyway, is there something I can help you with?"

"Where have you been? I have been trying to find you for an hour." She takes in the jacket and purse I'm holding with a sneer on her face. "Late lunch?"

"Um, no. I was...I was in the restroom. I must have eaten something bad at lunch because I wasn't feeling well. It was probably the seafood salad I ate," I say, squishing up my face.

"And you brought your jacket and purse with you?"

"I was, uh, on my way back when it hit me. I have been in there for more than an hour."

"Hmm. You seem fine to me now. Bradford asked me to join your meeting." She gets up and walks towards me. "Let's go before you make us both late. Don't forget your notebook."

"Got it," I say through clenched teeth as I grab my notebook, then throw my jacket and purse onto my liberated chair.

That was close. Way too close. I forgot I had forwarded my calls to my work number so my personal phone wouldn't be ringing throughout the day. I won't be doing that again.

I need to come up with a better system before someone catches on to what I'm doing. And by someone, I mean Carol.

SEVEN

Project Coco Fund = $119.20

WITH BRADFORD GONE on his business trip for the next week, I have additional time on my already idle hands. So I'm spending the morning researching how to run an errand service, properly. This involves consulting my silent, but extremely knowledgeable, business partner: Google.

The first thing I realize is that I need a higher-paying clientele. Charging ten bucks an hour won't cut it. If I focus on clients in the downtown core, I can charge at least twenty-five dollars an hour. And it will be easier to run errands during the day, as there will be less travel time between clients.

I also designed a flyer I'm planning to drop off at the main reception desks of the many companies downtown. I will ask if I can put up the flyer in their office kitchen. And if no one is around, I will sneak in and do it myself.

To jazz up the flyer, I added a cartoon image of myself wearing a superhero costume with a big "E" on my front and a cape on my back. I figure it works with my tagline. And because doodling is one of my mastered skills, it looks pretty good. But I hope I don't get any weirdos expecting me to show up dressed like that.

I found colour paper stock hidden away in the supply room. Carol must have been hoarding it. Initially, I chose pink, but my growing business sense said to go with blue. I want to attract male clients, too, and I somehow don't think pink is the way to do that. Carol is away this afternoon at a doctor's appointment, so I can print the flyers and deliver them without her prying eyes on me.

After loading the printer with the fancy blue paper, I run back to my desk to hit the print button. Then, I run back to the copy room to make sure no one else picks up my copies. All this running back-and-forth may raise some eyebrows, but I can't think of any way around it. The printer is finicky, so I can only print ten copies at a time. The last thing I need is a paper jam.

I'm printing a hundred flyers. I don't know when I will get another chance to print more. I can't rely on Carol being out of the office. This is the first doctor's appointment she has had in the time I have worked here. She even eats lunch at her desk. She is like a watchdog, always on duty.

My mission is to deliver at least twenty of the flyers today. I will drop off more each day until I run out. I'm focusing on companies that are part of the underground path. It will be faster for me to get around to a bunch of the office buildings, and there won't be any suspicious jacket-wearing required.

I love the underground path. It covers the majority of the downtown financial core and has lots of shops and restaurants, without ever stepping foot outside. It's amazing. It took me months to get the hang of it when I first started working downtown. I often had to come up to street level to find my way back to work. Since that time, I have had many occasions to explore on my countless long lunches and figured out how most of the paths interconnect.

This afternoon's flyer deliveries will be to First Canadian Place. My goal is to get the odd-numbered floors completed. The building has separate elevator banks for odd- and even-numbered floors. Tomorrow, I will do the even-numbered floors. And then, there is still Scotia Plaza, The Royal Bank Building, Commerce Court, Brookfield Place...so many office kitchens. So many opportunities!

Maybe I should print more flyers.

"Hello," I say, answering my phone.

"Hey, is this that errand service?" a deep male voice asks.

"It is! How can I help you?" Fingers-crossed he isn't baking a pie.

"I saw your flyer up in our staff kitchen. I want to create a standing order. I need someone to deliver my lunch daily. I can't leave my desk: I'm an equity trader. Ever since the *fuckheads* got rid of our receptionist, I don't have anyone to grab it. Coffee lunches aren't cutting it for me. What is your rate?"

I try to catch up. He saw my flyer: It's working! And a standing order: That is guaranteed business!

Think, Erin, think. Does that mean I should charge more or less?

I will stick with my new standard rate. I don't want to be greedy.

"Well, given that you want me to hold that time exclusively for you, I would have to charge twenty-five dollars an hour, plus the cost of food," I say, trying to sound confident, but that seems like a heck of a lot of money to deliver someone's lunch.

"*Fuck me!* That is more than I thought." (Dammit!) "But a guy has to eat, and time is money." (Phew.) "All right, let's say the cost of food and seventy-five bucks a week guaranteed, even if you take less than an hour to deliver. Deal?"

If I run the errand in half-the-time, I would get paid more than my standard rate. "Okay," I say, "that sounds fair."

We work out the details. Apparently, he is a health nut and likes to eat at this vegan joint that doesn't offer delivery. His office at First Canadian Place is near it, so I should make it under time.

"One more thing," he says as I'm about to end the call. "Will you be wearing that sexy costume when you deliver my lunch each day? I would throw in a bonus if you did."

Weirdo number one.

I need to deliver Mr. Trader's lunch any time between noon and two o'clock. I thought it was nice of him to give me this window because I would have the flexibility to run other errands on my lunch break. I calculated that given the distance from my office to his office, while stopping to pick up his lunch along the way, it shouldn't take more than half-an-hour to run the errand from start to finish.

But as I approach the vegan place, I see a bank line setup. *A bank line!* And the reason for the bank line is this lunch spot is so popular, they need to control the crowds. It isn't even an actual restaurant, just a food vendor at the end of a busy underground pathway.

Mr. Trader neglected to mention any of this. I might have to change his nickname to Mr. Traitor, instead.

I ask the girl ahead of me how long it usually takes. She tells me when it first opened, she once waited an hour-and-a-half for her Buddha bowl, but now, the wait was *only* thirty minutes. So much for making this a quickie.

As I'm fidgeting in line, my phone rings. "Hey," I answer absentmindedly.

"Hello, there. I am looking for Erin Girl. Do I have the correct number?" an indistinguishable, robotic-sounding voice asks on the other end.

"Yes, sorry, this is Erin Girl. How can I help you?"

"I came across your flyer. I recently purchased IKEA furniture. I would like to inquire whether furniture assembly is part of your service offering, and, recognizing that perhaps it is not feasible, your availability for tomorrow?"

This should be interesting.

For the record, it takes six hours and forty-eight minutes for someone with my skill level to assemble a dresser, two nightstands, a coffee table, and a bookcase. I know this because every single minute was being timed...and watched.

I spent the previous Saturday with one of those IKEA thingamajiggy tools, permanently attached to my hand. I developed two calluses, blurred vision, and mild dehydration. But I wouldn't stop until I finished. Not because I have a Puritan work ethic—I think that has already been established—but because I wanted to get the heck out of the client's apartment as fast as possible.

The entire time I was assembling said furniture, I had weirdo number two, standing over me, asking every few minutes whether I was doing it correctly.

Was I positive that piece belonged there? Perhaps I should take another look at the instructions?

So what if I messed up a couple of times. No one ever gets it right the first time. Everyone knows that.

Sunday was better. I had to water a client's houseplants and collect her mail while she was away on vacation. She asked me to stay for a few hours to make it appear someone was home. So I listened to loud music and danced around. I resisted the urge to go through her cabinets. I had a sneaking suspicion there were hidden cameras all over the place. (If so, I hope she enjoyed my rendition of *Swan Lake*.)

Then, during the week, I had an unpleasant mishap.

A client asked me to pick up his dry cleaning at the TD Tower building, which sounded easy enough. Except there isn't just one TD Tower, there are at least four. There is TD Tower North, TD Tower West, TD Tower South, and straight-up TD Tower. (I never found out if there is a TD Tower East.) And every single one of those towers has a thirtieth floor.

After finally finding the client in the right tower, he had the nerve to ask me if I was bonded. At first, I thought he was looking for sexual favours, and I was about to refuse when I clued-in that he meant bond insurance. He wouldn't let me take his expensive designer suits until I showed him proof. Well, of course, I didn't have any proof. Getting bonded costs money, and I'm trying to *make* money. So I lost a potential client and wasted a bunch of time.

I'm realizing entrepreneurship isn't easy. I thought I would have made more money by now. Even though I'm getting steady business and have some funds to show for it, I still haven't reached the halfway mark. Okay, so it hasn't been a full two weeks since Erin Girl launched, but this isn't a normal business. I'm on an extremely tight deadline. Eventually, my mom's bag will come back from repairs and someone will buy it. If I don't make money fast enough, it won't be me.

There is only one way I know how to make super-fast cash: I need to talk to Betty.

EIGHT

Project Coco Fund = $535.05

I'M SURPRISING BETTY at the airport. She always takes the same flight back from Boston on Sundays.

The best strategy is to do this face-to-face, even though getting to the airport is a major pain because I don't have a car, and I wasn't about to shell out my newly earned cash on a cab ride. An express train to the airport is being constructed, but, sadly, it isn't finished, yet. Very inconvenient *pour moi*.

Betty has been doing these weekend trips for months. This is the first time I have come to meet her. I was going to put her name on a piece of cardboard but thought that would be overkill. (Plus, she would probably get suspicious.)

I have been waiting at her arrival gate for so long that I'm running out of things to amuse myself with, and now my phone battery is dangerously low.

When she finally comes out of the gate, she looks worn out. Maybe this wasn't a good idea. It probably would have been smarter to wait until tomorrow. But it's too late, I'm already here.

"Betty! Betty!"

She doesn't immediately realize someone is calling her name. When she sees me waving while jumping up and down, she hurries in my direction.

"Erin? Is everything all right? What are you doing here?"

"I came to surprise you!"

"*Really?* Okay, phew. I thought something bad had happened," she says, visibly exhaling.

"Can't a big sister surprise her little sister at the airport, every now and again?"

"Well, you haven't before, so you caught me off-guard. But I'm so glad you are here. I needed to see a friendly face," she says, giving me a side hug with her baggage-free arm.

"And I'm glad to see you, sis," I say, hugging her back. "Hey, are you cabbing it or taking public transit?"

"Cabbing it. There is no way I can deal with other people after my flight. There was a baby on-board who cried the entire time. Babies shouldn't fly."

"*Betty!* Little people need to see the world, too."

"I know, I know. I'm just cranky and hungry."

Uh-oh. I should have brought her a snack. "Here, let me take your bag. How was your weekend?" I ask, taking the bag from her.

"Horrible. Matt and I got into a huge fight about this whole long-distance thing. He doesn't know when he will be back in Toronto. I'm so tired of going back-and-forth all the time."

"Yeah, it's rough, but you guys will work something out. You always do."

"I don't know. I have my limits."

We are the first ones in the taxi line and get a cab right away. We ride in silence for a while until I can't wait any longer. I need to ask her.

"Hey, Betty..."

"Yeah?" she answers as she is looking out the window at the passing horizon.

"I wanted to talk to you about Project Coco."

Betty turns towards me. "I knew you didn't come to surprise me. Seriously, this is becoming an obsession. Let it go. It's just a bag."

"It isn't 'just a bag,' and you know it, Betty." She can be so cold. "It's mom's bag. I need to at least try to get it back."

"It isn't 'mom's bag,' and you know that, Erin. Mom is gone, and you can't get her back by buying some bag. As far as we know, a posh socialite on the other side of the world is wearing it as we speak."

"I don't think so. I feel a connection to it. And I'm getting these signs from the universe. I know it sounds crazy, but there is a chance, a slight one I will admit, that it's really her bag."

"It does sound crazy. I'm sure the universe has better things to do than point you in the direction of a bag."

"Fine, let's agree to disagree on that. What I'm asking—and you can say no if you want—but I was thinking you could—"

"I'm not giving you the money."

"I wasn't asking you to *give* me the money. It would be more of a loan. I will pay you back with the money I'm making from the errand service. We can share the bag until I can buy out your portion."

"I'm not loaning you thousands of dollars so you can buy some silly bag."

"IT'S NOT A SILLY BAG!"

The taxi driver turns his head slightly. I lower my voice and say, "Whatever. You are the reason we don't have it anymore."

"I should have known you would eventually bring this up. Don't try to guilt-trip me. I *needed* braces. Don't you remember how bad my teeth were?"

"Yeah, but don't you see? This is our chance to get the bag back. After all these years, it can be ours again!" I hesitate before adding, "And you sort of owe me."

"For being orthodontically-challenged?"

"You know what I'm talking about."

"Oh, that is low!" Betty looks at me as if I slapped her on the face. "I was on an audit! I came *every* weekend. I took care of her, too. I don't see how one thing has to do with the other, but if we are keeping score, you owe me: nine thousand, five hundred, and thirty-seven dollars to be exact."

"For what?"

"Your share of mom's funeral and final expenses. I paid for everything."

"I didn't have any money! Not everyone gets a scholarship to cover their university expenses; some people need to get student loans."

"Yeah, well, not everyone adds to those student loans by backpacking across Europe for the summer, spending money they don't have, instead of getting a job to pay off their debts, like a responsible adult would."

"You suck, Betty."

"You suck more. This is the last thing I need to worry about right now. I think it's better if you take the subway the rest of your way home. I want to be alone."

"Fine."

We ride in silence until the taxi driver lets me off at the nearest subway station. I get out of the cab and take one last look at Betty, whose face is turned away from me.

Betty and I don't fight. Okay, we have had the odd disagreement, but this time is different. We went places that we have never gone before. I open my mouth to say something, but there is nothing left to say. I slam the cab door and make my way to the subway station.

NINE

Project Coco Fund = $535.05

I NEED TO STAY FOCUSED. I hate fighting with Betty, but there is no way I'm backing down now. She doesn't realize how important this "silly" bag is to me. It's the missing piece of a puzzle I can't solve. And until I get that final piece, I can't move forward. Plus, it's already led to a bunch of positive changes in my life: I started my own business, I made over five-hundred dollars, and I'm building a client base.

Erin Girl could end up becoming my full-time gig, and I could quit my job once and for all. So what if I haven't enjoyed most of the errands I have run. At least, it's my own show. I can't say that about my desk job.

I know I can do this. I just need to keep going.

And as the universe (no matter what Betty thinks) is in on this with me, my phone rings. Another client. Destiny.

"Hello, Erin Girl," I answer. I don't care if anyone hears me, not even Carol.

"Oh, hello. I'm so glad to have reached you. Is this the real Erin or one of her assistants?"

I never thought about having assistants. I could turn this solo operation of mine into an army of errand-running superheroes. But instead of assistants, they would be called sidekicks, obviously.

"In the flesh!" I say. I like this lady already. "How can I help you today?"

"I'm calling from Vancouver, but I'm originally from Toronto. My father passed away a year ago, and I haven't managed to get back since the funeral. My father *loved* daisies, and I feel horrible he has gone this long without any flowers. So I was wondering—I know it sounds somewhat unorthodox—but I was hoping you could plant daisies at his gravestone at Mount Pleasant—"

"I'm so sorry for your loss, but that is out of Erin Girl's jurisdiction. We focus exclusively on the downtown core. Perhaps another errand service can help you with your request. I'm so sorry," I say again and end the call.

I can't breathe. I need to get some fresh air.

I'm calling in sick. I have never called in sick before. Sure, I come to work late every single morning, but somehow calling in sick seemed like the last straw. As if once I started, I wouldn't be able to stop.

But I have a long list of errands to run today, and there is no way I can get them completed under Carol's watchful eye. It isn't a total lie: I'm not feeling the greatest.

So I'm leaving Carol a voice message, saying I won't be coming in. To play it safe, I'm calling at a quarter-to-seven. I hope she doesn't get in that early. I have no idea when she arrives at work, as I have never been there before her. Actually, I have never left work after her, either. She may never go home.

I have been practicing my sick voice, which is easy at this time of the morning: I already sound hoarse. My voice box doesn't normally open for business before eight.

The phone rings a few times, then goes to Carol's voicemail. Even her voice annoys me, so I hit the pound key to skip to the end.

"Hey, Carol. It's Erin." *Cough*. "I'm not feeling well." *Sniff*. "I think I have one of those twenty-four-hour bugs or something." *Gag*. "So I'm staying home today. Please let Bradford know. I'm sure I will be fine by tomorrow. Bye!"

My "bye" was too chipper. But there is nothing I can do about that now—except enjoy my first-ever sick day. Ah, the freedom! I could catch an afternoon matinée or spend the entire day in bed...

Oh, yeah, I have to waste it running crummy errands.

Even though I'm not going into work, I still need to go downtown.

My first errand of the day is to mail off a bunch of letters for a woman who lives in a suite at Trump Tower. I didn't think people wrote letters anymore. She tells me to call her M., so I automatically think she is MI6. (Her British accent supports my spy theory.)

M. has a stack of two dozen letters of various sizes, shapes, and thicknesses, with most going to different countries. I'm especially intrigued by the one addressed to the Embassy of the Republic of Yemen, but I resist asking. She isn't very...friendly. I get the impression I'm inconveniencing her by being in her presence.

M. trusts a specific post office to handle her complicated mailing instructions. She has a long list of which letters should be sent by registered mail, which ones must arrive by tomorrow morning, and which ones need a boring, old stamp. Her trusted post office is in the underground path. This makes me a bit anxious. Even though it isn't near my office building, it's still part of the same path. I wish I brought my sunglasses. I'm wearing a pashmina scarf, so I could always use that as a head cover, if necessary.

I make my way to M.'s special post office, passing two others along the way. When I find it, I see there is a long line. These guys must be really good at mailing. I hurry to join the line before it gets any longer.

As I'm wrestling with the letters, trying to keep them organized, I glance up and notice the back of a familiar head. It isn't until the person turns slightly that I can confirm it for sure. It's Bradford.

What is he doing all the way down here? Is he also in the know of these mailing magicians? Is this some private club that only a select few have knowledge of?

He is three people ahead of me. I don't think he has seen me. I will need to leave and come back when the coast is clear.

But I turn too quickly and bump into the person standing behind me. Some of the letters I'm holding fall to the ground with a loud thump.

Shit! I'm so getting caught!

Hastily, I bend down to pick up the letters. The person I bumped into has bent down, as well. I look up, and our eyes lock. I'm staring into the most beautiful blue eyes. I know *those* blue eyes.

It's Suit Guy.

"Here, let me help you with those," he says, grinning. Wow, even his teeth are gorgeous.

I inhale his intoxicating scent and get lightheaded. I'm about to thank him profusely, but then, I remember my boss is standing a few feet away from me. I can't risk Bradford recognizing my voice, so I nod and smile shyly as I reluctantly make my getaway.

Maybe the universe is actually conspiring against me.

Why doesn't anything ever go smoothly? Why was Bradford in my line, of all lines? And why did I have to run into Suit Guy for the first time outside of the subway today, of all days? I might have had the courage to finally—*finally!*—talk to him; ruined by the bad timing of my boss requiring postage.

The only positive thing to come out of this was that I touched Suit Guy. Okay, it was more of a body check, but, at least, I have that.

I hide out in a store across from the post office until I see both Bradford and Suit Guy leave. I wait a few extra minutes in case Bradford returns for another hit of magical stamps.

After I get the letters mailed, I make my way back to M. She has an envelope waiting for me with the exact cash required to reimburse me for the cost of the mailings and my time. She even marked the envelope with an "E." I should start referring to myself as that from now on to add an air of mystery.

I run Mr. Trader his vegan lunch, and then head for the subway to complete my final errands of the day.

As I'm about to pass through the turnstile, my phone vibrates, alerting me that I have a voice message. I turnaround to find a quieter place to listen to it.

It's the nice saleslady from the vintage shop. I left my name and number with her so she could let me know when my bag returned from repairs. She called to say it will be back by Friday and restocked for Saturday.

Saturday is only four days away. *It's too soon!* I need to step up things, or all of this would have been for nothing.

TEN

Project Coco Fund = $890.70

THE LAST FEW DAYS were spent running errand after errand. I'm willing to take anything at this point. It's getting harder and harder to come up with reasons I'm not at my desk when Carol says she has been looking for me.

My "in the washroom" excuse was wearing thin, even after suffering a couple of alleged stomach viruses, so I have been relying on my old standby of inventing fake meetings. And, yesterday, I called to say I would be extra, extra late to work because there was a burst pipe in my apartment. There wasn't a burst pipe in my apartment.

I'm becoming a rather adept liar. I may add it to my list of mastered skills. I contemplated taking another sick day, but that would have led to further suspicion.

Carol has been acting weird around me lately. I think she knows I'm up to something, but she can't figure out what that is. I hope she thinks I'm interviewing for another job, then she would leave me alone—or possibly even help me.

But I don't need to worry about coming up with any alibis today, because today is Saturday. My office job doesn't exist on Saturdays.

I'm heading to Yorkville this morning to confirm my bag has returned and maybe cast a spell on it so no one else buys it.

I counted up every nickel and dime I have earned: I'm almost at the halfway mark! Not bad for under three weeks' worth of work. If I can keep this up, I should have enough money within the next two weeks.

Just give me two more weeks.

—

When I get to the vintage shop, I don't see the nice saleslady. I hope she is the one working today; she has been so helpful in my mission. At this point, she is the only one in my corner rooting for me, and I don't even know her name.

I glance around the shop several times, but I don't see my bag anywhere.

"I will leave the Chanel bag out here while I try on these other items." I hear a woman say.

At the mention of Chanel, my ears perk up. With laser-eye focus, I zero-in on the bag. Yup, it's mine. My breathing quickens. There is a high probability I may pass out.

Someone is about to buy my bag. Someone is about to buy my bag!

What am I going to do? What *can* I do?

The mean salesgirl comes out of the fitting room area. She hasn't seen me, yet. My instincts tell me to hide, so I duck down behind a clothing rack.

Peeking through a slight gap in-between some hanging dresses, I see she has taken the bag from the woman.

"We can't leave a bag like this lying around," she says in her condescending tone. "I will put it behind the counter for you." She places the bag behind the counter, then goes back into the fitting room area with the woman.

I need to act fast. At the moment, I'm the only other person in the shop.

C'mon, Erin! Think! Don't quit now! You are too close to give up!

I know what I want to do, but that can't be the way I get the bag. Plus, I haven't stolen anything since high school: I'm rusty. Although stealing a Chanel bag worth two-thousand dollars hardly compares to stealing a five-dollar tube of lipstick.

As I look around the shop for inspiration, I'm hit with a stroke of genius.

I crawl on the floor until I'm behind the counter. I grab the bag and swing it around my neck. Then, I quickly crawl back to the other side of the shop where I spotted an ugly, oversized weekend bag in the colour of snot green. There is no way anyone would ever buy that bag. Once I place my mom's bag safely inside of it, I run to the door.

As I'm exiting the shop, I hear the mean salesgirl say, "Let me go grab that Versace evening gown you were admiring."

I hope they both somehow forget about the Chanel bag. I also hope there aren't any security cameras in the shop that witnessed what I did. But I didn't steal, and it isn't as if hiding merchandise is a crime...is it?

I spend the rest of the weekend hiding out in my walk-in closet. I even cancelled two errand jobs.

Part of me is afraid to leave my apartment in case the police are waiting for me outside, which I know is crazy. They wouldn't wait for me outside; they would just knock on my door. I fear my heart would stop if anyone knocked on my door right now.

And then, there is this other part of me, the one lying on the cluttered floor of my closet, staring at my shoe collection, wondering how the heck I got to this point. I almost stole a bag worth thousands of dollars. Worse than that, I *wanted* to steal a bag worth thousands of dollars. A bag. A silly, *silly* bag.

Betty is right. Betty is always right. I should stop with this obsession. I can't even call her to talk about it as we aren't, well, talking. This is the longest we have gone without speaking to each other.

If only I could stay in my closet forever and never have to come out again. Why is life so hard? Why can't the things we truly want, come to us—like magic? In real life, the things we need the most, the things we yearn for, can't be made to appear out of nowhere with a spell or potion concoction. Real life kind of stinks.

But there is another part of me, a much smaller, almost minuscule part, fading away as the years go by, that still believes magic exists. And that there is a reason I'm so drawn to this bag I don't fully understand. A reason I started this Erin Girl madness that has me running around like a fool completing errands for strangers. A reason strong enough to risk losing my job and jeopardizing my relationship with Betty. A reason proving all of this hasn't been for nothing.

And the only way for me to figure out what that reason is, is to get that silly bag in my hands.

Gazing up at my clothes hanging above me, I sigh. I wish I knew which part will win out in the end.

ELEVEN

Project Coco Fund = $1,017.35

EVENTUALLY, I CAME OUT of my closet. I'm too close to the finish line to give up. I can't give up. I won't give up.

What is the worst that can happen: I end up with two grand and no bag. Well, that is two grand I didn't have before. Even my job is more interesting now that I have this side hustle. I need to get my "real" work done quickly so I can go run errands. Work isn't that bad when there is something to do.

And, this morning, I received another sign from the universe to keep going in the form of a girl on the subway wearing a similar Chanel bag to mine. One day soon, I will be my own version of that girl.

In the last few days, I ran a bunch of errands, and I'm getting closer and closer to meeting my goal. All I need is one last push. So I'm printing more Erin Girl flyers and making the rounds again. There are buildings in the underground path I haven't gotten to yet.

It's almost lunchtime, so I take a chance and print the flyers. I walk nonchalantly to the copy room to make sure no one is around, then I load the printer with my special blue paper. I run back to my desk not-so-nonchalantly and hit the print button.

"Yes, of course, Bradford, I would be happy to grab you lunch. It isn't a bother at all." I hear Carol say as she exits his office.

Crap! She is in my line of path. I will have to wait until she leaves to get my flyers.

Nervously, I drum my fingers and sneak peeks over the top of my cubicle wall every few seconds to see if she has left.

The sound of my phone ringing interrupts my surveillance.

Before I get the chance to say hello, I hear a gruff voice on the other end say, "I have a job that needs to get done pronto. Are you my girl?"

"Um, yes, I'm your girl. I mean, Erin Girl. I'm sure I can help. What sort of errand do you need me to run?" I ask, lowering my voice, as Carol is still lurking around.

"I have a package that needs delivering, but only by someone who is discreet. Are you discreet, Erin?"

"Very discreet. Discreet is practically my middle name; that is how discreet I am."

"Good, that is what I wanted to hear. It's an easy job, too. All you got to do is pick up a package downtown and deliver it up to Finch. That is it. But it has to be done discreetly."

Yeah, yeah, discreetly—I get it. "No problem. I just need to get the addresses from you."

The first address he gives me is located somewhere in the entertainment district. The second address is at Jane and Finch. Eek, no one ever goes to Jane and Finch voluntarily...although I would be getting paid. I should tell him I can't do it. I can say I have another errand to run that I had forgotten about.

"Hey, you still there?" he asks.

"Yes, sorry. I just remembered I have—"

"Oh, yeah, I just remembered something, too. You will get three hundred cash at the first pick-up point and another seven when you drop it off. *Capisce?*"

That is...a thousand dollars! That would put me over the top. I would have enough money to buy my mom's bag!

Hold on a second. A thousand dollars for delivering a package?

C'mon, Erin. You have seen enough mafia movies to know there is something fishy going on here. He even said, "capisce." Your safety is worth more than a grand. You can't do this. You will have to say no. This is so wrong. Wrong! Wrong! Wrong!

"Um, capisce," I blurt out and end the call before I lose my nerve. I grab my jacket and purse and head for the elevators.

I want to get this mysterious "job" over and done with. Pronto.

—

This is really stupid. Not my ordinary, everyday brand of stupid—oh, no. This is horror film, run-to-the-basement-instead-of-outside kind of stupid.

I'm going to what I can only imagine is an abandoned warehouse to pick up a suspicious package for a guy who says, "capisce." Assuming I make it out of the warehouse alive, I'm then taking the package and delivering it somewhere near Jane and Finch.

Jane and Finch!

I have lived in Toronto my entire life, and I have never been within ten blocks of that area. I check over my outfit. I don't think I'm wearing any gang colours, although I'm not up-to-date on gang culture. Let's hope my beige trench coat is neutral.

The worst thing is, no one knows where I am. I can't call Betty. I couldn't tell Carol where I was going, but I should have at least told her I wouldn't be back this afternoon. I also forgot to get Mr. Trader his vegan lunch.

But there is nothing I can do now. They can read about my untimely death in the papers tomorrow. This is by far the dumbest thing I have ever done. Well, one of them.

Getting off the streetcar, I walk a couple of blocks until I find the abandoned warehouse. Except, it doesn't look abandoned. I can see into one of the units from the street. It's two-levels and has an enormous chandelier hanging from the living room ceiling. I guess they converted the warehouse into lofts.

Maybe there is nothing to worry about, and I'm imagining things.

I ring the buzzer. From the other end, I hear dogs barking wildly. Very big, very angry-sounding dogs. Then again, maybe there is something to worry about.

Why does everyone have to be a dog lover?

I get buzzed in without a hello. My legs are shaking as I make my way up the stairs. I wish I owned pepper spray. Why haven't I ever thought to buy some? I'm a single girl in the city without pepper spray. I reach into my purse and pull out my compact umbrella. It's something.

As I approach the top of the stairs, I see a door open slightly. One of the angry dogs tries to escape.

"Get back, Cake Pop!" I hear a woman say.

Cake Pop? Who names their killer dog, Cake Pop?

The dog backs off, and the woman opens the door wider. "Heya, you must be Erin."

She is barefoot, barelegged, and wearing a men's dress shirt with the sleeves rolled up to her elbows. Her hair is messy in a way that suggests she has just woken up. She is also tall and awkward pretty, so I assume she is a model or former model. (This is how my mind works.)

She reaches out to shake my hand.

This could be a test.

What if I'm supposed to know a secret handshake to confirm I'm the "real" Erin and not someone working for the Feds. As I don't know a secret handshake, I give her a standard one.

She glances down at my umbrella. "Is it raining out?"

"Um, no. I, uh, found it on the stairwell. Is it yours?"

"No, but I will take it. You can never have too many umbrellas."

Great. Taking one last look at my umbrella, I reluctantly hand it over.

"How do you know Frankie?" she asks.

Frankie? That must be the guy I talked to on the phone. "I don't. He called me about a job. I mean, an errand." I want to ask how she knows Frankie, but he told me to be discreet, so I'm being discreet.

"Cool. Wanna come in while I get you the package?"

I'm about to say yes because she seems nice, but then, I remember the dogs. "I'm okay waiting out here."

"Suit yourself. Back in a few."

She returns after a long while. I think she was talking to someone on the phone. It could have been Frankie. She might have told him she was getting a bad vibe from me and was calling the whole thing off.

When she opens the door again, one of the dogs is at her heels, trying to peek its head around it.

"Cupcake! *C'mon!* Go play with your brother; mommy is busy." (Craziness.) "Here it is, Erin. It's super fragile, so make sure you hold it like I'm holding it. No rocking it or anything like that. Mr. Kim is really picky. If it isn't perfect, he gets upset." She looks me in the eyes and says, "Very upset."

I take the brown, square box from her. It's smaller than I thought it would be and extremely light, as if it's filled with air.

What the heck is in here?

"No problem. I will make sure it gets there safe and sound. Um, bye," I say, walking towards the stairs.

I'm halfway down when she calls out my name. I jump, and the package wobbles in my hands.

Please don't let her of seen that.

I turnaround once I have the package in place.

She is standing at the top of the stairs with the two dogs on either side of her. I can now confirm they are rottweilers—or pit bulls—whichever type is scarier.

This is it. I'm finished.

"You forgot something," she says.

Keep the umbrella. Keep the fucking umbrella!

I just want to get out of here without being torn to shreds.

She comes down the stairs to meet me. Thankfully, the dogs don't follow her.

"You wouldn't want to leave without getting paid, would you?" She hands me an envelope.

No, no, I wouldn't.

One down, one to go. I'm so close: I can almost see the finish line. Too bad that to cross that finish line, I need to go to Jane and Finch first. I'm not sure how to get there. I settle on a combination of streetcar, subway, and, finally, bus.

Frankie didn't mention an exact time, but it's past four when I reach Mr. Kim's neighbourhood. That doesn't seem "pronto" to me.

It's been an interesting journey getting here. I have seen parts of Toronto I have never seen before. I rather enjoyed the experience, sort of like a day trip to another city. Maybe the media exaggerates how bad this area is.

But when I arrive at Mr. Kim's rundown apartment complex, I'm not so sure about that. I nervously smile at a group of teenage girls hanging out on the front steps. They mostly glare back.

As I'm about to enter the building, I hear what sounds like gunshots in the distance. I let out a scream and almost drop the package (and myself) to the ground. The girls laugh at my reaction.

Embarrassed, I quickly get inside and find Mr. Kim's name in the directory, buzzing his apartment.

"Hello? Hello?"

"Hi, Mr. Kim? This is Erin."

"I don't know no Erin. No soliciting."

"I'm not soliciting. I have a package for you."

"What package?"

Wouldn't I like to know. "A package...from Frankie."

"Okay, okay. Come in." He buzzes me in.

I take the elevator up to the eighth floor. When the doors open, there is a woman waiting with a crying baby in a stroller. After receiving another glare, I try to slide past her without getting run over as she charges into the elevator. What is the deal with all the glares around here? *Sheesh*.

Entering the hallway, my senses are overloaded. The smell of pot, garbage, and boiled cabbage fills my nostrils. I hear loud music and even louder arguing. The carpet below my feet is tattered and stained. I can't see much else, as there is a single light fixture in working order, and it's barely flickering, on the verge of giving up.

I know how it feels. I wish I were under the warm covers of my futon bed, watching bad television. And I don't even have my umbrella for protection anymore.

Once I locate Mr. Kim's apartment number, I knock on his door.

"Yes?" he asks, without opening the door. I can sense him appraising me through the peephole.

"Hi, it's Erin. I have your package."

"What package?"

Seriously? "From Frankie." I'm so over this.

"Okay, okay," he says as I hear him unlocking multiple locks behind the door.

I drop into a defensive half-crouch position—just in case.

The door opens.

I let out a sigh of relief when I see who is standing behind it: a tiny, old Asian man. Not that tiny, old Asian men haven't been known to be lethal in the past. I want to say he is Chinese, but I think I hit my stereotyping quota for the day.

Focusing on him, however, is impossible because I'm overwhelmed by the state of his apartment. It's completely packed with stuff in every nook and cranny from my vantage point. There is only a small pathway leading to the living room and another one to the kitchen. I label him an extreme hoarder.

"You wait here," Mr. Kim says. (Where could I possibly go?)

He takes a while to come back. I wonder if he has been toppled by his stuff, and whether I should go in search of him. But I stick to my instructions and wait by the front door.

When he comes back, he has an envelope in his hands that he places inside his front shirt pocket.

"Give me package," he says.

I do as I'm told.

He puts the package down on a nearby makeshift table made of stacks of old newspapers. He uses his exceptionally long pinkie fingernail to cut through the packing tape and opens the box. For a moment, a big smile appears on his face, and he looks like a small boy again.

I desperately want to know what is inside that box, but I'm too far away, and I'm not willing to risk taking a closer look.

"Okay, good. Very good," he says. The smile disappears. He takes the envelope out of his front pocket and hands it to me. "You count."

I open the envelope and begin counting the money to myself.

"Out loud," he orders.

"One, two, three, four, five, six, seven hundred," I say, finishing my recount.

I look at him. He looks back at me. This continues for a while. I hesitate, then do what most white girls would do in a similar situation: I bow my head.

He seems satisfied. "Okay, go."

I'm more than happy to oblige. When I'm out of his peephole view, I stick the envelope in my pants. I may be naive, but I'm not dumb enough to flash my new hundred-dollar bills in this hood.

My phone rings as I'm about to get on the elevator.

"Hello?" I whisper, so as not to attract any unnecessary attention.

"Erin, it's Frankie. Mr. Kim is happy. Great work, kid." He hangs up.

Some things are better left a mystery.

TWELVE

Project Coco Fund = $2,017.35!

THIS CRAZY DAY ISN'T OVER YET. I have my most important stop to make. But before making that stop, I had to go home and collect the rest of my earnings.

Tonight, I'm buying my mom's bag!

Assuming it's still there, and also assuming they don't arrest me for messing with their merchandise.

By the time I get to Yorkville, it's almost seven. I make a run for the vintage shop, hoping to get there before it closes. I can't wait another day. I need to buy the bag tonight.

The nice saleslady is locking the front door as I approach. She recognizes me and opens the door. "Hello, there! I was about to close up. It's been dreadfully quiet all day. Come in, come in."

I thank her profusely for letting me in.

"My pleasure...but I'm afraid I have some bad news." (Uh-oh.) "It's that bag you have been inquiring about, the Chanel." She looks at me with worried eyes.

"What about it?" I wait with bated breath.

"I'm so sorry, but it seems to have gone missing," she says, her voice full of concern.

I let out my breath. "Missing?"

"Yes, dear. One minute it was here, and the next—*poof!*—it vanished. Our camera system goofed up again, so we couldn't make out if it was stolen or what. A very bizarre situation."

"That is bizarre. But, um, I'm sure I saw it the other day when I was in. Somewhere over here..." I say, walking towards the ugly weekend bag. I block her from view as I unzip the bag and look inside.

It's still in there! It's still in there!

66

I turn around with the bag in my hands and the biggest grin on my face. "Here it is!"

"Oh, my! You found it! *You found it!*" She claps her hands. "Oh, thank goodness. I was worried the owner would think one of us had stolen it. Oh, thank goodness," she says again, placing her hand over her heart.

I never imagined she would get blamed for it. Thank goodness, indeed.

"Shall I wrap it up for you...or did you come by to have another look at it?"

"No looking today. Please wrap it up!"

I have never been prouder of myself. I did it. *I really did it!*

She takes the bag from me as we walk to the register. When we approach, she turns towards me and says, "This bag has quite the history. Do you know why it's called the 2.55?"

"Is that its version number?"

She chuckles. "Sort of. The number 2.55 represents February 1955, the date of its creation. And see the lining of the bag, this burgundy colour?"

"Yes?" I'm completely enthralled.

"That was the colour of the uniforms at the convent Mademoiselle Chanel was sent to after her mother passed away."

I never knew Coco was an orphan. My eyes get misty. Thoughts are racing through my mind.

"And how will you be paying for this today?" she asks, breaking my reverie.

I'm back to the present. "Cash. I will be paying with cash," I say, grinning again. I reach into my purse, which looks dingy compared to the Chanel, and handover the money, all two-thousand dollars of it.

She meets my eyes and says, "This bag suits you. It's a perfect match."

"Thank you, that means a lot." I'm getting misty again. It must be the built-up emotions of finally getting my mom's bag.

"Let me finish wrapping it up for you, then you can be on your way."

She places it into the original dust bag. None of my other purses have ever come with a dust bag. This is a whole new world for me.

"There you go!" she says, handing it to me.

"Thank you for your help. You don't know how important this bag is to me. It's like finding a lost treasure."

She gives me a warm smile and nods her head.

As I make my way towards the door, I remember that I forgot to ask her something. So I turn around and say, "I just realized, I never got your name."

"Ah, yes, they don't make us wear name tags anymore. My name is Elizabeth—but everyone calls me Lizzie."

My body tenses, but I quickly regain my composure. "Thanks, Lizzie. I appreciate everything you have done for me."

I head out of the shop and into the darkening evening.

THIRTEEN

I SLEPT WITH THE BAG last night. I must have passed out from the excitement because when I open my eyes in the morning, it's here, laying next to me, still in its dust bag.

So this is my first opportunity to see it up close. Every other time, it's been behind glass. The one time I had it in my hands, I was busy finding a hiding spot for it. But now, it's mine. I can look at it as often and as long as I want. I carefully remove it from the dust bag.

It's exactly as I remembered.

When I was a kid, I used to play dress up with my mom's bag for hours while she was busy working. She never knew, or, at least, I don't think she knew. I always put it back exactly the way I found it. Except for once, when I nicked it on my charm bracelet. It left a tiny snag on the bottom of the bag. My mom thought she was the one who did it.

I flip over the bag to see if it's still there.

It isn't. But that doesn't mean this isn't my mom's bag. The repair shop might have buffed it or something when they fixed the clasp.

Getting up for the day, I begin transferring the stuff from my old purse into my new (but technically very old) bag. As I do, I realize my lunch won't fit in it. But I can go back to buying my lunches now that Project Coco has been successfully completed.

I originally planned to save the bag for special occasions. But after spending all that money, I want to wear it as much as possible. (And I don't really have special occasions.)

Searching through my closet, I try to find something equally fabulous to wear. But my clothes seem shabby in comparison. Most of them don't go with navy, either. A black bag would have been a more practical choice. Maybe I should keep the errand service going until I can update my wardrobe to match my designer bag.

Eventually, I find a navy shift dress buried in the back of my closet. Not quite a little black dress *à la* Coco, but I think she would still approve. My trench coat and my painstakingly revived red ankle booties finish the look.

I'm overdressed for a Friday, as it's casual day at work. I normally never waste an opportunity to wear jeans. But today is different. Today is not only the launch of my new bag, but also the launch of the new me.

Before heading out, I give myself a once over in my full-length mirror.

Not bad, Erin. Not bad.

I'm in high spirits as I enter the subway station. Nothing can bring me down, not even being crammed into a tin can, like a sardine. And I'm early, so there is no need for pushing and shoving today.

As a reward for my good behaviour, I see Suit Guy standing inside my train car. He is wearing my favourite navy suit of his. We colour-coordinate.

I'm sick of calling him Suit Guy. I want to know his real name. So this morning, unlike so many mornings before, I'm going to talk to him.

No, really, I'm going to do it.

Squeezing my way past someone reading a newspaper, I narrowly avoid getting coffee spilled on me by someone else.

C'mon, people! The subway isn't your living room!

I take a breath and remind myself to think happy thoughts.

When I'm a few feet away from Suit Guy, he sees me and says, "Hey, you. You made it." And then, he smiles, a very, *very* sexy smile.

I'm taken aback. I'm sure my cheeks have turned bright red. This is going so much better than I ever imagined. He must remember me from the post office.

But as I'm about to respond in the sexiest voice I can muster, I hear a girl behind me say, "Hey, babe. Almost missed it."

Turning to my side, I see a tall, blonde goddess who is trying to get past me.

"Excuse me," she says, flashing me a dismissive glance, but then, she notices my bag and gives me a slight, subconscious nod of approval. She struts over to Suit Guy and kisses him full on the lips to mark her territory.

Suit Guy is taken.

On any other day, this would be a devastating blow. But his girlfriend's semi-acknowledgment of my bag helps to take a bit of the sting away.

Even the grey corridors and cubicles can't bring me down.

As I walk past Carol's desk, she looks up and takes me in, then glances down at her watch before saying, "Don't you look nice. Is that a Chanel bag you have there?"

"Yes, it is!" I say, modelling it for her. "It's a family heirloom."

"It's lovely," she says and goes back to her work.

Who would have thought, Carol, of all people, would be the first person to compliment me on my bag? It's a funny world. Guess she didn't realize I was gone yesterday afternoon, or, if she did, she isn't saying anything.

Maybe she and I can find a way to get along better after all these years. She seems to like it when I come to work early. I can try to do that more often. (No promises, though.) As a peace treaty, I should offer to buy her a coffee.

So I walk back over to her desk. "Hey, Carol!"

She looks up, startled.

"I was wondering...do you want to go downstairs and grab a coffee? It's on me."

She narrows her eyes at me repeatedly for several seconds; she probably thinks this is a trick. "I can't," she finally says. "I have to wait for Joe. The printer has been jammed since yesterday afternoon."

"Okay, some other time." At least, I gave it a shot.

I drop off my jacket at my desk before heading downstairs for my solo latte run. My first one *avec* Chanel!

Joe is at the end of the corridor as I'm coming out of my cubicle. We have so many printer issues that we are on a first-name basis with the repairman. I tell Carol that he is here.

She gets up from her desk and comes over. I ask her if she wants me to wait for her, but she says it will probably take a while and for me to go ahead.

As I'm walking towards the elevators, an image pops into my head. It is of me hitting the print button yesterday. I wonder if I was the one who caused the printer jam. What was I printing again?

NO! NO! NO!

I sprint back down the corridor and around the corner, coming to a halt outside the copy room.

I get there just in time. Just in time to see Carol holding one of my crumbled Erin Girl flyers.

Carol looks at the flyer, then towards me. It's as if I have been given temporary access to the recesses of her mind; all the puzzle pieces are connecting with the final piece, at long last, falling into place. She rushes out of the copy room.

"Carol! Carol! Please stop! I can explain! *Carol, please!*"

She doesn't stop, except for a split second to grab a red folder on her desk before continuing towards Bradford's office. I'm right at her heels.

"What's this?" Bradford asks in alarm as we both burst into his office.

"Bradford, I must speak to you, urgently." Carol turns and shoots me the death glare. "In private."

I flinch.

"Of course. Erin, please give us a moment," he says, a mixture of surprise and concern washing over his face.

I hesitate. If I leave his office, I know there won't be any way to unspin the web that Carol is about to weave. I *need* to defend myself.

But what could I possibly say? I have no defence. Not in their eyes, anyway. So I nod my head and slowly walk back to my desk.

And then, I wait.

After what seems like an eternity, Bradford appears at the entrance of my cubicle. "Erin, please come to my office," he says, without making eye contact with me.

Inside his office, waiting for us, is Michelle from Human Resources. I haven't seen her since my first day here, nearly five years ago. Carol is nowhere in sight.

Glancing down at his desk, I see my crumbled flyer. Crumbled, but completely legible. I also see the opened red folder. I'm close enough to make out it contains a bunch of timesheets, filled with row-upon-row of "time in" and "time out," confirming my suspicions Carol has been tracking my whereabouts.

Bradford notices me staring down at the folder and immediately closes it. He tells me to take a seat beside Michelle, then sits down in his chair.

Clearing his throat, Bradford says, "This will go a lot easier if you are honest with us." He still can't meet my eyes for more than a couple of seconds at a time.

Bradford has never been the best boss, but he has been (mostly) nice to me in my years here. So I tell them the truth—part of it. I leave out the real reason I started the errand service. Instead, I say I was bored and wanted something fun to do.

They say that they have to let me go, but that they have decided not to press charges. I never thought that was a possibility. But because I used company resources and time, I could have been charged with theft on top of being fired.

Afterwards, I'm given five minutes to grab my belongings. Michelle watches me the entire time (so I don't steal any more of those company resources), then she escorts me to the elevators, taking my security badge before I get on the first available one.

And just like that, I'm unemployed.

I ride the elevator down in a daze, only being jolted back to reality as it pings open at ground level.

That is when I see her.

Carol is standing in front of me with a coffee cup in her thin, veined hands. She shakes her head at me in disgust.

As I walk past her, I look down to avoid making eye contact.

I have never been more ashamed in my life...nor have I ever had a greater sense of relief.

FOURTEEN

WAIT, WHAT JUST HAPPENED?

I knew this *could* happen, but I didn't think it actually *would* happen.

Maybe I'm dreaming and none of this is real.

I pinch myself.

No, not dreaming.

Fuck!

I hated working there, but I always imagined I would leave on my own terms, not theirs.

Why couldn't I have picked up those stupid flyers?

I let myself get caught. I'm such an idiot!

What do I do now? Where do I go?

Home. I will go home. I need to lie down in my walk-in closet as soon as possible.

Once on the subway, I take a seat, not worrying about Suit Guy seeing me sitting anymore. Reality is setting in. No one will hire me with this mark on my resume and with no work references. Five years of my life eliminated from my record.

How will I pay my rent?

The errand service. I wasn't planning on continuing it now that Project Coco is over, but I guess I will have to keep it going. I look at my bag, laying on the seat beside me, next to a small box of my personal belongings from my former cubicle. I know how I could get some extra money, but I won't do it, not after everything that has happened. There is no way I'm selling my mom's bag. I worked so hard to get it. I lost my job because of it. I can't lose it, too. Or else, all of this would have been for nothing.

When I get home, I can call Betty. She will know what I should do. I will apologize, and everything will go back to the way it was between us. We will figure this out together. With a plan in place, I close my eyes. I'm so emotionally spent that my head starts bobbing up and down almost immediately.

Before nodding off, I hear the subway operator announcing that the train will be turning back at Davisville station due to signalling issues. One stop short of my own station.

Can't a girl catch a break?

I must have been out for a while because when I open my eyes again, I see we have arrived at Davisville station. Remembering the announcement, I dash out of the train as the doors are closing.

I need to call Betty. I have to talk to someone. As I reach into my bag for my phone, I'm met with air. There is no bag at my side.

Where is my bag?

Panic takes over as I try to remember where I left it.

Did I leave it behind at work?

They rushed me out of there so quickly, maybe I forgot it. I couldn't have—wasn't I just looking at it?

I spin around on the platform. The train is pulling away from the station. My heart races as I see the bag laying on the seat through the window. I attempt to pry open the doors, but the train is picking up speed. I run alongside of it, but I can't keep up.

And then, the train is gone.

My mom's bag is gone.

From somewhere deep inside of me, I let out a scream. I think I'm going to pass out.

"Miss, are you okay?"

I see the familiar uniform and realize it's one of the subway employees. "I left...I left...my..." I'm too out of breath to get the words out.

"Did your mother not get off the train in time?"

"Huh? What?"

"It sounded like you yelled, 'mom.'"

I stare at him in disbelief. "I did?"

"Well, it was more like, 'mommy.' That's what it sounded like, anyway," he says, blushing.

I'm losing my mind. I'm also losing time. "No, it was my bag. I left my bag on the train. It has my entire life in it. Is there any way you can stop the train at the next station, and I can go grab it? Or someone can get it for me before it's taken? *Please, you have to help me!*"

"I'm afraid that's against policy, but you can fill out a missing items report."

"A missing items report? I don't have time for that. I—I have to go!" I have already wasted too much time talking to him. I need to catch the train before it gets to the next stop.

I climb up the stairs and run out of the station, then down Yonge Street as fast as I can. I'm running, even though I know it's pointless. There is no way I can get to the next station before the train does. I'm already out of breath. But I can't stop running. I won't stop running.

However, my ankle disagrees with me, and I fall face first onto the hard pavement.

I hate these fucking ankle booties!

Sprawled out on the sidewalk, I admit defeat. I take a few deep breaths to calm myself down.

When I straighten up, I come face-to-face with a place I have spent years avoiding, even though I passed it at least twice a day on my subway rides to-and-from work. I always blocked it from my view or closed my eyes as the train went by before heading into the dark tunnel. It had become an ingrained reflex.

But my defences are down now; I can no longer avoid it.

I know where I need to go. And it isn't a subway station.

Crossing the street, I enter through the gated archway. I haven't been here in years. I'm not sure I remember where it is, but my feet seem to remember, as they take me the rest of the way there, down the winding paved paths.

The gravestone Betty picked out by herself comes into view. I was only here for the funeral service. It was such a small gathering. I wished more people could have come. And then, I never came back. I couldn't come back. In the beginning, Betty would invite me when she was going for a visit, but after I had given her the hundredth excuse of being busy, she stopped asking. And we never talked about it.

As I approach slowly, I see there are flowers planted in front of the gravestone, so she must still come here on her own.

I read the engraving:

Elizabeth Rose Bettencourt
October 10, 1961 – October 12, 2008
Loving mother to Erin and Beatrice

Yesterday was her birthday. I was so preoccupied with getting the bag that it never crossed my mind. And tomorrow marks the fifth anniversary of her passing.

Five years without an "I love you."

Five years of being caught between her life and death.

Five years of nothingness.

IT'S NOT FAIR!

She was all we had, and she was taken away from us.

I can't pretend anymore. A tear rolls down my face, then another.

There is a thunderous roar above, followed by rain, cold and heavy. Under its protective covering, and after years of holding in my tears, I let myself cry. I finally let myself cry.

My mom is gone.

Some time later, I'm awoken by one of the Mount Pleasant Cemetery security guards.

"The cemetery gates are closing," he says. "Looks like you have been here a while. You okay?"

I must be quite the sight. My arms are embracing my mom's gravestone, my legs are banged up from my fall, and my clothes are soaked through.

"I don't know," I say.

"You don't know if you're okay?"

"No. I never know how I really feel. I'm always pretending. It's like...It's like I have become a stranger in my own life."

He gives me a puzzled expression; probably thinks I escaped from the local loony bin. But then, he helps me to my feet and offers me a ride home when I tell him where I actually live.

FIRST INTERMISSION
September 2014

I WENT TO THE CEMETERY every day for a month after that. We had a lot of catching up to do. And now, I go whenever I want to talk to my mom or if I need a quiet place to think. It's so peaceful there, even though it's in the middle of this big, busy city.

After so many years, I finally allowed myself to grieve for my mom properly—if there is a proper way to go about it. I guess we each have to find our own way. I had denied her death because I didn't want it to be true. She was all Betty and I had. She gave up so much for her girls, and I never got to thank her for everything she did for us.

To me, the Chanel bag was a symbol of her former life. A life that didn't include raising two small kids on her own; a life where her dreams could still come true. Maybe I subconsciously thought if I got the bag back, I would prove it had been worth it. That she hadn't had to give up *everything* for us.

Although I eventually realized that my mom wasn't her Chanel bag, I filed that missing items report. I wanted my own things inside of it back.

The bag was never found.

In many ways, I also lost a part of myself on the subway that day. I lost my identity—literally, my I.D. was gone—along with my apartment keys, some money, and a lipstick. Oh, and a packet of gum. I hope whoever took my bag thoroughly enjoyed that packet of gum. My relationship with my smartphone came to an abrupt end, too. That really hurt. But mostly, I lost the old Erin; the one who had stopped living her life.

After the security guard dropped me off, I got Larry, the superintendent, to let me into my apartment. He changed the locks, but I didn't feel safe staying there. There was only one other place I could go: Betty's.

I used the spare key she had given me to get in. The look on her face when she returned from her Boston weekend to find me sitting on her couch, eating her *dulce de leche* ice cream, was priceless. Betty has the best ice cream stash.

I apologized for the things I said, and then she apologized for the things she said. I told her exactly what happened from the beginning. We cried for my mom, for our loss, for everything we couldn't change.

Poor Betty. She has her own issues to deal with, and yet mine always seem to take priority.

So we are best friends again. I don't know that we ever stopped. We love each other unconditionally if not slightly temperamentally.

I ended up giving notice on my apartment. I couldn't afford it without having a stable job, and I wanted that chapter of my life done with. Betty said I could stay with her rent-free as long as I applied half of any money I earned towards paying off my debt. That girl has a one-track mind. But it's working, I'm almost there! One day, I plan to pay her back, too. It's the right thing to do. In the meantime, I help out by cleaning the place and cooking the occasional meal. (I'm not a total mooch.)

The drawback of living with Betty is that she doesn't have a second bedroom. I sleep in the den. It isn't much bigger than my old walk-in closet, so I had to get rid of a bunch of my things before I could move in. At first, I didn't think I would be able to do it. But once I *really* looked through my stuff, I realized how much junk I had been holding on to. I kept picturing Mr. Kim's apartment; that motivated me to get rid of certain items I may not have otherwise. I felt so free afterwards, as though it was another necessary step to my fresh start. I needed a blank slate.

As for Erin Girl, I got spooked after that last errand. I was sort of glad I lost my phone and wouldn't be getting any more calls about "a job" from Frankie. So I ended it. I never enjoyed running errands; I was only in it for the money. I had already spent too many years doing something I didn't like for the money. I didn't want to fall into that trap again.

But I'm not a complete fool, either. Having no immediate job prospects, I kept Mr. Trader as my sole client. I needed that guaranteed seventy-five bucks a week. A couple of months later, he clued-in that spending that much money to have someone fetch your lunch was ridiculous. It was good while it lasted. And it might have lasted as long as it did because he hoped that, one day, I would show up in the superhero costume on my old Erin Girl flyers.

Eventually, I found a job as a barista at a coffeehouse near Betty's place. It seems fitting somehow. I love it there, but a girl can't pull espresso shots forever. I have dreams again.

When I was sorting through my things, before moving in with Betty, I came across my mom's old sewing machine. I contemplated donating it, but I remembered how my mom had taught me to sew with it. I used to spend hours making tiny outfits for my dolls. I even made some of my own clothes in high school. So I kept it. And then, I used it.

I reinvented a dress I already owned to spruce up my wardrobe, given my shopping days were on hold for the foreseeable future. I got so many compliments on it that I reinvented a couple more and tried to sell them. They did sell.

And so, a new business was born!

I opened my own online shop and named it, Lady Bettencourt, on behalf of my mom, my sister, and me. The dresses are now made from secondhand clothes I buy from thrift stores. There are three designs I reproduce that have been named after my favourite ladies: The Lizzie, The Betty, and...The Gabby. Who knew Coco Chanel's real name was Gabrielle?

Maybe the business will take off and I will become a huge success, or maybe I won't. It doesn't matter because I'm having a lot of fun with it; something that was lacking in my former working life. It feels as though I have been given a second chance to reinvent myself, kind of like my dresses.

For someone on the outside looking in, it may seem as if I have drifted off course. But the truth is, I'm finally getting back on track.

I was never meant to sit in a cubicle all day with those grey walls closing in on me. I'm getting claustrophobic just thinking about it. (I may still invent cubicle wallpaper for those that have to.) I took the first job that was offered to me after my mom died, and then I got stuck there. I was a round peg trying to fit into a square hole...or is it the other way around? Whatever. I was never going to fit. I was just going through the motions. I may have been there physically, but my mind made only the occasional appearance.

When we were kids, Betty would make me play Monopoly with her for hours. I never wanted to buy Park Place or Boardwalk; I was only ever interested in Kentucky Avenue. I don't know why, but it sounded like a place I might like to go. So if I got to buy Kentucky Avenue, I felt I won the game.

Life is like that for me again. I do what sounds interesting to me, not what others think I should find interesting.

Although I may not know exactly where I'm headed in the future, I know where I'm headed today. Today, I'm seeing my first-ever film at the Toronto International Film Festival—and not just stalking movie stars and pretending to be famous.

But, uh, I may be walking around Yorkville at this moment wearing dark sunglasses. Old habits are hard to break. Except, the coffee cup has been replaced with an organic apple, thanks to Mrs. O'Connor. (Some things do change.)

I'm finishing a single loop of this hamlet within a city before going downtown. Apparently, that is where most of the celebrity action happens now. (And sometimes change is forced upon us.)

From somewhere behind me, I hear someone huffing, and then I feel a tap on my shoulder. I turn around to see a young guy, holding a stack of eight-by-ten, black-and-white photos.

"Can I help you?" I ask.

"Aren't you that girl from that, um, movie?" He looks at me, then down at the stack of photos he has in his hands. He is shuffling through them, trying to find the right one. He isn't going to find it.

Part of me is flattered. After years of playing my little game, I have finally been spotted! But then, I realize something.

"I'm not who you think I am," I say. "I'm not that girl...not anymore."

But he has already taken off to find his next potential starlet, so I continue walking.

As I do, I catch a glimpse of my reflection in a store window. It's remarkable how much I look like my mom. She lives on through me: I am her legacy.

What a difference a year can make.

And it's all thanks to a silly bag.

PART II
LADY BETTENCOURT

"The most courageous act is still to
think for yourself. Aloud."
Coco Chanel

FIFTEEN
September 2015

RACHEL MCADAMS is wearing my dress.

Rachel McAdams is wearing my dress!

Is this really happening?

Maybe someone stole my dress design.

No, I remember those materials, taking them apart and putting them back together to sew my first-ever evening gown. And now, it's on Rachel McAdams' body.

Across the street from the Elgin Theatre, behind temporary fencing, a crowd is shouting Rachel's name, demanding her to "Look over here!" I'm blinded by camera flashes coming from every direction: from her fans across the street, from the media in front of the theatre, and from those, like me, standing in the ticket-holders line. The flashing stops for a moment, and I see Rachel wave to the crowd before making her way towards the red carpet.

It's a gorgeous Saturday evening in September, and I have been waiting almost two hours to watch a world premiere at the Toronto International Film Festival. Little did I know when I woke up this morning that I would be making my own world premiere.

The festival volunteers are telling us to move forward and to have our tickets ready. I'm near the head of the line and can catch glimpses of Rachel speaking with someone in the media about her film.

I *need* to know what she is saying.

Squeezing my way to the outer edge of the line, I get as close to the red carpet as I can without security stepping in. Rachel is moving on to the next entertainment reporter, but the current one stops her to ask who she is wearing.

This is it. I lean in closer.

"It's by a local designer," Rachel says. "All her dresses are made from secondhand materials. They have deep pockets, too. No need for a purse! The designer is...uh..."

Lady Bettencourt! LADY BETTENCOURT!

"Lady Bettencourt! Almost forgot that," Rachel says, smiling with those twinkly eyes of hers, then moves on to the next entertainment reporter.

Yes! Yes! Yes!

Should I jump the ropes and announce that *I am Lady Bettencourt*? I have always dreamed of walking the red carpet. But I would probably get arrested.

"Ma'am, please move along. You are slowing down the line," a festival volunteer says to me, drunk on his new-found power.

I head into the theatre with the other filmgoers while looking back repeatedly. I need to make sure it's real; that I'm seeing what I think I'm seeing. But there is no denying it.

Rachel McAdams is definitely wearing my dress.

I grab the first aisle seat I find in the beautiful, old Edwardian theatre, although I'm too preoccupied to appreciate its grandeur. Other filmgoers squeeze past me to find their own seats.

I wish I could call my sister, Betty, and tell her what just happened. But she is in Chicago with her fiancé, Matt.

Betty is engaged!

Finally. It only took thirteen years—they have been dating since the tenth grade. Matt even asked me for Betty's hand in marriage. Their wedding is next month. Matt's current management consulting project is wrapping up shortly before the wedding, and then he will be in Toronto full-time. That was the stipulation Betty placed on accepting his proposal.

Betty's "no calls unless it's an emergency" policy is still in effect whenever she is away with Matt. We have different definitions of what constitutes an emergency. We have different definitions of a lot of things. But she never said anything about text messages.

I reach into my purse for my phone. I lost my smartphone in the Great Subway Incident, two years ago, so now I'm using Betty's old Motorola Razr. And as it was Betty-the-accountant's phone, it's grey, not one of the fun-colour versions.

The theatre lights dim as I flip open the phone. Sadly, the backlight no longer works, so I'm not sure what I'm typing into the ancient keyboard. I'm tapping away, hoping I have chosen the right numbers, to make the right letters, to make the right words.

An older gentleman sitting next to me keeps glancing over and shaking his head. Probably because the keyboard volume has also malfunctioned and makes a loud, beeping noise every time I press a button. I have learned to tune it out.

"Do you mind?" he asks irritably.

And even though I do mind, I quickly send the message and flip the phone closed. "Sorry about that."

He nods his head.

I'm forgiven.

Betty is good at puzzles. She will be able to decode my message.

Sitting in the pitch-black theatre, I wonder what this means.

Am I famous now?

Not this very second, but it has to mean I'm going to become famous...well, famous-ish. People who have never heard of Lady Bettencourt will know it exists. They will know *I* exist. This is how it starts, isn't it?

Erin Bettencourt will finally be a somebody!

Not that I'm not a somebody already. I will just be a somebody, more somebodies, know about. And it's all because Rachel McAdams chose me. She had to know by putting on that dress and saying who she was wearing that she was about to change someone's life forever. She had to. Imagine having that kind of power.

What if I have a fashion show?

I can see it now: The models wearing my dresses as they walk down the runway, the *oohing* and *aahing* increasing with each

88

dress…and a juggler on a unicycle weaving in-and-out of the models? Hmm, I'm not sure what that is about. Or why there is a tightrope walker above the runway and lions roaring in the audience. Perhaps it will be a circus-themed fashion show? Really, you would think I would have more control over my own daydream.

At the end of the fashion show, I see myself coming out from backstage to take a bow. If only I could do a cartwheel and splits, like Betsey Johnson. Although, it is important to be original. So I finish the show by doing a cross between the Charleston and the Robot. (I will need to work on that part.) One of the lions is by my side as I walk the rest of the runway. For some reason, I'm not afraid of the lion. I wave at the audience, which is on its feet, applauding.

The daydream feels so real: I can hear the audience applauding and see everyone standing up. I'm about to take a final bow when I'm brought back to reality. And there is an audience applauding and standing up, except it's for the film and actors, not me.

I missed the whole movie!

How could that have happened? Unless, I fell asleep. My daydreaming may have been actual dreaming.

As I'm contemplating the probability of this, a spotlight comes on, and everyone turns in its direction. It's focused on Rachel McAdams and the cast of the film. She is several rows ahead of me, waving at the audience.

She was there, wearing my dress, the entire time.

I stare and stare, willing her to look over at me until…it works! I catch her eye and wave, then I yell out, "Thank you! Thank you!"

Rachel will understand one day.

"What did you think of the film?" the older gentleman beside me asks.

"Uh, I think it's Oscar-worthy."

It must have been good, given the standing ovation; festival audiences are critical. I will need to remember to watch it when it comes out to the general public next year.

And where will Lady Bettencourt be next year?

"I see it becoming a huge success," the older gentleman says, nodding.

I blush. But then, I realize he is talking about the film.

As I'm exiting the theatre, I'm questioning the events of the last few hours. Maybe it was all a dream; my imagination playing tricks on me. Maybe I saw what I wanted to see. I have been known to do that.

It couldn't be. My dresses are made from unique materials, and that particular dress was meant to be a practice run before making my maid of honour gown for Betty's wedding. But as it turned out so well, I put it up for sale on my online shop. Plus, Rachel specifically said Lady Bettencourt—unless that was part of the dream.

I need concrete evidence.

My text message to Betty!

Hopefully, people can't text while sleeping.

I flip open my phone, which causes a teenager walking past me to snicker at it. (I have gotten used to this.)

There are several messages from Betty, asking if I'm okay. The last one, sent a minute ago, says she is calling the police if I don't message her back in the next half-hour. Wow, that is dramatic, especially for Betty. I go back to my original text and realize why. It looks as though the message reads: "Ray hell mad warring my distress!!!"

Eek. I should text her back.

But before I can, I get an incoming call. It's probably Betty checking up on me. (My call display no longer functions, either. Every call is a surprise.)

"Hey, Bett—"

"Hello, I'm looking for Erin Bettencourt of Lady Bettencourt," a woman with a hypnotic-sounding voice says, cutting me off. "Is this her?"

"Yes, this is her," I say, waiting with bated breath.

"My name is Vanessa Moore of The Moore Agency. I want to represent you and the Lady Bettencourt brand."

I release my breath.

SIXTEEN

I HAVE SOLD OUT. All the dresses listed on my online shop have been purchased. That was fast. It's only been a few hours since I made my grand debut onto the world stage.

Most of the orders are from Canada, but there are a bunch from the U.S., a couple from Europe, and even an order from Japan. To think, someone named Mari will be wearing one of my dresses on the streets of Tokyo! It's almost too much to process. I have never had international orders before or this many emails. Emails from women saying they love my dresses and asking when there will be more in stock.

Vanessa Moore said this would happen. She said the footage of Rachel saying who she was wearing was live streamed. Plus, there were photos taken of her by the media that were posted online, and some of those photos mention Lady Bettencourt, too.

So while I was sitting in the theatre, not watching the film, my dresses were being snatched up. Now there is a waiting list. I'm so glad I added that function to the online shop. I can keep track of who wants a dress without (hopefully) losing a potential sale.

Vanessa and I are meeting Monday morning to discuss the future of Lady Bettencourt. She made me promise not to talk to anyone else until then. I'm not sure who she thinks I would be talking to. She wanted to meet tomorrow, but I have a shift at the coffeehouse.

I'm still pulling espresso shots to pay the bills. I'm also still living with Betty, in her condo, in the den. Although, Betty won't be living here for much longer. She bought a house with Matt; they are moving in just before the wedding. Their new house is cute and cozy, and it's in a great neighbourhood. But that means I may be homeless soon.

Betty is keeping the condo as an investment property. She is letting me decide if I want to rent it or if she has to find a new tenant. She is giving me until the end of the year to make up my mind, which is very generous of her. Betty is *very* generous.

I have been living in her den while getting back on my feet after losing (okay, getting fired from) my office job. I have paid off all my debt and built up some savings. I even have a credit card again. (Betty says it's important that I "reestablish credit.") But I still don't think I can afford her place. Even though she is generous, Betty needs someone who can pay the market rate for her condo. She can't carry me forever; I need to be able to make it on my own again.

It would be nice to have the whole place to myself, though. I could setup the den as my sewing room and take over Betty's bedroom as my own. Right now, my "workshop" is in the small dining room area. That is where I keep my mom's old sewing machine, along with a dress form (that goes by Sally) and a clothing rack (nameless) for finished items. I use the table for laying out patterns and cutting materials.

My teeny-tiny bedroom has just enough space for my old futon bed, but not enough space for my clothes. I store them in the front hall closet. Not only does my bedroom lack a closet, it also lacks a door. So I have hung a curtain for a bit of privacy.

Betty tells me repeatedly to use her bedroom whenever she is gone for the weekend, but I enjoy sleeping in the den. It's as if I'm in a cocoon. It's funny how I gravitate towards small spaces—I once had a walk-in closet I was particularly fond of—when I couldn't stand my former grey cubicle.

As I'm looking around my current work setup, my eye catches on a couple of large bags filled with secondhand clothes, beckoning me, on the dining room floor. So I grab my seam ripper (a horrible name for a tool that produces a calming, even therapeutic, effect) and begin taking the clothes apart to turn into usable material to make more dresses. A lot more dresses.

—

I need a new phone.

During my barista shift today, I kept wishing I could check my online shop to see how long the waiting list had grown to. But, no, impossible on a crummy, ancient flip phone with no Internet capabilities.

When I get back to the condo, Betty is sitting on the couch, eating a bowl of pasta. She is definitely not one of those brides who obsesses about their weight leading up to their wedding day.

"Tell me *everything*," she says, making room for me on the couch. So I do.

I tell her about the moment I realized Rachel McAdams was wearing one of my dresses, how I wanted to explode when she said Lady Bettencourt, then getting the call from Vanessa Moore, and, finally, coming home to find that my dresses had sold out.

"I wish I'd been there with you," Betty says when I finish my recap. "But what about this woman, Vanessa Moore? What is happening with that?"

"I'm meeting with her tomorrow morning. She wants to discuss how to grow the Lady Bettencourt brand," I say, throwing out the terminology Vanessa had used.

"I could take the morning off and come with you."

"Thanks, but it's only an initial meeting. We're just having coffee." Although I'm not entirely sure that is true, as I have never had a meeting like this before.

"Okay, but remember, you don't have to go with the first person who shows interest. Take your time finding someone who really gets you and what you want to do with Lady Bettencourt."

"*I know*, Betty."

Except, no one else has shown interest. Women want to buy my dresses, but I didn't get any calls or emails from anyone, besides Vanessa, who wanted to help with the business side of things. And if I'm being honest, I don't know where I want to take Lady Bettencourt. I'm still new to this. I need help.

SEVENTEEN

I GET TO the café at nine o'clock sharp. Vanessa is already there waiting for me.

I don't know what I was expecting, but I'm taken aback when she introduces herself. She asks me what I want to drink, then goes up to the counter to order. This gives me the opportunity to...stare at her.

She is captivating. Not beautiful. Not pretty. Not cute.

Captivating.

She has a mane of fiery red, curly hair. Hair that must be a pain to maintain, but is gorgeous to look at. Hair that makes you desperate to touch it, although the fear of getting your fingers ensnared in it, stops you. (And the fact it's someone else's hair.) Her eyes are a colour I have never seen before. Amber, maybe? I want to keep gazing at them; they are so cool. She is wearing a tailored, dark grey pantsuit with a beige blouse underneath. She looks polished and professional, but with a hint of something else...seduction.

I may have a girl crush.

Vanessa comes back to the table with our drinks. I try to stop gawking at her.

"So, Erin! It's great to finally meet you," Vanessa says, grinning.

"Me, too. I mean, you, too," I say, blushing.

Vanessa gives me a knowing smile. She must realize the effect she has on people. She has probably had to deal with it her whole life. We seem to be around the same age, but I haven't had to deal with that sort of thing.

"Sorry we couldn't meet at the agency. We're in the process of moving offices."

"No problem. I like cafés," I say, giggling. (I don't know why that is funny.)

"Good," Vanessa says with a cautious look on her face, as though she may have a nut job on her hands. "Well, I'm glad we're meeting because I have a ton of ideas on how to get the Lady Bettencourt brand out there. But we need to move fast on them before the hype generated from this past weekend dies down."

"You're a publicist, right?" I had just assumed she was when she called, but now I'm not sure. I have been so busy, I forgot to Google her and her agency before this meeting.

"Kind of, but much more. I oversee the *entire* brand. What is best for it and how far it can go."

"So like a super publicist," I say, making up my mind.

"I suppose so, if you want to view it that way. Do you have any branding experience?"

Now that is a tricky question. Technically, I worked as a sales and marketing coordinator for almost five years, but I didn't do much sales or marketing in that job. I mostly surfed the web.

"Not really," I answer. I want to impress her, but I need her help more.

"Okay, so we're starting from scratch here. I checked your online shop—nice design—but I couldn't find your social media handles anywhere."

I'm flattered she likes the website. I designed it myself over many, many long hours. All that web surfing had a benefit: I know what looks good.

"I'm not on social media," I say, sensing that is the wrong answer. Social media sites were blocked at my former job, so I never got into it.

"Not even a personal Facebook or Twitter account?" she asks hopefully.

"Nope, none of those, either." Why would I want confirmation of how few friends and "followers" I have?

She pauses before speaking again; she is probably wondering what she has gotten herself into.

"With an online dress shop, you should be on Instagram and Pinterest, at a minimum. Your dress photos are great, so it should be easy enough to get that up and running. Did you take the photos yourself?"

"No, all my photos are blurry. My sister, Betty, does the photography."

"Is she a trained photographer?"

"She's an accountant. She's just good at stuff."

A loud noise emanates from my purse. I feel the eyes of everyone in the café turn towards me. Opening my purse, I quickly take out my phone to power it off. The phone's latest malfunction is this loud, shrilling noise at random times. I will think I have a call or a message, but it turns out to be nothing. Maybe it's trying to talk to me.

"Is that—is that your phone?" Vanessa asks, the cautious look returning.

"Yeah...it's vintage," I say, joking.

"Hmm, perhaps we can work with that. Old becomes new, like your dresses. Let me have a think on it." Vanessa picks up her smartphone and starts typing.

"I guess, to me, social media is like this phone," I say. "At one point, everyone wanted it; it was the coolest thing. But today, it's pretty much useless. Social media seems as though it would be a waste of time."

Vanessa is still typing. I don't think she is paying attention to what I'm saying, so I stop talking.

"Uh-huh. I'll take that into consideration." She puts down her fancy phone and returns her attention towards me. "And now some exciting news: I got you a spot on *Breakfast Television* as part of their film fest coverage this week!"

Breakfast Television? I can't believe it! Erin Bettencourt on Breakfast Television!

I have always wanted to be on that show. (Any show, really.)

"That's amazing! Wait...what day this week?"

Vanessa gives me another cautious look and says, "Thursday at 8:15 a.m. Is that a problem?"

"*Dammit!* I'm on the early shift on Thursday."

"The early shift?"

"At the coffeehouse. I have a 6 a.m. start," I say, realizing how that must sound from her perspective. "But I can try to get it covered."

"Erin, I need your full attention if I represent you. I can't have you worrying about covering shifts. You can always get another coffee shop job, but you may never get another chance like this. You have to strike while the iron is hot; before people lose interest in indie designers with socially-conscious missions. Do you understand what I'm saying?" Vanessa asks, as though she is speaking to a four-year-old.

"Yes," I say, feeling like a four-year-old.

"Good." She reaches into her tote bag and pulls out a folder, removing a document from it. "I've put together a contract that lays out the terms of our working together. Take some time to read it over, but we can't move forward until it's signed. I also can't guarantee you the spot on *Breakfast Television* without a signature. I don't want to push you. I know this must be overwhelming for you, everything happening so quickly. But we *need* to get moving on this. Trust me when I say I'll do anything—*anything*—it takes to make Lady Bettencourt a success." She slowly slides the contract and a pen to my side of the table.

I flip open the document and pretend to read it. It seems legit, although I should probably have Betty take a peek at it before I sign, as she is better at this kind of thing.

But what if that is too late, and someone else gets my spot on *Breakfast Television*?

I glance up at Vanessa, searching her riveting eyes for a while. She never flinches or turns away.

"I trust you," I say, then sign my name.

EIGHTEEN

I CALLED JOAQUIN, my manager at the coffeehouse, and told him I had to quit, but that I found someone to cover my remaining shifts.

He said he was sad to see me go, but he understood. During what I hadn't realized was my last shift yesterday, I had filled him in on the events at the movie premiere. He told me he saw this coming, and that I would always be welcomed to come in for a chat and a latte on the house.

I thanked him for everything, especially for taking a chance on me when I didn't have any barista experience and no one else wanted to hire me. I loved working there. It was the first job I ever had where I could say that.

Now that I have officially quit, I'm not only sad, but worried about what this means for my finances. My job at the coffeehouse represented more than half of my income. I won't have that anymore. I will need to rely solely on Lady Bettencourt.

But I guess it's time I take a chance on myself.

Later that afternoon, I drop off a round of dress orders at my special post office in the underground path—an intricate network of tunnels covering most of the downtown financial core.

This post office and I have a history, and it isn't just because the employees are mailing magicians who never mess up a shipment. No, I go there hoping I may run into someone. Someone I refer to as Suit Guy.

Suit Guy is my long-standing crush. I used to see him on the subway, but ever since I moved downtown to live with Betty, I don't run into him anymore. The last time I saw him was almost two years ago, on a day that changed my life forever. That is also the day I found out he had a girlfriend.

But it's been two years; a lot can happen in that time. I'm proof of that. So I go to my special post office, hoping for another chance encounter.

What I don't hope for is an encounter with my former boss, Bradford, who has been known to frequent it, as well. That would be an awkward reunion. I'm still embarrassed by the whole "getting fired" situation, even though it turned out to be the best thing that could have happened to me.

And whenever I think of Bradford, I can't help also thinking of Carol, his evil administrative assistant and the person who got me fired. I thought I was done with Carol the day I left my miserable cubicle job, but she continues to haunt me in my dreams. Every time I have a nightmare with Carol playing the leading role, I always wake up in a pool of sweat, shivering.

If only I could have dreams starring Suit Guy, instead.

But I suppose I don't get to choose which people stay in the past, where they belong, and which ones I would give anything to catch the tiniest glimpse of...even if only in my dreams.

I need to pick a dress. It isn't as if I have many options. Three, to be precise. But considering tomorrow will be my first television appearance in my twenty-nine years of life, I want to pick the right one.

I love the Lady Bettencourt designs. They each hold special meaning for me.

To begin, I try on "The Betty," which was named after...Betty. It's a knee-length sheath with varying sleeve-lengths, depending on the season. I use secondhand wool skirts and dresses to make them. For the summer versions, I use linen whenever I'm lucky enough to find it.

The Betty is the most professional of the three. It's also the one I wear the least. Probably because I no longer have an office job, but I wanted to have a work-appropriate option in the line for those who do.

And it's perfect for when I want to look really put together. It's what I wore to my coffee meeting with Vanessa.

Next, I try on "The Gabby," named after the fashion designer Coco Chanel. Her real name was Gabrielle. It was only fitting to have a dress named after her, as her Chanel 2.55 bag led the way to my being fired and starting Lady Bettencourt.

The Gabby is a sleeveless shift dress that is suitable for work or cocktails, but can be dressed down, as well. I try to use darker materials for this design, *à la* little black dress, but I have done it in brighter colours and with cuts of different fabrics. It's my top seller.

Finally, I try on "The Lizzie," the one that has the most significance for me and my personal favourite to wear. I named it after my mom.

After pouring over countless old photos, I chose a shirtwaist dress for her design, as she seemed to gravitate towards that style. This dress also has varying sleeve-lengths, depending on the season. It's the fun design in the line, as it's more casual than the others. But it can be dressed up with the right shoes and accessories and made more formal depending on the fabrics I use. I mostly use men's dress shirts, which are always in high supply at thrift stores. Many of them have interesting patterns, like funky stripes and paisley.

Although I own all the designs in various materials and colours— I wear my dresses almost exclusively; it's been my only form of advertising—Vanessa asked me to make three new ones for the show. Whichever two I don't wear will be on mannequins on the set.

Vanessa also asked me to recreate "The Rosie," the dress Rachel McAdams wore to the movie premiere. She thinks viewers will get a kick out of seeing it, even though it isn't part of my regular lineup. She wanted me to rename it "The Rachel," but I said no. I'm grateful to Rachel, I am—eternally—but my dress names end in an "ie" or "y." I want to keep it that way. Plus, that dress already has a name.

The Rosie is named after the shared middle name, Rose, of my mom, my sister, and me. It's a halter dress with a partially exposed back and a full skirt that flows to the ground. It's beautiful.

But I'm not sure I want to add an evening dress to my online shop. They take me a long time to make, especially with the special pockets I add. Although, it would be a great use of the plethora of secondhand prom and bridesmaid dresses that I find. Maybe I could make one exclusive evening dress per season. Women love owning something exclusive. Actually, that is the cool thing about my dresses: Each one is unique, an original.

I have spent the last few days sewing the new dresses, taking my time with The Rosie, as I'm making it my official maid of honour dress for Betty's wedding. With the wedding being in a month, I needed to finish the dress, anyway.

Yesterday, Vanessa came by the condo to give me a bit of media training. We did a mock interview and everything. There is so much to remember. I don't want to let her, or myself, down.

Imagine: Tomorrow morning, I will be one of those people inside the television!

I take another look at myself wearing The Lizzie in my full-length mirror. Without realizing it until now, I know it's the one I was always going to choose.

NINETEEN

I BARELY SLEPT last night, fearing I wouldn't hear my alarm go off. So when it did at six in the morning, I was already awake.

Back in my cubicle days, it was a struggle for me to get up by eight. But when I started working at the coffeehouse, I became an early riser. Now I love the quiet of those morning hours while the city is still half-asleep.

I left for the *Breakfast Television* studio earlier than necessary. I had too much nervous energy to wait around at the condo.

My stomach is in knots. I haven't been able to eat anything. I almost forgot to use shampoo when I showered. Thankfully, they are doing my makeup. I hate to think the mess I would have made of my face, given my trembling hands.

Once I arrive at the studio entrance, I take a deep breath before opening the door.

Vanessa is waiting for me inside. "You're early, good. That gives us time to go over a few things." She takes the garment bags I'm carrying and hands them to a girl wearing a headset. "And you chose The Lizzie—excellent choice."

She is wearing her tailored, dark grey pantsuit. Come to think of it, I have never seen her not wearing it. Maybe she bought it in multiples and it's her uniform.

Vanessa reminds me it's live television, so there is no second take. No matter what happens out there, I have to go with it.

"What's rule number one?" she asks, quizzing me.

"Don't look directly into the camera for very long."

"So where do you look?"

"At the hosts."

"And what if you forget how to answer a question?"

"Take a deep breath and trust it will come to me."

"Okay, you're ready—well, almost. Let's find the makeup artist."

My makeup looks amazing. You can't tell I barely slept last night. Wouldn't it be great to have a personal makeup artist at your beck and call?

I met the producer while I was having my makeup done. He told me to relax and that the pros got nervous, too. That made me feel better. But as it's getting closer and closer to my segment, the butterflies in my stomach quadruple, and I'm feeling nauseous and lightheaded.

Oh, my god. What if I puke or faint on live television? Worse, what if I puke, and then faint on top of my puke on live television?

No, no, don't think like that.

During a commercial break before my segment, I'm introduced to the co-hosts, Dina Pugliese and Kevin Frankish. They are just as nice as I thought they would be. Dina is even prettier in real life and super tall, like more than six feet with heels. She towers over Kevin.

And then, the producer gives us a signal and says, "Show time!"

I can't believe this is really happening.

The first thing I do is look directly into the camera. And I keep looking into it.

Rule number one: broken.

I have also forgotten how to blink.

Dina is giving a brief introduction, but I can't hear what she is saying.

"So, Erin, it's been an exciting week for you," Dina says, trying to draw my attention.

Look at the host, Erin. Look at the host!

But the camera is so damn appealing. I slowly turn my head towards Dina, who is sitting on the opposite end of a light-blue sectional with Kevin at her side.

Deep breath. "It has been. Very exciting," I say.

It's boiling in here. It must be all the lights. I hope I don't sweat through my dress. Thinking about that makes me sweat more.

"How did you feel when you saw our hometown girl, Rachel McAdams, show up at the film premiere you were attending, wearing one of your dress designs?" Kevin asks.

"I was very...excited." (Note to self: Learn another word for excited.)

The hosts look at each other as though they have a dunce on their hands, which leaves me no one to look at. This is when I finally notice the big window behind us with a view of the street. There are passersby peering in, trying to get on television. One of them is a girl who reminds me of me. The old me. She smiles in my direction, and I smile back.

I can do this. I need to do this. For me and for her.

Trying to salvage the interview, Dina asks, "What inspired you to use secondhand clothes to make your dresses?"

"I, um, I use secondhand clothes because of the waste I saw in the industry. I didn't see the point of using new materials when there are so many clothes at thrift stores that have been worn for only a season or two. Sometimes they haven't been worn at all before being discarded. I wanted to give them another life," I say, getting the interview back on track.

Thankfully, Vanessa had prepped me on how to answer that question. My answer was partially true. It was the reason why I *continued* to use secondhand clothes to make my dresses, but it wasn't the reason why I started. In the beginning, I was only making a few dresses at a time. I couldn't buy materials in bulk, and new materials at fabric stores were too expensive. That is when I thought of using secondhand clothes because they often came with the bonus of zippers and buttons that I could also reuse. I was just trying to save money. Only later did I realize it was socially conscious.

"In fact, the dress you're wearing today was made from a man's shirt, isn't that right?" Kevin asks.

"That's right. And, some day, the one you're wearing may end up on a woman's body," I say, gesturing to his shirt, realizing after I have said it, how that must sound.

He laughs and says, "That would be a first!"

"Take us through your dress designs," Dina says, motioning me towards the mannequins on the set. The Rosie is in the middle, with The Gabby and The Betty flanking it.

We both get up, while Kevin stays seated.

I describe The Gabby and The Betty. When I say The Betty was named after my sister, I purposely look into the camera and say, "Hey, Betty!" I know Betty's watching, and she will get a kick out of my doing that, so I had to. Then, I share the significance of The Lizzie, the dress I'm wearing.

I'm really getting the hang of this television business. I even crack a couple more jokes.

"And now, the dress our viewers have been waiting for, The Rachel," Dina says.

The Rachel?

"You mean, The Rosie," I say, causing Dina to glance down at her show notes. "It's a duplicate of the dress Rachel McAdams was seen wearing, except this one is purple. It's made from old prom and bridesmaid dresses."

I'm about to add that it's what I will be wearing to my sister's upcoming wedding, but I have taken a breath, and Dina asks me about The Rosie's special pockets before I can.

"Those were sewn-in using a technique I invented," I say. "I think I invented it, anyway. Because of the full skirt and the pockets being reinforced, they can hold a lot without the dress looking or feeling bulky. It's perfect for those occasions when you don't want to carry a purse."

"I love that. Every dress should have that feature," Dina says.

"I agree!" Kevin shouts from the sectional. "I'm tired of carrying my wife's purse."

We laugh happily together. This is so much fun.

Dina guides me back towards the sectional, then says, "One of our lucky viewers will get to test out those pockets. Enter online at BT's website for your chance to win The Rach—Rosie, as well as two tickets to the closing night gala of the Toronto International Film Festival this Sunday. Contest closes tomorrow at midnight, Eastern-standard time."

What? No! That is my maid of honour dress!

I glance over at Vanessa, who is standing off-camera. She is making a rolling gesture with her hands and mouthing, "Go with it."

I'm furious, but I know there is nothing I can do.

"That's not all," Kevin says. "We will also be giving away two tickets to the Lady Bettencourt fashion show, featuring Erin's new spring line, taking place on…"

Fashion show? What fashion show? I don't have a spring line! It isn't even officially fall!

I don't bother glancing over at Vanessa this time. I know what she wants me to do.

Dina turns towards me. "This will be your first fashion show. You must be feeling…" She stops to catch Kevin's eye, and they both say in unison, "Very excited!"

I attempt a laugh, but it comes out sounding flat.

"Well, we wish you all the success in the world," Kevin says.

I mumble a half-hearted, "Thank you."

It had been going so well. I don't understand what just happened.

"Coming up…" I hear Dina say, but I can't make out the rest of her words.

My mind can focus on only one thing: I need to talk to Vanessa.

TWENTY

"IT WAS REALLY nice meeting you," I say, shaking Dina's and Kevin's hands, backstage. And it was. It's not their fault things went downhill. That credit goes to Vanessa.

"You did great," Dina says, as Kevin nods in agreement.

Vanessa approaches us. "Yes, she did," she says, beaming.

I avoid making eye contact with her. I need to calm down before I can look at her, much less speak to her.

"We had better get back," Kevin says. "We have to go pet some llamas or something."

I'm left standing with Vanessa in a hallway as various petting zoo animals and their handlers make their way around us.

Vanessa grabs my arm and pulls me into the now empty green room, closing the door behind us. "Okay, I know you're mad, but—"

"Mad? *Mad?* I'm not mad; *I'm furious!* Why didn't you tell me about the fashion show? Or that they were going to raffle off my maid of honour dress?" I'm pacing the room, but its size is too small to contain my anger.

"That was your maid of honour dress? I didn't know. I thought it was just a replica of what Rachel wore. The producer asked me at the last minute if they could give it away. I said yes, not thinking it was a big deal."

She seems surprised. And I never *actually* told her it was my maid of honour dress. But still, she isn't getting off that easy.

"What about the fashion show? Was that the producer's idea, too?"

"No, that was me. I felt we needed to announce something big to keep our momentum going. What better announcement than a fashion show. You said yourself that you wanted to have one."

"You should have asked me first. I have never put on a fashion show. I have no idea what to do!"

"But *I* do. That is why you hired me. It will take a lot of hard work, but we will manage. Together."

I stop pacing and look at her. She seems sincere. Maybe this is the right move; the next step for Lady Bettencourt.

Vanessa takes my hands in hers. "I'm sorry things got confusing out there. But you were great—well, except for the beginning bit. I promise I'll prep you better for the next show."

Next show? I'll be on television again?

"It's okay," I say. "I guess I'm partly to blame, too."

As I'm putting the remaining dresses into their garment bags, my phone rings.

"Erin, it's Betty."

"Hey, Betty Boop!"

"Really? We're still doing that?"

"You know you love it."

"No. I really, really don't."

"So...how was I?" Betty's opinion is always the most important to me.

"Amazing, considering you've never been on television before. I recorded the whole thing; we can watch it tonight. And thanks for the shout out—that was cool. There was just one thing—"

"*Oh, my god, what?* Was one of my buttons undone? Was there lipstick on my teeth? Please don't tell me my dress was in my tights!" I'm getting vivid mental images of everything that could have gone wrong.

"No, nothing like that. It's the fashion show—"

"*I know!* Vanessa surprised me with that. Can you believe it?"

"Not the fashion show itself, but the date of it."

"I sort of zoned out during that part. When is it?"

"The same day as my wedding."

Fuck!

"I'll get Vanessa to change it to after the wedding," I say quickly. "I'm so sorry, Betty, but I honestly didn't even know about it."

"It's okay. I knew it had to be a mix-up." She hesitates, then adds, "Are you sure about Vanessa? Something seems off with her."

"Don't worry, I have it under control. I've already exchanged a few choice words with her about...stuff." I was going to say the fact that Vanessa raffled off my maid of honour dress, but I don't think Betty wants to hear that right now.

"Hey, that wasn't your maid of honour dress that they gave away, was it?"

Crap.

"Um, no. It was a...replica. I haven't started sewing my dress, yet. I'm working on it this week."

"Okay, phew. I'm leaving for the office now. See you tonight at home," she says, ending the call.

Not only is the fashion show the same day as Betty's wedding, but that also means it's just a month away.

A month!

I need to have another chat with Vanessa.

"Ready to go?" Vanessa asks when she returns from the restroom.

"Yes, but I have to talk to you about the fashion show."

"Let's wait until we've left the studio," Vanessa says, sensing the seriousness in my tone.

When we get outside, we walk for a while in silence.

"So what did you want to discuss?" Vanessa asks, breaking the silence.

I take a deep breath. "I need to change the date of the fashion show."

"Not possible. I know it's only weeks away and that you're nervous, but we have to keep the momentum going while people are still interested."

109

"It isn't that it's just weeks away—although that's enough to give me a nervous breakdown—it's that it's the same day as my sister's wedding."

"Oh. Hmm. Is there any way she can change her date?"

"Of her wedding?"

"No, I guess not. What time is the wedding?"

"One o'clock, but—"

"Perfect! The fashion show is set for ten. You can do both."

"But there are things leading up to the actual ceremony, pictures and stuff. I have to be there. I'm representing our entire family."

"Erin, I've already booked the venue and some suppliers. It *has* to be that day because it *has* to be held around Fashion Week. All the key players will be in town for the shows. We need the press, editors, and buyers there for it to be a success. I barely managed to get us a venue."

We stop walking to wait for the streetlight to change.

Vanessa sees the conflicted look on my face and says, "I don't want you to stress out. We will make this work somehow. What I need *you* to do is focus on designing. Leave everything else to *me.*"

"But—"

"I know how to handle this; I've dealt with crazier scheduling before. It will work out. You'll see."

I can't see how it could possibly work out. But what if Vanessa is right, and it will only take an hour or so. How long are fashion shows? I should talk to Betty. We could make the day a two-part event: The morning for my fashion show and the rest of the day for her wedding. Although, she didn't sound happy on the phone at the prospect of having the fashion show on the same day as her wedding. It is supposed to be her big day.

But what about my big day? This could be my one and only chance to become a success. Can I really pass that up? Betty is getting on with her life. I need to get on with my life, too. Maybe I don't have to choose.

"I'm not missing my sister's wedding," I say, stating it for the record.

"No one is asking you to. Now let me buy you brunch to celebrate your television premiere!" Vanessa smiles her spellbinding smile, then links arms with me as we walk across the street.

TWENTY-ONE

Days to Wedding / Fashion Show: 26

THE BEST TIME to shop at my favourite thrift store is Monday mornings when it first opens. Hardly anyone is around, so I can take my time picking through items without having too much competition for the good stuff.

Since my appearance on *Breakfast Television* last week, Lady Bettencourt's waiting list has grown even longer. It's up to six weeks now. Not only do those orders need to be fulfilled, but I have to buy lighter-weight fabrics to create the spring line for the fashion show—which I also need to start designing. On top of that, I have to find replacement materials for my maid of honour dress, and then I need to remake it.

How am I supposed to get all of that done?

I wish I had remembered to bring a paper bag with me. I have started getting these mini-anxiety attacks and breathing into a paper bag really helps. Instead, I remind myself to focus on the task at hand. One step at a time. I can do this.

After browsing around the thrift store for a while, I spot some tablecloths. Maybe they could be made into dresses. Normally, I stick to clothes, but I'm not finding what I want, and I need a lot of material.

As I'm searching through the tablecloths, trying to find ones without any stains on them, I hear a woman beside me ask, "Are you Erin Bettencourt?" in a familiar accent I can't quite place.

Turning to my right, then down, I see an adorable, middle-aged woman gazing up at me. I don't recognize her. This must be...

My first celebrity sighting!

Well, I am a sort-of celebrity. I hope I look okay. I don't want this lady to be disappointed with the real-life Erin as opposed to the one she saw on television.

"Yes, yes, I am," I say, beaming.

Maybe she will ask me to sign something. I have been practicing my autograph (since I was seven years old). I should start carrying a Sharpie.

"You remember me?" she asks.

Do *I* remember *her*? Great, my first stalker, too.

"Um, no, have we met?" I ask, edging away slightly.

"It's Gloria! I work with your mom many years ago. I babysitting you and your sister sometimes."

Gloria...Gloria...GLORIA! The Portuguese lady!

"You used to bring us those delicious custard tarts!" I say, remembering her now.

She nods proudly. "How is your mom? I haven't seen her for so long."

Me, neither.

This is the first time I have to break the news to someone who knew her. It feels like opening up an old wound that will never truly heal.

"My mom...she...um...she passed away."

"Oh, no!" Gloria's hand raises to her chest and tears form in her eyes. "She was such a nice lady." She shakes her head in disbelief.

I reach into my purse and hand her a tissue.

"*Obrigada, querida,*" she says, taking the tissue from me.

I remember her teaching us the meaning of those words, "Thank you, sweetie," even though I haven't heard them in years.

"When did she die?"

Die. Now there is a word I wish I never learned the meaning of. I can't stand the sound of it. It sounds so ugly.

I do the math. "Almost seven years ago."

Wow, has it really been that long?

"Your mom and me used to be close, but then, she leaving the shop for new job, and we losing touch. I'm sorry I not there for you and your sister. That is bad time to lose your mom when life just beginning."

Now I'm getting teary-eyed. Things are getting quite deep at the thrift store, so I change the subject.

"Are you still working at the alteration shop? With the old man who had hair..." I was about to say, coming out of his ears and nose, but decide that might be rude and stop myself. Betty and I used to call him Hairy Scary because not only was he hairy, but he scared the crap out of us with his crooked fingers and clouded eyes. He was always offering us candy. We would take it, and then hide behind our mom.

"Anestis, the Greek with the hair," Gloria says. "He closing the shop and retiring few years ago. I do alterations from home now but little business. People don't want to fix clothes no more. They just throw away."

Wait a minute. What if...

"*Gloria!* How would you like to work for me?"

"Doing what?" she asks, looking a bit startled.

"Sewing dresses! I have my own online shop, Lady Bettencourt. I'm getting all these orders, and I can't keep up. Then, there is the fashion show and my sister's—"

She places her hand on my arm to stop me, meeting my eyes. "I help you."

"*Really?*"

"Of course!"

I let out a long breath.

She gives me her phone number, and I tell her I will call her to discuss the arrangements.

"I'm so happy to see you again, *querida*. I hope to see Beatriz soon."

Gloria always called Betty by her full name—the Portuguese version of it. My name was also a struggle for her, hence the default to *querida*.

"I'm glad to see you, too. But Gloria...how did you know it was me? You haven't seen me since I was a kid."

"Your face." She cups my chin and examines my features. "You look so much like your mom."

As she walks away, with a slight waddle, I can't help thinking this wasn't a chance encounter, running into Gloria after all these years.

Maybe my mom is still watching out for me.

Vanessa will be at the condo any minute now. Last night, she called to say she wanted to come over to take a look at my preliminary designs for the fashion show.

I had no designs. So I stayed up late sketching, and finished a few more this morning.

When she arrives, she is wearing her tailored, dark grey pantsuit (again) and has two coffee cups in her hands.

"I thought we could use these to get us going." She hands me one of the cups. "Lactose-free milk, right?"

"Yeah, thanks," I say, surprised she remembered. I take a sip. The effects are immediate.

I lead her into the dining room, where I have placed the sketches around the table.

She looks them over, taking in each one separately, as though she is at an art gallery. Occasionally, she points to a design and says, "Very nice."

I have never had someone scrutinize my designs before. I'm not sure I can handle the criticism.

"I haven't had a chance to name the dresses, yet," I say anxiously.

"Mm-hmm."

She circles the table again.

And again.

I can't take it anymore. "So what do you think?"

"They're great, but—"

"But, what? *But, what?* Please just tell me!" I knew it. My designs suck.

"Relax, Erin. I like what you've done, incorporating pockets into most of the designs is smart. It seems to be what women want. But can we make the dresses...sexier?"

"Sexier?"

"Yes, for example, with this dress..." She points to one of my designs. "Maybe take up the hem to mid-thigh. And this one—this one would look amazing with a lower neckline."

"My dresses aren't meant to be overtly sexy. I want classic designs women can wear for years, not something that goes in-and-out of fashion. It's *Lady* Bettencourt for a reason."

"Well, sex sells. But you're the designer, you get the final call."

Maybe I could shorten a few of the hemlines. "I'll think about it."

"I'll get you a list of the hot colours for next spring so you can be on the lookout for similar colours at the thrift store." She sees the face I'm making. "Or you can go with classic colours." Vanessa looks at the designs again, then asks, "Where is The Rachel? I mean, The Rosie?"

"I'm not sure I want to have an evening gown in the lineup. They are a lot of work to make."

"That's unfortunate. It would be a great way to cap-off the end of the show. Plus, the audience will be expecting to see it."

"I don't know..."

"Just think about it, okay?"

"Okay," I say, even though I already have enough to think about. I feel my chest tightening.

I need my paper bag.

TWENTY-TWO

Days to Wedding / Fashion Show: 24

GLORIA AND I have decided she will focus on fulfilling existing and new orders, while I mainly focus on the fashion show, Betty's wedding, and the business side of things.

I wasn't sure how to pay her, so I said she would get a fixed amount for each dress completed. She already finished one in the time she was at the condo. She is much faster than I am.

And here is the amazing part: She has a serger, a fancy sewing machine for finishing garments. This is taking my dresses to a whole new, professional level. I have wanted to buy a serger for a while, but they are expensive. Gloria is teaching me how to use it. And she has left it behind at the condo because she will be working with me here, for the most part. She said it's lonely at home now that her kids have moved out.

When she saw my mom's sewing machine, she gently caressed it and got teary-eyed again.

I have been having flashbacks of Gloria spending time at our old place when I was growing up. It's funny how things like that can hide in the recesses of your mind, only resurfacing themselves as needed.

When Betty came home from work that evening, she recognized Gloria right away, even though I hadn't had the chance to tell her about our reunion.

We chatted for a while, enjoying the yummy custard tarts Gloria brought us, and then, as she was leaving, Betty invited her to the wedding.

Great.

Now I will have to keep the fashion show date a secret from Gloria as well so that Betty doesn't find out it's still happening on her wedding day.

—

"Hey, Erin?"

"Yeah?"

Betty and I are sitting on the couch, watching television. She is working on the seating arrangements for the wedding, and I'm deconstructing secondhand clothes with my friend, the seam ripper.

"Do you think I could have my final dress fitting on Sunday when I get back from Chicago? I don't want to leave it to the last minute, given everything else you have going on."

"Um, sure. No problem."

There is a problem. Her dress is only half-finished. I had forgotten all about it. I count the days on my fingers. Five. I have five days to get it into final dress-fitting state. If I had nothing else to do, this wouldn't be a problem, but I do.

"Did you ask Lizzie to come to the wedding, yet?" Betty asks.

Something else I have forgotten to do.

"Um, no. But I told her I would drop by the vintage shop on Saturday. I will ask her then."

Okay, make that four-and-a-half days to get the wedding dress ready. Maybe I should tell Lizzie I can't come for a visit. But I haven't seen her in a while, and I miss her.

I met Lizzie two years ago. She works at the vintage shop where my mom's Chanel 2.55 bag turned up after so many years. (Betty still thinks it wasn't our mom's bag, nor that the universe had a hand in my finding it again. I strongly disagree on both counts.) Lizzie would keep me updated on whether someone had bought the bag while I tried to earn the money to buy it myself. And I did buy it, but then, I lost it.

Lizzie is my guardian angel—but the living kind. She also shares the same name as my mom. (See? Totally the universe working its magic.)

Speaking of names…"Have you decided what to do about your last name?"

"No. I sometimes think that's why I've waited so long to marry Matt."

Matt's last name is Getty, which would make her, Betty Getty.

"You could start going by Beatrice."

"Never."

"How are your other wedding plans coming along?" I have been so focused on myself that I haven't thought to ask her lately.

"Great! My list is almost all checked-off," she says, showing me a printed spreadsheet with a bunch of checkmarks on it. Betty is so organized.

"Sorry I haven't been able to help you more."

"Don't worry about it, Erin. It hasn't been that hard to organize. That's the best part of having a small wedding. I just need you to show up. Oh, and to finish my dress, obviously."

Obviously.

When Betty is safely asleep in her room, I begin my search. I check every conceivable location Betty's half-made wedding dress could be. I need to find it; it's irreplaceable.

Betty asked me to incorporate the dress she wore to prom with Matt and one of our mom's old dresses into her wedding design. Both of which are a light grey. She is going a less traditional route with her dress colour, although the design itself is classic. It's actually The Rosie but with added lace flourishes.

I search the condo three times, which isn't easy given all the secondhand fabrics and other half-finished dresses, laying around. I have to go through each piece to make sure Betty's dress isn't hiding in them. I even looked under my bed. But I can't find it anywhere.

Shit! Where could it be?

I need to find the dress before Sunday.

And before Betty does.

TWENTY-THREE
Days to Wedding / Fashion Show: 21

IT'S BEEN THREE DAYS, and I haven't found Betty's wedding dress. I even searched her bedroom from top-to-bottom while she was at work. I need a Plan B. Time is running out: Her fitting is tomorrow night.

But right now, what I need the most is a break. A break from cutting materials, sewing dresses, and packaging orders. A break from designing dresses for spring when the leaves outside are just beginning to change colour. Most of all, I need a break from the condo, as I haven't left in days.

So I'm on my way to visit Lizzie at the vintage shop in Yorkville: a little hamlet in the big city. A rich hamlet with designer and luxury goods, which means the vintage shop isn't filled with old housewife dresses from the 1950s. Instead, it's filled with vintage Dior, Yves Saint Laurent, and, of course, Chanel.

I used to be afraid to drop-in to visit Lizzie because of the mean salesgirl she worked with. But the mean salesgirl (and her hot-pink lipstick mouth) got fired a few months ago for being rude to the wrong customer. I guess some customers are worth more than others.

Whenever I come here, I'm reminded of the first time I realized this place existed. I was walking around Yorkville, playing this game (long story), when I noticed a flash in the distance. The flash came from the sun reflecting off the clasp of my mom's vintage Chanel bag in the shop window's display. Finding that bag again, after so many years, started a chain of events that has led me back here today.

Even though I don't have the bag anymore, I made a friend in exchange. But Lizzie knows that if a medium, navy, vintage Chanel 2.55 bag ever finds its way into the shop again, she is to call me immediately. While I know it's only a silly bag, a part of me still wants it back.

I walk inside the shop and look around for Lizzie. She is finishing up with a customer at the sales counter.

"Erin!" she says when she sees me. She comes around the counter to give me a big hug. Lizzie gives the best hugs.

"I'm sorry I haven't been here in a while. Things have been crazy," I say, holding her tightly.

"Aren't you a bundle of nerves?" She releases her grasp to look at me. "Are you all right, dear?"

I tell her about everything I have on my plate. How lucky I am to have Gloria helping me, but it still seems like too much to handle. How I'm having these mini-anxiety attacks and a hard time sleeping. I also want to tell her how I'm having my first-ever fashion show on the same day as Betty's wedding, but I'm not sure how she would react. I need Lizzie in my life. I need her to think I'm a good person.

When I finish, she says, "Oh, my. That does sound overwhelming. But I know just the thing." She goes back to the sales counter and writes something down on a piece of paper.

"What is this?" I ask as she hands it to me.

"It's a calming tea—soothes the nerves. Drink it before bed, as well. It will help you sleep. You can pick some up around the corner at Whole Foods."

"Thank you, Lizzie. You always know what I need. Oh, I almost forgot! I have something for you, too." I reach into my purse and give Lizzie the invitation to Betty's wedding. "We both hope you can make it. You're kind of my date."

She opens the envelope containing the simple yet elegant invitation inside. "October 17th. I just so happen to be free. Wait a moment...Isn't that the same day as your fashion show? Isn't that what they said on *Breakfast Television*?"

I didn't know she had seen it. I meant to call her, but had forgotten with all the commotion.

"Um, that was a mix-up. The fashion show is being rescheduled."

Lizzie looks at me for a while before saying, "Well, at least, that is one less thing for you to be worried about right now. By the way, you were great on the show. A real pro!"

More like a real fraud.

There was a time when Whole Foods was a mystical place to me. A place I liked the idea of, but not a place where I would actually *buy* anything. Mostly, I thought it was too expensive.

Then one day, I helped a little old lady who needed some apples (another long story) and became a semi-regular customer. And it turns out, not everything is that expensive, or, at least, not that much more expensive than what I would pay at a conventional, big-chain grocery store. Plus, the quality is so much better.

So I pick up some organic broccoli and fair-trade bananas before heading to the tea section, where I search row-upon-row of tea-after-tea until I find it. There is only one left. These must be stressful times.

As I'm reaching for the calming tea, my hand collides with someone else's. A man's hand. A very manly hand with long, squared fingers. My eyes slowly follow the hand up to the owner's exposed muscular-but-not-too-muscular arm, across his T-shirted broad shoulder, and finally land on his face, where a curious smile awaits me.

I know him. I know, I know him. But I can't remember from where because he is out of his natural habitat.

"See something you like?" he asks, in a deep voice with a wide grin spreading across his face.

That is when I realize who he is: Mr. Trader.

Mr. Trader was one of my former "Erin Girl" clients. I fetched his lunch on a daily basis for months, but then, he must have realized it was ridiculous to pay that much to have someone get your lunch, and, I guess, started getting it himself.

I call him Mr. Trader (not to his face) because he is an equity trader...and because I like to give people nicknames. But mostly because I feel weird using his real name.

"Hey, Erin, how are you?"

"Um, good," I say, embarrassed he caught me checking him out. He does look good, though. Scruffier than I remember him but better somehow.

"You still saving the day, one errand at a time?" he asks, grinning again.

That was the tagline from my errand service. I'm surprised he remembered.

"Nope, now I save it with dresses." He gives me a funny look. I guess he missed my television debut. "You still vegan?"

"Every day, except Thanksgiving and Christmas."

It's my turn to give him a funny look.

He shrugs his shoulders and says, "Nobody is perfect."

We both look over at the tea, waiting on the shelf.

"You have it," he says.

"No, you have it."

"Let's wrestle for it."

This is the Mr. Trader I remember. There was always a bit of harmless innuendo to our conversations.

"I'm kidding. Just take it," he says. "I still have half-a-box."

I thank him, but now, I'm wondering why he needs calming tea. He doesn't look stressed out. (This tea must really work.) But I probably don't look stressed out, either, and I clearly am. It's hard to know what goes on inside people's minds.

"Fuck, I'm late," he says, glancing at his watch. (He hasn't lost his potty-mouth.) "I'm headed to a barbecue." (Barbecued tofu?) "But I'm glad I ran into you, Erin. You look great!"

The last time he saw me, I was sporting my "grief weight." After my mom died, I had slowly put on a few extra pounds. I was never technically overweight, but I did look sort of puffy. I'm finally starting to feel like my old self again. Actually, that is what is also different about him. He has lost weight or toned up or something.

"Thanks," I say. "It was nice running into you, too...Aaron."

And that is why I call him Mr. Trader. Otherwise, it feels as if I'm talking to myself—not that I have ever been guilty of doing that.

TWENTY-FOUR

Days to Wedding / Fashion Show: 20

AFTER I HAD a cup of calming tea and a short nap, I came up with a solution to Betty's missing dress problem. I spent all night making her a mock wedding dress by sewing together two of the tablecloths I picked up at the thrift store.

It's an exact replica, including my special pockets incorporated into the design. It turned out so well that I may use it for the fashion show finale. It's The Rosie design, after all, and it's symbolic of my brand, as Vanessa would say. I will run the idea by her the next time we meet.

As I'm finishing placing the dress on Sally, the dress form, Betty arrives at the condo.

She puts down her weekend bag and says, "It's beautiful." But as she comes closer, she has a confused expression on her face. "These aren't my dress materials."

Here goes…"I've thought about it, Betty, and I want your final wedding dress, with all the extra little details, to be a surprise. It would be my special gift to you."

"Uh, okay…but how do I know the actual dress will fit?"

"We will do the fitting with this dress, and then I can make the final alterations based on that."

"And that will work, even though it's different materials?"

"The draping will be slightly off, but the fit will be the same."

"Well, I guess, if it means that much to you to keep it a surprise. So long as this isn't some ploy because you've lost my dress," Betty says, laughing. "You *are* famous for losing things."

I nervously laugh along with her. "Don't worry, Betty. Your wedding dress is safe and sound where I left it."

Which is most likely the truth. I just don't remember where that is.

"So when is the new fashion show taking place?" Betty asks. "You haven't given me an update."

She is standing on top of a stool, wearing the tablecloth dress and her new wedding shoes. I'm circling her, pinning the dress where it needs to be taken up or taken in. Luckily, I made the dress extra long, so it should work for the runway model when I unpin it, if we decide to use it for the show finale.

"Um, we haven't picked a new date," I say. "We're looking for a venue first." It's easier to lie when I'm looking at her feet.

"What about appearing on television again? Or is that on hold until you can announce the new date?"

"It's on hold."

It isn't on hold.

I'm actually appearing on a local cable program tomorrow morning. But I can't tell Betty, or she will watch and know the fashion show is still on her wedding day.

"Erin," Betty says quietly. "I did something you may not like."

I stop pinning the dress and straighten up so I can see her face. "What?"

What could Betty possibly have done that I wouldn't like?

"I found your contract with Vanessa, and I took it with me to Chicago. I wanted to read it over. You did read it before you signed it, right?"

"I, uh, glanced at it. It seemed official."

"*Erin!* I can't believe you signed something without reading it first! You can't do that. It's legally-binding."

"Was there something bad in it?" I say, starting to panic.

"You're lucky; it's a standard publicity contract. I looked it up."

I let out my breath.

"But do you know how much you're paying Vanessa?"

For some reason, I hadn't thought about that. I knew Vanessa wasn't volunteering her services, but I also never thought to ask. It hasn't come up, either. But she probably thinks I've read the contract and already know.

I shake my head.

"You're paying her a monthly retainer of two thousand dollars, for twenty hours of work, extra hours to be approved, for a three-month term, to be renewed upon agreement."

Two thousand dollars?

No, wait, it's actually six thousand dollars because the contract is for three months.

Where am I going to get six thousand dollars?

"Where are you going to get six thousand dollars?" Betty asks, echoing my concerns. "I know you've started saving, but it seems a waste to use them up."

My savings, yes! But I was kind of hoping to...save them. I think for a moment. "I may not have to. I've sold a bunch of dresses. Way more than ever before. And there is a waiting list with potential sales, too. I've been so busy; I haven't had a chance to look at the numbers, but maybe it will cover it. Anyway, don't I have to spend money to make money? I wouldn't have appeared on *Breakfast Television* without Vanessa's help, and that boosted sales a lot."

"I suppose, but I should start managing your books monthly, instead of only at tax time, now that your business is growing."

"Okay," I say, conceding.

"And make sure you're careful about how much you spend on the fashion show when you have it. You don't want that getting out of hand."

"I'll make sure."

Except, Vanessa already booked the venue and some of the suppliers; I have no idea what that is costing. If Betty manages my books monthly, she will see the invoices. I will have to hide them from her when I get them. I may have to put on a decoy fashion show after the real one to cover up everything.

"One more thing…" Betty says. (Oh, god. I can't handle anything else right now.) "I looked into Vanessa, as well. Did you know she was fired from her last job?"

She was?

"No, but I was fired. I can't really hold that against her."

"True, but the rumour is she was fired because she was having an affair with the president of her old agency. When he broke it off, she went nuts and started calling all the agency's clients, telling them he was running a side business selling child pornography."

"That doesn't sound like something Vanessa would do. It's probably just a rumour. How did you find that out, anyway?"

"I Googled her. I'm surprised you didn't. You Google everything. I read it on an online forum. Okay, *that* may be a rumour, but I do know for sure that her current agency, isn't *really* an agency. It's just her. And you may be her only client."

Hmm, that is a bit deceptive. But maybe she thought I wouldn't take her seriously if I knew she was a solo operation.

"Betty, everyone deserves a second chance. I got one."

"I still don't trust her."

"You haven't even met her!"

"Exactly. Why isn't she ever here when I'm around?"

"You can't expect her to wait until you get home from work."

"Fine. But something doesn't add up. Promise me you will never sign anything ever again without reading it first. This is *your* business. Don't let her run the show."

"I promise," I say, looking down at her feet.

"Look me in the eyes and say it again."

I look up and into her eyes, then repeat my promise.

TWENTY-FIVE

Days to Wedding / Fashion Show: 19

MY SECOND TELEVISION APPEARANCE wasn't as exciting as my first. Probably because the local cable program isn't as popular as *Breakfast Television*, but Vanessa said we needed to get as much exposure as possible leading up to the fashion show. She told me this, earlier this morning. She also apologized for not coming with me to the show because she had to attend an urgent client meeting. (Betty was wrong: I'm not Vanessa's only client.)

I had to bring my three dress designs, plus The Rosie, again. And as I needed to remake my maid of honour dress, that is what I brought with me. Luckily, there wasn't a surprise contest giveaway, and now I have that checked off my still-to-be-created list.

But the whole experience was upsetting. Before I got on-air, the producer told me to emphasize that Lady Bettencourt was started after the tragic death of my mother. He added that crying was good for both ratings and dress sales.

During the actual taping, when I was talking about what inspired me to start the business, the host kept trying to hand me a tissue. I refused to take the bait. I acted as if I didn't see it, even though she was practically shoving it in my face. I can't cry on cue, especially not for some jerks who want to exploit my mother's death.

The host also referred to The Rosie dress as The Rachel. That is the second time that has happened on-air.

I'm having lunch with Vanessa to review how the show went, so I will have to ask her about that. Actually, there are quite a few things I need to ask her about.

—

I spot Vanessa sitting near the back of the crowded restaurant. She sees me and waves me over.

Once I'm seated, I ask, "How did your meeting go this morning?"

"Fantastic! In fact, it had to do with Lady Bettencourt. But before I tell you, I want to hear how the show went."

"You had a meeting about *my* business without me? Vanessa, I—"

"Erin, I've had meetings without you before, remember? I found the venue, and I've spoken with the—"

"About that. I don't even know how much the fashion show is costing."

"I was able to negotiate better than market rates for the venue and most of the suppliers. I'm fully aware we need to be budget conscious. The deposits went on my company credit card, which I'll include in my bill to you, and you will receive the final invoices after the show to pay the rest. Exactly how it's set out in our contract."

"The one where I'm paying you two thousand dollars a month?"

"What is going on here? You're acting as if this is new information. I'll send you a breakdown of everything. But you should know that I've already passed my monthly retainer hours, and I wasn't even thinking of charging you. We're a team. I'm trying to help you."

Great, now I feel bad. I'm letting what Betty told me last night get to me. It's my fault I didn't realize what was in the contract. Vanessa is only following it. And it is nice that she is putting in extra time without charging me.

"I'm sorry," I say. "I guess I'm a bit upset because of what happened on the show."

"Why? *What happened?*"

"Don't worry, I didn't mess up," I say quickly. "But they kept pressuring me to cry over my mom's death to get ratings. They really wanted me to play it up."

"I see. I suppose that is the angle they took."

"Angle?"

"I gave them a brief, and that is what they decided to focus on."

"For future briefs, tell them to lay off the dead mom bit. I want to talk about it in a way that feels true to me, not as though I'm trying to make sales from her death."

"I completely understand your point of view, but it isn't in my control what they ask you once the camera starts rolling."

"Did your brief also include that The Rosie is named The Rachel? Was that out of your control, too?"

"Erin, think of the bigger picture. Try to be flexible with your naming conventions, especially as you still have so few dresses. Naming it The Rachel lets us leverage the Rachel McAdams story better."

"This isn't about 'leveraging a story' to me. It's about the direction I want to take Lady Bettencourt into the future."

"Okay, we will keep it The Rosie. I didn't know it was that important to you. Like you've said before, the dress isn't even part of your regular lineup."

A server breaks the mounting tension between us when he comes to take our orders.

Once he has left, Vanessa asks tentatively, "Do you want to hear about my meeting this morning?"

"Sure," I mumble.

"After the fashion show, we will likely be hit with a bunch of new orders. *Big orders*. There is no way you and Gloria can fulfill them on your own, so I've secured a factory to help us make the dresses. I'm still working out some of the details, but when I do, I'll need you to sign-off on it."

"But I want to make the dresses or, at least, have people I know make them. Maybe I could ask Gloria if she knows some other seamstresses who could help us."

"You're thinking like a dressmaker, not a fashion designer. Don't you want Lady Bettencourt to be an international success?"

"I do, but—"

"Then, we need to get a contract with a factory. And we need to get it soon before you and Gloria fall any further behind with orders and we start losing sales."

"Where is the factory located?"

As Vanessa is about to answer, our food arrives. We each take a few bites.

"So where is the factory located?" I ask again.

"Cambodia."

"Like a sweatshop?"

"You're thinking of Bangladesh. The working conditions are much better in Cambodia. You would be giving the women there a job and a chance at a better life, not only for themselves, but for their children, too."

"I'd rather production be local so I can keep an eye on it. I can't have my dresses made in a potential sweatshop. That goes against everything Lady Bettencourt stands for."

"Stop using the word 'sweatshop.' This is the way things are done in the industry, from the low-end to the high-end brands. Everyone does it."

"Well, I'm not everyone. I don't want to be. That is not my vision for Lady Bettencourt."

"Your vision? What is *your* vision? Because before I came along, you were an online shop with a couple of dress designs. Do you want to be a pattern-cutter for the rest of your life? Or do you want to be known as a world-renowned fashion designer?"

"I want to succeed. I really do. But this seems...wrong."

"Wrong? Where did you buy your cardigan?"

I glance down at my cardigan. "It's secondhand. I don't think there is a tag on it," I say, trying to reach around and look for one.

"What about your purse?"

"I, um, borrowed it from Betty. I'm not sure where she got it."

"The point I'm getting at is, we have all bought something we knew must have been made in an overseas factory with less than stellar

132

conditions because it was so cheap. It's hypocritical to think otherwise."

"But I want Lady Bettencourt to represent what I aspire to be, not what I currently am. I want to do better, to be better."

"Fine. But we will have to consider it for the initial run until we figure out a more sustainable, long-term solution. And we will have to move fast if we have any chance of meeting bulk orders."

"But how will the factory get the materials? Won't it be too expensive to ship them over there?"

Vanessa takes a bite of her meal, then says, "Materials will be sourced overseas."

"Secondhand materials, *right*? Because that is the whole premise behind my brand!" I say at the top of my voice.

A few of the other restaurant customers turn their heads towards us.

"Calm down," Vanessa says. "Some of the materials may be secondhand, but we can't guarantee all of them will be. But they will be cut to make it seem like—"

"What?"

"Erin, stop this. You know Lady Bettencourt isn't really about dresses made from secondhand materials."

"Huh? What is it about then?"

"It's about the feeling a woman gets when she buys one of your dresses. The feeling that she is doing something good, that she is good. We have to find a realistic way to meet the demand for generating that feeling."

"But it's a lie."

"I'll start brainstorming longer-term alternatives, but for now, this might be it. Just for now, not forever. I need you to at least consider it."

I reluctantly agree to give it some thought.

Vanessa has a way of making me question myself. I know where I stand on something, but then, she uses just the right words, in just the right order, to make me doubt myself and my way of thinking. As if I'm being naive and don't understand the way things are done in the industry.

And worse of all, that I would have blown this amazing chance I have been given if it weren't for her. It makes me angry that she has this much power over me.

Why can't I say no and stick to what I want to do? Maybe because I don't want to be the one who has to make the hard business decisions. Why did I pick a socially-conscious business to begin with? If I had stuck to regular fabrics, I don't know that I would have such an issue with using an overseas factory.

Vanessa interrupts my thoughts by insisting we share a piece of chocolate cake to end things on a happier note.

When it arrives, she says, "Okay, now for something lighter. Have you setup your social media accounts, yet?"

"No," I say sheepishly. "I've been so busy."

"Don't worry, I'll handle it for you...free of charge," she says, winking at me.

Vanessa calls me the next day.

She doesn't ask me if I have had a chance to think about the factory in Cambodia. Instead, she asks me how my designs are coming along and when she can take another look.

I'm hesitant to talk to her at first, giving her one-word answers. But then, I tell her that I'm almost there. That I have made half the dresses and an evening dress out of old tablecloths we can use for the finale.

She says she likes the idea. That it was clever of me and works well with the brand.

I tell her Gloria has made a serious dent in our back orders. And that Betty has taken photos of the new dresses that I will be sending to her to use on the social media sites.

She says perfect. And then, she says she has a contact at Flare magazine, and they want to do a profile of Lady Bettencourt. It will be months before it comes out, but it's still good exposure for the brand.

She didn't want to go ahead without my okay and asks if that is something I would be interested in.

She *knows* I would be interested.

And just like that, I'm caught back in her web.

TWENTY-SIX

Days to Wedding / Fashion Show: 16

THE CONVERSATION I had with Vanessa about the factory is on replay in my mind. I'm not sure I can go through with it. But what if there really is no other choice?

Sewing this morning was impossible. After I restarted the same dress three times, I realized I needed a break. So I grabbed a pile of finished orders and headed to my special post office.

I'm rounding a corner in the underground path, doing my best to balance the stack of packages I'm holding, when everything goes black, and I find myself lying on the cold, hard floor.

What just happened? Have I suddenly gone blind? Become spontaneously paralyzed?

"Hey, are you okay? I'm so sorry. I was in a rush and wasn't paying attention to where I was going."

At least, I'm not deaf because I heard that.

I feel a hand on my arm, trying to help me up. My legs seem to be functioning and things are slowly coming back into focus.

The good news is that I'm not blind. The even better news is who I'm seeing: Suit Guy.

"I feel like such a jerk," Suit Guy says, looking at me with those beautiful blue eyes of his. He has neatly piled the packages and placed them by my once-again-upright side. "Are you sure you're okay?"

I have gone mute.

Say something, Erin! Say something!

"Y-Yes, I'm fine. Totally fine." I smile as proof.

I inhale his intoxicating scent from where I stand, resisting the urge to go in for a closer sniff.

But he is the one who comes in closer and asks, "Don't I know you from somewhere?"

I want to scream: "Yes! From the subway! You know me from the subway! And our special post office, where *I* was the one who bumped into *you*!" But speaking to Suit Guy doesn't come easy to me. I give it a try, anyway. "We, um, we used to—"

"*BT!* You were on *Breakfast Television* the other morning! That's it, isn't it?"

Great. My first *real* celebrity sighting is by the guy who doesn't realize I stalked him for over three years.

"That's me," I say.

"It's...Erin, right?"

I feel my cheeks burning up.

He knows my name.

Wait. I still don't know *his* name.

I instinctively glance down to see if he is wearing his monogrammed cufflinks. He is. I can make out the "S," but what is the other letter? Is that a "B"? Or an "E"?

"Right, again," I say, hesitating before asking, "And your name is?"

This is it.

I'm finally going to know his name. I'm finally going to know his name!

He opens his mouth to reveal all that has been hidden from me for years, but what I hear, instead, is a loud, emanating noise coming from my purse.

Stupid, stupid phone!

I quickly reach into my purse to silence it.

"I'd better let you get that," he says. "I'm late as it is. My sincerest apologies once again." He begins to leave.

NO! Please don't go!

He turns back.

(Did I say that out loud?)

He reaches into the inside pocket of his suit jacket. "Here's my card. The least I can do is buy you a drink sometime." He flashes me a grin of his perfect, white teeth.

I definitely can't speak now, so I take the card while smiling and nodding at him, like a love-crazed fool. Then, I watch him walk away. Once he is out of view, I look down at the card he gave me.

Stuart Ellis, Vice-President of Mergers and Acquisitions.

Stuart. *Stu-art.*

Ever since our encounter a few days ago, that name has been on autoplay in my mind...and on my tongue. I will find myself doing something when a random "Stuart" escapes my mouth.

I have never actually liked that name, but the more I say it and picture the face that goes with it, the more it's starting to sound sort of sexy. I hope he doesn't go by Stu, though. That would never work for anyone.

And tonight, I'm calling him.

No, really. Right now, in fact.

As it's Sunday evening, I'm leaving a message at his work number. I'm not ready yet to have a full-on phone conversation with him.

I have written out a script. It's necessary, given my lack of skill at leaving unrehearsed messages. The script is covered with hand-drawn hearts. In the hearts are variations of "E + S," "Stuart + Erin," and "Mrs. Erin Ellis." (I have regressed to high school status.)

After rehearsing the script at least ten times using different inflections on certain words and testing out different pitches, I have settled on a lower, huskier version of my normal voice.

I dial his number.

I end the call before it rings.

I dial his number again and take a deep breath.

Four rings, and then it goes to voicemail.

God, I love his voice.

I can't think of anything I don't like about him. Although, I don't actually know much about him at all.

Beep.

"Hey, Stuart! It's Erin. You, um, ran into me in the underground path. I was the one with the packages...from *Breakfast Television*. I wanted to take you up on your generous drinks offer. I mean, drink, singular, not drinks, plural. One is more than enough..."

Oh, no! I have deviated from the script.

Wrap it up, Erin! Wrap it up!

"So, anyway, give me a call. My number is...um..."

Dammit! I never wrote my phone number on the script because I assumed I knew it. I, of all people, should never assume I know anything. And I have no idea how to check on this ancient phone without ending the call.

"Um, someone is at my door. I'll call you right back with my number!"

Quickly finding my phone number—and writing it down this time—I leave Stuart a second message.

Embarrassing. But, at least, I did it. Now I just have to wait for him to call me back.

He doesn't call me back. He sends me a text, instead, a couple of minutes later. I didn't think I would hear back from him so soon.

His message reads: "Thursday, Shangri-La bar, 6?"

Wow, he wants to take me to the bar at the Shangri-La Hotel! I have been wanting to go there ever since it opened, but I didn't have anyone to go with.

I force myself to wait a gruelling half-hour before responding. I don't want to seem too eager. Finally, I text him back: "Sounds good." My draft texts were much longer, but as his was short, I kept mine short, too. I also checked the message three times to make sure it wasn't jumbled up. My phone can't be trusted.

Imagine: This time, this Thursday, I will be on a date with Suit Guy!

I mean, Stuart.

How am I supposed to focus on anything else until then?

TWENTY-SEVEN

Days to Wedding / Fashion Show: 12

THERE IS A KNOCK at the door.

Gloria looks up at me from her sewing. "Are you planning on someone?"

"No." The condo's concierge usually calls to announce visitors.

I get up from the dining room table. I always get a little spooked when there is an unannounced knock at the door. I know it's silly, but I can't help it.

Through the peephole, I see a mass of red hair.

Phew, it's only Vanessa.

I open the door for her.

She walks in, bringing a chill from outside with her, along with a big paper bag.

"I hope you haven't eaten because I brought you—" She stops once she sees Gloria. "Sorry, I didn't know you had company."

Gloria is standing a few feet away from us with a pair of scissors in her hand. Apparently, she gets spooked by unannounced visitors, too.

"No, this is good," I say. "It's about time you two meet. Vanessa this is Gloria; Gloria, Vanessa."

"Nice to meet you," Gloria says, but something in her tone suggests the opposite. I wonder if she has been talking to Betty.

"And you," Vanessa says, flashing her mesmerizing smile.

Gloria isn't taken in by it.

Vanessa is the first to look away. She turns towards me. "I was hoping we could talk business. I have some news. But if you're busy, we can have coffee tomorr—"

"I have to go," Gloria interrupts.

"You do? I thought you were staying all afternoon," I say, confused.

"Sorry, *querida*. I forgetting I go to appointment."

"Oh, okay."

"Perfect!" Vanessa says.

Gloria eyes her suspiciously for a moment, then puts down the scissors. On her way out, she touches my arm and gives me a warning look. (She definitely has been talking to Betty.) It's probably good Gloria is leaving. If she stayed, I might have let something slip about the fashion show. Or Vanessa might have.

After Gloria has left, I ask Vanessa how she got in.

"I followed somebody up. I would have called, but I wanted to surprise you with the news in person."

I take the bag of food from her, placing it on the kitchen counter.

"What news? Is this about the factory?" I ask, grabbing us some plates.

Vanessa takes a seat at one of the bar stools at the counter. "No, it's something different. I'm not sure how you're going to react to this," she says, positively glowing, "but someone wants to buy Lady Bettencourt!"

I drop the plate I'm holding. It breaks on contact with the floor.

"That is one way," she says, coming around to pick up the broken pieces.

I'm too stunned to move.

"Say something, Erin."

"I need to sit down."

We move to the living room couch.

"I don't understand. Why would someone want to buy Lady Bettencourt?" I ask.

"There is a small but growing fashion house that is looking to add-on a socially-conscious division. Lady Bettencourt fits exactly what they are looking for."

"But-but why did they come to you?"

"They didn't. I went to them."

"You what?"

"Erin, I have been researching all possible avenues to make Lady Bettencourt a success. This is one of those avenues."

"Vanessa, I would never, *ever* sell Lady Bettencourt."

"But you haven't even heard—"

"Please, please stop. Don't mention this to me again. It is *never* going to happen." I get up from the couch. "Thanks for bringing lunch, but I'm not feeling well. I think you should go."

I don't want to hear anything else she has to say. I don't want her tempting me with whatever the fashion house is planning to offer. And I especially don't want to know which fashion house it is.

Vanessa stares at me for a moment, and then stands up. "All right, fine. I thought by bringing this to you, I was doing the best thing for Lady Bettencourt, and for you, but I see now I was mistaken. I won't mention it again."

Once Vanessa is gone, I go into the kitchen and throw the food she brought with her into the garbage because it feels as though it's tainted.

TWENTY-EIGHT
Days to Wedding / Fashion Show: 11

IT'S ALMOST LIKE I'm still an errand girl with all these package drop-offs I have to do. I have just completed another round at the post office when I decide to grab a latte before heading back to the condo.

Now that I don't work at an office job, I enjoy strolling the underground path, watching people scurrying, like the old me used to. Sometimes I have to move out of the way quickly when a large herd of them comes through, or I will risk getting trampled.

I'm trying to relax and not think about Vanessa because I have been spending too much time thinking about her and our latest encounter. I can't believe she actually thought I would consider selling Lady Bettencourt. Once our three-month contract is up, I may not renew it. She has really helped me, but she has also come up with some pretty crazy ideas. I'm not sure I can trust her anymore.

As I'm taking a sip of my latte, I glance up, and immediately choke.

Standing several feet ahead of me is Stuart.

I'm not sure what to do. A normal person would walk over and say, "Hi." But our date is only two nights away. What if I say something stupid and he cancels?

No, better not risk it.

With my decision made, I'm about to turn around and go in the opposite direction of him when I notice he isn't alone. He is with a tall, blonde goddess. The same tall, blonde goddess from that day on the subway years ago.

I thought they broke up!

Maybe they stayed friends.

I find a pillar to hide behind so I can spy on them properly.

They talk for a while, and then I see her lean in for a kiss.

Stop her, Stuart! Stop her!

He doesn't. And it isn't a just-friends kiss, either.

Are they still dating? Married?

He wasn't wearing a ring the last time I saw him. (I checked.) And he isn't wearing one now, according to his left-hand placed on her stomach, her very big stomach. Wow, she has put on some weight—

Oh, my god. She is pregnant!

Wait a minute.

Is that *his* baby? It has to be—hasn't it? Especially if they are making out in public like that. I'm so confused.

Why would he ask me out for a drink if he has a pregnant girlfriend, possibly, wife?

Unless...it isn't a date.

Maybe he really just wanted to buy me a drink to apologize for knocking me down. Or maybe he wants to know more about Lady Bettencourt. He seemed sort of interested in that. It may not be a date at all, but a business meeting over drinks.

Although I wish I could have gone to our date—meeting—without having seen that. Whatever that is.

I feel a tap on my shoulder and jump. I turn around carefully so I stay concealed behind the pillar in case Stuart walks by.

"Heya, Erin."

I don't think this is another one of my fake celebrity sightings because the woman who tapped me on the shoulder looks familiar. She also looks out of place.

Whereas everyone else around here is wearing dark tailored suits or boring business casual, she is dressed very bohemian. She is wearing a long, flowing skirt; a belted cardigan that is almost as long as the skirt; and a wool, cowboy-style hat to top off her tall, model-like frame. She is pretty, in an awkward kind of way. But mostly, she looks cool. And she somehow knows who I am.

"Um, hi," I say. "Sorry, but I'm blanking on your name."

"I don't think you ever got it. I'm Mila," she says, extending her multi-ringed hand.

I extend my own unadorned hand to shake hers. "How do we know each other again?"

She comes in closer and says in a low voice, "We've got a mutual acquaintance...Frankie."

My body freezes in fear; yet, my instincts tell me to run. But I think she could easily outrun me with her long legs.

Frankie was another one of my former Erin Girl clients. I never met him, but I delivered a mysterious package for him. In exchange, I got paid a thousand dollars. Cash. Mila was the one who gave me the package that had to be delivered.

"So what have you been up to?" she asks casually.

"Oh, you know, this and that," I say, trying to match her tone, but I don't want to give her too much information, either.

"You still running that errand business?"

"Nope. I got out of that racket, I mean, business."

She gives me a funny look. I think she knows I'm hiding something.

Maybe Frankie has been following me for the last two years, keeping an eye on me, making sure I didn't spill the beans on his operation. And I wouldn't even know because I have never met him. He could be anyone. I glance around the underground path, trying to find someone who looks like they could be mafia. There are a few contenders.

"You okay?" she asks.

"Me? I'm cool. Totally cool."

"Cool," she says. "Hey, you ever wonder what was inside that box?"

Shit. She brought up the box. Is this a trick question?

"What box?" I ask, remembering their number one rule: be discreet.

She raises her eyebrows. "You know, *that* box?"

"I completely forgot about that. So, no, not really."

"Really?"

"Okay, maybe I *have* thought about it every now and then. But only ever to myself and *never* with anyone else." (I told Betty about the box. But I will never reveal that, no matter what kind of torture they put me through.)

"That's good," she says. "But I can't tell you what was inside that box, or I'd have to kill you."

My heart stops beating.

She punches me in the arm. "Kidding."

My heart starts beating again. I give her a nervous laugh.

"Relax, Erin," she says. "It wasn't exactly legal, but you did a good thing. You gave someone back his life."

Honestly, I have wondered what was inside that box, and this new information makes me feel a little better about it, although the "wasn't exactly legal" part is worrisome. But there is something else I have spent more time wondering about.

"Why did Frankie pick me? How did he know I could be trusted?"

Mila glances around the crowded path and pulls me over to a corner. I look back, but Stuart and the blonde goddess are gone.

"Frankie checked you out before he called you," she says in a low voice. "He found something on you that he could use if he thought you'd blow his cover."

"Found something on me? What?" I ask. Surely, running an errand business from my cubicle, while not exactly ethical, wouldn't be enough.

She raises her eyebrows and says, "What happens in Europe, doesn't always stay in Europe."

Fuck! How did they find out about that?

I have never talked about it, or even thought about it, since it happened. I don't want to think about it now, either. I have too much on my mind as it is.

"Oh, right, *that*," I say, laughing it off as if it was no big deal.

"It was nice running into you," she says, reaching into her leather-fringed bag. "Here, take my card. Call me if you ever need anything."

I look down at her card, which I'm planning on getting rid of at the first opportunity.

C&C Dog Walking.

"You're a dog walker?" I ask in surprise. The C&C part must stand for Cupcake and Cake Pops, her very big, very angry dogs. (Maybe just the very big part.)

"I am—on the side. I also do a bit of modelling." (I knew it!) "Well, I gotta go. See ya," she says, walking away.

I stay in my spot. I want to give her some distance before I choose which direction to go in.

But when she is a few feet away from me, she turns around and says, "Hey, Erin?"

"Yeah?"

Now what?

"Congrats on Lady Bettencourt. I'm on your waiting list for The Lizzie. Your dresses are amazing." She winks and walks away.

She knew. That entire time, she knew about Lady Bettencourt. Which means, Frankie knows, too.

I hope they are harmless. They haven't done anything to me in the two years since the incident. It was probably just a reminder for me to keep things on the down low now that I'm in the spotlight. No tell-alls. That sort of thing. But I'm still freaked out. I will be watching my back; I may even start carrying that pepper spray I bought after our last encounter.

All I wanted was a little break from making dresses, but, instead, I got two unpleasant run-ins.

Am I destined to be haunted by the ghosts of my past forever?

TWENTY-NINE

Days to Wedding / Fashion Show: 9

I'M GOING.

Stuart sent me a text message earlier today to confirm if we were still on for drinks tonight. It was my chance to back out. But I didn't. Maybe I was wrong about what I saw in the underground path. I could be making assumptions.

And if he does have a girlfriend or wife or whatever, does that mean he and I can't be friends? Times have changed. Men and women can have platonic relationships now. Although I'm not really starting on the platonic side, but I bet with a little effort, I could get there.

Ever since I ran into Stuart again, my thoughts have been redirected to my subway crush. I'm still making dresses but mostly on autopilot. I have even stopped thinking about Vanessa. Well, nearly stopped.

I sent Gloria home early to give myself a few hours to prepare for tonight. My preparations included taking a long, hot bubble bath; blow-drying, then straightening my hair; full, but natural-looking makeup application; and, finally, wardrobe and shoe selection.

Originally, I planned to wear The Gabby and some fun heels, but then, I remembered this is after-work drinks, not Saturday-night drinks, so I'm wearing one of The Betty dresses. I am coming from work, even though I could do my job in my pajamas if I wanted to. I borrowed a blazer from Betty's closet. I had to roll up the sleeves because they were about an inch too short. I wish I could borrow a pair of Betty's pumps, but her feet are smaller than mine.

At the last minute, I change my mind about my hair. I pull it back into a *chignon*, instead; it goes better with the outfit. But it's a little too perfect-looking, so I mess it up a bit, like I had a hard day at the office.

And then, I'm ready.

Almost.

I give myself a head-to-toe examination in my full-length mirror to make sure there is nothing in my nose or teeth, no stray hairs from tweezing my eyebrows, no funny lumps under my dress from my padded bra, no deodorant stains—

Deodorant! How could I have forgotten to put on deodorant!

I rush back into the bathroom, which causes me to start sweating. I apply it carefully so as not to get any of those stains. I hope I haven't forgotten anything else. What a disaster that could have been.

Having completed my reexamination in the mirror, I give myself a nod of approval, then grab my purse and head out to meet Stuart.

I can't believe this is actually happening.

I get to the Shangri-La Hotel right on time. For what, I don't know, but this feels significant somehow, like a dream come true.

After taking a deep breath, I walk towards the hotel's bar while glancing sideways in case Stuart is arriving now, as well.

Once inside, I hide for a moment in a dark corner. I need to calm myself down. I'm about to step into the light when I see Stuart is already at the bar, waiting.

Waiting for me.

I catch a glimpse of his profile. It's beautiful. He is beautiful. He is wearing one of his tailored suits in navy. I picked out a navy dress because I had a feeling he would be wearing that colour from our days on the subway.

He is talking to a girl at the bar, but he keeps glancing at the door— the opposite door. I must have come in a different entrance.

There is something about the way he is standing next to her, just a little too close. I can't see his face anymore, but I can see hers. She is completely smitten by him. The look on her face triggers a memory to me. A memory from a long time ago.

When I was caring for my mom in her final weeks, I came across a big box in her closet. I opened it to find a bunch of old journals. And even though I knew they were likely her diaries, I couldn't resist taking a peek inside.

I only had the chance to read a couple of lines before my mom came into the room and told me to stop. I went searching for that box after my mom died, but I never found it. She wanted her secrets kept secret. But I will never forget what I read: "He didn't come home last night. He must be with *her* again."

While witnessing Stuart the other day with who must be his pregnant girlfriend-wife-whatever wasn't enough to make me cancel tonight, remembering those lines in my mom's diary is. I don't want to be another woman's *her*. And I don't want to be tempted to become another woman's *her*, either.

So I text Stuart that things got crazy, and I can't get away for drinks. I'm careful to muffle the beeping sound my phone makes with each tap, then I put it up to the light to make sure I tapped the message in correctly before hitting send.

I see him reach into the inside pocket of his suit and pull out his phone. He excuses himself from the girl and turns in my direction.

If he looks up, he will see me.

Going farther into the darkness, I watch him read the message. I see him frown at it, which gives me a pang of regret at sending it.

Stuart taps in a message, and then goes back to the girl at the bar, moving in even closer this time. He slowly places his hand on the small of her back. She nods blissfully at something he says.

Having seen that, I don't regret sending my text anymore. I turn and leave.

When I get outside, I read his text: "Some other time."

No, some other girl.

I delete the message and his phone number. I can't trust myself to hold onto it.

Two years ago, I felt I lost him. And now, I know I lost him for good.

I remind myself that I never had him, never even knew him. Only my illusion of him has been lost.

Maybe it's better to keep that illusion of someone than to find out the truth. But I *needed* to learn the truth so I could finally let go of this fantasy I have built up over the years.

Stuart Ellis turned out to be a jerk.

But Suit Guy will always have a small piece of my heart.

THIRTY

Days to Wedding / Fashion Show: 9

I'M NOT READY to go home, to have this night officially end.

It's still light out and warm for a fall evening. I want to enjoy this weather before it's gone.

And I'm starving. I barely ate anything during the day because I was so nervous about tonight. But now, my hunger hits me, and I'm ravenous. I'm also in pain. The bobby pins from my *chignon* are hurting my head, so I remove them, one by one, shaking out my hair.

Back to being me.

As I'm walking, trying to find somewhere to grab a quick bite to eat, I notice a penny on the ground. Normally, I don't bother picking up anything less than a quarter, but I could use all the luck I can get, so I pick it up and turn it over. It was made in my birth year.

The penny has been taken out of circulation; they aren't making any new ones. Soon they will become extinct. What will be my legacy before I become extinct? I thought I had figured that out, but, lately, I'm not so sure.

"A penny for your thoughts." I hear a man say.

Great. Now I have to deal with some weirdo.

I look up and am relieved to find it's one of my weirdos: Mr. Trader, no, Aaron. (I will never get used to calling him that.)

Smiling coyly, I say, "But I'm the one with the penny."

He returns my smile. "Okay, then I was thinking we should grab something to eat."

I contemplate this for a moment. I was about to get something. I might as well get something with someone else. And that someone else might as well be him. But I have one lingering concern...

"You mean, at like a vegan place?" I ask, wrinkling my nose.

He laughs at my expression. "At an *everybody* place."

"Sure. Why not?" I say and hand him the penny.

We take a short cab ride to a restaurant called Fresh. I have never been here before. It has a funky vibe. The hostess who takes us to our table has dreadlocks, a nose ring, and tattoo-sleeved arms. I immediately take off the blazer I'm wearing.

Once seated, the hostess places a jug of water and a couple of glasses on our table before walking away.

Looking around the restaurant, I evaluate the clientele. There is not a stitch of leather to be seen anywhere and a high percentage of feet are sporting Toms. I have been tricked.

I give Aaron a scornful look. "This is a vegan place." I used to have another nickname for him: Mr. Traitor.

"Would you have come here if I said it was?"

"Maybe. But you could have been honest and let me decide," I, the poster girl of honesty, say.

He raises his right-hand and says, "Okay, from now on, I promise to tell the truth, the whole truth, and nothing but the truth, so help me, God. Better?"

"Better," I say, hoping he doesn't ask me to take the same oath.

Opening the menu, I scan the items, praying there is something I can eat. Hmm, it's normal food, just without the meat. Sure, there are a few items I have never heard of, but I have eaten most of them. (I won't let Aaron in on my newfound knowledge, though.)

"Any recommendations?" I ask him.

"Any of the Buddha bowls are great." (Of course.)

A server with blue hair comes to our table to take our order.

"We should get some smoothies," Aaron says excitedly.

I let him choose mine.

There is a moment of silence between us after the server leaves, and I fear this may be an awkward meal. But then, Aaron breaks the silence by asking me what I have been up to. I tell him to go first. Too much has happened since I delivered his lunches. I need time to gather my thoughts.

"Well, I'm not an equity trader anymore," he says.

"*Really?* Why?"

For some reason, this is a bit of a shock for me. He seemed to fit the role perfectly—except for the whole vegan thing. That had always thrown me off as it didn't work with my perception of him.

"I grew up loving every-fucking-thing about the stock market. I'd seen every movie, read every book, with even the slightest mention of trading," he says; his brown eyes shining with the recollection. "But one day, I stopped believing in it. It didn't feel real to me anymore. I felt like a fucking phony every time I called up a client with the latest and greatest stock pick. So I had to get out."

I nod in agreement. Okay, so I don't know much about the stock market, that is Betty's domain, but I understand what it's like to feel like a phony.

"Sorry," he says, "I'm still working on the swearing thing. Old habits are hard to break."

"That's okay. We all have our vices. So what are you doing now?"

"After I quit, I took my savings and a small inheritance I received and became a micro-venture capitalist." He sees my confused expression and continues, "I invest in small startups that need funding to get off the ground. My latest project is a vegan food truck. Instead of picking stocks, I pick businesses I want to see in the world and that also happen to meet my needs. I help them become successful."

"Wow, that's amazing. You've really changed. It's like you're a different person."

He does seem different. Gentler somehow, not so brash as I remember. Maybe that was just a side effect of his unhappiness at work.

"I'm still me," he says. "But I'm trying to be a better version of me."

That is what I said to Vanessa the other day at lunch, or what I was trying to say.

Our smoothies arrive, and we toast to new beginnings.

I take a sip of my smoothie, and it's delicious. He offers me a sip of his, and it's even more delicious. He insists we trade. I want to refuse, but his smoothie is too yummy to not accept the offer.

"Enough about me," he says. "How about you? How does Erin Girl spend her days?"

Where should I begin? I decide to give him the Cliffs Notes version.

"I've changed my line of business, as well. I have an online shop where I sell dresses I make from secondhand materials." I emphasize that last part to show him I'm also trying to do good in the world.

"That's awesome, Erin," he says sincerely. "I need to start thinking about where my clothes come from. But I guess you can't change everything about yourself at once." He pauses, then asks, "You don't happen to have a men's line?"

"No, just women's. And it's only dresses, right now. I'm still sort of starting out."

"I'm tapped out for the year, but I know another investor who would be all over what you're doing. I could give you her name. That is, if you're looking to grow."

"I'm actually already working with someone. She is helping me with my brand, getting my name out there. That kind of thing."

"That's great. It's hard to find someone to work with who you can trust. There are a lot of crooked people out there."

I'm thinking of how to respond to that when our food arrives. Again, he offers me a taste of his food, but he prefaces it this time by saying he isn't trading if I like his better.

"Mmm, what is that?" I ask, after taking a bite of something I have never tried before from his Buddha bowl.

"Tempeh."

"What's temp-eh?"

"Fermented soybeans."

I gag a little, and then quickly swallow. I reach for my glass of water and gulp some down.

"*C'mon, Erin!* You liked it before you knew what it was. What's so bad about fermented soybeans?"

"The word *fermented*. It sounds gross."

"Didn't your mother ever teach you not to judge a book by its cover?"

His words sting. I know they shouldn't. It isn't his fault; he doesn't know about my mom.

"Speaking of words," I say, "if you eat meat at Thanksgiving and Christmas, can you really call yourself a vegan?"

I don't know why I asked him that. Maybe because of his comment. I want to take it back as soon as I have said it.

He doesn't seem offended. In fact, he lets out a laugh. "You remembered I said that. Normally, I don't let that slip, or else I get that question. It's just easier to give myself a label, like vegan, instead of having to explain that I eat a primarily plant-based diet with the exception of two days of the year. Once you tell people there is an exception, they want you to make one every time."

"I guess you must really love animals. I'm not that into them myself, so I'm okay with eating them."

"You're funny. I do love animals, but that's not the only reason, or I would be a strict vegan. It's just something that's in my control, that I can do for my health and the planet."

"So you're a hippie!"

"Not even close."

"A hipster?"

He throws his crumbled, biodegradable napkin at me. "You make dresses from *secondhand* clothes. That's some serious hipster behaviour right there."

We both start laughing.

"Maybe we are hipsters," he says when we stop laughing. "But, seriously, I think it's awesome what you're doing. You've changed, too. The world needs more people like you, doing what you're doing."

There is something so genuine about the way he says that, that I feel ashamed.

He is the one the world needs more of, not me. I haven't really changed that much at all. I'm still lying to get what I want and keeping secrets from the ones I love.

I'm still pretending.

And so, I tell him the truth.

The whole truth and nothing but the truth.

I don't leave anything out.

I tell him how I'm holding a fashion show on the same day as my sister's wedding, and she doesn't know. How I lost her wedding dress materials, so I made her a fake dress and have no idea what I will do for the actual ceremony.

Then, I tell him how I'm actually considering—*actually considering*—having a sweatshop produce my dresses from non-secondhand materials and lying about it.

Going further back in time, I tell him that Erin Girl was started while I was working a cubicle job, and that I got fired for using company resources for my own business.

I thought it would make me feel better, getting it all out in the open, but I feel worse. Listing my faults makes me realize I'm a horrible person.

He sits there and listens to everything I say, probably wondering what the fuck he got himself into. I turned a fun dinner into a therapy session. I wrecked it. I wreck everything.

After I finish my confessional, he clears his throat, then looks down at his half-eaten meal.

I guess I was hoping to receive some sort of penance, to be absolved of my sins, or, at least, for him to confirm that I am a terrible human being. Anything will do.

So when he doesn't react fast enough, I get up to go.

He gets up, too. "Erin—"

But I have already started for the door, squeezing my way past a group of people waiting to be seated.

When I finally make it outside, I start running.

I run for a long time, only stopping when I reach home.

THIRTY-ONE

Days to Wedding / Fashion Show: 8

I WAKE UP feeling hungover, even though I only drank a green smoothie last night. Maybe it was the spirulina. Or maybe I'm hungover from excessive thinking.

The closer the fashion show gets, the more I'm questioning why I ever agreed to have it the same day as Betty's wedding. But no matter how hard I try, I can't see a way out without looking like a complete flake for cancelling the show. I worry that it would be the beginning of the end for Lady Bettencourt.

Earlier in the week, I told Betty I changed my hair appointment for her wedding day. We were supposed to get our hair done together that morning, but I told her I wanted to go to my regular stylist, and he had an opening. She was disappointed, but said, as long as I was back in time for photos, it was okay.

So that is how I'm getting away to do the fashion show. And that is also how I'm the biggest jerk on the planet. What makes me an even bigger jerk than the biggest jerk on the planet (if that is possible) is that I haven't found Betty's wedding dress. I'm giving myself a few more days to find it, and if I don't, I will have to buy similar materials and hope she doesn't notice the difference.

Unforgivable, I know.

I make myself a cup of calming tea, and it has an instantaneous soothing effect on me. (I may start carrying it around in a flask.)

The calming tea reminds me of Aaron, which reminds me of my confessional. I can't believe I told him everything. I definitely shouldn't have told him about the sweatshop or about them not using secondhand materials, that would ruin my business if it got out.

It feels as if my closet is getting overcrowded, not with Lady Bettencourt dresses, but with all the skeletons I keep shoving into it.

—

There is a knock at the door.

Gloria raises her eyebrows.

I tell her that this time, I'm expecting someone. Although, Vanessa somehow managed to slip past the concierge again.

"Whoa!" Vanessa says when she sees the state of the condo.

The open concept kitchen, dining room, living room area has been overrun with materials and half-made dresses, as well as fully-finished dresses hanging on (newly-purchased) clothing racks. It looks like a gigantic walk-in closet.

It's a good thing Betty is officially moving out this weekend and taking the majority of the furniture with her because I need the space. I will miss living with Betty (and her television), but it will make it easier to hide the fashion show from her.

"How is everything coming along? All ready for the show?" Vanessa asks.

I flash her a warning look, which she seems to register.

"It's important to be proactive, to be ready for whenever opportunity strikes," she says, secretly winking at me.

Gloria watches us for a moment, then goes back to her sewing.

I take Vanessa over to one of the clothing racks. I have completed almost all of the dresses for the fashion show, including the tablecloth evening gown for the finale.

"These are fabulous," Vanessa says. "I appreciate that you took my suggestions to heart."

I beam at the praise. "Can I make you a cup of coffee or get you something?"

"Actually, I have to get going. I'm spending the long weekend at my parents' cottage before they close it up for the season. I haven't seen them in ages."

It sounds weird to think of Vanessa having parents. Silly, I know. I wonder if she has siblings, too. I really don't know much about her. Our conversations are always focused on business.

"But before I go," Vanessa continues, "I need you to sign-off on the contract with the factory we discussed." She reaches into her tote bag and pulls out a folder.

"Vanessa, I'm still not sure I want to go in that direction."

Gloria has stopped sewing and is watching us again.

"Erin, I need to fax this to them today, otherwise there won't be enough time." (I didn't know fax machines still existed.)

"Can I at least have the weekend to read it over?"

Vanessa takes a deep breath, then sighs. "I suppose I could come back early from the cottage and fax it on Monday morning."

She is trying to guilt-trip me into signing it. It isn't going to work.

Seeing the look of determination on my face, she adds, "But I will have to check with my contact first. Give me a moment."

Vanessa takes out her phone and turns away from me. And then, to my surprise, she is speaking Cambodian. Wait. Is that a language? She is speaking whatever language is spoken in Cambodia. (It's shocking how little I know about the other side of the world.)

Vanessa ends the call and says to me, "Sorry, Erin. Not possible. There's not enough time." She turns in the direction of Gloria, who is still watching us, and says slowly, "We have to get the contract in today so that we are ready for the fashion show next—"

"*Okay, okay!* Just give it to me!" I say, stopping her before she reveals that the fashion show is the same day as Betty's wedding. She has played me. And I gave her the ammunition to do so.

"*Er-in...*" Gloria says, cautioning me.

"It's okay, Gloria. Vanessa and I have talked about this. I know what it is."

Vanessa hands me the thick contract.

"It seems long," I say.

"Have you ever seen a contract like this before?" she asks, knowing I haven't. "They are long."

She points to the first place I need to sign.

I look at her for a moment, into those hypnotizing eyes of hers.

She doesn't flinch or turn away.

I close my own eyes to block her out, to block everything out. But I hear Betty telling me not to sign anything without reading it first, making me promise her.

When I open my eyes, I take a deep breath and quickly sign everywhere Vanessa points to.

She watches me as I do. I catch a glimpse of her expression. It's a look of complete triumph. She has won the battle.

And I barely put up a fight.

THIRTY-TWO

Days to Wedding / Fashion Show: 8

"YOU SHOULDN'T HAVE signed that," Gloria says after Vanessa leaves. "Beatriz will be mad."

Betty must have told her about my promise. "Please don't tell her. At least, not until after the wedding. It will just upset her."

"Okay, I won't. But I don't like that Vanessa. She sneaky, like *gata*, a cat." Gloria pauses a moment, then asks, "You go to cemetery tomorrow?"

At first, I'm not sure why she is asking me that. Then, I realize tomorrow is my mom's birthday, and, because of everything, I had forgotten. But Gloria, who hasn't seen my mom in years, remembers.

"Either tomorrow or Monday," I say to cover my embarrassment at forgetting. "She passed away two days after her birthday. I don't think I told you that."

"No, I didn't know," she says, getting teary-eyed. "I want to go see her. Can we go tomorrow? I don't know where to find her."

I reluctantly agree. I like to visit my mom's grave on my own, but I can see how much it means to Gloria. She has helped me so much; I can't refuse her this one request.

I made Betty a final breakfast in honour of our last morning as roommates. A moving company is coming to take her things to the new house this afternoon. I have taken the day off from making dresses to help her and Matt get settled.

It will be weird living on my own again. Even though she was hardly here on the weekends, I liked knowing she would eventually come home.

As I'm finishing loading up the dishwasher, Betty asks me, "Are you going to move into my bedroom now?"

"I guess so. I like the coziness of the den, but that probably makes more sense. I'll definitely be moving my clothes out of the hall closet."

"I'm leaving behind mom's painting," she says out of nowhere.

"*What?* You are? Why?"

"You like it more than I do. You're always staring at it, as though you're looking for clues or something."

My eyes tear up. I hadn't realized I did that. But it's true. I *love* that painting.

"It reminds me of us," I say. "I think that is why mom must have bought it."

The painting is of a mother holding a toddler and a baby. The mother's face is turned away. The woman always reminded me of my mom, and the two little girls of Betty and me. Betty took the painting after our mom passed away because she had the space for it, and I was still trying to get settled somewhere.

"Maybe you should keep it," I say, feeling guilty for wanting to have it, for so many things. "I already have her sewing machine. It doesn't seem fair."

"I'm not as attached to sentimental things the way you are—remember that Chanel 2.0 bag?"

"2.55," I say, correcting her.

We both laugh.

"Honestly, Erin, I already have a few of her things. I wear her earrings every day. And now, I'll have my wedding dress that combines the three of us. That will be my painting."

I want to burn myself to the stake when I hear this. I have to find her dress. *I have to.*

"I'll miss living with you," Betty says. "It was like when we were kids."

"I'll miss it, too. But mom would be so proud you're living in a house. She always talked about getting us one."

"I know. It's sad she isn't here to see us making our dreams come true. She is missing so much."

We both sigh.

"On the bright side," I say, "you will officially be a part of the Getty family."

"So will you. We're in this together. My family is your family, no matter what."

I give her a weak smile, but I suddenly feel all alone, as though she has already left.

Before Betty's move takes place, we have come to Mount Pleasant Cemetery. Matt meets us at the main entrance.

I run over and give him a big hug. "Hey, Matty Matt! I was beginning to think you were Polkaroo!"

He hugs me back, lifting me up off the ground. "I think you're the one who has been playing hide-and-seek. How is business?"

"Crazy. How did it go wrapping up everything in Chicago?"

"Let's just say, they asked if my wedding plans were set in stone." He bends down to give Betty a kiss. "Hi, honey."

Matt is super tall. He played basketball in high school and university. Betty is pretty short, so they are kind of an odd match physically, yet completely perfect for each other in every other way.

"Do you guys see Gloria anywhere?" I ask.

Betty points in the direction of a woman getting out of a car. *"Is that her?"*

"Ah, jeez," I say when I see her.

Gloria is dressed in black from head-to-toe, including a black, lace veil covering her hair.

She walks over to us. "Hi, girls." She kisses Betty and I on each cheek. "And you must be Matt-*chew*," she says, trying to reach up and give him a kiss on his cheek. "You are very tall."

He laughs at her comment, bending down to accept her kiss.

We walk the winding path towards my mom's grave, with Matt holding Betty's hand, and Gloria and I following along in behind.

When we arrive, Gloria starts to cry softly, and then takes out a rosary.

Betty places white roses (my mom's favourite) in front of the gravestone, and then her and Matt break out into a hearty rendition of "Happy Birthday."

Gloria and I stare at them in disbelief.

When they have finished, they see our expressions and say in unison, "It's tradition."

It reminds me of how many times Betty must have come here with Matt, and on her own, before I had come to accept my mom's passing. It makes me sad, happy, and jealous, all at once.

We wait for Gloria to finish her rosary, which takes quite a while.

I say my own prayer, begging my mom to ask whoever is in charge to help me find Betty's wedding dress.

As we are leaving, Gloria says our mom would be proud of the women her daughters have become.

I look down at my mom's grave. A single tear falls onto one of the white roses placed there. Because I know for me that isn't true.

The rest of the afternoon is spent setting up Betty and Matt's new house. It's a three-bedroom detached in the affluent High Park area, which is on the subway line and next to a huge park by the same name. There isn't that much to setup though, as Betty had already taken care of most of it.

I haven't seen Betty and Matt together like this in such a long time. They are so right for each other.

That is when it hits me. It finally hits me.

This is real.

My little sister is getting married in a week.

A week.

What have I done?

THIRTY-THREE
Days to Wedding / Fashion Show: 6

I SPEND THE REST of the weekend in my tiny room. I haven't showered. I have barely eaten. My body and mind have shut down.

All I want to do is sleep. Sleep and hope that when I wake up, all of this was a bad dream. That Rachel McAdams hadn't worn my dress. That I had never met Vanessa Moore.

So that is what I do. I go to sleep.

I'm in a large room. I'm floating above it, as though I'm a bird. Below me, I see row-upon-row of desks. School desks.

My thin wings flutter as I go in for a closer look. I'm not a bird: I'm a butterfly.

At each desk sits a little Asian girl, wearing a clean uniform, hair perfectly in place.

A loud, whacking noise comes from somewhere in the room.

All the girls sit up straight.

This is when I notice the woman. But her face is blurred. She goes down each row, hitting the ruler on the outer desks as she does.

In response, that row of girls quickly flip open their desks and pull out sewing machines and fabric. The room grows darker and becomes hotter in a matter of seconds. The children no longer look perfect in their uniforms. They look tired, beaten. They begin sewing frantically.

I fly towards one of the girls who has finished a garment.

She is affixing a label onto it: Lady Bettencourt.

It's a sweatshop.

My sweatshop.

I try to scream but nothing comes out. I'm voiceless. I try to fly away, but my wings feel as if they have been glued to my body. I can't move.

The woman rushes towards me and whacks me hard with the ruler.

Everything goes black until I come to. I'm being carried by the woman. I lay still so she doesn't hit me again.

Then, she throws me in the garbage, staring down at me, repulsed.

That is when her face finally comes into view, but I already know who it is.

It's Carol.

I wake up, screaming. But there is no one here to hear me anymore.

Laying back down on my sweat-soaked sheets, I try to stop my body from shivering. My heart is racing franticly.

Even though it may have been Carol's face in the dream, I know it wasn't really her.

It was me.

It was always me.

I'm back at the cemetery. Alone this time. I need to be with the one person who accepted me exactly the way I am.

My mother.

I need her advice, her strength. Although she can't physically give me those things anymore, I feel her presence whenever I'm here. And now, I feel her guiding me towards what I have to do. What I hope I was always going to do.

I take one of the white rosebuds from her grave for courage because what I have to do next scares me to death.

I have to tell Vanessa the fashion show is off.

THIRTY-FOUR

Days to Wedding: 5

VANESSA WILL BE here any minute.

I contemplated telling her about cancelling the fashion show in public—safety in numbers—but decided it would be best to do it at the condo. I didn't think she would get here so fast, though, as it is a holiday Monday and she was meant to be at her family's cottage. Or maybe that was a lie, too.

A call from the concierge announces her arrival. She is playing by the books today.

When I open the door, Vanessa has two coffee cups in her hands. Poison.

Don't be silly, Erin. People don't poison each other anymore.

She hands me one of the cups.

I grab the one in her other hand. "This one seems, um, hotter."

"But it isn't lactose-free."

"That's okay. I...took a digestive enzyme this morning."

She gives me a funny look with a hint of something else— disappointment? Maybe I was right about the poison. Okay, so it is probably not poisoned, but she could have done something to it. Perhaps a special concoction that gets me to do her bidding.

"What is this about?" Vanessa asks, as we move towards the dining room area. "You sounded anxious on the phone."

I close my eyes, take a deep breath, and say, "I'm cancelling the fashion show." There, I said it. It's done.

She chuckles. "Erin, you are just getting cold feet because the show is days away. Have a seat and drink your coffee. Let's talk this out."

I stay where I am. I refuse to sit (or drink).

"No, Vanessa. There is no 'talking this out' or talking me into it. I am not having the fashion show the same day as Betty's wedding. I won't do it."

She takes a long sip of her coffee, watching me the whole time. (The coffee is definitely *not* poisoned.)

"Fine," she says eventually. "We will have the fashion show without you."

"Huh?"

"I said, we will have the fashion show without you. It would be better if you were there, and it will require some explaining, but it isn't totally necessary at this point."

"Of course, it's necessary! I'm the designer. It's my dress line!"

"Technically, no, it isn't your dress line anymore."

My body stiffens. "You aren't making any sense. It is my dress line."

"Not as of Friday. Lady Bettencourt, including all of this—" she says, gesturing towards the clothing racks, "is now a subsidiary of—"

"*A subsidiary*? What are you talking about?" My breathing stops.

"The contract you signed on Friday. I may have led you to believe it was for the factory in Cambodia, but it was actually a contract for that other opportunity I told you about. The one where Lady Bettencourt would be bought out by—"

I gasp so loudly that Vanessa stops mid-sentence. I feel like I'm going to pass out.

Oh, my god. Is this really happening?

"No, that can't be right," I say. "I told you I wasn't interested!"

"You never heard the offer. You didn't even want to consider it. I couldn't let that happen to Lady Bettencourt. I know you can't see this now, but this is the best thing that could have happened to the brand."

"*The brand?* This isn't about the brand! It is about me and my company—*my name!*"

"No. It is always about the brand. Always."

"Why would you do this? *Why?*" I hold onto the table to steady myself.

"The fashion house needs someone to oversee and direct the brand, and, with my experience, I am the perfect candidate."

She is telling me this so calmly, as if it makes complete sense.

"So...I'm out?" I wipe a tear away from my cheek.

"Don't be silly. Here is the best part," she says excitedly. "We will still be working together! By signing the contract, you agreed to accept a lump sum payment—which I think you will be very happy with—as well as an equity share for the duration you remain the face of Lady Bettencourt. You will get to do all the fun parts, like magazine profiles and television appearances. And you will continue to have a partial say in the direction of the line, but you won't have to worry about making the dresses anymore. It's an amazing opportunity, especially for someone so new to the industry."

She is positively beaming. She actually believes I would want this. I don't know what to do or say. How could I have signed that contract without reading it?

I am such an idiot!

But then, an image pops into my mind, and I remember something. Something I did.

I let out a loud, crazy laugh.

"What's so funny?" Vanessa asks in alarm.

I can't stop laughing; now tears are really rolling down my face.

"Erin, stop it. Why are you laughing like that?"

"Be-because," I say, trying to get a hold of myself, "there is something you don't know."

"What?"

"I'm not really left-handed."

"I thought you were left-handed?"

"Okay, I am. I just always wanted to say that. But there is something you *really* don't know."

"Quit it with these silly games and get to the point."

"I never signed that contract. I mean, I signed it. But I didn't *sign it*, sign it."

"Yes, you did. I have a copy right here," she says, reaching into her tote bag and pulling it out. She looks closely at the first page, then flips through the others. "*What the fuck?* You little bitch!"

Vanessa draws back her lips, baring her clenched teeth. I never noticed how sharp her incisors were before. Her pupils are fully dilated, and there is a low, growling sound coming from her throat.

She is going to attack!

I look down at the dining room table for a weapon. *Shit!* The scissors are closer to her side of the table. All I have are the seam ripper and Sally, the dress form, that I can use as a shield.

We stand there, staring each other down for a long time.

Then, Vanessa's whole demeanor changes, and she regains her composure. "Don't be rash," she says. "Now that you know about the contract and the opportunity it represents, I think you should seriously consider it. I can get a new contract for you to sign."

A new contract? Phew!

I wasn't sure what I did would void the contract. I didn't know if by signing it, in whatever manner, still made it valid. I was only trying to buy time when I thought it was for the factory in Cambodia. But her saying she has to get a new one, confirms it isn't.

"Although..." she continues, "this may still be valid. I will have to get lawyers involved."

Dammit! Stop thinking, Erin. She can hear you!

But I have one more card to play, thanks to Betty and her love of legal television dramas.

"You could, but I will say I signed it under duress. Gloria will be my witness."

"It will be your words against mine."

"Maybe so, but how strong is the word of someone who wrongly accused her former boss of selling child pornography?"

She appears stunned. "That-that was just a rumour. It isn't true," she says unconvincingly.

Thank you, Betty! Thank you, Google!

"Well, then, let's see what the lawyers think. Because there is no way I will ever let you or anyone else *steal* my company!"

Vanessa throws the contract at my face, but it lands in my hands, instead. "Have fun being a pattern-cutter for the rest of your life," she hisses at me.

And I realize that is exactly what I want to be. Even if I never get to be in the spotlight again, this is what I was born to do, what I was meant to do. Being on television was a nice bonus, but that is all it was, a bonus, not the main event.

"You are fooling yourself, Erin, if you think you can change the world with some silly dresses."

"I'm not trying to change the world, Vanessa. I'm only trying to change myself."

She turns away from me as she gathers her things. "I will send out a press release announcing the cancellation of the show. I can't have my name associated with this or you anymore. You can deal with the venue and suppliers yourself. You will be getting my invoice."

"Perfect," I say.

Vanessa turns back towards me, giving me a final glare, before walking to the door and slamming it shut behind her.

Quickly, I lock the door, then slide down it until I'm sitting on the floor, where I try to return my breathing to normal.

I can't believe that just happened.

My hands are shaking as I look down at the contract I'm still holding. I have Betty to thank for making me promise to never sign anything again without reading it. And my phone. My stupid, ancient, wonderful phone.

Before "signing" the contract, I had closed my eyes. That is when I saw the jumbled text message I once tried to send with my name. My name came out as: "Er I Better Not."

So that is what I signed on the contract.

THIRTY-FIVE

Days to Wedding: 5

I RUSH OVER to my laptop, quickly changing the passwords to the Instagram and Pinterest accounts Vanessa setup. I can't take the chance she will try to retaliate somehow by using them.

There are photos of my dresses and information about the upcoming fashion show on both sites. I hadn't realized I had built up such a following. (That will always sound weird to me.) They should know the show is cancelled—but I need a photo.

Taking some leftover tablecloth material and cutting it to create a sash, I write "cancelled" across it using a red marking pencil. Then, I place the sash on Sally and take a photo. I have to take several more shots to get one that isn't blurry before posting it with the caption that the show is cancelled due to extraneous circumstances.

Dammit! What about the *Breakfast Television* giveaway to the show?

I call the studio and eventually get through to someone who connects me to the producer. I apologize profusely, and say I will make a custom dress for whoever won the contest as a consolation prize.

He says not to worry; these things happen all the time. He tells me to call back when the fashion show is on again, and he will have me on the program.

After thanking him and telling him that I will, I start making some more calls.

The rest of the afternoon is spent cancelling the venue and the various suppliers, trying to get my deposits back...unsuccessfully.

—

All around me are the clothing racks with the spring dresses I modified to Vanessa's specifications. I grab the dresses and throw them onto the hardwood floor. With my seam ripper in hand, I sit down and begin to take each one apart. Seam by seam.

The last one, at the bottom of the heap, is the mock tablecloth wedding dress I made for Betty. I hesitate a moment, then take it apart, too. It was a beautiful dress, but it was made of lies.

When I'm done, I fold the materials neatly and take them over to the bookcase, where I store fabrics. As I'm about to place the last batch on a shelf, I gasp and drop everything I'm holding onto the floor.

On the shelf, at the top of a pile, is Betty's half-made wedding dress.

That night, as I lie in my tiny room, I go over the events of the last month. *A month!* I can't believe this started just a month ago.

I could say Vanessa put me into a trance from the moment I heard her hypnotic voice and looked into her riveting eyes, but the truth is, I wanted to be seduced. I wanted to believe everything she was telling me because it made things easier; I didn't have to make any of the hard decisions myself. A part of me always knew she was lying. It is one of my mastered skills.

What is scary is how alike I now realize we are. We both tell people what they want to hear. We think we are doing it for their own benefit and there is nothing wrong with it, but we are really doing it for ourselves. Seeing it in someone else makes me ashamed to be that way.

Luckily, I have been given another chance. This time, I'm doing things right.

THIRTY-SIX

Days to Wedding: 1

I'M TELLING BETTY everything—after the wedding. There is no point telling her before just so I can feel better.

I spent the last four days finishing Betty's (real) wedding dress. As I was working on it, I got that feeling again. I haven't had it in weeks. Sometimes when I'm using my mom's old sewing machine, I feel connected to her, as though I'm channeling her spirit or something. I know, I know. It sounds crazy. But it's what I feel, real or not. Either way, it's amazing that I can take something that belonged to her to create new things, to give them life.

While I haven't told Betty the truth, yet, I did tell her I changed my mind about her wedding dress being a surprise. I couldn't have her walking down the aisle in a dress that didn't fit her properly. That would really be unforgivable. I also changed my pretend hair appointment back to her stylist. She was so happy when I told her.

Tonight, after the rehearsal, we are staying together at the Royal York Hotel—Toronto's oldest hotel and where the wedding is being held. Whenever our mom had some extra money, she would take us there for afternoon tea. It was our special place. And now, it's where Betty and I will spend our last night as the Bettencourt girls.

Tomorrow, my little sister is getting married!

THIRTY-SEVEN

Betty and Matt's Wedding Day!

IT IS JUST AFTER NINE on Betty and Matt's wedding day. Betty and I are finishing our room service breakfast when she looks at the time and asks, "Don't you have a fashion show to get to?"

My mouth drops open. "Betty, I can explain!"

She starts laughing. "Relax, Erin, I know you cancelled it."

"You knew about the fashion show this *whole* time?"

"I follow Lady Bettencourt on Instagram and Pinterest. You can't get away with anything these days."

Oops! I had forgotten Betty might have seen my social media accounts. Covering your tracks is a full-time job.

"I swear I was going to tell you everything," I say. "I was waiting until after the wedding. Are you mad at me?"

"I was. Really mad. But I knew you would make the right choice."

I think about that for a moment. "I'm not so sure I knew I would make the right choice."

"You do when it is important. I was actually more upset when I found my unfinished dress, laying around a week before my wedding."

"You knew about that, too?"

"What? Did you think the universe neatly folded the dress and placed it on your bookshelf?"

"Maybe," I say, shrugging my shoulders.

"Well, it was me. I found it when I was moving my stuff out. So I put it somewhere I knew you would find it. Your idea of a 'surprise wedding dress' always sounded a bit suspicious to me."

"I'm a horrible sister. It's almost like, you're the good twin and I'm the evil twin."

"First, we're not twins."

"We're Irish twins!"

"Second," she continues, ignoring me, "you're human. Humans make mistakes. Especially when they really want something."

"But, Betty, I can't think of any mistakes you have ever made."

"That's because I'm not human. *Mwahahaha!*"

"You're a dork."

"That, too."

We start giggling, like two little girls after a sleepover.

After we have our hair and makeup done, we go back to the hotel to get changed.

I help Betty get into her wedding dress. When she turns around, I get the full effect.

"You're beautiful," I say, tearing up.

She blushes. "I wish mom was here," she says in a whisper.

"Me, too," I whisper back.

No matter how old we get, no matter how many celebrations we have, there will always be something—someone—missing.

"C'mon, little sister!" I say to lighten the mood. "Let's get you to the church, I mean, banquet hall, on time!"

We link arms and leave the room together, not as little girls, but as women about to embark on the next stage of their lives.

"Hey, where is Mr. Getty?" I ask Betty. "I thought he was walking you down the aisle?"

"I changed my mind. I told him I wanted to walk on my own."

"Really?" That is odd. It isn't like Betty to change her mind at the last minute.

The music starts to play as the doors open slowly into the banquet hall that has been setup for the ceremony.

"Close them!" Betty shouts.

I turn around.

"Betty, are you okay?"

"I-I can't do it."

"*What?* Um, okay. Okay. Here is what we will do. We will leave. We will get a cab and bust this joint. And we will never talk about this day ever again." I grab her by the hand and start pulling her towards the other set of doors—the ones leading towards the hotel lobby.

"I don't mean that," she says, stopping me.

"No? I knew that. I was...testing you. No cold feet here."

"What I meant was, I can't walk down the aisle on my own. Everyone will be staring at me. There is hardly anyone sitting on our side."

"Oh, Betty. Do you want me to have them get Mr. Getty?"

"That doesn't seem right, either." She looks up at me. "Will you do it?"

I engulf her in a hug. "I do! I do! I mean, I will! I will!"

My little sister needs me! She still needs me!

"Okay, Erin. You can let me go now."

I wait a moment longer, and then I'm ready to release her, to let her go.

And for the second time that day, we walk together, arm-in-arm.

The rest of the ceremony was very sweet. I had to dab my eyes a few times when they read each other the vows they had written. Then, there were a gazillion photos taken, followed by the reception.

I sat with Betty, Matt, and his parents during the meal, but I switched to sitting at Lizzie and Gloria's table for the rest of the evening. Ever since dinner, though, something has been weighing on my mind.

So I walk up to where the band is playing and tell them to take five. (I have always wanted to say that.)

I see people chatting to each other across the room. I wish I had written something down. I was glad when Betty made the no speech rule, but now, I have to wing it. And I forgot to bring up my wine glass with me for the toasting part.

A kid walks by with a pop in his hands.

"Hey, kid," I hiss at him. "Give me your pop."

"No way!" he says, holding it tightly against his chest.

"I will give you five bucks for it."

"Okay!" He happily hands it over to me. "Where's my money?"

I check my dress pockets. *Crap.* I don't have any money on me. "I will, um, get it to you later."

He looks furious.

"It's an open bar. You can get another pop, *for free.* Now run along, young man."

He furrows his brow and mutters something about how *old* people can't be trusted.

Great. I will have to borrow five dollars from Lizzie or Gloria. I can't have this kid spreading tales about me.

I refocus, remembering why I'm up here.

"Hi, everyone," I say nervously. There is piercing feedback from the microphone, just like in the movies when a character goes on stage at a wedding to give a speech. (It's a real thing.)

People stop talking and turn in my direction. I wave, kind of like I'm the President, ahem, Prime Minister.

"Hi, I'm Betty's sister, Erin. Betty, where are you? There you are!" I say, waving at her.

She looks mortified.

"Betty said she didn't want any speeches. So this speech isn't about her and how she used to wet the bed until she was six."

"That was you!" Betty shouts.

"It was? Let's forget about that because this isn't one of those speeches. Instead, this is a speech about Matt." I search the crowd, finding Matt and waving to him, too.

He waves back as he walks over to take a seat beside Betty.

Everyone's eyes are on me. This is the first time I have had such a captive audience. Maybe I should sing a song or recite a poem. But I don't know any poetry...

Oh, right. My speech.

"I didn't like Matt when I first met him. It wasn't anything he said or did. It was the fact he was dating my little sister. Up until that point,

180

it had been the three Bettencourt girls, taking on the world, and here came this tall guy who played basketball and loved peanut butter. I mean, *loved* peanut butter."

The wedding guests laugh and nod in recognition of Matt's love of peanut butter.

When they stop, I continue, "I guess I was jealous and thought he would take Betty away from us. I wanted things to stay exactly the way they were. But as the years and years *and years* went by—" (More laughter.) "—I knew he wasn't going anywhere. That's when I realized that Matt wasn't taking Betty away from us—from me—he was becoming one of us."

I pause to take a deep breath.

"When our mom got sick, Betty and I took care of her...but so did Matt. He gave us a break whenever we couldn't handle it. And then, when our mom passed away, and I zoned out for a while, a long while, he was the one who was there for Betty, not me. My mom loved Matt. Everyone loves Matt. And now, he is officially a part of *our* family. So thank you Matt, for coming into our lives and for taking care of my little sister. To Matt, my brother!" I say, raising my drink.

"To Matt," rings out across the room.

"Betty," I say, looking directly at her. "Mom would be so proud of the woman you have become. I won the lottery the day I got you as a sister. To my sister, Betty Getty!"

"To Betty Getty," rings out across the room.

Betty dabs her eyes. Actually, there are quite a few people doing the same thing.

Matt takes Betty's hand and guides her towards me. I jump off the stage and meet them halfway on the dance floor.

The three of us form a hug, which must look sort of awkward from the outside but feels really nice and special on the inside.

Now I'm in tears, too. Tears of happiness with a touch of sorrow that our hug is short by one.

THIRTY-EIGHT

IT'S MONDAY MORNING, and I'm back to business. But I'm not sure what my next steps are now that I'm fully in control again. So I start brainstorming ideas in my head.

"You okay, *querida*?" Gloria asks with a look of concern on her face.

"I'm thinking."

"About what?"

"What I should do with Lady Bettencourt."

"Oh, the fashion show. I knew," she states matter-of-factly.

"You did?"

"Of course! I'm on Pinterest—for the recipes. But I follow you, too."

She knew, and she didn't say anything, either. I wonder if Lizzie also knew.

"Is Vanessa finished for us?" Gloria asks.

"Yeah, she is gone for good." (I hope.)

"Why don't you have another fashion show?"

"It isn't that easy. I would have to get a venue, suppliers, buyers to come..."

Wait a minute. That is the way you are *supposed* to have a fashion show, not the way you *have* to have one. What if I kept things simple?

"Gloria! You're a genius!"

She shrugs her shoulders.

I get up to pace the room. It would have to be the least expensive fashion show of all time, as in, zero to very-low cost. Most of my savings have already been spent on the one that got cancelled.

Hmm, what do I need to hold a fashion show?

A venue. No, I only need some sort of a location.

Lots of dresses. Gloria and I can make those or get extra help.

Shoes and accessories. *Lizzie?* We could borrow them from the vintage shop in exchange for advertising or something.

Models.

Where the heck am I supposed to find models?

Wait.

No.

Maybe?

Mila did say to contact her if I ever needed anything. Aren't you meant to keep your enemies close? Is she an enemy? I don't know what she is. I will keep her as a potential option.

But what I really need is a hook. My time with Vanessa wasn't a total waste. I did pick up a few things from her. I'm brainstorming possible hooks when a loud, shrilling noise comes from somewhere in the room.

"What is that?" Gloria asks, looking around in alarm.

"Don't worry, it's just my phone. It's old and makes weird noises."

Hold on a second. It isn't old. It's vintage.

That is it! I have found my hook!

But can I actually pull this off?

I ask Gloria if she knows any other seamstresses who could help us. She says she will call her sister, Natalia, as well as Sophia, a niece of Anestis, the man who ran the alteration shop my mom worked at. She says they are both very good dressmakers.

Then, I call Betty and Lizzie to ask if they can come to the condo at six. Thankfully, they are both free.

I'm getting excited. This is going to work. I can feel it. But in order for it to work, I will need publicity. So I take a deep breath and call the producer of *Breakfast Television* to share my plans with him.

He says he loves the idea and will fit me in Friday morning as part of their Fashion Week coverage. I thank him a million times over.

Finally, I call Mila. It's risky, but something tells me it's okay. She doesn't seem surprised to hear from me. She is coming to the condo tonight, too.

After everyone has been called, I sit down at the dining room table and start sketching. I need to have my new designs ready by our meeting tonight. Before I thought a month was too short to put together an entire fashion show. Now I have just three days.

The condo is in total chaos.

There are materials and people everywhere. A big worktable has been setup in Betty's old bedroom. Luckily, I hadn't moved my things into it, yet. This is where most of the sewing is taking place. The model fittings are happening in the living room.

At the meeting I called last night, I shared my idea with everyone and asked them if they wanted to be a part of it. I explained that they would get compensated for their work, but I wasn't sure how much that would be, and I would understand if they weren't interested and wanted to leave. No one left.

I told Mila I needed ten models of various sizes, ages, and ethnicities. The models would have to be okay with being compensated by getting to keep their dress and another one from the line.

Lizzie talked to the owner of the vintage shop, and he agreed to let us borrow shoes and accessories. We don't need purses, as most of the dresses have pockets, but I want to include one, a very particular one. Lizzie said she would see what she could do.

There are ten dress designs for the show, including updates of the original three. It's all we could manage in the time allowed. The Rosie will end the show. It's earned its place in the line.

Betty is in charge of photography and social media. She actually *likes* social media. She used it to gather ideas for her wedding planning and has become a bit of an addict.

Mila and I are working on getting the secret extra supplies we need for the show.

Betty asked at the meeting if what I planned to do was legal. She mentioned something about getting permits.

I had glanced over at Mila, who said, "It's cool. I know a guy."

Betty gave me a worried look, but I ignored it.

So it's all been settled, and we each have a job to do. We also have a codename: Operation Reissue.

THIRTY-NINE

EVERYTHING IS UNDER CONTROL. Tomorrow is the big day.

But before then, I have a special delivery to make, and if I don't mail it out today, it won't arrive in time.

I hesitated about whether or not I should send it. It almost seems as if too much time has passed, even though it was only a couple of weeks ago. But it feels like the right thing to do. And so, I once again find myself at the post office.

Joining the long line, I realize who is standing directly ahead of me: Bradford, my former boss.

I turnaround to leave, but then, stop. I need to face him. It's part of the twelve-step program I have created for myself.

Step one is to tell the truth. Step two is to face my fears. (I'm not sure what the other steps are, yet. It may just be a two-step program.)

I tap him on the shoulder.

He turns around and raises an eyebrow. "Yes?"

He doesn't recognize me. I worked for him for almost five years, and he doesn't recognize me.

"It's Erin, Erin Bettencourt. I used to work for you."

He wrinkles his forehead. "Erin! Right, right. How are things?"

This is so awkward. Does he remember firing me? It doesn't seem like it. But I still want to say what has bothered me for the last two years.

"Bradford, I-I wanted to apologize for how things ended. It was totally my fault. I'm really sorry."

He looks confused. "These things happen. People move on."

He doesn't remember!

I have been worried about this, this whole time, and he doesn't even remember. I can't resist asking him, "Um, how is everyone back at the office?"

"Everyone is good, good."

I'm going to have to say it. "And Carol? Your administrative assistant?"

"Actually, she is the marketing coordinator now."

I knew it!

I can't really be mad. I'm sure she is doing a much better job than I ever did.

"Okay, great," he says and turns back around.

I guess that means our conversation is over.

Maybe I never needed his forgiveness. Maybe I was the one who needed to forgive myself.

FORTY

(Anti) Fashion Show Day!

I'M BACK at the *Breakfast Television* studio. It feels so different this time around. I'm still nervous, but nothing like the first time. My hair and makeup are done, and I'm about to go on set.

I walk towards Dina and Kevin, who each greet me with a hug, as if we are old friends. We move towards the light-blue sectional. I take my spot, along with a deep breath.

In five, four, three, two—

Dina gives a brief introduction, welcoming me back to the show.

"So, Erin," Kevin says, "your original Lady Bettencourt fashion show was cancelled because you decided to take a different approach. Tell us about that."

I'm looking at him as he says this, instead of directly at the camera. (Progress.)

"It's an anti-fashion show during fashion week," I say. "We will be showing dresses women can buy and wear now, not next spring. It's a fashion show for the people, not those in the industry. And each show will have an old-to-new theme, just like my dresses."

"I love it!" Dina says. "And the show, or should I say shows, will be held in various secret locations around Toronto, is that right?"

"That's right. Each of the locations has significance to me and the Lady Bettencourt brand. The first show starts soon. Very soon, actually."

"Can you give us a *tiny* hint where that one will be?" Kevin asks.

I pause, as if I'm debating whether or not to tell them, even though we planned this part out in advance.

"Okay, a *tiny* hint...Ride the Rocket."

"Oh-oh, I know!" Dina and Kevin say in unison, jumping up and down in their seats.

We laugh happily together.

"And will The Rosie, the dress Rachel McAdams wore to TIFF that started all of this, be in the show?" Dina asks.

"It will. A slightly updated version. The Rosie is now a permanent addition to the lineup. I think every woman should own at least one fabulous evening gown."

"With pockets," Dina says, grinning.

"With pockets," I say, grinning back.

"Well, we should let you get to that first show. It was a pleasure having you back," Kevin says.

"It was a pleasure to be back." I turn and look directly into the camera, and then I wave.

I couldn't resist. Plus, I know my ladies are watching.

Operation Reissue has assembled at Bloor subway station. It's a quarter-to-eight. We do a final check, then the models take their positions on the platform.

Betty has taken the day-off work to photograph everything. Mila and Gloria are also here for support and any dress adjustments.

The subway train pulls into the station. The models are lined up and wearing (secondhand) men's grey trench coats.

I give the lead model the signal.

One by one they slowly take off their coats, revealing a newly designed Lady Bettencourt dress underneath.

A few people notice something is happening, but continue onto the train, as do we.

Mila, Gloria, and I quickly collect the coats from the models. Then, the models open magazines—magazines from the sixties to today—and pretend to read them. They are mostly fashion magazines, but The Betty model has *The Economist*.

The real Betty maneuvers through the passengers, taking photos of each model.

Now people are paying attention. I hear different variations of "What's going on?" (along with a couple of grumbles).

189

And then, as I hoped, the passengers pull back to watch, creating a small clearing. The newer subway trains, without separate cars, make a perfect runway.

The models begin walking down the train while passengers farther along, crane their necks to see what is happening.

I keep waiting for someone to say it's the Lady Bettencourt fashion show. But the models have been walking for a while, and no one has said anything. I'm starting to get worried.

Finally, someone shouts, "It's the Lady Bettencourt fashion show! I see this morning on Brunch Television!"

I gaze in the direction of the voice.

It belongs to Gloria, who is ducked down in a group of people. I can't help letting out a small laugh. I will have to tell her later that it's actually called *Breakfast Television*. But her announcement has a ripple effect throughout the subway train. There is *oohing* and *aahing* at the dresses—and even clapping! Like, a *real* fashion show!

Mila, Gloria, and I hand out Lady Bettencourt business cards, shaped like dresses. The models continue to walk down the train until we reach Union station, where we get off.

Anti-fashion show number one: completed.

We are doing the whole thing again. And again.

Each time we do, the same pattern emerges. People are confused at first, then slowly recognize what is happening, and, eventually, someone (usually Gloria) announces it's the secret Lady Bettencourt fashion show.

And, at one of the shows, someone asks me to take a bow. I'm overloaded with grey trench coats but somehow manage to do a curtsy. Unfortunately, it's at the same time the train jerks, and I find myself sitting on the lap of an amused, older gentleman.

I definitely need to work on that part.

—

I'm nervous about this second set of shows. I hope we can repeat this morning's success.

Operation Reissue has convened at the lower level of First Canadian Place in the underground path. It's a wide-open space that gets a lot of foot traffic. And, as it's almost noon, office workers will soon come out in droves to grab their lunch.

The models, wearing their grey trench coats, are assembled in a line, overlooking a tiered water fountain.

Workers begin spilling out from different areas of the concourse. Some of them glance over at this line of grey women but keep walking.

Once I give the signal, the first model takes off her coat, followed by the next model, until all the grey trench coats are laying on the ground.

This is when people take notice.

One of the models hoists a boom-box from the ground onto her shoulder and presses play. A mixed tape of music through the ages that Mila cut together, rings out through the path.

More people have stopped to watch.

Another model is listening to a Walkman, another to a Discman, and yet another to an iPod. The other models are pretending to talk into cell phones from the '80s, '90s, and early 2000s, as well as the latest smartphone. All the while they are walking and spinning, spinning and walking.

When the show is over, there is applause.

I go "on stage" and take an awkward bow. As I do, I search the crowd, but I can't find who I'm looking for, who I'm hoping is here.

Afterwards, Betty shows me the photos she took, capturing everything. They are amazing. But she wasn't the only one taking photos. There were people in the crowd taking them, as well, and they have posted them to various social media sites.

"Who's that guy?" Betty asks out of nowhere.

I glance in the direction she is pointing to. "Oh, that's Joaquin, from the coffeehouse."

"I *know* who Joaquin is," she says, rolling her eyes. "I meant the guy standing beside him, talking to him. Is that his boyfriend?"

I let out a gasp.

He came! He came!

"No, that's Mr. Trader, remember me mentioning him? The guy I used to deliver lunches to?" I try not to sound too excited. I never got around to telling her about our disastrous dinner.

Aaron sees us looking in his direction and comes over with Joaquin.

"That was fabulous!" Joaquin says. "Makes me want to wear a dress."

"I wouldn't put it past you," I say, giving him a hug, which I immediately regret. Aaron is standing right there, and it doesn't seem appropriate to give him a hug. "Joaquin, you remember my sister, Betty." They shake hands. (Phew, we are back to the safety of handshaking.) I turn towards Aaron. "And this is Aaron Novak."

"*Aaron?*" Betty's eyebrow raises as she shakes his hand. "Interesting. Nice to meet you."

"And you." Then, he turns towards me. "Can I talk to you for a minute?"

We walk away from the others.

"I guess you got my package, huh?" I'm still embarrassed by my behaviour from a couple of weeks ago.

"I did. Thanks for the box of calming tea. I was running low," Aaron says, smiling.

I smile back nervously. "Thank you for coming on such short notice. I'm sorry I went a bit crazy at dinner that night. It wasn't fair of me to unload my crap on you. But I wanted you to know I made it right."

"Erin, sorry," Mila says, interrupting us. "We have to get going."

I reluctantly agree. "Can you come to the next show?" I ask him.

He looks at his watch. "Sorry, I can't. I want to, but I'm meeting someone—a client."

"Okay...I guess I'll be bumping into you."

"Be bumping into you," he says, chuckling before turning to go.

I hesitate a moment.

"Aaron, wait!"

He turns around.

"Here." I hand him a Lady Bettencourt business card. "Just in case that takes a while."

As he reaches for the card, our hands brush. I feel a tingle of electricity course through my body. I can't tell if he felt it, too.

"Good luck with the rest of the shows, Erin. You *deserve* this."

"Thank you," I say, blushing.

I head over to Scotia Plaza for the next show with my ladies. And I know we are about to put on a good show. No, a great show.

Operation Reissue is at the final secret location for the anti-fashion shows: Yorkville.

It's an outdoor show, and, luckily, the weather is cooperating on this beautiful, sunny afternoon in late October.

Our other shows have already gotten some press. I can't help wondering if Vanessa has heard about them. But I put her out of my mind just as quickly as she has entered it. I don't want to think about her today.

I wanted to have this fashion show in Yorkville for both the rich and the gawkers who hang out in this area. And appropriately, although I resisted the idea when Betty first suggested it, the old-to-new theme is dogs. They aren't actually old dogs. They are dogs that were or need to be adopted from a local animal shelter.

Betty asked her coworker Greta if she had any contacts. It turns out Greta's dogs, Huey, Dewey, and Louie, who I walked once (another one of those long stories), were adopted from the shelter. As were Mila's dogs. So even though I'm not a fan of dogs in general, I agreed.

The models are wearing their dresses without the grey trench coats for this show. But there is one addition. One of the models will be carrying a vintage Chanel 2.55 bag...in black. It was all Lizzie could get. But if things continue to go as well as they have been, I may be buying it as my reward. My keepsake from this wonderful day.

The dogs are wearing coats made from the same materials as the models' dresses, with either "I'm adopted" or "Adopt me" embroidered on them. Greta's and Mila's dogs represent those that have been adopted, and the shelter brought a few others that need adopting. I have also been assigned my own dog to appear with me for the show finale bows.

We have convened at the gigantic, artificial rock hill on Cumberland Avenue before the start of the show. It's pretty chaotic with us and the dogs. The plan is for the models to do a lap of the main loop, with the finale happening back at the artificial hill.

Once the show begins, Betty follows the models around the loop, taking photos of them as if they are famous movie stars.

Almost right away, we hear someone say, "This must be one of those Lady Bettencourt shows!" without Gloria having to announce it.

Mila, Gloria, and I stay behind at the hill with Lizzie, who has popped out of the vintage shop to attend these shows.

The little dog that is assigned to me, a black cavalier with splotches of white and brown, keeps loyally to my side. My right side. Kind of like, and this is weird, this is also *her* fashion show. I think it's a her, given what she is wearing.

Sophia, one of the new seamstresses, took care of making the dog clothes. I wasn't interested in going anywhere near them.

Lizzie bends down to pet the cavalier. "What's your name, pretty girl?" She looks up at me, expectantly. I shrug my shoulders.

"I used to know a dog who looked exactly like this," Lizzie continues. "The shop owner's wife had one. She would bring her in every now and again. Even has the same demeanor: a bit snobbish."

I laugh because it's true; this dog does seem snobby.

We see Betty coming around the corner, followed by the models, followed by a small group of people.

God, this is fun.

Once everyone is back at the hill, the snobby cavalier and I head to the front and take a bow. At least, it seemed as if she was bowing, too.

By six o'clock, the final show of the anti-fashion shows is over. I can't believe we did it. We actually pulled it off! Everything went (almost) exactly as we had planned. Silently, I thank the universe. Then—out loud—I thank my ladies and the models for their hard work. Hugs and kisses are exchanged.

The van from the animal shelter arrives. I glance down at the cavalier and say, "Time to go home."

She looks up at me with her big, brown eyes, and tilts her head to the side. My heart melts. She doesn't have a home to go to. Not a real home. She is in an orphanage for dogs.

I bend down and pet her for the first time. "Sorry, kid. I know what it's like to feel alone. But you will be okay. Someone will adopt you soon. Just look at those lashes!"

She seems to nod slightly in agreement.

The volunteer from the shelter has rounded up the other dogs. He turns towards us and says, "C'mon, Coco. C'mon, girl!"

Coco? Her name is Coco?

Coco looks at me once more, then runs towards the van, leaving me standing there.

"Ready for our celebratory dinner? Matt is saving our table at the restaurant," Betty says. "Erin? Did you hear me?"

"Um...yeah. Yeah, I'm ready," I say, starting to walk away with her.

But then, I stop to glance back at the van as it turns the corner and disappears into the darkening evening.

FORTY-ONE

BETTY CALLS the next day for an update.

"How are sales?" she asks.

"Through the roof! Thank goodness I have Gloria and the new seamstresses helping me. We shouldn't fall behind on orders like last time."

"That's awesome! I'm so proud of you. What you did yesterday was really cool. I knew you had it in you."

"Thank you, Betty. That means a lot." My voice catches. Her opinion matters more to me than anyone else's.

"Did you buy the bag?"

What bag?

Oh, yeah, the Chanel bag. I had forgotten all about it. "No, but I have made a decision about the condo."

"And?"

"I want to stay. I think I can manage the rent. There is just one, small thing."

"What?"

"Is it okay if I have a roommate?"

"You are going to rent out the den?"

"What's wrong with the den? I have slept in there for two years. It's cozy. And I'm going to keep sleeping in there because I'm turning your old bedroom into Lady Bettencourt's sewing workshop. There is more space for when the ladies want to come over."

"Great, idea! You can claim a portion of the rent as a business expense!" (I totally thought of that, too. Right.) "But where is this roommate supposed to sleep? Is it that guy, Aaron? Is he moving in?"

"Aaron? I barely know him."

"Then, who is this roommate?"

"It isn't actually a person; it's a dog. But she seems to act a lot like a person."

"You are getting a dog?"

"I'm adopting the little cavalier from the Yorkville show. We bonded. I get her officially in a couple of days."

"But you don't like dogs."

"I like this one. Plus, she needs somewhere to go, and I don't want to live on my own. We are a perfect match."

"She is cute."

"Super cute. And she appreciates fashion. I can tell. Here is the crazy part: Her name is Coco. *Can you believe it?* It was meant to be."

"With you, Erin, I'm starting to believe anything."

SECOND INTERMISSION
November 2015

COCO AND I are on our way to visit Lizzie at the vintage shop before heading to the dog park. Coco has a play date with Greta's dogs: Huey, Dewey, and Louie.

Who would have thought I would ever want to spend a Saturday afternoon at the dog park? It's a strange world. But it's important that Coco has friends. We all need friends. Sometimes Mila and her dogs join us, too, but they mostly just stand guard, waiting.

Since the anti-fashion shows, Lady Bettencourt dress sales have been growing steadily. I was afraid I was going to be a one-hit wonder. I know it's still early, but I think women want an ethical alternative. As long as I keep the dresses affordable and well-made, I don't see why Lady Bettencourt won't continue to grow. I finally feel like a businesswoman who (mostly) knows what she is doing. What I don't know or can't do on my own, I get help from people I trust.

I could never fulfill the new orders without Gloria, Natalia, and Sophia. And the dresses are of higher quality because their skills are superior to mine.

I could never source the secondhand materials I need without Mila. She has a great eye for finding stuff.

I could never take (non-blurry) photos of the dresses for the website or maintain Lady Bettencourt's social media accounts without Betty. She has really taken to it. And my "followers" enjoy interacting with the person who inspired The Betty dress. Plus, she is the only one I trust to manage my numbers.

We are a team. My success is our success.

And then, there is Aaron.

He called me a few days after the show to say if I ever needed any business advice, to let him know. So for the cost of a few vegan dinners (and the promise to get my first-ever menswear creation), he has been helping me, too. Except, lately, there hasn't been that much talk of business. I'm not sure where that is headed, but I think I like where that may be.

"Time will tell," I say out loud as a man walks past me.

He gives me a funny look.

Bending down quickly, I pet Coco and say, "Isn't that right, girl?"

I do this whenever I talk to myself out loud and someone catches me. It happens quite a bit. I'm not sure Coco appreciates being used like this, but then, I have to pick up her poop, so she doesn't get a say.

We are almost at the vintage shop when a woman hurries towards me.

I'm used to this. It happens all the time now. But it isn't because they recognize me. It's because of Coco. Everyone loves Coco.

Instead of petting Coco, however, the woman opens her coat and flashes me. I'm taken aback at first until I realize she is showing me her dress.

"It's The Glory!" she says excitedly.

She is wearing one of my new dress designs named after Gloria. This is the first time I have seen a customer wearing a Lady Bettencourt dress out in public. It feels so good.

I pull open my own coat and say, "Me, too!"

We both burst out laughing.

"I love your dresses and what they stand for," she says.

I blush with pride and thank her. It's nice to be recognized, to be *almost* famous. But the thing is, I was always somebody. And I will always be somebody, no matter what happens.

She glances down and finally notices Coco. "How cute is she! Do you design dog clothes, as well?"

She is referring to Coco's coat, which matches the dress I'm wearing. I used the leftover materials to make it. When I first got Coco, I decided I wouldn't dress her up in dog clothes. But she kept draping materials over her little body and going over to my full-length mirror to check herself out. I think she likes it, so I do it every now and again. Plus, it's getting chilly out. She *needs* a coat. Well, another one.

"No," I say. "I only make things for Coco here."

"Lucky dog."

We say our goodbyes, and then Coco and I are on our way again.

Hmm...maybe I *should* start a dog clothing line.

Or create my own signature perfume.

Or custom shade of lipstick—definitely not hot-pink.

I could diversify and get the Lady Bettencourt brand out there, *everywhere*!

Maybe I shouldn't be putting the horse before the cart...or is it the other way around?

What I mean is, I should probably stick to figuring out this whole dressmaking business first. Because if there is one thing I have learned in the last few weeks, it's that more isn't always better. But better always is.

PART III
HOUSE OF BETTENCOURT

"Beauty begins the moment you
decide to be yourself."
Coco Chanel

FORTY-TWO
August 2017

MY HIP IS VIBRATING.

At first, I think I'm having some sort of localized seizure. But then, I remember it's my phone in my dress pocket. I thought I had turned it off. There is nothing I can do now, not while my segment is being taped.

What was I saying? Something about...

"So, um, that's how to incorporate patterns into your wardrobe."

"*Ooh*, I love this paisley one," Marilyn Denis, the television show host, says as she reaches out to touch the Lady Bettencourt dress worn by a model on the set.

"Me, too. It's such a happy pattern."

"It is. Thanks for being back on the show, Erin."

"Thanks for having me back."

"Coming up, a hundred-and-one ideas on how to manage unruly, curly hair...or maybe just five," Marilyn says, winking at the camera.

When the taping stops, Marilyn and I walk past the live audience, where one of the women yells out, "I love your dresses!" Another one says, "I'm wearing The Cindy!"

I yell to them, "Thank you!" and "Looks amazing on you!"

Once Marilyn and I are out of view, she air-kisses me on both cheeks. "That was great, kiddo. See you in a couple of months."

"Thanks, Marilyn. Great shoes, by the way," I say as she turns to go.

In response, she waves her hand over her shoulder, without turning around, and returns to the studio.

I still can't believe I have a regular segment on *The Marilyn Denis Show*, a national lifestyle program. I'm inside people's televisions all across Canada!

This reminds me of my hip vibrating earlier, which could have potentially led to my not appearing inside those televisions anymore. I check my phone to see who the culprit was. My new smartphone.

My "vintage" Motorola Razr flip phone finally conked out, but it's been given a place of honour in my sewing workroom. It acts as a constant reminder to never let anyone else tell me how to run my business.

The call was from Brian, the owner of the frame shop where I'm having a painting reframed. My heart races as I listen to his voice message.

I listen to his voice message again because I have to make sure I heard him correctly. Because if I heard him correctly, I need to get to the frame shop as soon as possible.

It's probably nothing. I mean, why would a package be hiding behind the painting?

Not any old painting, *the painting*: The one that belonged to my mom, depicting a mother and her two young daughters. The one that hung on our living room wall throughout my childhood.

Unless...she never knew the package was there.

Oh, my god. What if it's drugs?

It is probably not drugs.

But it could be drugs.

Or money.

What if it was my mom's secret hiding place and the package is full of cold, hard cash?

I could be rich.

But what I want to know the most right now is, why did I take the subway? I should have taken an Uber. Our train has been at a standstill for ten minutes due to someone having a medical emergency. I hope the person is okay, but I may pass out from anticipation if we don't get moving soon.

I *need* to know what is inside that package. It feels as though my own life depends on it.

"Where is it?" I ask as soon as I'm inside the frame shop.

"Where is what?" Brian, the owner, asks.

"Sorry," I say, catching my breath. "Let me start again. I'm Erin Bettencourt. You left me a message about a package you found behind the painting I brought in."

He looks confused.

How many packages do they find behind paintings?

This can't be an everyday occurrence.

"Package...package. Oh, that package!" he laughs. "I'm only fooling with you. It's right here." He reaches under the counter and places the package on top.

I don't know what I was expecting, but it's a normal, padded envelope. I guess I thought it might look special somehow, and that by looking at it, I would know what was inside.

"Do you know what's in there?" he asks, echoing my thoughts.

"No idea."

"Well, if it's anything good, we take a fifty-percent finders fee."

"Really?"

"Fooled you, again!" he says, chuckling to himself. "But you would be surprised how often this happens."

I want to ask what sorts of things he has found, but he keeps talking.

"We're having some issues sourcing the frame you requested. It may take a bit longer than we quoted, but we should have it ready for you in a few weeks."

"That's okay. No rush. Thank you for letting me know about this," I say, taking the package into my hands for the first time.

Again, I feel nothing when I touch it. I was hoping for an electric spark or something, but it feels like...an envelope. What I do know is that I shouldn't open it in here. Not in front of "Funny Man" Brian.

So I clutch the package to my chest and leave the frame shop.

—

When I get home, Coco, my cavalier, is there waiting to greet me with her big eyes and wagging tail. I give her a few cuddles, and then place the package I have been holding tightly on top of the dining room table.

Maybe I won't open it right away. Maybe I will make myself a cup of tea and catch-up on some business.

Instead, I pace around the condo while looking at the package, then away from it, then back at it. This goes on for some time. Coco follows my every movement.

You are being silly, Erin. Just open it. It's only a package.

A mysterious package. I have had a somewhat sordid history with those. But this one is most likely from my mom. Which means, I should probably tell Betty, my sister, about it.

Except, I have no idea what is inside of it.

What if it's filled with that deadly white powder stuff, Amtrak? That doesn't sound right. *Anthrax!* That is it! What if it's filled with that? I can't expose Betty to Anthrax, not while she is pregnant. (Or ever, actually.)

Oh, yeah, Betty is pregnant!

Very pregnant—with twins! I'm going to be an auntie, multiplied by two. And I'm pretty sure one of my chief duties as Auntie Erin is to not bring harm to my unborn nieces or nephews or some combination of which.

Betty is keeping their sex a secret. I tried getting it out of her OB-GYN by pretending to be Betty on the phone, but she didn't fall for it. (How was I to know Betty was sitting in her office at the time?)

So opening the package, without my sister present, wouldn't be to quell my own curiosity. No, it would be to protect the next generation.

With my decision made, I stop pacing and resist the urge to rip the envelope open.

Coco senses something is on the verge of taking place and makes her way to my side.

"If anything bad happens, Coco, call 9-1-1."

She lets out a small bark.

Having received her confirmation, I slowly cut open the envelope and peek inside.

It is full of paper. And not the dollar-bills kind.

I reach in and pull out a small bundle of various stocks of paper, held together with an elastic band. The elastic band breaks once it's been freed from the envelope. It must have been in there a while.

As I try to keep my grasp of the now loose sheets of paper, my eye catches on the top sheet. That is when I see something I haven't seen in a very long time.

My mom's handwriting.

FORTY-THREE

~Letter~

SEPTEMBER 21, 2008

My beautiful girls,

I suppose you are not girls anymore, although it's hard for me to think of you any other way.

Last week, I found you, Erin, in my closet, reading one of my journals. I was upset at first, but then, it confirmed something I had been debating for a while.

I know I haven't shared much about my past; however, there were things I always planned to tell you when you were older. Sadly, I no longer have that option. And for that, I'm sorry.

During the summer, when you were both away and I found out I was sick, I began going through my things. I didn't want you to have to deal with it once I was gone. But I kept a box of journals I contemplated sharing with you.

It's taken all my remaining strength to go through that final box of journals and select only the most important things I wanted you to know. The things I felt affected you the most. Not everything, of course. Every woman must have her secrets. But those things that may make you understand me, and yourselves, better.

Why hide the package behind a painting, instead of giving it to you? For one, that painting is very special to me. And for another, I have been using it as a hiding spot for years. I manipulated the paper-backing specifically for that purpose. So it felt like the right place to keep my final secret.

I figure if you are meant to find it, you will. And if not, then you will remember me the way that I am—or rather—the way I was.

My diary entries are addressed to Elizabeth, as though I'm writing to an older version of myself, or an older sister. I always wanted a sister who I could look up to. I suppose this was my way of having one.

Please read these together so you can lean on each other should something you learn upset you. You are blessed to have one another.

Regardless of what you read, know that I don't regret anything that has happened in my life. Everything happened as it should.

You girls gave my life purpose, reason, and meaning. You have been the loves of my life. I'm honoured to have been your mother.

Love you always,
Mom

P.S. All of my other journals have been destroyed. There are no more "hidden packages." I don't want you having any false hope you might find something more. And should someone else be reading this letter right now, please destroy it. If it wasn't found by my girls, it wasn't meant to be found.

P.P.S. Give my love to Matt. He is one of the good ones.

P.P.P.S. Know that I tried to do my best for you both.

—

I wipe a tear from my face. I hadn't realized I was crying. It's just that, as I read the letter, I could actually hear my mom's voice again, almost like she was talking to me.

And I don't want her to stop talking to me, so I turn to the first diary entry before remembering that she wanted Betty and I to read them together.

Betty! I have to tell her what I found!

She won't believe it. I can hardly believe it myself that I will finally get to read some of the diaries I went searching for after our mom died. Betty will be as excited as I am to read them, too.

I reach for my phone, but then, hesitate.

At least, I think she will be as excited as I am. But what if she doesn't want to read them? She wouldn't say no, would she? And if she doesn't want to read them, does that mean I can't, either? Is that what our mom meant?

I don't know.

I'm not sure what Betty's feelings are on diaries. The topic has never come up. She is definitely not into Hollywood gossip—not that that is the same thing. Plus, she isn't in the best position to make this sort of decision at the moment, being on bed-rest.

Did I mention Betty is on bed-rest?

When Betty found out she was pregnant, she wasn't very happy. It wasn't because she didn't want to have kids, but because she hadn't planned on having them so soon in her married life. Betty likes to plan things.

Then, just as she was getting used to the idea, she found out she was having twins, which was another bit of a shock. And now, a few weeks before her delivery date, she has had to go on bed-rest. (I didn't know that was still a thing.)

So I have been visiting Betty a lot because she isn't used to having nothing to do. Basically, she is only allowed to get up to use the bathroom or take a shower.

When I visit her tomorrow, I will gauge her general feelings on diaries before I reveal the discovery I have made. I want to go tonight, but it's getting late, and it might make her suspicious.

Even though I'm desperate to begin reading the entries now, I need to handle this properly.

Matt, Betty's husband, is coming out of their front door when I arrive the next morning.

"Hey, Matty Matt! How is she doing today?"

"You know Betty, she wants those babies out now."

"I can imagine. Well, sort of." I wave him off to work before heading inside the house.

When I reach their bedroom, I see a humongous bulge coming from the middle of the bed. Betty's face is completely obscured. I creep over to the top of the bed.

"Hey, Betty Boop!" I say, popping my face in front of hers.

She jumps a little. "*Erin!* You are not supposed to scare a pregnant woman. I almost peed!"

"Sorry," I say, trying to suppress a giggle. "I didn't think of that. How are you feeling?"

"Horrible. I'm so bored. Extremely, extremely bored," she says while staring blankly up at the ceiling. "You think they would have invented a cure for pregnancy bed-rest by now." She slowly sits up and begins maneuvering the many pillows around her to get into a comfortable half-sitting, half-lying position.

Hmm, she isn't in a good mood. Actually, she hasn't been in a good mood for weeks now. I guess having to stay in bed all day will do that to you, especially when you have a Type-A personality.

After I finish helping her setup the pillows, I place both my hands on her belly and say, "Hello, Baby Coo-Chi! Hello, Baby Chi-Coo! It's your Auntie Erin. See you soonish!"

I want them to recognize my voice when they are born. I have been doing this same routine from the moment I found out Betty was pregnant. (I found out even before Matt did. It's one of those long stories I might tell you about one day.) I used to say, "Baby Coo-Chi-Coo," but I had to split it up once we knew she was having twins. I will be upgrading their nicknames once I officially meet them.

"How did your segment go on *The Marilyn Denis Show*?" Betty asks.

"Good, except that—" I was about say that my phone almost went off during the taping, but that might lead to questions regarding the framing of the painting, which could lead to the package behind that painting. So instead, I say, "I messed up one of my lines. Nothing major but still."

"I'm sure you were great. Let me know when it airs so I can watch it. How are the new girls working out?"

The "new girls" are Trendy and Leo.

Betty used to take care of Lady Bettencourt's social media accounts. Although she could technically do that from her bed, we wanted to have someone trained before her maternity leave. So I hired a recent college-graduate as an intern. I thought it was really cool her name was Trendy and she worked in social media. But she told me it's her nickname and her real name is Trindade. She made me promise to never tell anyone.

I also had to hire a freelance photographer named Leo because Betty took our dress photos, and she can't exactly take photos from her bed. Leo's full name is Leonilda. She didn't ask me to keep it a secret, but she prefers Leo.

Not only was Betty in charge of social media and photography, but she is Lady Bettencourt's accountant (her regular day job), as well. Thankfully, Betty is still able to do my bookkeeping and payroll. She says she can do numbers in her sleep...and I believe her.

She has been a big help to my business, with all of these multiple talents. Her absence is missed. And no wonder she is bored; she is used to having so much to do.

"The new girls have turned out amazing!" I see Betty's face fall a bit, so I add, "But they're not as amazing as you. Oh, yeah, I brought you a treat. I left it in the kitchen. Do you want me to go get it? It's your favourite!"

The purpose of the treat is two-fold: First, to cheer her up. Second, and more importantly, to sweeten her up before getting to the purpose of my visit. The way to Betty's heart is generally with food.

"Thanks, I will have it later, maybe. I'm too full of babies to eat right now."

I didn't anticipate this. Betty is *always* hungry. And now, I don't have a backup plan. "Um...read anything interesting lately?"

"Just some parenting books."

This isn't going well. How am I supposed to ask her what her thoughts are on diaries? But maybe reading the diaries will entertain her, give her something to look forward to each day.

"Hey, Betty, remember when we were kids and mom gave us both a diary for Christmas? What happened to yours?"

"I shredded it."

"*You what?* Why?"

"Because I didn't want anyone finding it. It was so embarrassing. All these petty grievances I had because this person did this or said that. Imagine if someone read what I had written years later and thought that was what I actually felt."

"So you don't regret not being able to go back and reread it now? To see what the old you was like?"

"No way. Diaries are specific to the time in your life when you wrote them. It's almost as if they aren't real, as if they are an exorcism of your demons. Honestly, I've always thought there was something a little sad about them. Why are you asking?"

This is it. I should tell her now. Maybe Betty would feel differently if she knew the diaries belonged to our mother. But maybe not. I can't risk it.

"Um, no reason," I say.

When our mom wrote her letter, she hadn't anticipated it would be found when one of her daughters would be heavily pregnant with twins, full of excess hormones and other weird stuff happening to her body, and not in the right frame of mind to make this sort of decision.

Our mom wouldn't want her other daughter to have to suffer by making her wait an extended period-of-time before reading the diary entries.

Wouldn't she?

I am the older sister. I should get to make the final call. Betty can always read them after the twins are born, at her own leisurely pace.

Or I could shred them after I have read them, like Betty did with hers, and she never needs to know they existed. She doesn't seem to appreciate the importance of diaries. It doesn't matter to her, like it does to me. To me, it matters more than anything else at the moment.

But would that be a horrible thing to do?

I'm never quite sure. I need to talk to someone impartial. I need to talk to Aaron.

FORTY-FOUR

AARON AND I have taken an oath. An oath to always tell each other the truth, the whole truth, and nothing but the truth.

The oath is really for his benefit, not mine. He doesn't have trouble with this truth-telling business. But it was part of the deal when we first got together—I was the one who suggested it.

I should probably mention that Aaron and I are "official." Like boyfriend and girlfriend, official. Which may sound kind of immature and very high school, but as I haven't had a boyfriend in forever, I don't care.

I have a boyfriend! A boyfriend!

Okay, now that that is out of the way, back to the oath. Because of this oath (that I sometimes wish I had never suggested), I need to tell him about finding my mom's diary. I actually want to tell him because I could use his advice on what I should do.

There is only one, teeny-tiny problem with that: Aaron is in East Africa.

He is volunteering with a non-profit organization that is trying to bring clean water to remote regions in that area. He had been planning this trip for a long time, even before we became a couple. It's been two weeks since he has been gone, and he won't be back for another few weeks. Hopefully, before the twins are born.

We decided on weekly Skype calls while he is away, but let's just say, East Africa not only needs clean water, but could also benefit from a better Internet connection.

I'm at my laptop at our scheduled time, but I have already been disconnected twice. I try again. Finally, Aaron appears on the screen.

God, I have missed his face.

He grins and says, "Hey, Lady B." (That is his nickname for me.)

"Hey, Mr. Trader," I say, beaming back.

When I told him the old nickname I had for him, he said he thought it was funny. I use it now because it reminds him of how far he has come: How he traded-in his old life of being an arrogant equity trader, for a new life of helping fund small startups that share his values.

But I think the real reason we use nicknames for each other is because it would be weird to regularly use our birth names. It seems redundant somehow.

"And hello there, Mademoiselle Coco," he says to Coco, who is sitting on my lap.

Coco looks down and blushes. Or, at least, appears to blush. I sometimes feel as though she thinks Aaron is *her* boyfriend.

"I don't have long to talk; we're moving camps tonight. But I have some bad news—"

Nothing.

"Wait, the screen froze," I say. "What's the bad news?"

"The camp I'm moving to doesn't have any Internet, and phone service is unreliable. I don't know when I'll be able to call again."

I feel my face fall at his news.

"Sorry, babe. I thought I would be staying in one place the whole time. But we finished up earlier here than expected, and there is another location that needs our help."

"I understand." I *mostly* understand. But I can't deny someone clean water, just so I can Skype with my boyfriend.

"How is everything over there? How is Betty doing?"

"Betty is bored out of her mind." This reminds me of what I wanted to talk to him about. I have to tell him now, or I might not get the chance. "Remember how I told you I wanted to get my mom's painting reframed? Well, when the framer took off the paper-backing, he found...a package!"

I wait for Aaron's reaction, but his face is frozen on the screen again.

"Aaron? *Aaron?* Can you hear me?"

Nothing.

"Aaron!" I say louder, as if that will help.

The call disconnects.

Dammit!

I spend the next hour, trying to get him back, both by Skype and by phone. Neither works. Now he can't help me figure out what I should do.

Coco, who has been waiting patiently for Aaron to return to the screen, looks at me with wondering eyes.

So I say to her, "And in that package was a bundle of my mom's old diary entries. My mom wanted Betty and me to read them together. But when I talked to Betty, she said she didn't believe in diaries. Do you think I should read them on my own?"

Coco turns to the side, almost as if she is about to shake her head. But then, she lets out a little bark.

"I will take that as a 'yes,'" I say before she does anything else.

But I can't read them, yet, as I need to take Coco for her walk. Plus, it will give me a chance to clear my head, to make sure I'm doing the right thing. Because I know that once I read my mom's words, I can't unread them.

What if I find out something bad? Or what if what I read changes the way I remember her?

Maybe Betty is right; she usually is. Maybe diaries should be kept secret, even if you have permission by the owner to read them.

But I can still hear our mom's voice in the letter she wrote to us, replaying in my mind. I want to hear her voice again. It's like having a piece of her back after so long.

I'm walking down the street in a daze, debating what to do, when a little girl of about five comes running up to Coco and me.

"Mommy!" she says excitedly. "Look at this cute doggie!"

The little girl's mother catches up with her. She is carrying a baby in a sling. "He is very cute," she says.

Coco looks offended. (I think this is why she likes it when I dress her up.)

"'He' is actually a 'she,'" I say, correcting her.

"Oh, sorry. *She* is very cute," the woman says, bending down awkwardly to pet Coco.

Coco lets her, so I guess she is forgiven.

"We better get going," the woman says as she starts to walk away. But the little girl is still at Coco's side, petting her. The woman turns. "Come along, honey. Mommy is waiting."

Mommy is waiting.

"Yes, mom-my," the little girl says, in her sweet, sing-song voice. She runs to her mother, then reaches up to take her outstretched hand.

When they are almost at the end of the street, the little girl turns around and sees I'm watching them, so she waves. I wave back.

I know what I'm going to do. What I was *always* going to do.

For the first time in years, my mommy is waiting for me, too.

I have to know what she wants to tell me.

One. I'm reading only one of my mom's diary entries.

That way I can get a sense of what they are about, and if I can't handle it, I will stop. Then, after Betty has the twins and is fully recovered, I will tell her what I found.

Given the present circumstances, with Betty not really being Betty at the moment, I think this is the fairest solution for all parties involved.

It's only one.

What harm could that possibly do?

FORTY-FIVE
~Diary Entry~

AUGUST 27, 1982

Dearest Elizabeth,

Sorry I haven't written in a while. I know, I know. I promised to write every day to remember my time here in Paris, but things have been crazy. Okay, so I forgot about you until I found you hiding under my bed when I was looking for my missing shoe. And now, I have so much to tell you.

I'm in love with Paris! I wish I didn't have to leave in a week. My summer living in Montmartre has been everything—*everything*—I wished it would be.

Most of my days are spent sketching portraits of tourists in the *Place du Tertre*. I speak to them with a fake French accent and wear a black beret tilted on my head. I get better tips that way. Occasionally, I even pretend to smoke using one of those long cigarette holders, like in *Breakfast at Tiffany's*. It adds to my character.

I have also spent countless hours painting at the Louvre, copying from the great artists. I can only dream that one day, I will be half as good as them. I have already learned more in the short time I have been here than in the past three years at school.

It doesn't seem possible that in a couple of weeks, I will be sitting in a classroom again. I want to stay here forever. Runaway for good. Especially now that I know I can make it on my own.

Sure, money has been tight, but what do I really need to live? I have cheese, baguettes, coffee...and *pain au chocolat*! I could live on *pain au chocolat* alone. And I can speak the language, so that has made things easier. The studio I'm renting is tiny, but it's cheap and full of charm. That is all I need to make me happy. And my art. I *need* my art.

My *maman* is still angry. *Quelle surprise.* But I thought she would be over it by now. She doesn't understand why I would run-off to Paris when she had lined up an internship for me at her friend's art gallery. But I didn't want to spend my summer in a stuffy gallery, trying to sell paintings. I wanted to create them.

We haven't spoken in weeks. The last time we did, she threatened not to pay my tuition and housing fees for the upcoming school year. I told her to do whatever she felt she had to do.

This summer has taught me that I don't need her money. It isn't even her money: It's my stepfather's. But she definitely acts as though it's hers. I hate how having money has changed her. Or maybe that is what she was always like underneath.

I can't wait until I'm officially done with school in the spring, then I will get to start living my life the way that I want to.

Love you always,
Lizzie

P.S. So much more has happened while I have been here. I have met so many interesting people. One in particular has caught my eye. *C'est l'amour!* But I'm too sleepy to write about it now, I need to go to bed. I will write more later. Promise.

—

My mom was an artist!

How come I never knew that? She made the best Halloween costumes and was really good at decorating our birthday cakes, but I never saw her paint or draw or anything. When did she stop?

She also never mentioned spending a summer in Paris. I would have remembered if she did. As far as I knew, she never left the continent. If it was the summer of 1982, that would make her...twenty-years-old. She was so young! For some reason, it's hard for me to picture my mom being young.

I knew she spoke French, although never with Betty and me. To my knowledge, she only ever spoke it when talking on the phone.

Sometimes when she did, I would creep behind her bedroom door to listen, more out of curiosity than anything else. But she spoke so fast, I couldn't understand what was being said, except for a word or two. Those conversations always made her angry and often ended with her slamming down the phone.

Maybe she was talking to someone she had known back in Paris? Or maybe it was her *maman*, my grandmother.

My rich grandmother. Or, at least, her husband was. But what happened with my mom's *real* dad? She never talked about him. I never met either of my maternal or paternal grandparents. I thought they passed away before I was born. Isn't that what my mom told us? Had she told us? Or had I assumed they passed away?

They could still be alive. I could have grandparents!

Although if they are, my mom's mother doesn't seem very nice. I guess it makes sense she was rich. She is the one who gave my mom the Chanel 2.55 bag that I tried to get back a few years ago. I do remember her telling us that story.

Well, I remember the part where she said her mother had given her the bag when she got her first job. That is all I really remember.

Why hadn't I paid more attention?

The weird thing is, as I was reading what my mom wrote, I couldn't help thinking how much the younger-version of her sounded like me. I always felt that her and Betty shared the same kind of personality, whereas we just looked alike. Maybe when she became a mom, she changed. Or was forced to change.

I have so many questions I wish I could ask her: What happened when she came back? Did her and her mother make amends? And this *amour*, could it have been my father? After all, he was from France. But mostly, I want to know why she stopped painting if she loved it so much.

Maybe some of those answers can be found in the rest of the diary entries she left us.

As I'm about to turn to the next sheet of paper to read it, Coco places her little paws on my knees, tilts her head, and barks.

Right. I said I would read only one. It's better I stop, anyway. I need to process what I have learned. I can decide later what I will do next, if anything.

Carefully, I organize the sheets of paper to keep them in the order they were in and grab a binder clip to make sure they stay together. I put everything back in the original envelope, then I take the envelope to my room and hide it under my futon mattress.

I don't know why I'm hiding it. But I feel I'm suppose to. Plus, I want to keep it somewhere safe, where I won't lose it.

And somewhere only I know where to find it.

FORTY-SIX

I LOVE MONDAYS.

When I had a cubicle job, Mondays were the day of the week I dreaded the most because I knew I had another five days to go before I could be free again. Now that I love what I do, I love Mondays, too.

Actually, since I no longer have a regular workweek, all of the days kind of get mixed up together. I can work whenever I want to, as long as the work gets done. It doesn't matter if it's Monday or Saturday, morning or night; I get to choose. I can't believe how much my life has changed in three years.

Every now and again, I pinch myself to make sure I'm not dreaming. Praying, I won't wake up to find myself sitting in my old cubicle, in a job I hate, with Carol—my former work nemesis—peeking over my cubicle wall, reminding me of some boring meeting I had forgotten about.

"*Querida*, you okay?" Gloria asks.

Phew! Definitely not a dream. There was no Gloria in my past working life.

I smile and nod in her direction.

We are seated at either end of a long, wooden table that has been setup in the only real bedroom of my condo. (I still sleep in the den.) Okay, so it isn't actually my condo. It's Betty's. She decided to keep the condo as an investment property after she bought a house with Matt. I'm her tenant.

The "bedroom" is the official headquarters of Lady Bettencourt. There are sewing machines at both ends of the table; the middle portion is used for laying and cutting out patterns. On the side walls, there are bookcases holding sewing supplies and the deconstructed secondhand materials we use exclusively to make our dresses.

Finished dresses, go on row-upon-row of clothing racks in the living room.

Thankfully, I never replaced the furniture Betty took with her when she moved out. I didn't realize how much space I would need to run my online shop once business took off.

Gloria is the first seamstress I hired to work with me. She had worked with my mom at an alteration shop, but with time, they lost touch. Years later, through the power of my friend, the universe, Gloria and I were reunited.

Soon after that, I hired her sister, Natalia, as well as another former coworker from the alteration shop named Sophia. In the beginning, Natalia and Sophia worked out of the condo, too, but there isn't enough room anymore. We are (figuratively) bursting at the seams.

There has been so much demand for our dresses that I had to hire two more seamstresses, Patricia and Ming, who work on a piece-work basis from their own homes. Patricia is Sophia's cousin. I found Ming through Patricia, as they once worked together at a bridal shop, making wedding gown alterations. Ming sews the majority of our evening gowns because she has the most experience working with finer materials.

They all magically came into my life when I needed their help the most. The universe—and my mom—definitely had a hand in making that happen.

But it does make me wonder how my mom ended up at the alteration shop in the first place. She was going to be an artist.

When did that change?

Wait a minute. Not only was Gloria my mom's former coworker, she was also my mom's friend, and even babysat Betty and I when we were kids. She may know something.

"Gloria!" I say, startling her. "Did you know my mom was an artist?"

"Yes, she was very good at making clothes."

"No, what I meant was, did you know she was a painter?"

She thinks for a moment. "Oh, yeah, I remember her telling me one time she had to paint your bedroom because you drew over the walls with crayons," she says, giving me a scornful look, as if this happened recently.

"I don't mean a painter of walls," I say. "But a painter of paintings, of pictures." Gloria's English is pretty good, but some things still get lost in translation.

"No, I never know she do that."

This isn't going anywhere.

"What about her mother? My grandmother? I know they weren't close, but do you know anything about her?" I ask, hoping to get at least something out of her.

She stops sewing the dress she is working on. There is a blank look on her face as she gazes out the floor-to-ceiling windows. It's as if I can see her replaying a memory in her mind. But then, she shakes her head and looks towards me.

"Why you ask me these questions, *querida*? What happen?"

Dammit! She is on to me.

"I was wondering if you knew anything. That's all. I'll, um, go make us some more coffee." I get up quickly from my chair and leave the room.

Gloria has a way of knowing when I'm not being a hundred-percent truthful. It's better I drop it for now. I hadn't thought out what I would say to her. I hadn't known I was going to say anything; it just sort of came out. But I can tell she is hiding something, too.

I can feel it.

I'm in the kitchen, making Gloria and I coffee, when there is a knock on the door.

It's Mila. She walks in, carrying several full bags from the thrift store.

While I occasionally go out on hunts for the secondhand materials needed to make our dresses, Mila does the majority of the scavenging now. She is really good at finding stuff at low prices. It's helped our profit margins a lot.

In greeting, she air-kisses me on both cheeks.

I used to think Mila was this super cool model-slash-dog-walker-slash-illegal-package-handler, but she is actually kind of goofy.

"Coffee?" I ask.

She nods her head vigorously, then walks towards the living room area to find someplace to put down the bags. I see her struggle to find a spot because of all the clothing racks.

"Erin, we need a bigger space."

For some reason, her vocalizing what I had already known to be true, makes me look around in an entirely new way. This place is a gigantic mess.

"Yeah, I know," I say.

It isn't that I can't afford to rent out a proper workshop; business has been growing like crazy. It's just that I'm, well, a little afraid. It's scary making major business decisions. I'm always worried they won't turn out, especially when they involve spending significant amounts of money.

"I could talk to Frankie," Mila says. "See if he can find us some old, abandoned warehouse on the cheap."

"Maybe, but, uh, give me a bit of time to think about it first."

I definitely don't want to get Frankie involved—unless I have to. Frankie is...actually, I don't know who Frankie is. I still haven't met him. I only ever talked to him on the phone that one time when he asked me to do "a job" for him, delivering what I later found out was a "not exactly legal" package.

That is also the short version of how I met Mila, the illegal package handler. Although Mila and I don't share that particular story of how we met with other people. We tell them we used to work together and let them assume it was at my old job. People love to assume.

Maybe finding new headquarters for Lady Bettencourt is what I should be focusing on right now. It will distract me from what I read in my mom's diary.

I have to stop thinking about how her life took such an unexpected turn. Because if I think about it, really think about it, I already know the answer to that. It's as obvious as my needing to find a bigger space.

My mom stopped being an artist because Betty and I came into the picture.

FORTY-SEVEN

LIZZIE CALLED. Not Lizzie, my mom—obviously—but Lizzie, my friend from the vintage shop, who shares her name. She called last night to say they were running low on Lady Bettencourt dresses and could use another batch.

A few months ago, I began selling my dresses at the shop; the higher-end ones, including The Rosie and two new evening wear designs that they carry exclusively.

I came up with the idea and convinced the owner, Arthur, it was still in keeping with the concept of the shop and would help bring in a younger clientele. He said he would take the dresses on consignment and that I had a month to prove myself.

I did prove myself. So much so that he gave me my very own rack. I love seeing my dresses in a real-life, bricks-and-mortar store. I never thought that would happen.

So whenever Lizzie calls to ask for more dresses, I make sure to have some on hand to be delivered at a moment's notice. I would hate to lose my rack.

And that is why I'm standing outside the vintage shop in Yorkville, in the early hours of this summer morning, with a pile of garment bags in my arms.

I knock on the glass front door to get Lizzie's attention, as the shop hasn't officially opened for the day.

As she comes into view, a wide smile spreads across my face. Even though there is a significant age difference between us, we were friends right from the start. She is always looking out for me.

When she sees me, she returns my smile and hurries to open the door.

"Hello, you!" she says once she has let me in.

I place the garment bags on top of the sales counter so I can get a hug from Lizzie. Lizzie's hugs are the best kind of hugs.

"How is Betty?" she asks when she releases me.

"Ready to give birth."

"Poor thing. It must be dreadful having to stay in bed all day. Tell her to keep a bottle of peppermint oil next to her bed. She can take a whiff of it whenever she needs a little pick-me-up."

"I'm visiting her after I leave here, so I'll tell her then."

"Oh, I almost forgot. I have some news!" she says, clapping her hands together.

"Spill," I say conspiratorially.

"Arthur is selling the shop," Lizzie says in a whisper, although we are the only two people in here.

"The shop? *This shop?*" I ask, not in a whisper.

"*Shhh!* He hasn't put it on the market, yet. He doesn't want it getting out there until it is official. He has to ready himself for the vultures who will swoop in."

I can see why there would be vultures. Yorkville is one of Toronto's prime real estate locations. Because it's a hamlet, it's limited in size, so there isn't much land available, making anything that comes onto the market, extremely desirable.

But if the vintage shop is sold, it's unlikely whoever buys it will want to keep it as such. They will probably turn it into a designer clothing store, like the others on this street. I would lose my beloved rack. But that also means...

"Lizzie! You will be out of a job!"

"It's all right, dear," she says, patting my arm to calm me down. "I will be okay. I have some savings. I have been thinking about retiring soon, anyway. I'm getting too old to stand on my feet all day."

Lizzie is old. I always forget that because she has such a youthful spirit.

"But I'm sorry you may not be able to sell your dresses here anymore," she continues. "Which gave me an idea...I think you should buy the shop!"

"*Me? Buy the shop?* With what money?"

"That part, I haven't quite figured out. But I'm sure you will come up with something. I have a good feeling about this. What if I arrange for you to have a chat with Arthur before he places it on the market?"

"I don't know, Lizzie. That would be a huge step for me to take."

"It's just an idea for now. There is still a bit of time. Let it steep, like a cup of tea."

"Fine, I will. But only to humour you."

As I'm leaving the shop, I can't help wondering if it would be possible. Could I find some way to do it? It would solve the space issues I'm having. There is a back room that could be used as the sewing workshop and for storage. And Lizzie once told me there is a small apartment upstairs Arthur uses whenever he is in town. That could be additional workspace...or I could live there to have one less expense.

Imagine: My own bricks-and-mortar store full of Lady Bettencourt dresses!

No, no, it's just a fantasy. There is no way someone like me could own a place like that. That sort of thing doesn't happen. Well, it does, but only in the movies. And this is definitely not a movie.

I haven't been in Betty's bedroom for more than a few seconds when I blurt out, "Did you know mom was an artist?"

"What? She was?" Betty asks as she tries to sit up in bed.

There is something wrong with my brain. I reminded myself not to say anything as I walked in the room, and there I go opening my big mouth. I need to divert her attention. "Hey, is that a new pillow? It looks super comfy."

"Erin, why do you think mom was an artist?"

I should know by now, there is no tricking Betty. That once I made that kind of statement, I would have to back it up.

"Um, I was going through some of her things when I came across it. Apparently, she went to Paris and painted at the Louvre."

"*Really?* Wow. I always wondered where you got your artistic talents."

"You're artistic, too. You take amazing photos."

"I guess, but what was this 'it' you came across?"

"Just, um, a note she wrote."

"A note? Cool! Can you bring it the next time you come to visit? I would love to see it."

Crap. How am I supposed to do that?

"Okay, sure. I'll bring it. It isn't that big of a deal; just something she wrote down."

"Still, I want to see it. I'm missing her a lot lately. Being pregnant makes me realize how much. There are so many things I wish I could ask her about her own pregnancies. Like, were we breastfed? I never thought to ask her."

"We weren't exactly thinking about that kind of stuff at that age."

It never occurred to me how hard this must be for Betty; her being pregnant and not having our mom here to give her guidance. She has to rely on her parenting books, as most of her friends haven't had babies, yet, and I don't think she would feel comfortable talking to Matt's mom, even though they get along well.

Maybe I should show her the diary entries, in case there is something in there about that. But how would I explain that I have already started reading them? She will know I kept it from her. She always knows. I need more time to think it through before I tell her. I don't want to make a hasty decision.

"Oh, yeah," I say, wanting to change the subject. "Before coming here, I went by the vintage shop to drop off some more dresses. Lizzie told me to tell you to take a sniff of peppermint oil whenever you feel down."

"Hmm, I hadn't heard of that. I think we have some, so I'll give it a try. I'll try anything at this point. Tell her, thank you for me."

"I will. She mentioned something else, too. Apparently, the vintage shop is going up for sale and—get this—she thinks *I* should buy it. Isn't that crazy?"

Betty thinks for a moment. "Interesting. It isn't completely crazy. It depends on the numbers. Get me the numbers, and I will tell you if it's crazy or not."

I can't believe Betty actually thinks there is a chance.

Has the whole world gone insane?

"Betty, I don't exactly have millions of dollars laying around."

"Obviously. But there might be another way. We can figure something out...once we have the numbers."

The only numbers I can see making this happen are lottery numbers.

Maybe I should buy a ticket.

FORTY-EIGHT

FOR MOST OF the next day, instead of sewing dresses, I brainstorm ways to tell Betty about our mom's diary. She got so excited when I told her our mom had been an artist; there is no way she wouldn't want to know more.

So once Gloria leaves for the day, I go to my bedroom and look for the package underneath my mattress.

It is still there.

I don't know why it wouldn't be. Maybe because losing things is one of my mastered skills.

As I remove the little bundle of papers from the envelope, Coco peeks around the corner of my (non-existent) door, and then comes to lie on the small patch of floor beside my bed.

I place my hand on top of the letter our mom wrote us. And I know this sounds weird, but it makes me feel as though I'm touching her hand.

My plan is to practice reading the artist diary entry out loud, so I can read it to Betty during my next visit, sort of like a performance. I'm dramatic that way. But as I finish removing the binder clip from the bundle, my phone rings.

Setting everything aside, I search the room for my phone. It isn't in here. I follow the rings until I find it on the workroom table.

"Hello," I say hurriedly, hoping whoever is on the other end hasn't disconnected.

Please let it be Aaron.

"Erin! Brian from the frame shop here!"

"Oh. Hi, Brian."

"I'm calling because I found a hidden message in the canvas of your painting."

"You what?" I instantly feel lightheaded, so I take a seat at the table.

"A secret code, like, you know, in *The Da Vinci Code*."

A secret code? Is this another clue from my mom?

But she wrote that we wouldn't find anything else.

"Hello, Erin? Are you still there?"

"What does—what does the code say?" I close my eyes in anticipation.

"The code says...fooled you again!"

I'm going to kill this man!

I'm never framing anything at his shop ever again!

"Ha-ha. Good one," I say, even though I'm annoyed. He doesn't realize the significance of his joke.

"By the way, what did you find in that package I gave you?"

"Just some, um, old receipts." And he won't get to know the significance after that little prank he pulled.

"Well, that's no fun. What I actually called to tell you is that your painting will be ready for pick up on the first of September. Come by anytime after ten to get it."

"Okay, thanks. I will."

"You have a super-duper day now!" he says, ending the call.

I'm so gullible. I can't believe I bought his "secret code" joke. I guess when it comes to my mom, I will believe anything if it means I will get something more from her.

When I go back to my room, the diary entries are no longer on the bed. I check the envelope, but it's empty. Then, I check underneath the mattress. But they are not there, either.

Where could they possibly have gone?

They couldn't have disappeared into thin air—could they?

No, they couldn't.

Coco!

"Coco! Where are you, honey? *COCO!*"

Even though I consider Coco to be human-like, every now and again, she reminds me she is still a dog.

My first stop is the bathroom, her favourite hiding spot, but she isn't in there. I already know she isn't in the workroom, so I walk towards the open concept kitchen-living room area.

"If you come out from wherever you are, I'll give you a treat."

Nothing.

"I'll make you a pretty pink bow so people will know you're a girl."

Coco comes wandering out from behind the kitchen counter with a guilty look on her face.

I squat down to her level. "Coco, that was a very naughty thing you did. Very naughty. You know not to do that."

She tilts her head to the side and bats her long lashes at me. It's impossible for me to be mad at her. I get up and go around the kitchen counter.

Maybe it is possible.

My mom's diary entries are scattered across the floor and some of the papers are torn. Tears are burning in my eyes.

"*Go to your bed, Coco!* You have been a naughty, naughty dog! No pink bow for you!"

A double insult: calling her a dog and denying her fashion. She whimpers, then heads off in the direction of her dog bed.

Picking up the sheets of paper, I place them on the kitchen counter. Everything is out of order, although I have no idea what order they were meant to be read in. I know that my mom's letter and the artist entry go first, so I search for those in the pile.

And, of course, as my bad luck would have it, most of the damage Coco inflicted was to the artist entry. The one that Betty wants to see. I find some of the pieces and put it back together, but there is a huge chunk missing.

So I get down on my hands and knees, searching the area. But after looking everywhere, I don't find anything.

Oh, my god. Did Coco eat it?

My heart fills with sadness.

How could I let this happen?

Quickly, I scan the other diary entries, putting the remaining ones into chronological order, as I have no idea what order my mom wanted us to read them in. The pile seems lighter than I remember.

Did I pick them all up?

I count them. There are five, plus my mom's letter. Only five. But I never thought to count them before, so I have no way of knowing if this is everything. It also could be lighter because of the missing pieces.

After finding some tape, I try to repair the torn artist entry. Then, I take a clean sheet of paper from the printer tray and sit down on a stool at the kitchen counter.

I begin rewriting the entry, adding in the missing section from memory. It's all I can think to do. I remember a lot of what she wrote, which surprises me, but not everything.

Once I'm finished, I allow the tears that have been patiently waiting to finally fall.

Why wasn't I more careful?

There are so few diary entries as it is. What if something else happens, and I lose the rest of them before having the chance to read them?

I imagine all the possible horrible scenarios that could take place, from a raging fire to invading zombies. I can't let that happen. I won't let that happen. If I hadn't already read the artist entry, I wouldn't have been able to recreate most of it. What if that had happened to one I hadn't read?

These diary entries are the last thing I will ever receive from my mom. I can't risk not knowing what she wanted to tell us.

I need to keep reading them. All of them. *Right now.*

Betty will understand. I will explain to her what happened, and she will understand why I did what I did.

She has to.

FORTY-NINE

~Diary Entry~

OCTOBER 10, 1991

Dearest Elizabeth,

It's official: My last name is now Bettencourt. I signed the papers today, ironically, on my thirtieth birthday. I suppose this signifies a sort of rebirth, although I'm still processing how I feel about it. Just hearing that name generates so many different emotions in me. But it isn't as if I would ever stop hearing it, after all, it's the last name of my girls.

I always assumed it would become my last name, too, when I married their father. But we kept putting off getting married because of one excuse or another. Not enough money. Not enough time to plan with two small children. And then, he left, and there was no one there to get married to anymore. Given the circumstances of his leaving, I guess I caught a lucky break. But the name issue remained.

Originally, I thought about changing the girls' name to my own, but that isn't really my last name, either, is it? I remember how mad I was when my *maman* changed it to my stepfather's name after she remarried. I wanted to keep the last name of my *papa*, in his memory and because it was the only one I had ever known. But I was too young to get to choose.

So I decided not to choose for my girls, and chose for myself, instead. Besides, Betty has already learned how to spell Bettencourt, not an easy feat for a four-year-old. It may have led to questions from her about why it was changing; questions I didn't have the energy to answer.

And, hopefully, it will also stop the unspoken questions from the other mothers at their school. It's the 1990s, for Pete's sake, not the 1950s. I didn't think people cared about this stuff anymore. But I see the questions wash over their faces, and I know it still does. If it comes up, which I doubt it will, I will say I finally got around to changing it to my married name. They don't need to know the truth. Most of them address me as Mrs. Bettencourt, anyway.

The main point is, my daughters and I now share the same last name. That is what matters. At the end of the day, a name is just a name.

Isn't it?

If that is true, then how come I feel as if I have lost another piece of myself?

Love you always,
Lizzie

—

I'm illegitimate. This bothers me for some reason. Even though, I know it shouldn't. As my mom wrote, this isn't the 1950s—or whatever decade it was when people frowned upon this sort of thing.

Maybe it bothers me because I didn't know until now. I had always assumed my parents had divorced after my father left.

Does it really make any difference?

No, but it almost feels as if I have just been told I'm adopted, and now I'm wondering who my real parents are.

What else was my mom hiding from us? What else does she want to share with us through these diary entries?

Maybe I don't want to know what that is.

Hold on a second.

If I'm illegitimate, that means Betty is illegitimate, too. Given she is on the verge of having children of her own, I'm not sure she would be happy to find this out right now. I should probably keep this particular diary entry to myself. Her OB-GYN said Betty has to keep her stress levels to a minimum so that she doesn't go into early labour. Plus, Betty has always been more conservative than I am. So if this new information bothers me, and it does, it would definitely bother her.

My poor mom. I can't imagine what it would have been like having her name taken away from her as a kid after her father passed away. There is no way for me to ask her, either. And now, I know for sure, I don't have a grandfather on my mother's side.

It is too much to take in. I had planned to read all the diary entries straight through, without stopping, but I can't. I need to process what I learned. Honestly, I'm afraid of what I may learn next.

So I put the diary entries back into the envelope, then place the envelope on the top shelf of the front hall closet. I figure this is the safest place for it. I can easily reach up and grab it in the event of an emergency, like a fire (or zombie attack). And there is no way Coco can get to it.

Coco!

I find her sleeping on her dog bed and give her a kiss on her tiny head. She opens her eyes for a moment before closing them again.

The best thing about dogs is, even though they may eat your mom's long-lost diary, they won't lie to you. They don't know how.

"Did you bring it?" Betty asks.

"Bring what?"

She rolls her eyes at me. "The note about mom being an artist."

She remembered. Of course, she remembered. I have been avoiding visiting Betty for the last few days. I wasn't ready to face her, given what I had recently learned. I was hoping she had forgotten about the note, but I guess "baby brain," or whatever it is called, hasn't kicked-in, yet.

"Sorry, Betty. But I don't have it." I see her face fall in disappointment. "I...I placed it by my bag so I would remember to bring it, but then, Coco got a hold of it and tore it to shreds. She even ate part of it! I'm really sorry."

This is mostly the truth, although I'm totally throwing Coco under the bus.

"That is too bad," Betty says, looking as if she may cry. "I would have liked to have seen it."

"I know." I sit on the bed beside her, giving her an awkward side hug. "Hey, how is the baby-naming coming along?" I ask, trying to cheer her up.

It works! Her face immediately perks up.

"Actually, I've made a spreadsheet." (Betty loves spreadsheets.) "I have a list of names, along with the meaning of each one."

"Cool! Can I see it?"

"Nice try, Erin. You can't fool me that easily. But I did want to get your opinion on middle names."

"Okay, shoot!" I say, happy to be involved in some way. Plus, this might give me a clue about the sex of the babies.

"Matt and I are leaning towards having Bettencourt for both of their middle names. What do you think?"

I freeze. If Betty and I had this conversation a week ago, I would have been completely in favour of it. But now, things are different somehow. Which is stupid because my whole business is based on our last name. And it isn't as if I didn't know it was our father's last name when I decided to use it, regardless of him being married to our mom or not. But it does seem a bit tainted now.

"It's kind of long," I say finally.

"Yeah, that's the drawback if we choose it. Remember how long it took us to learn how to spell it properly?"

No, it took me forever to learn how to spell it properly. I can still hear Betty's little voice, instructing me: "It's like the start of Betty, B-E-T-T, and then an E for Erin…" Even though she was almost a full-year younger than me.

There is a slight tap on the door before Matt comes in with a tray of food.

"Sorry to interrupt, ladies, but someone has to eat," Matt says, placing the tray on Betty's belly, which makes the perfect resting spot.

"I hate food," Betty says.

"Think of our unborn children. I'm sure they don't hate food."

Betty gives him a scornful look, and then takes a bite.

"Can I get you anything?" Matt asks me.

"No, thanks. I should be going, anyway." I say, heading for the bedroom door.

"Don't forget to get me those numbers!" Betty yells out to me.

"What numbers?"

Betty rolls her eyes at me for the second time that day. "The numbers for the vintage shop."

"Betty, it isn't going to hap—"

"It could happen. You're just suffering from Impostor Syndrome."

"Impostor-what?"

"Impostor Syndrome. I learned about it while listening to a podcast. It's where you don't feel as if you're good enough and think everyone is going to find out you're a fraud. Just get me the numbers."

"Fine. I'll get you the numbers," I say, forcing a smile on my face as I wave goodbye from the bedroom door.

My smile fades as soon as I turn my back to them.

Impostor Syndrome.

That sounds about right. Except, I am a fraud.

FIFTY

I'M STILL Lady Bettencourt's official errand girl. Although the business has graduated to using a courier service for picking up most of our dress deliveries, whenever there is a special or rush order, I like to handle it personally by taking it to my trusted post office in the underground path.

The underground path is actually more of a maze, connecting the majority of the office buildings in the downtown financial core, with a bunch of shops and restaurants along the way to tempt you. I spent many lunch breaks back in my cubicle days wandering in this maze...and being tempted.

Because it's summer, the path isn't as busy as usual. The office workers are outside, trying to get in some sun before it goes away. Without those office workers swarming around, it feels sort of like an underground ghost town. It must be spooky down here at night once the (living) inhabitants of the surrounding buildings have cleared out for the day.

After delivering the packages to the post office magicians and grabbing a latte (iced with almond milk), I decide I also want to be enjoying the sun, so I head for the nearest exit.

In my eagerness to get out of this subterranean maze, I bump into someone who is just as eager to get into it.

"Oh, sorry," I say, turning slightly to acknowledge the person.

All I see is red.

Fiery red.

A fiery red mane of curly hair.

Vanessa!

I have been dreading this moment ever since our last confrontation. I knew the odds of running into her at some point were likely, but as it hadn't happened in almost a year, I had let my guard down.

She hasn't seen me, yet. She doesn't know I'm the one who bumped into her.

Please don't let her turn around.

Maybe I should make a run for it.

Would she recognize me from behind?

I can't risk it. If I show any sign of weakness, she will pounce.

"Watch where—" she says as she turns in my direction, then stops. Her striking, amber eyes bulge for a moment when she recognizes it's me.

"Hi, Vanessa," I say casually, deciding to play the sports(wo)man card. She won't be expecting that.

"Erin."

This is awkward. We should walk away from each other, but neither one of us does. It's as if a force field is keeping us here, locked together for a certain amount of time before we can be released.

"I hope you've been well," I say. And I do, even after everything that has happened, I do want her to be well, to have found some happiness in her life, instead of trying to take the happiness of others away.

"I'm great—really great. Just had lunch with a client. A very big client. We're working on something that's going to be *huge*."

"That's great, Vanessa. I'm glad you've landed back on your feet." I immediately regret my choice of words. She won't like them.

She narrows her eyes at me. "I heard you added a *few* more designs to your lineup. So I see things are pretty much status quo for you."

Don't let her intimidate you, Erin! She is not the boss of you!

"Actually," I say, "I have something big of my own I'm working on."

"Hmm, what's that?" she asks, pretending not to be interested.

Yes, what is that?

"I'm...um..." *Think, Erin, think!* "I'm—I'm opening a flagship retail shop for Lady Bettencourt. I signed the lease on a space this morning. You heard it here first!" And so have I.

"Well, good luck with that," she says sarcastically, although I know I have taken her (and not only myself) by surprise with my little announcement.

"Thanks! And good luck with your client thing."

There is another awkward pause where we linger, staring at one another, wondering what to do next.

"I should probably—" I say.

"I have a—" Vanessa says.

And then, the force field breaks. We are released. We turn away from each other without saying goodbye, to reenter our own universes.

Except, in my universe, I now have an imaginary flagship retail shop to open.

Why would I say that?

I can't believe I'm still trying to impress Vanessa. Still trying to make her see I'm not just a pattern-cutter with an online shop, carrying only a *few* more dress designs than when her and I worked together.

That was really dumb.

Or was it?

Maybe this is the next step for Lady Bettencourt. We do need more space. Why can't that space also include a retail setup? Haven't I always wanted a bricks-and-mortar store of my own? Having a rack of my dresses at the vintage shop is great, but having a store full of them would be even better.

Betty is right. I am suffering from Impostor Syndrome.

Maybe running into Vanessa was the push I needed to realize this is exactly what I'm meant to do.

So I reach into my dress pocket and take out my phone.

It rings a couple of times before I hear her voice on the other end.

"Lizzie, it's Erin. Tell me everything you know about the sale of the vintage shop."

—

After my conversation with Lizzie, I have enough information to start working on a plan to make this impossible dream possible. Lizzie shared "the numbers" she has heard being batted around. The very large numbers. Even Betty will be daunted by them.

However, an idea is forming in my head to workaround that. But I need it to steep a bit more, as Lizzie would say, before I reveal it. I know that somehow, I will find a way to make this work. I know it.

Even with my excitement at the prospect of having my own retail store, I can't get my encounter with Vanessa out of my mind. It's playing on a constant loop in my brain.

But I don't want her connected with my decision to try to get the vintage shop, anymore. I want that decision, going forward, to come from a pure place. And I know the *perfect* way to forget about Vanessa.

I need to read another one of my mom's diary entries.

So the moment I'm settled back at the condo, that is exactly what I do.

FIFTY-ONE
~Diary Entry~

JANUARY 4, 1998

Dearest Elizabeth,

My apologies for my absence. It's been a very confusing and emotional few weeks. I wasn't ready to write about it until now, but now, may be the only chance I get.

It turns out, I have—I can't believe I'm writing this—I have cancer. Ovarian cancer, if you want to be specific, and I'm finding cancer is quite specific. I found out a couple of days before Christmas.

And, of course, I couldn't tell the girls. How would that go? "Merry Christmas, darlings! Looks like mommy has been naughty this year because she got cancer. Let's open your presents and see what you got!" No, I couldn't do that to them. But it was so hard watching them open those presents, wondering if this would be our last Christmas together.

Tomorrow, I'm having a hysterectomy. There was a scheduling mix-up, and now I have to go in earlier than I had planned for, making me have to rearrange so many things in such a short period of time.

Honestly, I haven't really processed any of this. I'm just following the steps I have been told to follow, doing my best to cope, and trying not to be bitter.

When I found out I had cancer, I asked the doctors if I would need chemotherapy. But they said they had caught it early enough that it could likely be avoided by having the surgery and, if necessary, a few rounds of radiation. So I chose the surgery.

It isn't for vanity purposes that I don't want chemo. I'm not worried about losing my hair. It's that I don't want Erin and Betty to know I'm sick. I don't want to place that burden on them or for them to see me suffering like that, especially as everything will probably be okay.

But I had to explain why I would be away for weeks, so I told them I was going on a holiday because I needed a little rest. Even telling them that has made them anxious, given that their father went on a "holiday" and never came back. So I promised to call every day. I hope that puts them somewhat at ease.

Gloria has agreed to watch them. She is my saviour. I will be staying with Victor while I recover from the surgery. Things have been tense between us. My getting cancer has tested the strength of our relationship.

Everything is being tested by this.

I hate to admit it, but a small part of me wouldn't mind not waking up from the operation. It's just that I'm always so tired. It would be nice to get to sleep for an eternity.

But that part is minuscule in comparison to the part that wants to live and see my children grow up. They are not even teenagers, yet. They need me. They don't have anyone else to look after them.

If only I had planned ahead for the possibility of something like this happening. I don't even have a will! Or life insurance. And now, the chances of my getting life insurance are slim. I have failed my girls in that regard.

I know my *maman* would take them if the worst was to happen. But that is the last thing I would want. They don't even know she exists. I have talked to Gloria, and she said she would watch over them. I know it's too much to ask of a friend, but I'm desperate, and Gloria is a good person. Let's pray it doesn't come to that.

Pray. I have been doing a lot of that lately. I'm not a big believer in religion anymore, but God, if you are out there, please let me live. Please let me live for my girls.

Love you always,
Lizzie

I'm dumbfounded. This doesn't make any sense. Our mom had cancer—in 1998? She never told us, not even after what must have been a relapse, ten years later. Betty and I thought she had gotten cancer for the first time.

And that holiday she took, I do remember that. I was so worried she wouldn't make it back for my twelfth birthday. How selfish of me. But how was I to know?

She did make it back in time for my birthday, but she was really skinny and didn't look like herself. I thought her break must not have been very restful.

What I had forgotten was Gloria taking care of us. We stayed at her house for weeks. It was such a weird, confusing time. Maybe I blocked it out because I was scared our mom wasn't coming back for us.

And who was Victor? I never knew my mom dated after my father. She never introduced us to anyone. It's strange, but the idea of my mom having a boyfriend, makes me think of her—and this should be obvious—but it makes me think of her as...a woman. I know, I know. But to me, my mom was always just my mom. My everything. I'm beginning to realize she was more than that. She had a separate, private life of her own.

Apparently, Victor wasn't the only one she didn't introduce us to. *I have a grandmother.* Not a very nice one it seems, but somewhere out there, I have a grandmother!

Tomorrow, when Gloria comes to work at the condo, I'm asking her a bunch of questions. She can't deny Betty and I lived with her. That will be my "in." She has to know more. And this time, I'm getting it out of her.

The next morning, I get a message from Gloria saying she is working from home because she has a dentist's appointment that afternoon.

Now I have to wait a whole day more before I get answers to my many questions.

But there is one other person who might remember something from that time: Betty.

FIFTY-TWO

FIVE MINUTES. That is how long I force myself to wait after I have settled into Betty's bedroom. She is propped up with her pillows, and I'm sitting beside her on top of the bed covers.

"Hey, remember when we were kids and mom went away on vacation?" I say, trying to sound casual.

"Vacation? I don't remember mom *ever* taking a vacation," Betty says, flipping through a parenting magazine.

"When we were eleven or so. We stayed with Gloria while she was away."

She puts down the magazine and turns towards me. "I had completely forgotten about that."

"Don't you think it's strange she went away without us? That wasn't like her."

"Didn't she go to Florida or something? She probably needed a break. What made you think of that?"

"Because I found mom's diary, and she wrote about that. Except, she wasn't on vacation, she was recovering from *cancer*. Isn't that crazy?"

That is not what I actually say. What I do say is, "Um, it just popped into my head. Maybe because of working with Gloria. I don't know." I shrug my shoulders to support my fake confusion.

It doesn't seem Betty remembers anything more from that time than I do. It's almost as though the both of us have blocked it out. Which is normal for me, but not so normal for Betty. Maybe she was afraid our mom wouldn't come back, either.

But there is another reason why I wanted to visit Betty today. "Guess what?" I say excitedly.

"What?"

"I'm buying the vintage shop!"

Her eyes light up at my news. "Awesome, Erin!"

"Okay, not officially, but I want to try to get it. Arthur, the owner, is away on business for a few days, so there is still time to come up with a plan before he puts it on the market. Oh, and I got the numbers from Lizzie."

"And?"

I go over to my bag and pull out a pen and a scrap piece of paper.

"What are you doing?" Betty asks, confused.

"I'm writing it down," I say, scribbling the number on the paper.

"But I'm right here. Just tell me."

"It's more fun this way." I fold up the paper and hand it to her.

She rolls her eyes at me. She has to stop doing that. But as she unfolds the paper, instead of her eyes rolling, they are practically bulging out of her head.

"Wow, that is more than I thought. Erin, I don't think..."

"I know, I know. Impossible."

"What if you looked at some other locations? What about Queen Street West? Lady Bettencourt would be a total fit in that area."

"But I don't feel as if *I* fit there. Not that I feel as if I fit in Yorkville, either, but it's the vintage shop, itself, that I want. I have a connection to it. I need to at least try to get it before I look for something else. Plus, I have an idea. I need to do a little more research before I tell you, but when I do, I was hoping you could go over the numbers with me."

"Of course."

"Thanks, Betty. You're the best."

"So much secrecy," she says, laughing in a conspiratorial manner.

But her words hit me hard. She doesn't realize their double-meaning. I laugh, too, but I know my face reveals everything. Luckily, she has turned away from me in time to keep my cover.

We reassume our positions. Whenever I stay for a longer visit, I lie down next to Betty, and we read magazines or books or, in my case, surf the web on my phone for a couple of hours. We used to do this when we were kids. We would choose one of our twin beds and spend entire afternoons lying there, reading (Betty) and daydreaming (me). Or sometimes in our mom's bed, and she would come join us.

Betty is right. There is so much secrecy. Too much secrecy.

I have to tell her. This has gotten out of hand.

For the next ten minutes, I lie there thinking about how I will do it until finally I say, "Betty, I have something to tell you, but please don't say anything until I'm done." I'm looking up at the white ceiling. It's easier to admit my sins without having to face her. (I understand now why they have those dark confession booths in churches.)

And then, I tell her.

I tell her about the painting and the package. I tell her how I was only planning to read one, but then, I read another one and another one. How I couldn't stop myself because it was like getting a piece of our mom back. And how I kept coming up with justifications as to why it was okay for me to do what I was doing.

Then, I apologize for not telling her sooner. How I shouldn't have been so selfish, keeping this last gift from our mom all to myself. I should have shared it with her. Or, at least, given her the chance to refuse it. But I tell her I was afraid of what she would say. That maybe she wouldn't want me to read them, either.

When I'm finished, I turn my head towards her. "I'm so sorry, Betty. I've messed up...again."

Her face is turned away from me.

She must be really mad.

I sit up in bed. "Betty, please, you have to understand!"

She still doesn't say anything.

Her hair is covering part of her face, so I gently pull it back.

Dammit! She is asleep.

I finally told her the truth, after all of that agonizing over what I should do, and she slept through it.

But as I gaze down at her and see how peaceful she looks as she sleeps, how innocent, I realize another stronger truth: I don't want to take that away from her.

Maybe the universe didn't want me to tell Betty; didn't want her to know what I have learned.

Every time I have tried to tell someone about my mom's diary (excluding Coco), something always stops it from happening.

Maybe my mom's diary is meant just for me, and I am the only one who is supposed to read it.

So when I get back home, I take the package out of the hall closet and go into the bathroom, closing the door behind me. Then, I sit in the bathtub with the shower curtain drawn around me, shutting me off from the rest of the world. Well, except for Coco, who I can hear whimpering on the other side of the door.

"Sorry, Coco. But I need some alone time. Go play!" I yell from the tub.

She whimpers a bit more before going off to do whatever she does when I'm not watching.

There are two diary entries left to read. Only two. I want to read them slowly, to savour them. But it isn't in my nature. And some things never seem to change.

FIFTY-THREE

~Diary Entry~

FEBRUARY 13, 2002

Dearest Elizabeth,

Today was one of the strangest days of my life. In the morning, I went to my mother's funeral. And then, in the afternoon, I celebrated Erin's sweet sixteen.

When my *papa* died, I was overcome with grief. Grief that has never fully gone away. Grief that is always in the shadows, waiting to make an appearance when I least expect it to. I idolized and adored my father. And I was certain of his love for me. Our time together was cut short, but it was filled with so many wonderful memories.

With my *maman* now gone, the situation is completely different. Our relationship had always been strained. In my mind, I had convinced myself that her passing wouldn't affect me; that attending her funeral would feel like attending the funeral of an acquaintance.

Silly me. There is so much I still don't understand about this life. These things never hit us the way we imagine.

I hadn't spoken to my *maman* since I told her I had cancer. I was angry and hurt at her reaction, even though I should have known to have expected it. So I said I wanted her out of my life, once and for all. That getting cancer made me realize I was being reborn, and I wanted to be reborn motherless. I said some other dramatic nonsense in the heat of the moment that I didn't really mean. But my pride stopped me from reaching out to her again. Likely, hers as well.

Perhaps we were too similar. Too stubborn to let the other get her way. We spent four years not speaking to each other, and now that silence is permanent.

It's so pointless. So stupid. We have cost my daughters the chance to have a grandmother, to have a part of their history. *And for what?* I will never get the answer to that question, to any of the many questions I have.

At the funeral, I found myself shedding the tears I had bottled up all these years. They came pouring out of me. My stepfather was kind, but I think he was suspicious of my emotions, given our estrangement...and so were his adult children.

They probably thought I was hoping to get something from her will. I wanted to scream at them: "I don't want money! I don't want anything from any of you! All I want is another chance with my *maman*!"

But, of course, I didn't say any of that.

And then, I had to put a cap on my bottle of tears and reapply my "happy face." The girls weren't aware of any of this. I promised Erin the three of us would go to the Royal York Hotel for afternoon tea, our birthday tradition.

The thing is, I got that tradition from my own mother. That is how we had celebrated my birthdays after my father died, in those couple of years before she remarried, when it had been just the two of us. At least, I have those memories, so that is something I can cherish.

As I write this, I'm shedding a few more tears. I don't think I tightened the bottle cap tight enough. No matter her wrongdoings, she was my mother, my *maman*. The only one I will ever have.

Love you always,
Lizzie

—

That is not how I remember my sixteenth birthday.

The way I remember my sixteenth birthday is as one of the best birthdays of my life. Both Betty and I got to skip class. (Betty wasn't as excited about that as I was.) Ever since we began school, the deal was

I wouldn't have to go to class on my birthday if it fell on a weekday because Betty always got her birthday off.

Did I ever mention Betty was born on Christmas Day?

She was the best Christmas present I don't remember receiving. My own birthday was almost on Valentine's Day, but alas, I was a few hours short from being born on the day of love.

Back to my sixteenth birthday. I had made myself a dress—my first one ever—to replicate a design I had seen in *Seventeen* magazine. I loved that dress. I had also taken the time to properly straighten my naturally wavy hair. There were no kinks: a small miracle. I felt so grown-up.

At the Royal York Hotel, I remember us getting my favourite table, eating the delicious tiny sandwiches and scones, and having sips of our mom's mimosa.

I even remember the presents I got. Betty gave me Clinique Happy perfume and my mom gave me a necklace I still wear sometimes.

What I don't remember was our mom being sad. But I wasn't looking for her to be sad, either. If she had been, I would have assumed it was because her daughter was growing up.

I was just so excited to be sixteen. After so many years of waiting, it was here. *I was sixteen!* My life would officially start. Or, at least, that is what I thought.

But maybe kids, especially teenagers, don't really want to know what their parents are going through because they are so self-absorbed in their own lives. Looking back now, that day must have been so hard for her. And she had to go through it on her own.

Her mother had died. *My grandmother had died.*

Now I will never have the chance to meet my grandmother, either. To see what she was like for myself. To ask her my own unanswered questions.

There is no one left in our mom's family who knew her, except for Betty and me.

I lie back and close my eyes. It's too sad to think about, but I can already feel the tears falling down my face.

—

Everywhere I look, I see white. Bright white. I'm freezing, and my body is aching from being contorted into a weird shape.

Where the heck am I? Have I been kidnapped? Is this...Is this heaven?

Oh, right, I'm still in the bathtub. I must have dozed off.

What time is it?

I reach for my phone: 4:44 a.m.

There is something about being awake at four-anything in the morning that gives me an uneasy feeling. It's almost as though I'm caught in-between two worlds: the sleeping and the waking. The feeling is amplified by the fact I'm in an enclosed space.

I stretch out my sore limbs, then pull back the shower curtain. As I open the bathroom door to make my exit, I narrowly avoid stepping in poo. Dog poo.

Coco!

I deserve it. I never took her out for her walk yesterday. After I clean it up, I find Coco sleeping soundly in her bed. I stroke her head softly so as not to wake her.

Then, I return my mom's diary to the hall closet without reading the last entry. I'm too tired and anxious to read more.

Once in my room, I lie on my bed, even though I know I won't fall back to sleep. But I need to rest before Gloria gets here in a few hours. She is the only chance I have to get answers to those unanswered questions.

FIFTY-FOUR

"NATALIA? WHAT ARE you doing here?" I ask as I open the front door. I was expecting Gloria, her sister, to be on the other side.

"For the meeting. Is not today?" she asks, making a confused face.

Crap. I forgot about our monthly team meeting. I guess some things never change. But I have been so preoccupied, it didn't cross my mind, and now I haven't prepared anything.

Because we can't all work out of the condo anymore, once a month we meet in-person to see each other's faces and discuss any important issues. I try to make the meetings fun, given that I hated them back in my cubicle days.

"No, no, it is. Sorry, "I say. "Come in, come in!" Another thought occurs to me. "I forgot to get the donuts."

"No worry, *querida*. Sophia say she bringing *loukoumades*, is like donuts."

Better than donuts, like super Greek donuts.

Natalia calls me *querida*, too. I think it's an older generation Portuguese thing. I mean, I am their boss, and they go around calling me "sweetie" all the time. But I don't mind. It's a term of endearment. There is something motherly about it, something protective. Especially how they pronounce it: lower than their regular tone of voice and drawn out.

As I'm closing the door, I see Sophia coming down the hall, carrying a covered aluminum tray. Reopening the door, I say, "Hi, Sophia! Long time no see!" It does feel as though I haven't seen her, or my team of ladies, in a long time.

"Erin! You look tired. You work too hard," she says as she approaches me.

Sophia doesn't call me *querida*, probably because she is Greek, not Portuguese, but she has her own special way of talking to me. Half the time, I'm not sure if I should be offended at the stuff she says, although I know it also comes from a concerned, motherly place.

I thank her for bringing the *loukoumades*, taking the aluminum tray from her so she can get settled in. I bring the tray into the kitchen, where Natalia is already getting plates and mugs out of the cabinets and placing them on the counter.

"I start the coffee," she says, smiling.

How could I not love them?

They take care of me.

I go into the sewing workroom to setup chairs around the large table for the meeting. I'm a chair short now that our team has grown so much. But that is okay, I can stand.

In quick succession, everyone else arrives. First, Trendy, the new social media intern. Then, Mila, carrying a bunch of bags of secondhand clothes for the seamstresses to take home with them. Followed by, Leo, the new freelance photographer, and the two part-time seamstresses, Patricia and Ming. The new team members seem to be shy at first, but slowly, they start to mingle with the others.

Where is Gloria?

She has to make it. I need to talk to her when the meeting is over.

After several more minutes, she arrives.

"Sorry, sorry! There was accident on highway," she says breathlessly as she rushes in through the door.

Once everyone is settled in the sewing workroom, I look at each of their faces. It's still weird to think I have a staff.

As I'm about to begin the meeting, Mila asks, "What about Betty?"

Oh, yeah, Betty.

I dial Betty on my phone, putting her on speaker when she answers.

Another several minutes pass as everyone asks Betty how she is doing. They are (almost) as excited as I am about the twins. The twins will be the first babies from the Lady Bettencourt team. Possibly, the only ones for a while, given our older demographic.

When the chatter dies down, I finally begin the meeting.

Item number one on the agenda is to properly introduce the new members to the rest of the team, as this is their first face-to-face meeting with everyone.

I'm always anxious when I bring on someone new. All of us get along so well, I don't want to wreck our dynamic. But I can already see that they are a fit. They have that Lady Bettencourt vibe. I can't define what that is, but I know it when I see it.

Afterwards, I tell the team about some upcoming orders we are getting, then share the designs I worked on over the summer for our fall lineup, which is going into production the following week. I mention the space issues we are having, saying that I'm working on a plan to address that. I worry Betty may let something slip about the vintage shop, but there is nothing for me to worry about. Betty doesn't let things slip.

Once everything has been covered off, I ask if anyone has any issues or concerns. There aren't any, so I call the meeting to be adjourned.

No, really, I actually say, "This meeting is now adjourned!" Then, I slam my empty coffee mug on the table to make it official.

What? Not professional?

Whatever.

If we have to have meetings, and we do, then there has to be something entertaining about them. And there also has to be donuts, or, in this case, yummy *loukoumades*.

After everyone has filed out, Gloria and I are left alone in the condo. I wait as long as I physically can before I bring up the subject.

"Gloria, can I talk to you about something?"

She stops cutting the pattern she is working on and looks at me. "What is it, *querida*? You okay?"

"I'm fine. It's just—it's just I remembered something."

"What you remember?"

"I remembered living with you for weeks when I was almost twelve. And I know Betty and I were with you, not because our mom was on vacation, but because she was sick." I wait, but Gloria doesn't respond, so I go on. "I'm sorry to put you in this position, but my mom isn't here for me to ask her these questions. I only want to know the truth." Before I can stop them, I feel tears beginning to form.

Don't cry, Erin. Don't cry!

But it's too late, a few tears have already escaped. I can't help it. For one, I didn't sleep very much last night, which makes me extra emotional. And for another, everything that I have learned from my mom's diary is getting to me. It's a one-way form of communication. I can't ask her, why this? Or, why that?

It's not fair.

"I told her to tell you girls. I told her." Gloria shakes her head. "But she didn't want you to worry. I promised on my children's life I say nothing." She stops for a moment before continuing, "But, maybe, a promise like that breaks when someone dies. I think, anyway. So, yes, she was sick, and you girls stayed at my house. Okay?"

"Okay, thank you! Do you—do you know who Victor was?" I ask, pushing my luck.

"Her boyfriend."

"For how long? Was he still her boyfriend when she died?"

"No—unless they getting back together when I lose touch with her. They breaking up a little bit after your mom's operation."

"Do you know why?"

"Not really. He was younger. Maybe he want kids, and your mom couldn't have them anymore."

Something occurs to me that has never occurred to me before: Gloria knew my mom more than anyone else I know, except for Betty and me. But she also knew her on another level, a woman-to-woman level. She is a potential wealth of information—if she is willing to give it.

"What about her mother, my grandmother? Did you ever meet her?"

"Once. She was rich! A big shot."

"And?"

"And what? She was not a nice lady. I'm sorry, *querida*, I know she was your grandma, but she don't take care of your mom when she was sick. She never want to see you girls. When she died, she left nothing for any of you. Nothing for her only daughter! She just think about herself. And everything was about money, money, money."

Maybe it's better that I never got the chance to meet her. Although, to be fair, Gloria's information is based on what my mom told her. And at that time, she was really angry with her mother.

"Anything else?" Gloria asks.

So much else, but nothing immediately comes to mind. But then, I do think of something. "Did our mom breastfeed us? Betty has been wondering." I figure Betty should get something out of this, too.

"Let me think...yes, she did! I remember talking one time about our boobs and how they used to be nicer."

I start laughing. I can't help it. Gloria joins me.

When we stop, she comes over to me and places her hand on my cheek. "Anytime you have questions about your mom, you ask me, okay? I think she be happy for me to do that now."

I place my hand on top of hers, look into her eyes, and say, "*Obrigada*."

FIFTY-FIVE

"MS. BETTENCOURT, there is a delivery here for you," the concierge says, as I enter the condo building after having taken Coco for her afternoon walk.

"*Ooh,* I wonder if it's those new scissors I ordered!" I say excitedly at the prospect.

He doesn't respond. I guess he doesn't think new scissors warrants this level of excitement. I thank him as he hands me the package, which is larger and heavier than what I imagine a box containing scissors to be.

Did I order something else?

I must have. I'm always ordering something for the business. But only my name and address appear on the package; there is no other label to give me a clue.

Once I return to the condo, I check-in on Gloria, who is busy sewing away in the workroom. I head back to the kitchen to open the package, carefully removing the label and tape so that I can reuse the box. Inside, I find a sheet of paper and some folded clothing.

I definitely didn't order this.

As I look closer at the paper, I see it's actually a typed letter. A typed letter signed by—my eyes must be playing tricks on me, because it's signed by Carol Devall.

Yes, that Carol.

Why would Carol send me a package? And how did she get my home address? There is only a postal box address on the Lady Bettencourt website.

Wait. I *gave* her my address. After I was fired, Betty told me to contact my former employer with my new address so I wouldn't miss receiving any final tax documents.

The only phone number I had was Carol's, so I left her one of my famous, early morning, unscripted voice messages. I pretended to be someone else calling on my behalf, using a fake accent. But then, I kept slipping in-and-out of other various accents. Let's just say, I'm pretty sure she knew it was me calling.

Before reading whatever Carol has written in her letter, I feel the need to take a seat at the kitchen counter. It could be anything, and I still find her kind of scary.

Erin,

I saw you on television. I am glad you are finally making something of your life.

This box contains clothing that I have held onto for far too long. I needed to finally rid myself of them or have them turned into something useful. I have chosen the latter.

They belonged to my daughter, Emily, so please take great care with them. They mean the world to me. I would like you to make me something I can wear to remember her by. But not one of your dresses. I don't wear dresses. I trust your judgment—in this matter.

Once completed, please send to my attention at the office, along with how much I owe you for your time. Cost is not an issue.

Regards,
Carol Devall

I try to take in what I read.
Carol has a daughter?
I knew she was divorced, but she said she didn't have any children. I remember thinking she was so cranky because she didn't have a life;

all she had was work. Or maybe, Carol *had* a daughter. She did write "to remember her by." Her daughter must have...

Carefully, I remove the clothing from the box.

There are cute jumpers and patterned dresses with tags from newborn to nine months. There is nothing past nine months.

My heart hurts and tears come to my eyes.

I worked with Carol for almost five years, day-in and day-out, and I knew nothing about her. Maybe she was cranky not because she didn't have a life, but because she had one, and it was taken away from her. Maybe Carol and I aren't as different as we always assumed we were.

How little do we know about other people. We only know what they tell us...or what we eventually find out.

Of course, I can't help thinking how little I knew of my own mom. How I'm finding out aspects of her life only now that she has left us some pieces of a much bigger puzzle.

And I realize, I'm ready. I think I have been subconsciously putting it off because I know it's the last diary entry. There won't be any more words after reading it. My mom will be taken away from me, once again. But I'm ready now to read those final words she wanted to share about her life.

So after Gloria has gone home for the day, that is what I do.

FIFTY-SIX
~Diary Entry~

AUGUST 24, 2008

Dearest Elizabeth,

Erin is back from Europe! How I have missed her! Betty, Matt, and I went to the airport to pick her up. As she came out of the arrival gate, I could see the sadness behind her eyes, even though she welcomed us with a great, big smile. I don't think she found the answers she was seeking while she was over there.

She thinks I don't know why she went to Europe. But I know my daughter. Before leaving, she said she wanted to backpack across Western Europe, taking the train from country-to-country. But I knew which country she really had her mind set-on: France.

I had hoped Jacques wouldn't be too cruel; that her father wouldn't completely ruin her expectations of him. I wanted to stop her from going, to keep her all to myself for these last few months I have remaining. But she didn't know I was sick. And I knew this was something she had to do. So I let her go. Like her, I hoped they would reunite. They are so similar in many ways. I wanted Erin and Betty to get reacquainted with their father, now that their mother was the one leaving them. He is all they have left.

But alas, things don't always go the way we plan or the way we hope. Now I have to tell her that I have to leave her and her sister, too. And I have to do it soon, as our time together is running out.

Perhaps it has been running out from the first time I became sick, and I was only ever granted an extension until my girls were old enough to manage on their own. Maybe that was the actual plan.

Love you always,
Lizzie

—

She knew. My mom knew the reason why I went to Europe.

But how could she have known?

Because it's true: She knew me better than anyone else. She understood me.

I have never admitted to anyone the real reason why I went to Europe, not even to Betty. It was such a foolish (and expensive) thing to do. I actually believed my father would want to see me, to get to know me. I thought now that I was older, we could be friends or something.

Unfortunately, he turned out to be nothing like what I had built up in my mind. He wasn't this charming Frenchman. He was an insensitive jerk.

But I don't want to think about him. Or that other thing that comes to mind whenever I recall my trip to Europe. I want that particular secret to stay in Europe forever. (And inside Mila's and Frankie's heads forever, as they somehow found out what happened when I was there.) Because this isn't about an uncaring father or poor decision-making while travelling, it's about my mom. The one who stayed. The one who gave up her dreams for us. And even though she wrote in her letter that she didn't regret anything, I regret it for her.

What I regret the most for myself is that while I was searching for my father, who didn't care about me, I could have been spending that last summer with my mom, who loved me unconditionally.

I hope one day, I can forgive myself for that. But I didn't know. I didn't know.

I'm so sorry, mom. I'm so sorry.

—

It's starting to get dark, a hint of summer's impending end. A sign on the Mount Pleasant Cemetery main entrance states that the gates close at eight. I check my phone: I have twenty minutes. Thankfully, I got here in time. I needed to come here tonight, after what I read. After everything I have read.

I didn't have any flowers at home, and there wasn't enough time to pick some up on the way. All I have to offer is myself.

And Coco. I brought her along with me for company and for comfort. (Definitely not for protection. Coco would totally save herself.)

As I make my way down the winding path, I realize I have never come here this late before. It's sort of spooky. Maybe it's the overwhelming feeling of being surrounded by so many hopes and dreams, fulfilled and unfulfilled, simultaneously.

But then, I reason, it isn't any spookier than being anywhere else at this time or being here in the daylight. The fear is only in my head.

When I find my mom's grave, I touch it gently, and then I sit on the grass. I see the flowers I planted earlier in the summer because Betty wasn't in the position to do so. I reassure myself it's okay that I didn't bring any. My mom is taken care of.

This whole time, while I was reading my mom's diary entries, I knew she was gone. I couldn't deny it, not like in the past. I knew I wasn't getting her back.

But I did get her back: a part of her I never knew before. And I have come here tonight to say goodbye to that part. I'm not sad. I'm so grateful to my mom for giving me the chance to learn more about her as a woman.

I sit a while longer until one of the Mount Pleasant Cemetery security guards drives up and brakes in front of me. His window is rolled down, and he calls out, "The cemetery closes in five minutes."

Looking closer, I recognize it's him: The same security guard who gave me a ride home all those years ago. I haven't seen him since that day.

"You okay, miss?" he asks, probably because I can't stop staring at him.

He doesn't recognize me. *How could he?* I'm a different person from that day.

"Yeah, I'm okay. Thank you," I say, getting up and wiping the dirt and grass from my legs.

He drives on.

I turn to Coco, who is beginning to nod off. "Wake up, girl. It's time to go home."

She gets up and wanders away from me. I catch up to her just as she is about to pee on someone's gravestone. I quickly grab her leash to pull her away from it, out of respect.

As Coco does her business, I glance towards her intended target. The gravestone is very ornate with lots of flourishes and a script font that makes it difficult to read the person's name, especially as it's getting dark. I take a closer look.

A small gasp escapes when I finally make it out.

Rose Le Duc.

I check the dates.

It's her. It's my grandmother.

This whole time, her grave has been across from my mom's, and I never noticed. Maybe because there is a road that divides them (even in death), but at least they are close together, facing each other, for all of eternity.

Could Betty have known this when she selected our mom's plot? No, she would have mentioned it at some point. It was definitely the universe playing its hand, making sure things were righted in the end.

I walk back to my mom's grave, taking a flower from her planted lot, then return to place it on my grandmother's grave.

My mom would have wanted me to do that.

And I also needed to do it for myself.

FIFTY-SEVEN

I AM AWAKEN BY the sound of my phone ringing.

Who is calling me at this hour?

Through squinting eyes, I look at the screen. It's an unknown number. Maybe I shouldn't answer it. But what if...

"Hel-lo," I say groggily.

"Hey, Lady B."

"*Aaron?* Aaron!" In zero-to-two seconds, I'm fully awake and sitting upright in bed.

"Sorry to wake you, babe."

"No, no, it's okay."

"Listen, I only have a minute. I borrowed a satellite phone from this film producer guy I met here—long story. How are things over there?"

"Everything is good. No babies, yet." It's the overall truth. Anyway, I can't explain my own "long story" in the length of a minute. But there is something I was hoping to ask him, if by chance he called, and him saying "film producer" has triggered it. "Hey, Aaron? *You still there?*"

"I'm still here."

"What was the name of that film you made me watch, the one about the financial crisis?"

"The what?" he asks. There is some static on the line.

"The film about the financial crisis. The one with Ryan Gosling?"

Okay, so I mostly remember the Ryan Gosling part and not the movie itself. But I have a vague memory of the plot, and I want to watch it again as research for my idea to get the vintage shop.

"*The Big Short?*"

"That's the one!"

"Why are you asking me that?" His tone sounds suspicious of my motives.

Should I tell him about the vintage shop?

There is not enough time to go through it all. I have to figure this out on my own...well, with Betty's help. I always have Betty. So I say to him, "I will tell you when you get back."

"Do *not* buy any stocks until I get home!"

I chuckle. "You definitely don't have to worry about that happening." (Does he actually think I would buy stocks on my own? Silly guy. I'm buying an entire retail store, instead!)

"All right, good. I have to give back the guy's phone. But I wanted to tell you, I'm coming back on...*static*...day."

"What day? There was static."

"On...*static*...day."

"Aaron?"

Static.

And only static until the line goes dead.

But he is coming back.

Aaron is coming back!

I knew he was coming back, eventually. I'm just glad that eventually is almost here.

There is no way I will be able to fall asleep again after our call. So I get up from bed and go into the sewing workroom, turning on the lights. It takes a few seconds for my eyes to adjust to the brightness.

I search for the external hard-drive Aaron gave me, containing his downloaded "must watch" films. Once I have found it and connected it to my laptop, I grab a pen and a pad of paper. I need to take notes as I watch.

Most of the films on Aaron's "must watch" list are documentaries. When we first got together, we took turns picking films on movie night. My choices were either lighthearted romantic comedies or action-adventure flicks. His choices, at least in the beginning, were always documentaries on animal cruelty.

I thought he was trying to convert me to his vegan ways, but he said he only wanted me to know the truth, and then I could decide for myself. Well, after like the third documentary (I think it was *Earthlings*), I couldn't not know the truth anymore, and I became a vegan.

For a week. But then, I ate fish.

I reasoned with Aaron that I would be willing to kill a fish. In fact, I'm pretty sure I killed our goldfish when I was a kid. So now I'm a pescatarian. And whenever I get tempted to slip up and eat meat, I look at Coco and say, "I wouldn't eat you Coco!" She usually runs away from me whenever I say this. I don't think she is convinced.

Besides the documentaries on animal cruelty on the external hard-drive, there are documentaries on the financial crisis and regular movies about the stock market. Aaron used to be an equity trader, so he has a fondness for the subject matter.

Scrolling through the list, my eyes fall on *Trading Places*. I'm almost tempted to watch it, instead. It was made in the 1980s and is hilarious. (Just thinking about the movie gives me a sudden craving for orange juice.) And I believe it's related to my research, too. But I have to stick to my original plan, so I find *The Big Short* and click play.

After watching both movies and drinking a tall glass of orange juice, I get a couple of hours more of sleep before starting my workday. Gloria isn't coming to the condo today, as she works from home on Fridays. I quickly complete some pressing administrative work, then head over to Betty's house. I'm finally prepared to share my idea with her.

It takes me a while to get settled-in once I arrive at her place because of my anxious energy. I almost forgot to give my customary hello to the twins. I can't believe that in a few more days, they will be outside of Betty's belly. It's actually kind of weird to think about.

"Are you ready now?" Betty asks impatiently.

"Uh, one more minute," I say, getting up from sitting on her bed and walking to the foot of it. I should do this presentation-style, although I wish there was a white board or a projection screen behind me, instead of a television on top of a dresser. So, not really presentation-style, just me talking at the foot of Betty's bed. I grab the remote and turn on the television.

"What are you doing?" Betty asks, confused.

Yeah, that is not going to work. Maybe if I had thought to have *The Big Short* playing in the background, and then I could have pointed out crucial moments to support my strategy. I turn off the television. It will only distract me.

"Okay, I'm ready," I say. "*Wait!* I forgot to tell you something. Mom breastfed us!"

"How do you know that?"

"I asked Gloria. She knew. You should ask her stuff like that about mom, in case she knows anything."

"Gloria! Of course." She looks relieved. "I will ask her. Thanks, Erin."

I'm so happy at her reaction that I sit back down on the bed, smiling in her direction.

"Erin, your idea?"

Right. I stand up again. "So I plan to buy the vintage shop by...not buying it."

"That doesn't make any sense."

"Hear me out. I'm going to propose to Arthur that I lease it, instead."

"But doesn't he want to sell the building?"

"He does. So I have come up with a solution to that, too."

"*And?*"

"In five years, if the market price of the building goes down, I will pay him the difference between the current market price and whatever the future lower price is. Sort of like—but, not totally—a short sell option. And in the meantime, he will get the cash flow from the rent I will be paying to lease the building. He can't lose."

"Yeah, but you can lose, a lot, depending on how much the price goes down. And what happens after the five years? You will be out of money, and you won't have the shop anymore."

"I have also thought of that. Part of the deal will be that after the five years, I get first right of refusal to buy the building at today's market price or the future market price, whichever is higher. So he still can't lose."

"Hold on a second, this is hurting my pregnant brain." Betty takes a moment to digest what I have said. "Okay, assuming you find the money to buy the place in five years, you may be overpaying for an undervalued asset. It's too much of a risk to take."

"I know. But I'm taking it. I'm the one who has to. There can't be any risk for him. There is no other way someone like me could get a shop in an area like that. And I believe in Lady Bettencourt. I believe this will work out. I can feel it. That is why it doesn't seem that risky to me."

Betty is quiet for a while before saying, "I guess if the worst happens, you will find a way to pay the difference. Or you can buy the building and add some condos on top of it to increase its market value."

I knew she would come around.

"But, Erin, you still have to come up with the monthly rent on the shop."

"I figured that out, too. Both my ideas involve adding dresses that sell at a higher price point. The first way is to add a line of—"

"Wedding dresses," Betty says, finishing my sentence.

"How did you know I was going to say that?"

"It's obvious, when you think about it, given where the shop is located and the ridiculous markup on wedding dresses. But I didn't think you wanted to include wedding dresses in your line."

"It isn't that I didn't want to sell them—I like designing them—it's that I don't have the skills to sew anything more elaborate than what I made for your wedding. But I have Ming now, and she is a pro. I will assign her exclusively to wedding dresses. And if there is a lot of demand, I will hire someone else."

"What is your other idea?"

"Made-to-order, custom dresses."

Betty raises an eyebrow in question.

"I don't know why I never thought of it before," I continue, "but it makes so much sense for Lady Bettencourt. Instead of us having to source all of our own secondhand materials, we will have customers bring in their own materials that have special meaning for them that they want turned into something they can wear. Either to remember a person they have lost, or, if it's their own clothes, to remember important events they have attended throughout their life. Because we will be making them a custom dress, not one of our off-the-rack designs, we can charge a higher price. And if that custom dress is also a wedding dress, the price point will be even higher!"

The credit for sparking that idea goes to Carol. After I received the package of her daughter's clothing, it began to form. I haven't decided yet what I'm making for Carol, as she doesn't want a dress, but I'm sure an idea will begin to form on that, too. It just needs time to steep.

"Hmm, this could actually work," Betty says. "I will run some preliminary numbers based on the average lease rates in Yorkville, along with projected sales on the wedding and custom dresses."

"Thanks, Betty. You are the best little sister a girl could have." I go over to her side of the bed to give her a hug.

"Yeah, well, you are not so bad, yourself. You definitely keep things interesting around here."

FIFTY-EIGHT

"I'M WATCHING YOU, Louie. No running off," I say with a stern look on my face. He sort of nods, so I release him. "Okay, go play!" He turns and heads for the wading pool to join the others.

I'm at the dog park. Louie is a terrier. I'm also here with his brothers: Huey, a pug, and Dewey, a chihuahua. And, of course, Coco is with us. It's a play date.

Greta, the "mommy" of the *DuckTales*-named dogs and Betty's coworker at her accounting firm, asked if I could take them today because her regular dog walker was sick. It's funny (and somewhat awkward), but whenever I take the dogs on a play date without Greta joining us, she always tries to pay me for my time. I guess because once, only once, I was her paid dog walker.

Another funny thing I never thought would happen is that I actually like hanging out with dogs now. Well, some dogs. They remind me of people with their own little personalities.

For instance, I can tell Coco has a crush on Louie. I finally made her that pink bow, so she is wearing it with pride as she splashes around, following Louie wherever he goes. But Louie doesn't seem to notice. I think he is a player. She was spayed when I got her, so I'm not concerned in that regard, I just don't want her heart to get broken.

Huey doesn't seem to understand why Coco wouldn't be in love with him. Everyone loves him. So there is a bit of a love triangle thing happening, or maybe it's more of a love line.

And then, there is Dewey. It's embarrassing to admit, but I used to be afraid of chihuahuas. Now he is my favourite of the three boys. (Don't tell.) I think it's because he is so self-conscious and nervous all the time. I'm trying to build up his confidence by giving him positive remarks. He and Coco get along really well, too. When I see their tiny heads come together, it looks as if they are gossiping about the other dogs at the dog park. It looks like that, anyway.

My psychoanalyzing of canines is interrupted by my phone ringing.

"Hi, Liz-zie!" I answer in a sing-song voice when I see it's her calling.

"Erin! You have to get to the shop, right away!"

"*Why?* What's wrong?" I have never heard her sound so panicked before.

"Arthur is here, but he is leaving soon. I heard him talking on the phone. He is putting the shop on the market on Monday!"

"Oh, no! Okay, I will get there as soon as possible!"

"I will stall him until you do, but hurry!" She hangs up the phone.

This is happening faster than I anticipated. Betty hasn't even had a chance to finish running the numbers. I quickly grab my stuff and get up to go, then stop because I remember I'm not here on my own.

For a split second—not even a full one—I contemplate leaving them behind and coming back for them later. But I know I can't do that. So I call out their names, and they come to my side...except for Louie.

"Louie! Get over here!"

He doesn't come over.

He is doing this to me again!

But I don't have time for his games. Not now. Luckily, I'm wearing one of Lady Bettencourt's summer sundresses, so I kick-off my flip flops and hike up my skirt, then go into the wading pool.

From somewhere behind me, I hear a man shout, "Hey, lady! Dogs only! No humans allowed!"

Why is that guy always here?

Maybe he is some sort of lifeguard for dogs.

When I reach Louie, I realize there is no way to avoid getting wet. I release my skirt and scoop him up, then make my way out of the pool.

Once the dogs are on their leashes, we head out of the park, with me assessing the situation as we do.

Should I take the dogs back to Greta's place before heading to the vintage shop? What if she isn't home? There isn't enough time. I will have to bring them with me.

Another problem: The dogs are wet. *I'm wet.* No Uber or taxi driver will take us. That leaves us with only one option: the subway.

When we near the edge of the park, I look down at my gang and say, "This is your last chance to do your business. I don't want any 'accidents' on the subway. Go pee!"

And to my surprise, they do. All of them.

We make it out of the subway without any incidences to my great relief. And then, I start running the best I can while wearing flip flops and being trailed by four small dogs.

When we near the vintage shop, I collect my breath. I'm a mess. This is not how I imagined this would go. My plan was to come wearing The Betty, my most business-like dress, carrying some sort of a briefcase, and pitching my strategy to Arthur in true presentation-style. I never envisioned I would be wearing a sundress with flip flops and have a pack of dogs with me.

Why can't anything ever go as planned?

The good news is, I'm not wet anymore, neither are any of the dogs. We have dried out along the way, but, unfortunately, we still smell like wet dog.

Once we arrive, I don't know what I should do with them. I can't tie them up to a bike rack—Louie can't be trusted not to runaway. I will have to bring them inside with me. We climb up the steps to the shop door.

Before opening it, I turn around and say, "Please be good in there." I'm met with blank stares. "If you are good, I will give you a treat after." They open their mouths, panting. I guess, that is the most I can hope for.

As we enter, Lizzie comes rushing towards us.

"He is upstairs in his apartment, but is packing up to go. Oh, dear!" She has finally taken in my physical state and my army of dogs.

"I know. Sorry, it couldn't be helped."

"I will hide them in one of the fitting rooms, so you can—you can freshen up!"

"Great idea!"

"If he comes down by chance, remember to act as though you don't know the shop is for sale and you are only making an inquiry."

"Right. Okay, I got it."

Lizzie goes into the fitting room area with the dogs. I look around the shop—what could be my shop—and I get butterflies in my stomach. I'm really nervous. I definitely don't look the part of a future shop owner.

My eyes fall on my clothing rack. To think, in a few months, this whole place could be filled with Lady Bettencourt dresses.

Wait.

Those are my dresses.

I race to the rack and try to find the least formal design in my size. I settle on The Annie. I named the dress after Rachel McAdams, whose middle name is Anne. It was my way of thanking her (without her knowing it) for putting Lady Bettencourt on the world stage. It's a 1920s-inspired flapper dress, with a dropped-waist. It's a little fancy for a business meeting, but it's the best option of the bunch. I could always say I came from an afternoon at the opera. No, bad idea. I don't know anything about the opera, and he probably does.

There is no one else in the shop, so I take off my sundress and put on The Annie. It's a very cool dress, but it makes me want to breakout into the Charleston. I take my own clothes and hide them behind the counter.

Next, I go over to the vintage shoe section. I glance at some of the sticker prices on the shoes and get shocked. I decide to borrow a pair for the meeting; I will put them back after. It isn't as if they haven't already been worn. Finally, I fix my hair in one of the shop mirrors, then apply some lipstick and perfume I had in my bag.

Lizzie comes out from the fitting room area and stops in her tracks when she sees me, then says, "Oh, good, you are ready."

I take a deep breath.

I'm ready.

FIFTY-NINE

THIS IS DEFINITELY not how I imagined things would go.

When Lizzie called Arthur to say there was someone downstairs to see him, I thought that is where we would meet, downstairs. But instead, when he asked who it was and found out it was me, he told her to send me up to his place.

So I find myself sitting in a Yolk (or maybe it's Egg) chair in the living room of his apartment above the shop. His very minimalist apartment. The walls are painted white and the only furniture, which looks vintage, includes four chairs surrounding a coffee table and a bar cart along the wall.

"Can I offer you a drink? A bourbon?" Arthur asks as he pours himself one from the bar cart.

A bourbon? I have never had a bourbon before. Maybe I should try...

"I'm fine, thank you," I say. I have to keep this professional.

"How is the dress business?" (Good, so is he.)

Arthur comes over and sits across from me in a Madrid-style chair—or is it a Barcelona-style chair? (Note to self: study chair designs.) He is very dashing for his age, which I would put at late sixties. His wavy, white hair has silver highlights running through it. The few times I have seen him, he has always been impeccably dressed, and today is no exception. He reminds me of a composite of every old, rich, white guy who has ever appeared in the movies and on television. That is who he reminds me of.

I take a deep breath. "Very well, actually. That's why I'm here."

"I'm intrigued. Go ahead."

"Arthur, I want to—"

"Call me Art."

"Okay, uh, Art." What is my next line again? I wish I had my notes. "Art, would you ever consider selling the vintage shop?"

He chuckles to himself. "Ah, that Lizzie."

Dammit! I wasn't smooth enough. I feel my face turning bright red. "I, um, no, she didn't—"

"It's all right, Erin. I have known Lizzie for years. I know how her mind works."

The way he says this causes my eyebrows to raise. Now I'm wondering how *well* he knows her. Maybe Lizzie has some secrets of her own.

"If I were to say I was considering selling," he continues, "what would you propose?"

This is it. This is my chance.

Somewhat awkwardly, I extract myself from the chair. This isn't a sitting-down matter.

Standing up, I begin. I tell him about my short-sell strategy, just like I explained it to Betty. I emphasize that there is no way he can lose, and he will get additional funds each month from the lease.

Then, I share with him something I hadn't planned on sharing, something that had been subconsciously steeping in my mind: I share my vision of what I see the shop becoming.

I tell him how I want to have a glass window in the shop, looking into the sewing workroom, so people can see the dresses being made by the seamstresses. Sort of like, open kitchens in restaurants. I'm making wild hand gestures, as I move around the room, demonstrating how I would setup the shop if it were mine.

Finally, I share my dream of creating a place where everyone feels welcomed when they walk in, not intimidated, and how I want to sell ethically-made dresses at price points all women can afford. Through the shop, I want to show how things can be different.

There, I have said my piece. I gave it everything I had. And I somehow resisted the temptation to end it with the Charleston, even while wearing a flapper dress.

He takes one last sip of his drink, finishing it, then places the glass on top of the coffee table.

"I will have to think about this. Send me some numbers—some real numbers—and I will have a look."

"I will! Thank you so much for meeting with me. I really appreciate it."

"You remind me of myself when I was young." (That is a good thing, *right*?) "Foolish. Naive." (Crap!) "But I like your spunk." (Phew.)

"I know it may sound crazy and idealist, but I believe it can be that way. I just need someone to give me a chance. Did someone ever give you a chance when you were young and foolish?"

A haze falls over his eyes, then he says, "Yes, in fact, someone did." He returns to his composed self. "Here, let me walk you out."

When we reach the shop level, we hear them before we see them.

Somehow, all the dogs have gotten loose. I'm pretty sure I can guess which one of them orchestrated their escape. Lizzie is chasing after them, trying to grab their leashes.

This can't be good.

"What is going on here?" Art asks, alarmed. "Whose dogs are these?"

Coco comes up to me and licks my leg, then she looks up at me with her big, beautiful eyes.

I know this may blow my chances, but I can't deny Coco. "They are my dogs. Well, this one here is. I'm watching the other ones."

"Looks like you aren't doing a very good job in that department," he says.

It's over.

But then, Art lets out a boisterous laugh. And as Louie runs past him, he reaches out and grabs his leash. *"Gotcha!"*

Lizzie comes towards us with Huey and Dewey, who she has managed to catch.

I see her and Art exchange meaningful glances, and I definitely know there is a story there. But I will let Lizzie keep it to herself unless she ever chooses to share it with me.

Art is on his knees, petting the dogs. And he doesn't look so debonair, anymore. I can picture him being young and foolish at one time.

His eyes fall on Coco, who is tilting her head and flashing her long lashes at him. "My ex-wife had a dog like this. I don't miss her, but I miss her dog."

Maybe Coco and the other dogs haven't wrecked my chances. Maybe they have improved them.

After I dropped off Greta's dogs, I came home and called Betty to give her the news. She got really excited and said she would email me the final numbers in the morning.

I tried to eat some dinner, but I had too much energy from the day's events. So, instead, I'm doing something I have avoided for a very long time: cleaning the condo.

But as I'm vacuuming the kitchen floor, I hear a strange sucking noise. I switch-off the vacuum and bend down to see what caused it; a piece of paper that must have been hiding under the oven.

How did it get under there?

I pull it out of the vacuum to get a closer look. It isn't any piece of paper: It is another one of my mom's diary entries. It must have slipped under there when Coco took the package.

Using all of my strength, I move the oven to see if there are any others. There aren't. Then, I move the refrigerator. There is nothing under there, either. But I had to check. I had to be sure.

I thought I read everything there was to read. That I was done with this. I am almost tempted to get rid of the diary entry without reading it.

Almost.

But I am young and foolish. So I read it.

SIXTY
~Diary Entry~

APRIL 4, 1999

Dearest Elizabeth,

My bag is gone. The last physical connection I had to my *maman*, sold to a man wearing an excessive amount of cologne and gold jewellery.

I remember the day she gave it to me: my twenty-second birthday. I had graduated from university the spring before, and after months of drifting from place-to-place, I finally accepted a job at an art gallery downtown owned by one of my stepfather's friends. She was so happy I accepted it; she gave me her most prized possession: a navy Chanel 2.55 bag. She said it was the sort of thing I needed as I started to make my way in the world.

Maybe she always planned to give it to me. I don't know. I never knew with her. What I do know is that on that day, she said she was proud of me and the woman I was becoming.

But she didn't stay proud for long. Not after Jacques came into the picture and my life went in a direction she didn't approve of. A life she hadn't *chosen* for me.

I wonder if she ever regretted giving me her most prized possession. She would be mortified if she found out it now belonged to the gold-chained man's bleached-blonde, leopard-wearing bimbo. All right, perhaps not a bimbo. I am being mean. Regardless, my *maman* wouldn't approve. That I do know for sure.

But getting her approval was always so damn hard, much less trying to keep it. So it is probably for the best the bag is gone.

It seems symbolic, as though this is the official end of our relationship. We haven't spoken in over a year as it is, not since I told her I had cancer. And neither one of us is likely to bend on that front.

The important thing is, Beatrice will get her braces, and that is all that matters now.

Love you always,
Lizzie

P.S. The man paid for the bag in cash. His name was Alto. He owns a dry-cleaning business, "Alto's Dry Cleaning." It is located at the corner of College and Ossington. That is the only information I have on him.

P.P.S. I don't know why I added that. Okay, I do know. A part of me hopes that I can get the bag back one day; that not everything has been lost.

—

Oh, my god. *Oh, my god!* I can't believe it!

I knew that day when I saw my mom's bag in the vintage shop's window that she wanted us to have it.

I knew it!

This diary entry confirms what I have always known. Why else would she have included it with the other entries? She *wants* us to get the bag back!

But if the bag was sold to this man and his lady friend, does that mean the Chanel bag at the vintage shop wasn't actually my mom's?

No, no, that can't be right. I felt such a connection to it. The man or the woman must have sold it to the shop at some point.

But if they didn't, that means...they might still have it.

I could still have it!

There is only one way for me to know for sure: I need to talk to Alto.

—

In ten seconds flat, I'm Googling: "Alto's Dry Cleaning."

My eyes widen at the search results.

It is still there! It is still there!

As I'm writing down the address, my gaze falls on their business hours.

What time is it now?

According to my phone: 7:01 p.m. They closed a minute ago.

Dammit!

I will have to wait until tomorrow. Except...they are closed on Sundays.

Double dammit!

I will have to wait until Monday to launch my mission, which I have codenamed Mission 2.55. I hate waiting. It is the hardest part.

On Monday morning, I arrive at Alto's Dry Cleaning at exactly eight o'clock, just as the door is being unlocked.

The woman who unlocked the door, greets me without a smile. "Morning. Pick up or drop off?"

Why didn't I think to bring something with me?

I could have used it as a segue or to buy some time. I look down at what I'm wearing—a Lady Bettencourt dress, of course. But if I give her that, we will be headed in the completely wrong direction.

"Neither, actually. I was wondering if I could speak to Alto?" I ask.

The woman looks at me with suspicion. Her name, Rita, is embroidered on her uniform shirt. For a moment, I wonder if she is the "bleached-blonde bimbo," but she doesn't fit that description. She has short brown hair and a bit of a limp. Although, it has been years. She may have adapted her look...and picked up a limp somewhere along the way.

"Which one?" she asks, narrowing her eyes at me.

"Which one, what?"

"Which Alto do you want?"

"There is more than one Alto?" I ask in surprise. "But, um, the sign says—"

"There are two. Brothers. Alto is their last name. Which one do you want?"

Two brothers? How am I supposed to know which one?

"Uh, I don't know..."

"Choose," she says impatiently.

"I guess whichever one knows about a vintage Chanel 2.55 bag. A navy one. Medium in size."

She doesn't seem fazed by my answer. She just makes a note on a piece of paper. "What's your name and number?"

I give it to her.

"One of them will give you a call. Have a nice day," she says, again without a smile, effectively ending our conversation.

"Okay, um, have a nice day," I say, and head for the door.

That didn't go anything like I thought it would. Truth be told, I thought I would be leaving with my mom's bag. And now, I have to wait for a call that may never come.

It is completely out of my control.

SIXTY-ONE

EVERYTHING IS ON HOLD.

First, there is the status of the vintage shop. Betty sent me the numbers, which I forwarded on to Art. Now I have to wait for him to make his decision.

Then, there is Betty and the imminent birth of the next generation of Bettencourts.

Finally, and if I'm being honest, this one is causing me the most distress at the moment, I haven't gotten a call back from either of the Alto brothers. Two days have already passed.

My mind keeps wandering as I sit in the workroom, trying to sew a dress, but not getting far with it, until my phone rings. It could be in regard to any of the aforementioned three. My heart races as I turn over my phone.

Betty's name appears on the display.

"Is it time?" I ask, getting up from my chair.

Gloria gets up from her chair, too.

"No, no," Betty says. I shake my head in Gloria's direction, and she sits back down. "I just wanted an update on the vintage shop. I thought you were coming over yesterday?"

"Sorry, Betty, I forgot. But there is nothing new to report."

"Can you come by today? I'm so bored."

"I can't today. I have to finish some rush orders, but I will swing by tomorrow."

This is mostly true. I do have rush orders to finish. But I'm also worried I will get the call from the dry cleaners while I'm at Betty's. I can't exactly have that conversation in front of her.

"Okay, I'll watch Netflix or something," she says. *"Ouch!"*

"Betty! Are you okay?" I ask in alarm. "Is it starting now?"

Gloria gets up again.

"No, this is normal." I shake my head once more in poor Gloria's direction. "But my OB-GYN said if I don't go into labour by the weekend, she will have to schedule a C-section. Either way, I'll be out of this bed soon."

"And I'll be an auntie! All right, call me if anything starts to happen."

"I will. Or I'll try. I have no idea what it will actually be like. But Matt will call if I can't."

"So exciting!"

Betty laughs. "Yeah, and a bit scary. Bye, Erin. Love you."

"Love you...always!"

Almost as soon as I have ended the call with her, another one comes through. This time, it's a blocked number.

"Hello," I say with bated breath.

"Erin, it's Frankie. How you doing, kid?"

I have made my way to the kitchen. I can't have this conversation in front of Gloria.

"Frankie? How—how are you?"

How did he get my new number?

Mila. She must have given it to him.

Ah, jeez, why is he calling me after so long?

"I'm good," he says. "And you?"

"Um, I'm good, too. So...what can I do for you?"

Eek. I shouldn't have offered to do anything for him. He may give me another "job," and I'm no longer in the mysterious package delivery business.

"I think it's more like what can *I* do for *you*."

What is he talking about?

Then, I remember Mila mentioning a few weeks ago that he could help us find a new workspace. "Oh, right, about that...I'm on top of it. I don't need your help anymore."

"Lemme get this straight, you *don't* want the Chanel bag?" he asks, sounding confused.

Wait. What?

I'm slowly connecting the dots. "You're...you're Alto? Frankie Alto?"

"The one and only. So do you want the bag or not?"

"You still have it?"

"It's been sitting in my hall closet for years. I bought it for this woman I was seeing. She wore it, once or twice, then said it wasn't her style. How did you know I had it? Mila tell you?"

How doesn't he know? He knows everything.

"No, it wasn't Mila. Um, that bag belonged to my mom. She sold it to you. Years ago. Do you remember?"

"That bag belonged to *your* mother? Not possible."

"Why not?"

"I never forget a name. I would have remembered if she said 'Bettencourt.' I would have made the connection."

"What was the name of the woman you bought the bag from?"

Without hesitation, he says, "Elizabeth Condé."

Condé. I search my mind. "That was my grandfather's last name," I say. "She gave you her birth name."

"Well, that explains it. If I had known, I would have given you the bag. I lost my mother, too. I know what it's like."

"Thanks, Frankie. And sorry about your mother."

"Yeah, me, too. But I guess we can't dwell on these things. We gotta keep going."

"I guess so," I say. "Please let me know what you want for the bag, and I will get you the money. I'm just so happy to have it back."

"Money? Erin, I'm offended. I can't take your money."

"You can't? But I have to give you something for it."

Great. Maybe I am back in the mysterious package delivery business.

"I'll tell you what you can do for me. You can name one of your dresses after my mother."

I breathe a sigh of relief. "Of course, of course, I will! What was her name?"

"Francesca."

"What a beautiful name. But do you want me to name the dress The Franny—or The Frankie?"

"Uh, let's go with The Frankie," he says sheepishly, then adds, "My mother was a princess. So it has to be a dress fit for a princess."

"That I can manage. Thank you so much. I really appreciate this."

"Forget about it. Come by the shop tomorrow morning. The bag will be waiting for you."

"I'll be there." Now I'm wondering if the dry-cleaning shop is a cover for his other "business" activities.

"You know what, Erin? I remember your mother. She was stylish. Very stylish."

"She really was. Thanks for saying that."

"No problem. One last thing: You ever wonder what was inside that box?"

I can't help freezing. I always do at the mention of "that box." I'm about to respond with my standard, "What box?" (Rule number one: be discreet.) But then, for the first time, I understand something.

"I know what was inside that box."

"You do?" he asks, surprised. "What was it?"

"Hope. That is what was inside that box."

"Smart kid." He pauses a moment. "It's a small world, huh, Erin?"

"Very small. Tiny."

SIXTY-TWO

TODAY IS THE DAY.

Today is the day I'm getting my mom's bag back!

I still can't believe it. It seems so surreal. Although, a part of me is wondering about that *other* Chanel 2.55 bag. The one I lost on the subway all those moons ago. I had felt such a strong connection to it.

For a delusional moment, I imagined the bag had wandered out of Frankie's hall closet, made its way to the vintage shop so I could buy it, and then went back to Frankie's hall closet after I lost it.

Maybe the connection I had felt wasn't to the bag itself, but to what it represented. And maybe I wasn't ready to get the bag back until I truly knew what that was. Anyway, I'm glad it's finally returning to where it belongs.

Rita is standing behind the counter as I enter the dry-cleaning shop. I smile at her. She gives me a nod. I thought we might be on a smiling basis this time around, but I guess not. She places a box on the counter.

I definitely know what is inside *that* box. Mission 2.55: accomplished.

"Mr. Alto said you'd be by to pick this up."

"Yes, thank you so much!"

"Have a nice day."

"Oh, okay. Uh, yeah, have a nice day," I say, taking the box and turning to leave.

"Mondays, skirts and dresses are fifty-percent off," she says, catching me by surprise. I thought I had been dismissed.

I look back at her, and although she isn't smiling, there is warmth in her eyes. "I'll remember that," I say. "Thank you."

When I'm outside, I see there is a note written on the box. It reads: "If you ever need anything, you know who to call. Frankie."

If I had received that note a week ago, I would have been in a panic by what it meant; what I would have to do in return for his help. I have often wondered whether Frankie was a "good guy" or a "bad guy." Maybe because I sometimes wonder the same thing about myself. But I have decided that, for me, Frankie is a good guy, and I know now if I do need anything, I will ask him. He is my kind of people, even though we have never actually met in person.

Hold on a second.

We have met in person!

Or, at least, *I* have seen Frankie.

I was there when he came to pick up the bag with the bleached-blonde bimbo. I was thirteen or so. I had stayed home from school because I was sick. (Or, maybe, pretending to be sick. I was never a fan of school.) My mom thought I was napping in my room when they came by, but I was hiding behind our kitchen wall, witnessing the whole transaction.

Now that I know that was Frankie, he looks exactly like what I had imagined. But I guess I can't really say I imagined he looked like that when I actually saw him in real life.

Something else from that day has been burned into my memory. It was the way my mom held onto the Chanel bag, almost as if she couldn't physically let it go, as if it pained her to do so.

Mom, I got it back!

No, *we* got it back. I never would have found it without her diary entry. Okay, so it took seventeen years, but we did it.

We did it!

Not everything has been lost, after all.

Before I can return home and examine my new most prized possession, I have another stop to make.

My mom's painting is ready!

Of course, I have to deal with Funny Man Brian to get it, but that is okay. This is turning into such an amazing day, I'm in the mood for his cheesy jokes.

So as I enter the frame shop, I say, "Good morning! Have you found any more secret codes hidden in paintings?"

He makes a confused face. "Uh, no. Is there something I can help you with?"

"Maybe you can. You know how I said there were receipts in that package you found? I lied. It was a treasure map. A treasure map leading to the lost paintings of the world. All we have to do is find 'X.'"

"I'm not, I'm not following..."

"Brian! *C'mon!* I'm joking."

"I'm not Brian. I'm his twin brother, Stephen."

"Oh! I'm so sorry! I thought..." I feel my cheeks turning bright red. This is embarrassing. "Anyway, I'm here to pick up a painting. The name is Bettencourt, Erin Bettencourt."

He disappears into a back room and returns with the painting wrapped in packing paper.

"Thank you," I say, taking the painting from him. It will be awkward juggling it and the box with the Chanel bag, but I will manage. "Um, have a nice day." I head for the door.

"Erin?"

I turn back. "Yeah?"

A grin forms on his face. "Gotcha, again!" he says, laughing to himself.

This man is insane!

"That you did," I say, rolling my eyes. "Have a nice day, *Brian.*"

And by day, I mean life, because I'm never coming back here again.

"Hello?" I say, answering my phone as I walk in the door of the condo, carefully putting down the two packages.

"Erin, it's Art."

My breathing quickens. "Hi, Art!"

"I will get right to the point. I don't want to keep you in suspense any longer. I have spoken with my business advisers, and I have decided to proceed with your plan."

"So it's-it's a yes? The shop is mine?" I ask. I need to be a hundred percent sure I'm understanding him correctly.

"It's a yes. The shop is yours. Well, once you have signed the paperwork, which will be ready for you early next week."

I let out a scream. "*Sorry!* I'm just really excited! Thank you! *Thank you!*"

"I understand. But you should know I'm adding a condition to your offer."

Uh-oh. "What kind of condition?"

"I want to be your mentor for the first year, to provide you with training on how the world of retail works. It won't be written into the contract, and I won't charge a fee, but someone did that for me at the beginning of my career, and now I would like to do that for you."

"Wow, of course, I accept your condition."

"This is your chance, Erin. I hope you know what you are getting yourself into."

"I'll figure it out," I say, knowing that somehow, someway, I will.

When I get off the phone, I jump up and down. Coco comes over and barks at me. I take her front paws into my hands and start dancing with her, singing, *"We got the shop! We got the shop! We got the shop!"*

I wanted to tell Betty first, but Gloria has probably already heard me screaming.

"Gloria!" I shout towards the sewing workroom. I don't get a reply. "Gloria?"

The workroom is empty when I enter it. Then, I remember Gloria said she would be working from home today. I hear my phone ringing, so I run back to the kitchen to answer it before it stops.

"Hello," I say breathlessly.

"Erin, we're at the hospital. It's time," Matt says in a rush from the other end.

"It's time? *It's time!* Okay, I'll be right there!" I end the call, then scramble around to quickly pack a bag until I realize I'm not the one having a baby. I don't need to pack an overnight bag.

"Sorry, Coco. I have to go, and I don't know when I'll be back. But when I do, I'll be an auntie! And you will have cousins! Sort of."

As I'm heading out the door, my eyes fall on the unopened packages containing the painting and the Chanel bag. I circle back and put them both into the hall closet. I can't risk leaving them out in the open, where Coco may enact her revenge for my abandoning her.

"Please try not to make too much of a mess," I say to her.

She tilts her head one way, then the other, as if to imply, "Who me?"

"Yeah, you. Be good!" I say, closing the door behind me.

But whatever mess she does get into, I will happily deal with. Nothing can bring me down.

This is turning out to be one of the best days of my life!

SIXTY-THREE

I HATE HOSPITALS. I haven't had many experiences in them, but the main experience I had wasn't a good one.

But as I'm walking through the institutional, cinderblock corridors, I remind myself that this time is different. This time something good will come of my visit. Two little something goods.

When I reach the maternity ward, I'm not sure where I'm supposed to go. Betty and I had decided I would be in the delivery room, but if I couldn't handle it, then she wouldn't be upset if I left. She would have Matt with her.

Finally, I spot Matt, standing behind the plastic window of a hospital door.

"Matt!" I yell, pushing through the door and rushing towards him. I give him a hug. His body is tense. He must be getting nervous. I have to admit: I'm getting nervous, too. "Where is Betty?"

I'm looking behind him, half-expecting to see her wandering the corridors, but she is probably already in the delivery room.

"Erin, uh, there has been—" Matt's voice trails off.

"There has been what? *What?*" I say, my own voice comes out louder than I anticipated.

"Hi, Erin, do you remember me?"

I turn my body. In my excitement at finding Matt, I didn't realize someone else is standing there, as well. "Um, yes, hi, Dr. Yamin," I say, a bit shamefaced for having called her office multiple times in the last few months, trying to find out the sex of the babies. "What is going on?"

"Your sister's blood pressure is quite elevated," Dr. Yamin says calmly. "It's higher than it should be at this stage. So we are prepping her for surgery."

"Surgery? Like, a C-section?"

"Correct. And I need to go check on how it's progressing. Matt, are you ready?"

"Yeah, I'm ready," he says in a tone that implies he isn't ready at all.

"But Betty?" I ask. "My sister will be okay, *right*?" My breathing is quickening, and I feel lightheaded.

Dr. Yamin gives me a reassuring look and says, "We will come find you in the waiting room after the surgery, okay?"

"Okay."

"Don't worry, Erin. Everything will be fine," Matt says, but he doesn't sound convincing, nor does he seem convinced himself. I have never seen him so frazzled like this before.

I watch them until they disappear behind two other doors. And then, I'm left standing on my own in the hospital corridor with the same question swimming over and over in my head.

Women don't die in labour anymore, do they? Do they?

It's completely dark in here. I find a spot on the cold floor and sit down with my back against the door, trying to get comfortable, even though I don't deserve comfort.

This is my fault.

Betty and the twins are going to die, and it's my fault.

So I have decided to stay in this janitor's closet, or whatever kind of closet it is, until I also die. That will be my penance. My punishment. I *have* to stay in here. If I come out, then I will be putting the lives of all the other people I love at risk, too. It's safer for everyone.

I should have known something like this would happen. Things were going *too* well for me. I should have learned by now when the universe gives you something, it takes something else away. That is how it works. It's a rebalancing. And you don't get to choose how it decides to rebalance things.

The process started when I didn't tell Betty about our mom's diary, when I kept our mom all to myself.

I did this. I am a bad guy.

It is as though I can hear the universe mocking me, saying, "You may have gotten your mother back for a bit, but now, you have to sacrifice Betty and the twins."

And I want to scream, "Stop picking on me! Why are you always taking everyone I love away from me? *WHY?*"

But I don't scream. I am afraid of what else it will do if I did.

So I close my eyes and sit.

SIXTY-FOUR

I DON'T KNOW how long I have been sitting in here, but I think I'm starting to go crazy because I hear someone saying my name. Then, my phone makes a ping sound.

I'm being pulled back to reality, where I don't want to be. When I go to power-off my phone, my eye catches on the text message notification on the display.

It's from Aaron and reads: "I know you're in there. Please open the door."

I jump a little.

Aaron? He is back? Wait...is he outside the door?

How is that possible? Maybe I am going crazy.

Another ping and a text that reads: "I can hear your phone. Please come out."

I'm not sure what to do. I'm happy he is here, but I'm scared. What if I open the door, and the universe zaps him down on the spot? Maybe this closet is the only safety zone.

"I will open the door," I say. "But you have to come in here, where it's safe. Okay?"

"Okay," he says from the other side.

I get up and open the door a crack. Then, I rush to the far end of the closet, turning around and closing my eyes so I can't look at him, in case that effects things.

He comes in.

"Close the door!" I yell.

I hear it close. We are safe. I risk turning around, now that it's dark again. And while I can't see him through the darkness, I can smell him. "Aaron, you stink!"

"I came straight from the airport and haven't had a proper shower in weeks. Give a guy a break. Come here," he says.

I can sense his arms reaching out for me, but I pull myself farther into the corner. "No," I say. "Don't touch me! I'm poison."

"Erin, you are *not* poison."

"I am poison."

"What's going on with you?"

"I can't tell you or else it will make it true."

We stand in silence for a while. Then, I hear him rustling about, but I can't see what he is doing.

"Reach out your hand," he says.

"No."

"Erin..."

"Fine." I reach out my hand into the darkness. I feel his hand touch mine, and there is a spark. There is always a spark when we touch. He places something cold in my hand. I use my other hand to pick it up. "Is that, is that a coin? Are you giving me money?"

"It is a coin. A penny, actually. The penny you gave me the night we ran into each other on the street."

"You kept it?" I ask in surprise.

"I thought it might come in handy one day. So Lady B, I have given you a penny, now tell me your thoughts."

I'm so touched he kept it that I start crying. But my tears aren't only about that, they are for everything that is happening or has already happened. Through my sobs, I manage to get out, "I-I killed Betty and the twins."

Aaron finds me in the darkness and takes me into his arms. He whispers into my ear, "How could you have killed Betty and the twins if I just saw them?"

I pull back from his embrace and look up at where I imagine his face to be. "You-you saw them?"

"Yup."

"And they are okay?"

"They are great! Betty is a bit out of it from the surgery, but they are all doing fine."

I can't believe he met the twins before me. Another thought enters my mind. "What did she have? Girls or boys? Both?"

"You will have to leave this closet to find out."

Dammit! He has got me.

I take a moment to think things through. Maybe—just maybe—I overreacted a little. But I was so scared the worst thing possible in the world was happening.

"Okay," I say. "I'm ready to come out of the closet."

He takes my hand and opens the door.

My eyes need a second to adjust to the light. When they do, I look at Aaron and blurt out, "What happened to your face?"

"Do you like it?" he asks, caressing his beard. "Shaving was too much of a hassle over there."

"I'm not sure, but I think it might *grow* on me."

"Funny girl. Now give the bearded man a kiss."

I pretend to pull away, but I can't resist, bearded or not.

God, I have missed those lips.

"Where is the penny?" Aaron asks after we have stopped kissing.

"Um...I just had it...maybe it's..."

We both turn towards the open closet door and see it laying on the floor.

"Oops! Sorry," I say, wrinkling my nose.

Aaron shakes his head, then walks back to pick it up. "I may need to use this again some day," he says when he returns.

I punch him in the arm.

"How did you find me, anyway?" I ask.

"Matt. I was planning to surprise you at the condo, but Matt told me you were here and that Betty was in rough shape. I figured you would need to see a familiar face."

"I meant: How did you find me in the closet?"

He looks me in the eyes. "Seriously, Erin? If I have learned anything about you, it's that whenever trouble strikes, you look for the smallest room to hide in."

We both laugh because it's true. So true.

"Let's go find the twins!" I start running down the corridor.

He bursts out laughing again before calling out, "Uh, Erin?"

I slow my pace and turnaround. "Yeah?"

"You are going the wrong way."

I burst out laughing, too, then run back towards him.

It's also true that sometimes I go the wrong way before I can manage to get things right.

SIXTY-FIVE

"GIRLS!" I yell as I come rushing into Betty's hospital room and see the pink balloons that someone—Matt? Aaron?—must have gotten. I would have (probably) been just as happy if she had boys or a combination of the two. But it's girls! *Girls!*

"Hey, Erin," Betty says groggily from her bed.

I go over to give her a hug. "Oh, Betty! I'm so glad you're okay." My eyes tear up.

"Yeah, I'm okay. What about you?"

"I'm okay now. Can you believe it, Betty? *You're a mom!*"

"It's sinking in," she laughs softly.

I see Matt sitting in a chair, looking weary.

"Congratulations, Matty Matt!" I say, walking over to give him a hug, too.

"Thanks, Erin. Sorry about being freaked out earlier. I just didn't know what was happening."

"It's all right. Everything worked out in the end." I remember what my mom wrote in her letter, so I add, "You're a good man, Matt."

He smiles at me.

With congratulations out of the way, it's time. Time to officially meet the twins.

I walk towards their tiny hospital cribs and peek inside.

They are so small! So adorable! And they are part mine!

"What is your name little girl?" I ask the one on the left, half-hoping she will say it.

"Georgina is the one on the left, and Charlotte is on the right," Betty says from her bed.

"Georgina and Charlotte! No...Georgie and Charlie," I declare their new nicknames. "Nice to meet you, I'm your Auntie Erin." Wait a minute. "Betty? You do realize you have chosen the names of...um, nothing. Forget it." Of course, she wouldn't have realized. I'm pretty sure she doesn't follow the happenings of The British Monarchy.

"Their middle name is Rose," Betty says. "Like mom and us."

And our grandmother, their great-grandmother.

But Betty won't understand the significance of that. Not right now, anyway.

"That's perfect," I say. "Can I pick them up?"

Everyone in the room, except the twins, looks at me apprehensively.

"What? I have held a baby before."

"Okay, but be careful," Matt says, coming over.

"Who came out first?" I ask.

"Georgina," Matt answers.

I take her out of the crib, then hold her up in the air—while supporting her head—and start singing "Circle of Life" from *The Lion King* while slowly spinning around.

In the background, I hear:

"Erin! What the f—" from Aaron.

"What is she doing?" from Betty.

"Don't worry, I'm spotting her," from Matt.

But I ignore them. This has to be done. And then, I do the same thing with Charlotte.

Once I have finished and have placed Charlotte safely back in her crib, I turn around to face them. They are looking at me incredulously.

"What?" I ask. "It *is* the circle of life. It's proof that it continues. Our family continues."

I can see their eyes tearing up, especially Betty's. But before things can get too emotional in here, a nurse walks into the room.

"You must be the famous Auntie Erin who Betty has been talking about," she says with an Irish accent. I beam. Betty has been talking about me. "Aren't the twins gorgeous?"

"Very," I say. "Most newborns are pretty ugly, but these came out already cute."

The nurse raises her eyebrows and says, "Well, twins are a blessing, ugly or not."

"Twins run in our family," I say. "Betty and I are also twins."

"You are?" The nurse asks, surprised. "Then that is a double blessing."

"We're not twins," Betty says to her.

"We're Irish twins!" Really, you think she would have accepted it by now. I remember the nurse is actually Irish and that it might not be a politically-correct term, anymore, so I add, "We're not Irish-Irish. I, um, didn't mean..."

The nurse chuckles. "It's fine. No offence taken. I hate to break up the fun, though, but Betty here needs to get some rest."

"Okay," I say, disappointed that we have to go so soon.

I give Betty a goodbye hug and whisper in her ear, "You are going to be the best mom. I know it."

When I release her, she says, "Thanks, Erin."

And I know we are both thinking the same thing: We wish our own mom could be here, too.

To stop things from getting emotional again, I give her some important news she doesn't know about, yet. "Betty, I got the vintage shop!"

"*You got it?* Congratulations! I knew you could do it!"

"Thanks to your help," I say.

"Wait, you got *what*?" Aaron asks in confusion.

Turning towards him, I say with a big grin on my face, "I will tell you on the ride home."

As Aaron and I sit in the backseat of an Uber, returning us to the condo, I explain how it came to be that I'm the proud future owner (renter) of the vintage shop.

"It's risky," he says when I finish. "There was no other way?"

"I could have leased another retail space somewhere else, but I wanted the vintage shop."

"Have you signed anything, yet?"

"No, but I'm going to. As long as it states what Art and I agreed to, I'm signing it. I really want this."

"Then there is no point trying to change your mind. But can one of my lawyer friends look at the contract before you sign?"

"Of course. I was going to ask you about that. I have learned my lesson when it comes to signing contracts without reading—or understanding—them first."

"Wow, you got yourself a retail shop! Anything else exciting happen while I was away?"

Do I tell him about my mom's diary?

"Yes, something did happen, but I can't tell you." I see the worried expression on his face. "It's just that I need to tell Betty first, but she has more important business to take care of at the moment."

"You know, Erin, we don't have to tell each other *everything*. I know you are set on the oath we took, but every couple has some secrets."

"*Secrets?* What kind of secrets do you have?" I ask accusingly.

He looks uncomfortable. "It's no big deal. Well, it's sort of a big deal, but...let's not talk about it now."

I knew it. This thought had lingered in the back of my head the whole time he was away, and I can't stop myself from voicing it. "You fell in love with a beautiful Ethiopian woman named Farhiya, didn't you?"

"That is where your mind goes to? You even named her? No, that is not it. I...I ate goat."

"*You ate goat?*" I try (unsuccessfully) to suppress a giggle.

"It isn't funny. I wanted to refuse, but how could I? They killed the goat for us, as a thank you. Plus, they *literally* put it into my mouth! I couldn't spit it out!"

I place my hand on his arm. "It's okay. But no turkey for you this Thanksgiving. You have used up one of your two exceptions."

He laughs, but then, in a serious tone says, "I've missed you, Erin."

"I've missed you, too," I say, laying my head on his shoulder. "Are there any other sins you want to confess to me while you are at it?"

"No, not a sin, but I've been thinking about something. I think I want to make films. Or, at least, try to."

"Really?" I say, lifting my head in excitement. I'm visualizing him producing these big Hollywood blockbusters and us attending fabulous parties, hobnobbing with celebrities. Except, this is Aaron, so…"You mean, like documentaries?"

"Yeah, and maybe some short films. What do you think?"

"I think you should go for whatever makes you happy." And I mean that. (Even though, I still think Hollywood blockbusters would be more fun.)

"There is something else I wanted to tell you. Remember how I borrowed that film producer's satellite phone to call you?"

I nod my head.

"It turns out…"

I, Erin Bettencourt, am walking the red carpet at the Toronto International Film Festival next week!

The producer Aaron met in Ethiopia is friends with someone who worked on a film that is being premiered at the festival. And because Aaron helped him out of some sort of a pickle—which he was sworn to secrecy about—we get to walk the red carpet at the premiere. So maybe there are some secrets I don't need to know about, especially if it means I get to walk the red carpet.

That also means, I will need something special to wear. But I will worry about that tomorrow. I have had enough excitement for one day. And what a day it was, with its highs and lows, it still turned out to be the best day of my life. I give a silent thank you to the universe. (We are friends again.)

But now, all I want to do is sleep.

SIXTY-SIX

IT TAKES ME a moment to realize where I am. I haven't been here in years.

The first thing I recognize is our old couch, but not everything is the same. I don't remember those curtains; the items in the display case are different; and there are a bunch of toys scattered on the floor.

What am I doing here? How did I get here?

Out of habit, I go to mine and Betty's room. I'm expecting to see our old twin beds, but, instead, there are two cribs against each wall.

My blankie!

I pick it up and smell it. It smells just like I remember. I was so sad when I lost it. It was like losing a friend.

I hear laughter coming from my mom's bedroom. I walk in slow motion back across the living room, although I'm trying to run. Trying to get there as fast as I can.

Finally, I do get there. In the room, I'm playing on the floor: the two-year-old version of me. Beside me is Betty, who is barely one. And then, I see her.

I see her!

"Mommy?"

She turns around. "Erin, my sweet girl." She comes over to me.

We are hugging. I can actually feel her hugging me, and I never want to let her go.

"Oh, mom, I've missed you so much. *So much!*" I say, crying into her hair. "I'm sorry you didn't get to have the life you wanted. I'm so sorry."

She releases me and looks into my eyes. "Of course I had the life I wanted. I chose my life."

"But your art, you gave up your art."

"Erin, I could have kept painting. I'm the one who decided to stop. Consciously or subconsciously, *I* decided to stop. I was done."

"So you're not sad you gave up everything for us?"

"Look, Erin," she says, pointing down at Betty and me, playing on the floor. "Don't you see? I got what I always wanted the most: a family."

I hug her once more because I know I'm dreaming. I also know I will wake up soon, and I can't let this moment pass without holding her tight before she is gone again.

As I'm hugging her, I look over her shoulder and see she had been painting before I came into the room.

Without her turning to see what I'm looking at, she says, "It was my last piece. My masterpiece," she adds with a laugh.

How I have missed her laugh.

I look at the painting again, but it is blurry, I can't make out what it is. Everything is getting blurry, fading out. I'm waking up.

"No!" I scream.

But it is too late, I'm awake.

I try to fall back asleep, to get back there. But it's hopeless, I can't.

Aaron is sleeping blissfully beside me, unaware of anything. He is a very deep sleeper. So I get up and go to the kitchen for a glass of water.

The clock on the oven reads 4:44 a.m. Those numbers again. The death numbers.

Since my mom passed away, I have never had a dream about her. I wanted to, desperately, but it never happened until tonight.

I got to see my mom! I got to hold her!

I'm so grateful to whoever is in charge of dreams for giving me that. I only wish I had seen what she had been painting, her masterpiece.

Then, like a shock, it hits me.

Rushing towards the hall closet, I take out the painting I left in there, earlier the previous day.

310

My mom's painting.

How have I never made this connection before?

Once I tear off the packing paper, I hang the painting in its proper place on the dining room wall, then I stand back and look at it. Really look at it.

It is still the same mother with her head turned away while holding a toddler and a baby on her lap. But now, I see that the little girls are Betty and me, and the woman is my mom. Maybe she is looking away because she is saying goodbye to a part of herself. I glance down and confirm it for sure. I never noticed the signature on the painting before. I never thought it was important. But it was always right there.

Condé.

My mother's birth last name. This was her masterpiece. We were her masterpiece.

I find myself crying once more. That is the thing about grief: When you think you have finally come to terms with it, it comes back to bite you. It never really goes away; it just changes form.

I will never be completely over my mom's passing.

How could I be?

And I will always be afraid the people I love will be taken away from me.

How couldn't I be?

But I know that is the way things go. It is the circle of life.

SIXTY-SEVEN

I NAME THE DRESS The Penny.

It's a one-shoulder, Grecian-style dress that has a long, flowing skirt...with pockets. It's made from silk curtains in a beautiful bronze colour that I found at a thrift store. I have sewn-in a band of pennies under the bust line and at the shoulder of the dress.

Definitely, one of my most difficult sewing projects to date. But I had to do it on my own, and I also had to incorporate pennies into the dress somehow, given its name and the meaning behind it.

I thought about including the original penny Aaron has been holding on to, but I want to auction off the dress after the film premiere and donate the proceeds to charity. So I let Aaron keep his penny for future use and, instead, sewed the meaning of it into the dress.

When I found that penny on the ground, not even a year ago, I had been struggling with, well, my existence. When I saw my birth year on it, knowing that pennies had been taken out of circulation, I realized that my time was limited, too. And that I needed to do something worthwhile with whatever time had been allotted to me on this Earth. I feel as though I'm finally becoming the person I was always meant to be. The dress is a symbol of that.

Along with the dress, I will be carrying my mom's Chanel bag, which I have converted into a temporary clutch for the occasion.

When I had taken the bag out of the box it was in, I had held it in my hands for a while before removing it from its dust bag. (I still get way too excited about dust bags.) I lingered in that moment because it had taken me (and my mom) so long to achieve that goal.

I know what you may be thinking: It's only a silly bag.

But not to me. It changed everything for me. So when I removed it from the dust bag, I held it close to my chest, as if I were hugging a friend, then I flipped it over.

The tiny snag was still there. And I knew all was right in my world.

The film premiere we are attending this evening is *Queen of Katwe*. It's based on the true story of a young girl, living in the slums of Katwe in Uganda, who rises up from poverty by mastering the game of chess.

At first, I will admit, I was a bit disappointed I wouldn't be walking the red carpet with big, Hollywood movie stars I recognized. But this is the perfect film premiere for me to attend because it's about changing your life by believing in what you are capable of achieving.

Whatever money is raised from selling The Penny will be donated to allow more girls (and boys) to try to change their lives, too.

"Lady B, the car is here. Are you ready?"

I come around the corner, then pose against the dining room wall, Marilyn Monroe-style, and whisper breathlessly, "I'm ready, Mr. Trader."

"Wow, you look beautiful! Come here," he says, moving closer towards me.

"*No!* You will wreck my makeup—and hair! Do you know how long it took me to do this?"

"This" is a braided side bun, which I learned to do by watching and studying countless YouTube videos.

"I do know how long because I've been waiting this whole time."

I ignore his comment. "Actually, you look very handsome yourself," I say, as I take him in properly.

He has kept the beard he grew while in East Africa, but he has trimmed it so it's neat and tidy. It has *grown* on me. He is wearing a black tailored suit with a bow-tie that matches my dress. As his former office job was business casual, this is the first time I'm seeing him in a suit. And, well, I find it hard to resist a man who looks good in a suit.

So I go over and plant a big kiss on his yummy, full lips.

When we pull away from each other, he makes a face.

"What?" I ask.

"I wrecked your makeup."

"Aaron!" I run back to the bathroom.

When I return, it's finally time for us to go.

I can't believe I'm about to walk the red carpet!

It's really all happening.

"Erin! Erin! Lady Bettencourt!"

Camera lights are flashing in my eyes, blinding me. I try to hold my smile and not turn away in reaction.

They know who I am. I didn't think they would, but they do.

I look over at Aaron, who is standing a few feet away from me. He grins and comes to join me.

Wait a minute.

"Aaron, how do they know my name?" I ask suspiciously.

He shrugs his shoulders, but his grin grows wider.

I punch him playfully on the arm. But I'm grateful. It adds to the fun of the experience.

We walk the remainder of the red carpet together, stopping every now and again to pose for a photo.

It feels as if I'm in a dream.

Am I dreaming?

I have to be. How else would I, Erin Bettencourt, be walking the red carpet at the Toronto International Film Festival?

This can't be real.

I pinch myself.

No, not dreaming.

We are about to enter the theatre, Roy Thomson Hall, when an entertainment reporter I have met before reaches out and grabs my arm.

"Erin?" She looks surprised to see me. "I guess I don't have to ask who you are wearing."

I laugh. "No, but I will say it, anyway: Lady Bettencourt. This dress is a special edition named The Penny. It's made from old curtains! Oh, and my bag," I pause to hold it up for the camera. "My bag is a vintage Chanel 2.55. It belonged to my mom."

EPILOGUE
October 2018

"ON THE COUNT of three. One...two...three!" I say.

Aaron and I jump out of the fitting rooms at the exact same time.

I burst out laughing uncontrollably.

"What's so funny?" he asks, placing his hands on his hips and puffing out his chest.

"You're—you're," I say, trying to get a hold of myself. "You're wearing tights!"

"Every worthy superhero wears tights. It demonstrates our confidence," he says in a superhero-style voice, then adds in his regular tone, "Besides, you designed this. You knew about the tights."

"Yeah, but knowing and seeing are two different things."

"Well, you look hot. I guess I finally owe you that bonus."

"You don't look so bad yourself. Maybe you should wear tights more often."

Let me back up a moment and explain...

Aaron and I are attending a Halloween party at Betty and Matt's house tonight. I designed both of us superhero costumes à la the original Erin Girl flyer, complete with tights and capes—the works. Mine has a big 'E' on the front and Aaron's has a big 'A.' And I didn't forget about little Coco; she has a 'C' on her cape. Together, we form: The ACE Team!

After all these years, Aaron gets to see me dressed up like the cartoon-version of myself I drew on the flyer, and I get to fulfill my promise of designing my first-ever piece of menswear for him. Although, this probably isn't what he envisioned when he had made that request.

I also made Georgie and Charlie a bunch of different costumes. Once I started making them, I couldn't stop. Before the party, we are taking the twins trick-or-treating for their first time. It will be fun to go trick-or-treating. It's almost like getting to be a kid again...but without the candy.

Except, maybe there will be candy in my future. The twins are only fourteen months old; they shouldn't be eating that stuff. And if you are wondering, would I really steal candy from a baby? The answer is yes, yes, I would. From two babies, actually. Double the candy!

I have fallen in love with those two babies. I love being an auntie! I have always known I'm not mommy material—there are some things you just know—but I completely excel in the auntie department.

Okay, I *mostly* excel in the auntie department. There was that incident about a month ago.

Long story short, I lost Georgie. As the twins are identical and move around super fast now that they can walk, I thought I was seeing both of them—not the same one in a new location. I eventually found Georgie hiding inside the linen closet, fast asleep.

Needless to say, when Betty found out, she wasn't very happy. She decided it would be best if I had supervision whenever I babysat them in the future. Aaron has to be with me now before she will let me watch them for more than five seconds on my own. *Sheesh.* I mean, Georgie was never in any *real* danger.

And I would have gotten away with it, too, if Charlie hadn't ratted me out when Betty got home, by saying, "Georgie lost. Georgie lost." Betty figured out what had happened based on that alone.

Even though the twins are barely more than a year old, I can already see their personalities forming. Georgie is definitely an "Erin." (Reference her interest in hiding in small spaces.) And Charlie is totally a "Betty." (Reference her need for law and order.)

But I love them both equally. They are my future heiresses.

After her maternity leave, Betty decided not to return to the accounting firm. She said I inspired her to be her own boss. So she started a part-time bookkeeping business, and also works as a freelance photographer.

She realized she had been suffering from impostor syndrome herself when it came to her photography. She thought it was something she could only do for fun and not make any money from. That she couldn't be a real photographer because she never had proper training and because she always thought of herself as analytical, not creative.

But she is lucky: She is both left-brained and right-brained. Whereas, I'm totally left-brained. Or am I right-brained? I'm whatever side is the creative side.

Both of her businesses are doing really well. So well that I had to keep Trendy and Leo on board the Lady Bettencourt team. But Betty is still the only one I trust with "my numbers."

Six months after the twins were born, I finally told her about finding our mom's diary. I explained why I read the entries without her and apologized for what I had done. And, of course, she forgave me. She understood that I would need to read them, but she wished I would have told her from the beginning. She said she would never have prevented me from reading them.

As my penance, I have taken the "truth oath" with her, too, with the additional clause that she has to be awake when I reveal these truths. We limited it to anything to do with our mom, which was kind of a relief. I'm definitely still working on adding "telling the truth" to my list of mastered skills. After I "lost" Georgie, she made me include the twins, as well.

But every woman—every person—has to have some secrets.

Are secrets, lies?

I don't know. Maybe they are hidden truths waiting for the right moment to be revealed.

As for Betty, she decided against reading our mom's diary. She said she didn't need to. She wanted to keep her memory of our mom the way it was. I guess we both always had to choose for ourselves.

She does know I have our mom's original Chanel bag and that one of the diary entries helped me find it. I'm glad because one day I hope to pass down the bag to the twins, and I want them to know the significance behind it. That is a secret I don't want to keep.

And she also knows about our grandmother's grave being across from our mom's. She admitted that maybe—just maybe—the universe had a hand in that happening.

"We should go; it's beginning to get dark," Aaron says, breaking through my reverie.

"All right," I say, heading for the door. "*Crap!* I forgot the twins' costumes upstairs."

"You forgot something? I'm shocked."

I roll my eyes. "Very funny, Aaron boy. I will meet you out front of the shop."

My shop.

It's still hard to believe I own this place—okay, lease. Although, in a few years from now that may be true, as well.

After signing the contract, getting the keys, and making the necessary renovations, my shop officially opened on my birthday. I figured it was a great way to kick-off another year in the life of Erin Bettencourt.

The shop looks completely different from before. We tore down a wall and replaced it with a window so customers can see the clothes being made. There is a curtain, though, for when things get a bit crazy.

The seamstresses don't mind. They pretend as if they are putting on a show. Gloria has especially taken to giving her daily performance. And when they want more privacy, they can always work from home.

Actually, it isn't all seamstresses anymore, we have a tailor named Bernard on the team. (He refuses to let me call him Bernie.) He had been a tailor for years when the place he worked at closed down. That is when I snatched him up. He is really good at making our more structured dresses and our coats.

Coats! We have coats!

Or rather, cloaks. Carol inspired the idea. As I couldn't make her a dress with her daughter's clothing, I made her a cloak, instead. I had seen her wear one many times before, so I knew she liked the style. I used secondhand grey wool for the outer material and her daughter's clothing for the lining. I figured it symbolized Carol's whole demeanor: stern on the outside, (possibly) warm on the inside.

But I didn't tell her any of that. Nor did I make her pay for my work. I did, however, tell her I was adding a dress named "The Emily" to our new baby line.

We have a baby line of dresses!

That was obviously inspired by Georgie and Charlie, who have their own dresses named after them. There are mini-versions of some of our women's dresses, too, so that mothers—as well as, aunties and grannies—can dress the same as their daughters. Sort of cheesy, but customers love it. *I love it.*

And our wedding and custom lines have turned out to be a huge success. I'm easily making my monthly lease payments, which is a great relief. I also love that instead of just carrying dresses with names like The Barbie or The Lucy or The Frankie (a princess-cut wedding dress), any woman can have her own custom-made Lady Bettencourt dress named after her.

Another cool thing is getting to work with Lizzie. I know she stayed on longer than she would have because of me.

But given that our staff does skew to an older demographic, one evening a week, when the shop is closed, I have begun training at-risk youths on how to sew. A skill they can use eventually to get a job, either with us or for themselves.

And, in a few weeks, we are launching a series of workshops, both in-person and online, for anyone who wants to learn how to make their own clothes. Mila is helping me organize those. She is very multi-talented, kind of like Betty, but in her own (not-always-legal) way.

Aaron will be recording the workshops and including parts of them in a documentary he is making about me and the shop for one of his film classes. The working title is, *The Making of Erin Bettencourt.* He is really getting into it and developing his own unique style.

With all of the changes to my shop and business, the name Lady Bettencourt didn't fit anymore. Lady Bettencourt had become a division of something larger.

So what did I change the name of my business to?

House of Bettencourt.

That way, we can grow without worrying about having to stick to any one thing. (Although, having a menswear or dog-clothing line would be in the very, *very* distant future.)

I was hesitant to use the name Bettencourt again because of what I had read in my mom's diary. But I came to understand that when she took on that name, it changed its meaning. It was no longer the last name of the father who abandoned us. Instead, it became the last name of the mother who stayed. She took it on because of her love for us.

"I thought you were going upstairs?" Aaron asks.

"Huh? Oh, yeah, sorry," I say. "I will be right back."

Zoning out: another mastered skill.

I turn and race up the hidden stairs to the small apartment above the shop, where I now live. It worked out because Betty wanted to sell the condo to help with her financial transition to becoming an entrepreneur, and I finally live in a place that feels like my own. That feels like me.

The apartment is no longer minimalist the way Art had it. But he did leave behind the vintage Egg chair and the bar cart, which may have had something to do with me gushing on-and-on about them when I came to sign the contract. He also left behind a bottle of bourbon. I have learned a lot from him in the last year he has been mentoring me. He has become a friend.

I redecorated the apartment by painting one of the walls in the living room in colourful stripes, wallpapering the bathroom in a paisley print, and—

Focus, Erin. Focus.

Right, the costumes. I should probably get those.

Once I'm downstairs again, I pause near the front of the shop before heading outside. Through the window, out on the street, I see Aaron playing with Coco.

I'm reminded of everything that has happened over the past few years, from that day when I was standing alone, on the other side of this window, looking in. But I'm not alone anymore, my life is filled with so many people I care about and love.

Without realizing it until this very moment, I know that is what I had been actually searching for that day, searching for this whole time: a family.

I head out of the shop and into the darkening evening.

THE END...MAYBE

ACKNOWLEDGMENTS

I WOULD LIKE TO THANK: The Academy.

Now that that is out of the way, I would also like to thank:

My family and friends, for putting up with my quirkiness over the years. Especially my sister, Elizabeth Cunha, who has endured the longest, and, my niece, Sophia Rose, who will spend a lifetime having to account for her crazy Auntie Sandy C. (Sorry, kid.)

My Tia Gloria and Tia Natalia, as well as my favourite cousins, for being there for my sister and me after our mom passed away. (My mom would thank them, too.)

My prereaders—and friends—of the different parts of this novel: Diana-Marie Bombardieri, Sherry Chang, Anukriti Mishra, Pam Romano, and Pranya Yamin. Their suggestions made the story better than it would have been.

A second round of applause (you are clapping after each mention, *right*?) goes to Diana-Marie Bombardieri and Pranya Yamin, who also assisted with editing.

My former writing group members: Ariel Balevi, Hardish Dhaliwal, Carrie Oreskovich, and Susan Regular. The story changed from when we first met as a group years (and years) ago, but I finished it. And as we promised to include each other in our acknowledgments if we ever published our books, they can consider themselves acknowledged.

Anthony Del Col, for sharing with me what it's like to be "inside the television."

Luvbug and Hugs, for inspiring the Mademoiselle Coco Bettencourt character and for being my pooch sisters. Sadly, they are no longer with us.

Madison Dechief, a then fashion student, for answering my (many) questions while we waited in line at the Toronto International Film Festival. The film was *The Dressmaker*. *Très à propos*.

Fred Betterman, for helping me relearn the grammar lessons I only half-paid attention to in elementary school. All errors are my own.

Alan Watt, for writing *The 90-Day Novel*, which guided me towards finally completing my first draft after trying to do it on my own for far too long. I'm very, *very* much obliged.

Caro Soles, one of my past writing instructors (and an author), who told me years ago she hoped I would write this story. She may not remember saying it, but that simple remark stayed with me and kept me going. Well, I wrote it. And I think it has turned out better for having waited this long.

Lastly, I would like to thank Mademoiselle Chanel, for illustrating that sometimes we think the stories we make up about ourselves are more interesting than the reality, but there is nothing more fascinating than the truth.

Here is to all of us living our truth!

WAIT! Like any Oscar-inspired speech, I almost forgot to thank the most important person.

Thank you to my mommy, for everything she did for me.

ABOUT THE AUTHOR

SANDRA CUNHA is the author of *The Making of Erin Bettencourt*. She has never started a business from any of the many grey cubicles she has inhabited, but she has signed a contract without reading it first. She doesn't recommend doing this. Nor can she recommend reading other people's diaries—or, maybe, just not her diaries.

Sometimes Sandra lives in Toronto, and sometimes she lives in Waterloo. Other times she doesn't live in either.

As well as not knowing where she should live, she also can't make up her mind about being (and staying) on social media. The best place to find her is at her website: sandracunha.com.

AUTHOR'S NOTE

DEAR READER,

I hope you enjoyed reading *The Making of Erin Bettencourt*. Please consider leaving a review where you purchased the book and/or on Goodreads.

Reviews are really helpful to get other readers to discover new books by independent authors.

Thank you for your support!

Sandra

www.ingramcontent.com/pod-product-compliance
Lightning Source LLC
Chambersburg PA
CBHW051335250626
47155CB00007B/2603